T0328980

The darkness is coming . . .

The old house near Hode's Hill, Pennsylvania is a place for Madison Hewitt to start over—to put the trauma of her husband's murder, and her subsequent breakdown, behind her. She isn't bothered by a burial plot on the property, or the mysterious, sealed cistern in the basement. Not at first. Even the presence of cold spots and strange odors could be fabrications of her still troubled mind. But how to explain her slashed tires, or the ominous messages that grow ever more threatening?

Convinced the answer lies in the past, Madison delves into the history of the home's original owners, only to discover the origin of a powerful evil. An entity that may be connected to a series of gruesome attacks that have left police baffled. No matter where she turns—past or present—terror lingers just a step away, spurred on by a twisted obsession that can only be satisfied through death . . .

Books by Mae Clair

Weathering Rock
Twelfth Sun
Myth and Magic

The Point Pleasant Series
A Thousand Yesteryears (Book 1)
A Cold Tomorrow (Book 2)
A Desolate Hour (Book 3)

The Hode's Hill Novels
Cusp of Night (Book 1)
End of Day (Book 2)
Eventide (Book 3)

Published by Kensington Publishing Corporation

Eventide

The Hode's Hill Novels

Mae Clair

LYRICAL PRESS
Kensington Publishing Corp.
www.kensingtonbooks.com

LYRICAL UNDERGROUND BOOKS are published by
Kensington Publishing Corp.
119 West 40th Street
New York, NY 10018

All Kensington titles, imprints, and distributed lines are available at special quantity discounts for bulk purchases for sales promotion, premiums, fundraising, educational, or institutional use.

Special book excerpts or customized printings can also be created to fit specific needs. For details, write or phone the office of the Kensington Sales Manager: Kensington Publishing Corp., 119 West 40th Street, New York, NY 10018. Attn. Sales Department. Phone: 1-800-221-2647.

Lyrical Underground and Lyrical Underground logo Reg. US Pat. & TM Off.

First Electronic Edition: December 2019
eISBN-13: 978-1-5161-0729-2
eISBN-10: 1-5161-0729-2

First Print Edition: December 2019
ISBN-13: 978-1-5161-0732-2
ISBN-10: 1-5161-0732-2

Printed in the United States of America

For Bob,
My brother, My brother

Chapter 1

May 15, 1878

Hollande Moore twisted the doorknob with her good hand. The room was locked from the inside, the same as all the others she'd tried in the long hallway. Behind her, Sylvia plodded down the corridor, the iron fireplace poker held lax at her side, droplets of her son's blood glistening on her face. No rush in her step.

Dear God, how had it come to this?

Hollande sagged against the door, pain from her shattered wrist spiking to her head. Dizziness was a luxury she couldn't afford. A blast of vertigo weakened her knees and made the floor heave beneath her. Perspiration beaded her brow in fat, cold droplets. Gummy with sweat, her palm stuck to the glass knob.

Pat-tap. Pat-tap.

Sylvia's footsteps echoed softly, a harbinger of doom.

Hollande staggered away, every movement sending a fresh jolt of pain through her butchered wrist. At the end of corridor, the door to Darrin's study gaped wide—the single room consistently locked throughout her brief tenure. No matter. Anywhere she could hide was welcome. She slipped inside, then slammed the door. When she gripped the knob, it came apart in her hand.

"No! Please, no!" Someone had battered it repeatedly, making the lock useless.

Tears blurred her vision. Had Sylvia planned this killing spree? What would Nathaniel think if he could see the depths of depravity his mother had succumbed to?

She spun, her gaze raking the room. There had to be something she could use as a weapon.

In mockery, the fireplace stood cold and black, both the poker and ash shovel missing. Cobwebs sprouted from lampshades and glommed into corners. Dust lay thick and undisturbed on a cherry desk. Across the room, the balcony doors yawned open to the night.

She rummaged through the desk, shoving aside papers and correspondence emblazoned with *Stewart Quarry* at the top. In a left-hand drawer, she located a letter opener. The blade was blunt, but with enough force, it might do the same damage as a knife.

The steady tramp of Sylvia's footsteps drew nearer.

Hollande backed toward the balcony, the makeshift weapon clutched in her good hand. Even if she managed to clamber over the railing, the drop to the veranda was too great, the unyielding surface sure to break bone. Darrin was proof of that. Her best chance was to stand and fight.

Pat-tap. Pat-tap.

So close now.

Sweat trickled down her neck. Her heart beat faster and mushroomed into her throat.

Sylvia flung the door wide. She paused on the threshold, hair sweat-matted to her temples, eyes stygian in the sallow mask of her face. Her fingers twitched on the iron poker.

Hollande forced herself to block the image of Nathaniel—his skull crushed, blood pooling on the floor beneath him. "Please, Sylvia. It doesn't have to end this way. I can help you."

"I don't need help." Her voice was dispassionate, tainted by the cancer of madness. "You never should have come here. I can't change the past, but I can make certain this house becomes your tomb." With a grunt, she lurched forward, swinging the rod like a club. A violent displacement of air fanned over Hollande's face.

She hurled herself onto the balcony—

—a step from death on the unforgiving stones below.

* * * *

Present Day

Madison Hewitt stood on the balcony and breathed the air wafting from Yarrow Creek. The heady scent of leafy green plants twined with the sweetness of Spanish bluebells and catmint, warmed by the heat of a late spring day. Elsewhere in Hode's Hill, people took advantage of the long Memorial Day weekend by mowing lawns, opening backyard pools, or gearing up for three days of family cookouts. She'd chosen the stretch to move.

"This one is marked *bedroom*." Her sister Jillian breezed through the doorway carting a cardboard box. She plopped it on the bed, then paused to swipe a strand of hair from her brow. "That's the last of them. Roth left to take the truck back to the rental company."

"Thanks."

Jillian joined her on the balcony. "I love the view."

It was one of the many things that attracted Madison to the house. A lot of people would have been bothered by the isolation, tucked outside of town on a dead-end road. She found it relaxing.

"I noticed there aren't any streetlights, and the nearest house is over a mile away." Jillian worried her bottom lip between her teeth. "It's going to get dark at night."

"I'm a big girl. All healed." Madison tried to keep the edge from her voice. "I can take care of myself."

Jillian flushed. "You don't have to say that."

"Yes, I do." The stigma of being mentally broken wasn't easily set aside. "Sooner or later, I have to start over."

"You have started over. You're working again."

"Real estate's only part of it." Madison brushed past her, angling for the bed. Her career had enabled her to learn about the property the moment it came on the market. In search of something small and inexpensive, she'd met one of those goals. The house was far larger than she needed, but the price had been too good to overlook. The previous owner passed away in a nursing home, her only relative a distant cousin who lived out of state. Anxious to divest of the house quickly, the cousin had been willing to negotiate on most of the furnishings.

"The place is kind of creepy." Jillian scuffed her arms. "Did you see the burial plot in the back?"

"It's only three graves." Madison dug a pale green sheet from the box. "A lot of people had backyard cemeteries in the eighteen hundreds." She fanned the cover over the bed.

Jillian caught a corner on the other side. "I still think it's creepy."

"Why? We're used to tending graves. What about Gabriel?"

"That's different. Our ancestors were tasked with that obligation centuries before we were born."

"A person dies three times." Madison tucked a fitted edge around the mattress while reciting a piece of folklore their mother taught them. "Once when he dies. Once when he's buried. And once when there's no one left to remember him." *The Final Death.* She reached for the flat sheet. "I'll make sure the people in those graves are never forgotten." The same way she carried on the tradition for Gabriel Vane long after his tragic death in 1799.

"Grave-tending is a serious responsibility." Jillian smoothed the sheet over the bed, the compressed line of her mouth telegraphing tension. "You should leave them alone."

"Maybe I want the responsibility. I'm sure the woman who lived here before me did the same."

"You don't know that. Besides, sometimes it's best for the departed to embrace Final Death. You don't know anything about those people or the lives they lived."

"I know their names. Darrin and Sylvia Stewart. I think they must have been husband and wife. Their son is buried there, too." In some strange way, the wind-pitted stones had spoken to her. "You were worried about me being by myself out here, but I'm not."

"Now you're being ridiculous."

"Says the woman in love with a practicing medium." Madison quirked a smile.

"Dante only experiments."

"Maybe, but when he gets back from his art exhibit, I'd love to get his impression of the house." Madison tossed her a pillowcase. "I've never seen him read a folk memory."

"Sometimes there aren't any to be found. And sometimes folk memories are better left alone. I have an uneasy feeling about this place."

"No, you have an uneasy feeling about me living by myself after four and a half years under someone's nose."

"True."

Madison huffed out a breath. "Roth asked me to move in with him." Her boyfriend was cut from the same cloth as her sister.

"What?" Jillian shot her a startled glance. "I didn't know you'd grown that serious."

"We haven't. At least, I haven't. I told him I needed a break."

"You've been together six months. And it's been over four years since Boyd was killed."

"Boyd has nothing to do with it. I need time to myself." She didn't want to dwell on how supportive Roth had been—was *still* being—by giving her the space she needed. He'd said the L-word, and the prospect terrified her. She was stupid for bringing up the subject when her emotions were in a quagmire. Not something you wanted to broadcast when your younger sister possessed empathic abilities. "Let's finish and grab lunch." She reached for the bedspread. "I picked up some chicken salad and fruit."

Afterward, they tackled more boxes. By the time evening settled, Jillian's dog, Blizzard—who alternately stayed clear of the mess or trailed room to room—was ready for an overdue dinner. Madison hugged her sister goodbye, watched as Jillian got the husky settled in the backseat of her Accord, then pointed the car down the narrow lane, headed for Hode's Hill. Madison waved from the driveway.

There would be fireworks over the Chinkwe River tonight, something Jillian could catch from the stoop of her brownstone. She'd invited Madison and a few mutual friends to join her, but Madison preferred to spend the first night in her new home without distractions.

She strolled around the side where an expansive stone veranda overlooked Yarrow Creek. The second-floor balcony ran the length of the house. From what she'd been able to deduce, the upper section had once been two bedrooms. Somewhere in the past, the smaller chamber had been converted into a bath, creating one large master suite. By contrast, the rest of the house had seen little, if any, remodeling. Peeling wallpaper, hardwood floors in need of refinishing, and old kitchen cabinets with lopsided shelves were just a few of the problems she'd inherited. The master suite with its rambling balcony and view of the creek had sold her.

That and the graves.

Madison followed a trail past the veranda and up an embankment to the rear of the property. The small graveyard—nothing more than a patch surrounded by a knee-high wall of limestone blocks—had been situated above flood levels in the event the creek should rise. Grass grew high and spiky at the edges, reminding her to invest in a weed trimmer. In the center, three tall slabs dotted with lichen stood as testament to another century.

Based on the dates, Darrin had died first, passing in 1865. Sylvia, and their adult son, Nathaniel, thirteen years later. Something tragic must have happened for mother and son to pass on the same day. A fire or accident, perhaps even illness. She could imagine Nathaniel trying to save his mother, or Sylvia succumbing to a fatal ailment while glued to the bedside of her dying son. She might never know the truth, but she would care for the graves as if they belonged to her ancestors.

Madison breathed deeply, savoring the quiet. Already, the air grew heavy with the heady mustiness that blooms around water at dusk. She loved the smell. Relished the fickle skip of breeze wafting from the creek. A few bats flitted between trees. Further away, a mourning dove cooed from somewhere among the branches.

As much as she enjoyed being outside, there was still unpacking to do. Maybe later, she'd relax on the balcony with a glass of wine and watch night settle. Alcohol didn't mix well with meds, but she'd been off her pills long enough. She deserved the treat.

Warmed by the thought, she headed toward the house. The sight of a dead squirrel sprawled by the front door crushed her sense of tranquility.

"Damn." The animal must have been injured, crawled up on the porch, and died. It was an odd place for a wild creature to seek shelter in the waning moments of life, but the area was infested with small rodents. The poor thing had probably tussled with a fox or a raccoon. She peered closer but didn't see a mark on it. As unpleasant as the task was, she'd have to dispose of it. Part of living so far from town meant dealing with the occasional critter in her yard or home.

Inside, she located a trash bag and a pair of plastic gloves. When it came time to put the carcass in the sack, she averted her eyes. The little body hung limp in her hand, faintly warm through the thin layer of her gloves. She bundled the bag shut and glanced to the rickety floorboards, praying she wouldn't discover blood.

A chill prickled her spine.

The squirrel's body and tail had concealed a single word stenciled in capital letters on the doormat. One that might have been inviting under other circumstances, but now seemed sinister.

WELCOME

Madison glanced over her shoulder, the swiftly falling night abruptly unsettling. She sprinted across the driveway to the detached garage, then dumped the bag in a trash can. Of course, no one was watching her, but it was hard to squash old fears.

How many women survived seeing their husband butchered with a knife? How many people knew what it felt like to be murdered?

Chapter 2

March 20, 1878

"It's a good position." Edgar used his knife to slice a piece of pot roast.

Hollande gave no outward sign of distress, her gaze trained on her brother rather than his pregnant wife. She'd known all along this day was coming. "A companion to Sylvia Stewart?" Thank heavens her voice didn't tremble.

"You'll like the family, and the fit couldn't be better. You possess a gentleness when looking after others that Carolyn can vouch for with her bouts of morning sickness and vapors. And I remember how you tended to Phillip when he was ill."

Hollande flinched involuntarily at the mention of her departed fiancé, but Edgar failed to notice. He forked a chunk of potato into his mouth, the glow from the gas-lit chandelier gleaming off the high dome of his forehead with a sheen that reminded her of sweat.

That was an illusion, of course. Her brother would have no qualms about ousting her from the house their parents once owned, no more than he had in selling it. Mama and Papa would have expected Edgar to provide for her, and in his own distorted way he was—by securing a position for her that included a room and meals.

She shifted her attention to the claret wallpaper festooned with intricate swirls of gold. Her mother had loved the dining room with its deep tray ceiling and pendant chandelier. Each holiday the table brimmed with platters of fruits and nuts, soft cheeses, and a fat turkey or glazed ham. Drinks sparkled in crystal glasses on the cherry sideboard, waiting for friends or family to claim them. Such laughter and joy.

As a child, she'd scampered barefoot across the hardwood floor on Christmas Eve, a frilly white nightdress swirling around her ankles. It was usually Papa who scooped her into his arms, laughing as he carried her up to bed. Christmas morning, Mama would dish up bread steaks, Swiss eggs, and jugs of sweet milk. Because it was a holiday, there would be smoked salmon and a bowl of spiced apples or candied potatoes.

So much had changed now that her parents were gone. Her meals with Edgar were polite, even somber. She'd once hoped the mood would change when he wed Carolyn, but Hollande's sister-in-law was every bit as reserved as the man she'd married.

"I spoke to Nathaniel—one of the brothers—at length." Edgar's knife scraped across the blue-and-white dinner plate as he made short work of his wife's pot roast. "There are two of them. Twins. Tristan wasn't there, but I met the mother, Sylvia. Upstanding woman, though somewhat frail. She's taken a sickly turn, according to Nathaniel, and remains isolated most days." He used the meat to sop up gravy, then forked the dripping lump into his mouth. His jaw worked as he diced up turnips and carrots. "She's lonely for company. Understandable, given the size of the estate. You've seen the place out by Yarrow Creek."

A rambling home at the end of a lane. Remote. Few people went out that way. Hollande set her fork down, heart thumping against her ribs. She had only herself to blame for her predicament, twenty-eight and unwed, dependent on an older brother. That may have been fine when it was just the two of them, but his marriage to Carolyn changed the dynamics of the household. As upset as she was, she couldn't fault her sister-in-law for wanting to move closer to her parents, especially now with a baby on the way.

"When the house is settled, I'll see that you receive a share, of course." Having finished with his meal, Edgar pushed his plate away and leaned back in his chair. "Mother and Father would want to know you've been properly cared for."

Hollande dabbed a napkin against her lips. It seemed her fate was sealed. She felt light-headed, but it may have been the gas lighting leeching oxygen from the air. It wouldn't be the first time.

"When do you plan to begin advertising the property?"

Edgar added cream to a cup of tea at his elbow. "I've already met with an estate agent. He's begun looking for a prospective buyer."

"So soon?"

"We thought it best." Carolyn ventured her first words since Edgar's mention of the Stewarts. She fiddled with her napkin, lacing it between her fingers. Red spots bloomed on her pale cheeks as she averted her gaze.

It wasn't her house to sell, but Edgar would have discussed options with her. Hollande had become excess baggage in her brother's marriage. He was ready to move on, grow his family, but not until he'd secured accommodations for his unwed sister. If only Phillip hadn't died, they would surely be married by now and started on a family of their own. Since her fiancé's death, she hadn't the heart to look at another man.

No matter. Fate was fate. She could stay and dawdle, but arguing wouldn't change her brother's mind.

"When did you tell Mr. Stewart I would be available to start?"

Edgar shifted. For the first time that evening, he appeared uncomfortable. "I, uh..." His gaze skittered to his wife before he refocused on Hollande. "The timing is up to you, of course, but Caro and I felt—"

"I see." She cut off his squirming. "The sooner the better."

"Hollande, you needn't leave until the house is sold." Carolyn reached across the table to grip her fingers, her gaze a simpering match for her voice. "We just thought you might like to get settled as soon as possible. It will surely be difficult seeing your parents' home sold."

"You needn't worry about me." Hollande pulled her hand away. Briskly. "Edgar, you may inform Mr. Stewart I will be available by week's end. That will give me ample time to have items in order." She preferred to remain no longer than necessary where she wasn't welcome.

"You'll adjust." Edgar sounded as if he was trying to convince himself. "It's for the best."

"Of course." If only Phillip was at her side. If only her parents hadn't met their end in a carriage accident. She stood, appetite gone.

If only.

Hollande set her napkin on the table. She walked stiffly to the door, the sound of some long-ago Christmas Eve echoing faintly in her ears.

* * * *

Present Day

Madison spent her second day in the house sorting boxes, moving furniture, and tossing things she didn't need. The previous owner left behind a number of odds and ends, including a hodgepodge of old tools, rusted paint cans, and plastic bins in the basement. It was dirty work rummaging through it all, and she felt grimy by the time she walked upstairs for a bottle of water.

A quick check of the time told her it was nearing two o'clock. After a short break, she tied her hair in a ponytail, ready to tackle the project fresh. Before she could head downstairs, the chime of the doorbell drew her to the foyer. She peered through a leaded-glass window to spy Roth McGrath on the front porch.

Surprised, Madison opened the door. "Hi. What are you doing here?"

"Not exactly the greeting I was hoping for." He flashed a smile that sank a dimple into his cheek. "Would you believe I was in the area?"

"I'm at the end of a dead-end road."

"Okay, I lied. I wanted to see how you were doing. Can I come in?"

She stepped aside to make room for him to enter. "It's only been one day, Roth."

"I know, but it's an isolated property." He looked around the foyer as if taking stock of the house, his gaze sweeping past the staircase to the drawing room. He'd helped her move, securing the rental truck and doing the heavy lifting. "Everything go okay last night?"

"Fine." She avoided mentioning the dead squirrel. "I was exhausted by the end of the day. Thanks for your help with the move."

"No problem. I guess you still have a lot to do."

"That's an understatement. I'm working in the basement right now."

"Need some help?"

Madison hesitated. They'd agreed to take a short break from each other, but that didn't mean their friendship had to end. She cared for Roth a great deal. She just wasn't ready to live with him.

"Sure. There's a lot of junk down there I want to toss."

"You sort, I'll toss."

They worked together for the next few hours, pushing unwanted items to the side, bagging and hauling smaller ones to the rear yard for trash. Roth kept her entertained talking about the antics of his students. As a middle school math teacher, with the year winding to a close, classes were mostly fun and games.

Madison originally met him through Tessa Camden, Jillian's next-door neighbor and a mutual friend. Six months ago, as a favor, she'd driven Tessa's son to school on a rainy Monday, ending up with a flat tire in the parking lot. Roth helped her out, and their relationship escalated from there.

"I think I'm ready to call it quits for the day." Madison swiped sweaty hair from her brow. "Or at least get out of this basement." The place was dank and dingy even with several pull-chain lightbulbs overhead. Rough stone walls and an uneven floor made the dreary space unsuited for anything other than storage. By the looks of the metal shelving units and boxes of old Ball jars, the previous owner had done a lot of canning. A set of squat steps on the right led to storm doors that opened to the rear yard. Roth had been using the exit to haul unwanted junk out for trash.

She needed a shower, followed by a relaxing dinner on the veranda. The time was nearing five, and with nothing but coffee and yogurt in the morning, her stomach demanded attention. "I've got some chicken I could throw on the grill. Want to join me for dinner?"

"Best offer I've had all day. I think I'll run home first, clean up, and get out of these grungy clothes." Roth swatted dust from his jeans. Sweat soaked the ends of his black hair and gummed the front of his T-shirt. "How about if I pick up a bottle of wine on the way back?"

"That sounds great." Madison stooped to shove a box out of the way. A low gurgling made her pause. She'd heard the same noise a while ago but thought she'd imagined it. "Did you hear that?"

Roth closed the storm doors. "What?"

"That sound. I thought I heard it before. Listen."

Silence dragged for several seconds before being broken by a wet burbling.

"It's coming from over there." Roth headed to a section of basement housing the mechanicals. Hot water heater, oil tank, furnace. Even with light from the rafter bulbs, shadows nested in the corners. "Look at this." He moved an old tool chest out of the way.

Madison joined him, staring down at a round stone lid, roughly three feet in diameter. Massive bolts secured it to the floor.

"Any idea what it is?" Roth crouched beside the cover.

Madison had skipped a home inspection, something she'd never advise a buyer-client to do when purchasing property. But the house was old and would have thrown up too many red flags. If she'd had an inspection done, she'd know exactly what she was looking at. "Maybe an old cistern, but it's odd the top is bolted down. It looks like it hasn't been used in decades." The gurgle exploded again, reminding her of air bubbles trapped in a water tank.

Roth located a rag near the toolbox, using it to wipe the bolts free of cobwebs. Like the lid, they were heavy, industrial things, thick with the patina of age. He'd almost finished when a distinctive clang echoed from the depths of the cistern.

Madison drew back. "What was that?"

"I don't know, but I vote we open this thing and find out."

"It must be sealed for a reason."

"Maybe the previous owner had kids. Or pets. It could have been a safety issue."

Madison was sure Vera Halsey didn't have small children. She'd ended up in a nursing home. Maybe grandchildren or pets. Roth seemed intent on unbolting the lid, and she was curious enough to stand aside while he rooted through the toolbox. After several failed attempts with a socket wrench, he shook his head.

"The bolts are rusted in place. When I come back tonight, I'll bring something to loosen them. I've got better tools, too."

Madison stared at the lid. "Do you think all that's necessary?"

"Aren't you curious what's underneath there?"

"I guess so." The clanging and burbling had stopped, but something was responsible for making those noises.

True to his word, when Roth returned, he came prepared with tools and a can of WD-40. He soaked the bolts, leaving the oil to dissolve the rust while they shared a glass of wine. Afterward, he went back to work, more focused on opening the cistern than she was. Madison guessed it had become a challenge for him and busied herself tossing a salad. She was adding the finishing touches when he yelled up the stairs.

"Hey, come here. I think I've got it."

Drying her hands on a tea towel, she picked her way down the steps. Roth had hooked a cage light to an overhead beam for more illumination and had a variety of tools strewn around the cistern. He'd managed to remove all eight bolts. Looking at the long ends scattered by the lid, Madison was surprised by how deeply they'd been threaded into the floor.

"Did you hear anything while you were working?" she asked.

"Nothing." Roth sat back on his haunches. He'd drudged up a sweat again, the knees of his jeans grimy with dirt, black muck freckling his hands. The least she could do was offer him a place to shower when he was through.

"Ready?" He indicated the lid with a grin.

In many ways, it felt like opening a treasure chest. A long time ago someone had taken extra effort to secure the lid in place. Maybe it was nothing more than she thought. An old cistern, decades or centuries out of use. And yet—

She nodded.

With effort, Roth shoved the heavy cover aside, back and shoulder muscles bunching with the exertion.

"What the—" His face contorted. Gagging, he recoiled.

A noxious cloud of sulfur and decay engulfed Madison.

"Oh, that's awful!" She pressed the tea towel to her nose and mouth. "It smells like something died."

"Not even close. It smells a hell of a lot worse." Roth snatched a flashlight from the floor. With one hand cupped over his nose, he angled the beam into the hole. "I can't tell if anything's down there. It looks about ten feet deep, maybe more."

"Is there water?" Despite the stench, Madison inched closer.

"Not that I can see. If there is, it's a long way down."

A blast of cold air hit them in the face, strong enough to make Madison backpedal. The bare bulbs dangling from the rafters flickered then died. Roth's flashlight sputtered, failing altogether.

Chilled, Madison hugged her arms to her chest. "What was that?"

"Hell if I know." He rapped the barrel of the light against his palm until the beam reignited. Gradually, the odor faded, and the temperature returned to normal. Overhead, the lights powered on.

"That was weird." Madison eyed the cistern. A creeping sensation spread through her gut.

"Do you see anything that could have made the noises we heard?"

Squatting beside the hole, Roth swept the beam of his flashlight from side to side. "Nothing. It just looks like a pit in the ground. Limestone walls, though it's hard to tell from all the grunge. I guess it is just an unused cistern someone covered up."

"You sound disappointed."

He shrugged. "You never know what you might find in these old houses."

"You were thinking a cache of money or jewels?"

"Better than a dead body."

"That's horrid."

He shot her a grin as he gathered his tools.

Madison shook her head. "I'm going upstairs to finish getting dinner ready. When you're done cleaning up, if you want a shower, feel free to use the main bath. There are fresh towels in the linen closet."

"Thanks. Do you want me to seal that thing back up?" He nodded to the cistern.

"No. Just cover it." As she headed upstairs, her mind tracked to the clanging and gurgling noises. She hadn't imagined those, and Roth had been certain they'd come from the cistern. The result of something mechanical most likely.

For surely nothing living could exist in such a wretched, polluted pit.

* * * *

After a week in the house, Madison forgot about the cistern. She'd grown accustomed to the creaks and groans of settling floorboards and joists, but the sound that woke her this night was different. She bolted upright in bed, heart pounding in the quiet. Dream images flitted from her grasp, nothing she could pinpoint, only that the memories disturbed her. The feeling clung, thickening the air with an oppressive weight. If she didn't know better, she'd think someone was in the room with her.

The noise came again, shattering the stillness. A strange rustling she couldn't identify, almost like something sweeping over the floor. One second, two.

Loud, close.

She switched on the bedside lamp, her gaze raking the room—bureau, armoire, an oval standing mirror inherited from the previous owner, a tufted chair, and a dressing table. All that remained was the shadowed arch into the bath.

A place for someone to hide. A man with a knife and murder on his mind.

Stop it!

Boyd's death was years in the past. She'd survived that butchery. Was stronger for putting the carnage behind her.

Heart triple-timing, she swung her legs to the floor. The scuffed boards were cool against her bare feet as she padded toward the bathroom.

"Hello?"

Idiot. Did she really expect someone lurking in the dark to answer? The dream was getting the better of her, turning her palms moist with sweat. She'd probably imagined the noise. If someone was skulking in the shadows, she had no weapon to defend herself. Foolishness on her part. She was tired of being a victim. Of being broken, relying on meds for recovery. She'd put the ugliness of those days behind her. Determined, she strode into the bathroom and boldly flipped on the light.

The room was empty.

Laughter bubbled into her throat. Spilled over in a gasp that bordered on hysteria. She clamped a hand to her mouth, mentally chiding herself for being on edge. Her reflection in a large wall mirror startled her. Now and then, caught by surprise, she didn't recognize herself.

Her red hair used to be lighter, woven with gold. The staff at Rest Haven had cropped the length for easy care. It had since grown out but was darker now, merlot without the threads of brass. For a moment, she imagined someone else staring back. A woman with fuller lips, skin like warm honey, and hair that tumbled to her waist. A stranger.

She blinked, and the image flitted away like a ghost.

Madison switched off the light. In the sudden shadows, a spark of yellow gleamed through the window. Surprised, she brushed the curtains aside, opening the lacy panels against the night. The glow came from the creek, a small rectangle of amber-gold that made her think of an old-fashioned lantern. There were no lights to indicate a boat. Could someone be prowling the perimeter of her property?

She hurried back to the bedroom, switched off the lamp, then opened the doors to the balcony. Darkness draped her like a cloak when she eased outside. The temperature hovered in the low sixties, seasonal and mild, but the air sketched goosebumps on her arms. A few spring crickets chirped among the trees, backed by the occasional croak of a bullfrog. Moonlight splattered the wide expanse of ground before her, Yarrow Creek black and unreflective in the distance.

Had she imagined the light the same way she'd imagined the noise?

It had been a long week. She'd been working extra hours to close a few deals hovering on the fence. An indecisive buyer, a home inspection that called for a new roof, and a seller with limited funds. The evening brought hours of cleaning, scrubbing out cupboards, and weeding through bric-a-brac left by the previous owner. Purchasing a home mostly furnished had benefits, but also a downside. In addition to furniture, she'd inherited old pots and pans, moldy linens, and closets filled with faded holiday decorations and knickknacks.

No wonder she was imagining things. She'd been told not to overdo it by her medical doctor and her psychologist. Roth had been persistent too, wanting to help but determined to give her space.

She stepped back into the bedroom and closed the balcony door. When she crawled into bed and closed her eyes, she had the distinct impression someone watched silently from the corner.

Crazy.

And crazy was something she wasn't.

* * * *

Madison gathered her hair into a high ponytail, banding it with a pine-green scrunchie as she hurried down the hallway. If she skipped reviewing her email, she probably had enough time to down a cup of coffee and few spoonfuls of yogurt before her appointment with Dr. Kapoor. Once she'd drifted off last night, she'd slept soundly, dozing past her alarm. She was almost to the end of the hall when something banged loudly behind her. The door to her bedroom somehow managed to slam shut.

Great. Another item on a growing list of problems and repairs.

She retraced her steps, but the door wouldn't budge, not even when she jiggled the handle and added her weight. Somehow, she must have flipped the lock while rushing to leave. She tried again, butting her shoulder against the wood. The knob spun effortlessly, spilling her into the room with an abruptness that made her stumble. Immediately, an invisible cloud of sulfur and worm-rot engulfed her.

Please, not a sewage problem.

She crossed to the bathroom, checked the toilet, then flushed. No issues that she could see, but the odor could be funneled up from the basement. She should have never let Roth open the old cistern. As she stood debating the matter, the reek gradually faded. Within seconds, she could almost believe she'd imagined it. Already behind for her appointment with Dr. Kapoor, she decided to worry about the problem later.

Downstairs, she gobbled vanilla yogurt while waiting for her coffee to brew, added a lid to the cup, then hurried outside. Chunks of gravel crunched under her shoes as she hurried down the drive to the garage. A carriage house at one time, the stone building had been converted sometime during the last century. An exterior door on the side was locked at all times, mostly because the wood had warped, making it hard to open and close. She'd yet to have an automatic opener installed and was forced to set her coffee down, then use both hands to heave the main door upward on its tracks.

The moment light hit the rear of her Honda, she knew something was wrong. The Civic listed to the side, looking like a drunk unable to stand upright. A heavy sense of foreboding settled in her stomach. There was only one reason a car would lean like that.

Both right-side tires had been slashed.

* * * *

"You seem ill at ease." Dr. Kapoor was a fiftyish woman of Indian descent. Her shoulder-length black hair carried a smattering of gray, and her eyes reflected the tawny brown of licorice root.

Madison sat across from her in a cushioned chair placed before a large window. She fought the urge to fidget, normally soothed by the comfortable surroundings. There was nothing remotely clinical in the plush taupe carpeting, soft heather paint, or furniture crafted of honeyed wood. Pastel paintings of sandy beaches and wind-swept dunes hung on the walls, and a row of potted succulents occupied the windowsill. The side table sported a box of tissues in a cut-glass caddy along with a few magazines.

She resisted the temptation to snatch a tissue and twist it between her fingers. "It's been a hectic morning. Thanks for fitting me into your schedule."

"I'm happy I could accommodate you. It worked out well that I had a cancellation." Dr. Kapoor crossed her legs, shifting a yellow legal tablet onto her lap. The top page contained several scrawled lines of writing, but she'd yet to add any since Madison arrived. "You said you had a problem with your car."

"Yes." Madison didn't care to elaborate. She'd called AAA to change out the tires, storing the damaged pair in the back of the garage. She should have notified the police but feared opening herself to a larger investigation. Jillian would overreact, insisting she install multiple security measures, and Roth would swing into hover mode. The less they knew, the better. The whole incident might be nothing more than random mischief, once and done. A teenager could have noticed the house was occupied and thought it fun to put a scare into the new owner. That would explain the light by the creek.

Stupid kids. She'd stopped thinking of herself as fragile over a year ago and had no desire to sink into that mindset again.

"It was just a flat tire." She avoided mentioning the second and gave in to the compulsion to snatch a tissue. "Triple A changed it out in no time, but it put me behind on everything."

"I see. How are things going with the new house?"

"Fine." Madison thought of the atrocious smell and the dead squirrel. Now two slashed tires. She hoped her smile wasn't strained. "Because I bought the house furnished, there's a lot to sort through. It's keeping me busy."

"No new nightmares?"

She shook her head. She couldn't remember last night's dream anyway, only that it left her uneasy.

Dr. Kapoor consulted her notes. "You've been off your medication for two months. Any anxiety attacks?"

"None."

"Do you feel you've finally managed to put Boyd behind you?"

"I do." If only everyone else would. She shifted her attention to the window with its pristine view of the Chinkwe. This far from the center of Hode's Hill, only a smattering of cars traveled past on River Road. Roth's condo was several blocks away, tucked in a community of quads with an HOA and pristine landscaping—the complete opposite of the home she'd bought. They had dinner plans later that evening, the break she'd wanted from their relationship no longer an issue. With one exception.

She crumpled the tissue in her hand. "Roth asked me to move in with him."

Dr. Kapoor's normally neutral expression betrayed her surprise. "Was that before you settled on your home?"

"Shortly after I signed the contract."

He'd done his best to be persuasive.

I'm worried about you being alone out there. The place is isolated. It isn't too late to change your mind and back out of the deal. Then, within hours of settlement, when the keys were in her hand: *You can always flip the house. I'll even help you.*

"I care for Roth a great deal. It's scary to admit, but I love him. I just don't want to give up my independence. Jillian and I lived together after our parents died. I went from there to being married to Boyd, then to Rest Haven, then Jillian again. I've never had a chance to see what I can do on my own."

"And that's important to you?"

"You know it is." They'd discussed her determination at length. "I made a mistake when I married Boyd, letting myself get swept up in his lifestyle." Looking back, Madison couldn't imagine why she'd been attracted to her husband's rough edges, his need to push boundaries and skirt the law. "I should have walked away when he started dealing drugs." It wouldn't have changed anything for Boyd—he'd still be dead, butchered by Kirk Porter—but it would have saved her from three years as a mindless husk, unable to speak or communicate.

Like Jillian, she'd had the gift of empathy. That aptitude was gone now, shattered when she'd witnessed her husband's murder. She'd felt Boyd's pain, his horror, *lived* his death. For three years, she'd recreated it almost daily in her mind. When she'd finally emerged from the bleak cocoon that comprised her world, her talent for empathy was gone. She couldn't say she missed the ability. It wasn't easy to absorb the emotions of others and remain sane—God knew how Jillian managed with her added trace of psychic power—but the sudden lack was an adjustment.

"I'm starting over. In more ways than one." Her gaze flashed to Dr. Kapoor. "Roth is important to me, but it's also important that I regain my sense of self. The house is just one step in that direction."

Dr. Kapoor nodded, jotting a few notes on her tablet.

"I used to worry someone from Boyd's past would come looking for me." Madison stared at the cheerful succulents on the windowsill. "He made so many enemies."

"Kirk Porter and his brothers are dead."

"I know." Madison had watched Kirk stab Boyd—over and over again—while Clive restrained her. She'd learned to block that memory, banishing the images when they floated to the top of her consciousness. Now they only haunted her dreams, occurrences that had gone from almost weekly to rarely ever. She shifted her gaze to Dr. Kapoor. "The kind of people Boyd crossed are ones who hold a grudge. I never had anything to do with them, but..." She swallowed, thinking of the light by the creek, the butchered tires on her Civic. "Maybe I shouldn't have bought such an isolated property."

"That's Roth talking. And your sister."

Madison looked up sharply.

"A moment ago, you told me you'd put Boyd behind you. Now"—Dr. Kapoor lifted her shoulders—"you're clinging to the past. Worrying about the people he associated with, people who have no connection to you. We've talked about this, Madison. As long as you allow Boyd's life and death to haunt you, you're never going to rise above a victim mentality."

Her spine stiffened. "You're right." It was too easy to sink into that mode of thinking. Like an alcoholic falling off the wagon. "It's an adjustment, stepping out on my own after so long." Two months ago, she'd been babbling her excitement to Dr. Kapoor, giddy at the prospect of living alone.

The older woman smiled kindly. "You've taken a major step in reclaiming your life. I'm going to leave our next session up to you."

"Pardon?"

Dr. Kapoor uncrossed her legs, palms flat on her tablet. "You've been off your medication with no side effects or setbacks. You haven't had any panic attacks, and you're no longer troubled by dreams. The nerves you have related to the house and the move are typical for a new homeowner, nothing out of the ordinary as far as I can see. I'm available if you want to continue our sessions, but I don't believe they're necessary, especially on a regular basis. I'll leave the scheduling up to you. Down the road, you're more than welcome to call if you feel the need."

Madison stared openly. "You're pushing me out the door?"

"Like a mother duck urging her duckling into the pond. It's time for you to swim on your own."

Independence. It's what she'd wanted, what she'd aimed for from the start of their sessions.

Madison drew a steadying breath and nodded.

Mission accomplished.

Chapter 3

March 24, 1878

Hollande's first impression of Nathaniel Stewart made her wonder if her new home would be as somber as the one she'd left. Her brother had paid for a hansom cab, having the driver deliver her to the Stewart estate on a gray, rainy Saturday. Nathaniel met her outside, an umbrella raised over her head as he took one of her bags to carry indoors. The driver brought the other two, accepted a tip from Nathaniel, then departed into the downpour.

She untied her bonnet while Nathaniel set her luggage at the bottom of the stairs. Though she'd caught only a glimpse of his features outside, stoic was the word that sprang foremost to mind. When he faced her, grim and impassive, she decided she wasn't far off the mark.

"Welcome to Stewart Hall, Miss Moore." His hair, the dark gold of an autumn harvest, glistened with rain in the glow of several wall sconces. Given the size of the parlor, she was surprised by the lack of a ceiling chandelier.

"Thank you." The room was staid, even dismal, dressed in solemn hues of russet and bronze. A patterned carpet covered the floor and acted as a runner on a central staircase with braided wooden balusters. She had a vague impression of doors somewhere off to the left and a corridor disappearing into shadow. Tugging off her gloves, she forced a smile. "I'm sure my brother told you this is the first time I've taken employment. I'll need to know what's expected of me."

"Of course. Let me hang your cloak, then we'll discuss the details."

Hollande passed him the garment, along with her bonnet. After he'd secured both in a closet, she trailed him to the drawing room.

"Would you like some tea?" He motioned to a sideboard set with a china pot, cups, and saucers.

"Yes, please." A chill pressed into her bones. She couldn't say if the cold was prompted by the dismal weather or her equally dismal surroundings. Not even the fire, crackling in a large stone hearth, seemed capable of chasing away the perpetual frost. "Sugar and cream are fine." She settled onto a stiff burgundy divan, arranging her skirt for modesty.

Nathaniel passed her a cup, then sank into a high-backed chair. "I trust the carriage ride was manageable."

"Of course." Hollande sipped her tea, thankful her fingers didn't tremble. "When will I meet your mother?"

"Later. I prefer to address a few concerns first."

Straight to the point. She replaced the cup in the saucer, watching him expectantly. Would he want references, ask who she'd cared for before? Or had Edgar already told him about Phillip? Did he take pity on her—the lovesick woman who'd watched her brave cavalry captain succumb to a wasting disease?

"I'm sure your brother told you my mother is not well." Nathaniel's pronouncement drew her from her thoughts. "She has good days and bad, but in her mind, all days are the same."

"I don't understand."

"She doesn't think she's ill. She doesn't want you here."

"But then why would you..."

"Pay to have someone act as her companion?" His lips turned in a grim smile. "She's aging. Whether she knows it or not—accepts it or not—continued isolation is an unhealthy habit."

"Doesn't she go into town?"

"This estate is her world. She's been that way since...my father died."

Hollande tried to remember what Edgar told her about the Stewarts. The father—Daniel? No, Darrin, had died years ago. Sylvia Stewart lived alone with her twin sons, Nathaniel and Tristan. The family was well-off but reclusive, the sons occasionally seen in town, but never the mother.

Hollande set her cup and saucer on an end table. "I don't mean to second-guess your plans, and I certainly need employment now that my brother and his wife..." She tightened her hands in her lap, trying not to think of the way Edgar ousted her. "If your mother doesn't want me here, how do you expect me to—"

"I only ask that you do your best." Nathaniel's expression was set, but there was a weariness in his eyes she hadn't noted before. "Tristan and I have both tried to make my mother understand why your presence is important."

"Is your brother here?"

"I expect him back after dinner. Tristan is often out during the day attending to matters of business."

She didn't inquire after the type of business or where that business might take him. As neither brother frequented town, it was possible he had contacts elsewhere. Rumor said most of the Stewart wealth was generated by shrewd investments.

"Because my mother can be"—Nathaniel grimaced—"difficult, Tristan and I have tried to adapt our schedules around her needs. I spend days with her. He sits with her in the evenings."

Surprising. "Are you saying your mother requires attending each hour?"

There was nothing humorous in Nathaniel's short laugh. "It isn't a matter of necessity, so much as what she desires. Since my father's death, she's become dependent on us."

"How long has it been?" Hollande was uncertain if she should press the matter.

"Since my father died? Thirteen years. My mother has not left the property in all that time. Now you understand what you're up against. Tristan and I have coddled our mother for too long. We both feel it's time she stood on her own." As if to cement the matter, Nathaniel rose to his feet.

Hollande stared up at him. "Then she's not sick?"

"Not physically. If there is an illness that plagues her, it is an ailment of the mind. I need you to befriend her, Miss Moore. If she can adapt to change in her own home, there is hope she'll eventually embrace life as it should be. For thirteen years, I've tended to her needs. I am not ashamed to say I've wearied of the task."

He was blunt if nothing else. Sylvia Stewart had become inconvenient to him. Given the stance Edgar had taken, perhaps she had more in common with Nathaniel's mother than she originally thought.

Hollande sat straighter. She prayed her distaste did not show. "What of Tristan?"

Nathaniel's mouth twisted. "He will tell you the same when you meet him."

* * * *

Present Day

After her session with Dr. Kapoor, Madison stopped by her office. The realty company she worked for wasn't large, an independent firm on the plus side of thirty agents. The occasional part-timer came and went, but most of the full-time agents had been with Hode's Hill Realty Group for years. Gaining a foothold was tough for anyone starting out in the business, especially in the current market, but the broker had added two new agents over the last month.

Madison had yet to meet either—agents came and went at differing hours throughout the day and evening—but wished them well. It had taken a full year for her to get her business back on track. Thankfully, she'd had the luxury of living with Jillian during the lean months. Many times, new agents didn't have a cache to tide them over until the first commission checks started to appear.

Once in the office, she said hello to Betsie, the receptionist, then headed down a hallway to a large room in the rear. Madison's cubicle was on the left in a quad with three others, two on each side, back to back. Bruce Horton, who sat beside her, was nowhere to be seen, but the half-empty water bottle by his phone indicated he'd probably been there earlier.

She dumped her laptop and several files on the desk as she slid into her chair. First things first. She wanted to call Lou Keaggy, the contractor she used for odd jobs, and have him install an automatic opener with a lock on her garage. That should prevent a repeat of last night's vandalism. Afterward, she needed to contact the Martins about the latest round of listings she'd emailed for review, then follow up on the status of a closing scheduled for the end of the month.

Lou's contact information was stored on her cell. As she rooted through her purse for the phone, an attractive brunette rolled her chair around the corner of the cubicle.

"Hi. You must be Madison."

"Yes. Hi." She offered a smile. The woman had to be one of the new agents Glen hired.

"I'm Karen Randall. I just started last week." The woman extended her hand, confirming Madison's suspicions. "It's nice to meet you." She looked to be somewhere in her midthirties, with light brown eyes and a sprinkling of freckles over her nose.

"Welcome." Madison shook her hand. "Are you brand new to the business?" Through networking and association, she'd come to know a good percentage of agents in competing firms, and Karen's name didn't sound familiar.

"Yes. Newly licensed."

"Congratulations. It's a great field. If I can help in any way, let me know."

"Thanks." Karen's eyes lit with warmth. "Everyone's been so helpful. It's exciting to try something new."

Madison set her phone on her desk, then fished in the top drawer for a pen. "What did you do before?"

"I had a residential cleaning business. Nothing large. Just two employees. I did okay, but it took a toll on my back. My husband was the one who suggested real estate. Which reminds me." Karen sat up straighter, suddenly animated. "I saw on the sales board you closed that old home on Yarrow Creek Road."

"Yes. A few weeks ago."

"That must have been difficult. I can't believe someone actually bought the place."

"Why?"

"Well, you know...all the rumors and odd things that happened there." Karen's reaction was not at all what she expected.

"What are you talking about? I'm the one who bought it."

"You did? Oh...I didn't know. I..." A wash of red stole over Karen's cheeks. "I'm sorry. I should get back to work. It was nice meeting you." Quickly, she scooted her chair behind the cubicle.

Madison walked around the partition. "Karen, what did you mean? What happened at the house?"

The woman did her best to look busy, shuffling through several multi-list printouts. The crimson stain had yet to fade from her cheeks. "Nothing. Really." Her laugh was high and fluttery. "Just ignore me." The phone at her elbow beeped, flashing with a green light.

"Karen," Betsie's voice came through the intercom. "Mr. and Mrs. Blocker are in the lobby to see you."

Karen depressed a button. "I'll be right there." Gathering the printouts, she shot to her feet and offered Madison a wobbly smile. "My first appointment. Wish me luck."

As she hurried from the room, Madison wasn't sure if Karen's nerves were from the appointment, or her discovery that Madison was the new homeowner of 2 Yarrow Creek Road.

* * * *

By the time Madison finished at the office, it was after three. Before heading home, she swung by the grocery store for more cleaning supplies and a few toiletries. As she passed the floral section, a bright yellow spray of daffodils caught her eye. She added the flowers on a whim, tucking them in with her other purchases.

She was halfway to her car in the parking lot when she spied a man wearing ratty jeans and dark sunglasses approaching. Something about the way he moved with his shoulders hunched forward, dragging his feet rather than lifting the heels, was familiar. She tried to latch onto a memory, regretting the effort the instant it clicked into place. Quickly, she averted her eyes.

"Hey." He halted as she reached her car. "You look familiar."

"Sorry. I don't know you." Madison clicked her electronic key fob to open the door. She dropped her bags into the backseat.

"Sure you do." The guy stepped closer. "You were with Boyd Hewitt. That jerk stiffed me for a wad of cash."

"I don't know what you're talking about." She slid into her seat and reached for the door handle. But the man—she couldn't remember his name, just that she'd seen him with Boyd before—had bullied into the open space, making it impossible to close the door. Her heart heaved into her throat. "You're in my way."

"Got any cash?"

"No. And I wouldn't give you any if I did. Now get out of the way or I'll scream."

"Whatever." The guy seemed to realize he would be an idiot to force a confrontation in broad daylight in a parking lot. He held up his hands and stepped backward. "It's not worth it."

Madison slammed the car door and hit the lock. As she jabbed the button for the ignition, he leaned down to peer through the window.

"You should know there are a lot of people out there still ticked at that dead husband of yours." He pitched his voice to be heard through the glass. "If I were you, I'd be careful, pretty lady."

He cast her a smug smile, then sauntered away, across the lot to the store. Madison watched his slow progress, hands latched onto the steering wheel, her heart drumming out an anvil beat. It took a full five minutes before she was able to collect herself and back out of the space.

The encounter clung and was still swirling in her head when she pulled into her driveway. A single glance at the house helped her breathe easier. The property represented starting over, free from her past and the ugly tragedies connected with those years.

Feeling better, she carried her bags inside, then instantly drew up short. The sound of a man and woman arguing drifted from the drawing room.

"Hello?" Had Jillian stopped by with Dante?

The voices fell silent.

"Jillian? Is that you?" Her sister was the only person she'd given a key.

Madison dumped the bags on a small table, then strode across the foyer. The pocket doors—always open—were shut. Her sister must have done that, too.

"Jillian?" As she stepped inside the drawing room, a prickle of warning coiled around her stomach.

Something was out of place, though the room looked as it always did, formal and staid with claw-footed furniture, oversized moldings, and worn rugs. Almost as an afterthought, she noticed the drapes. Someone had drawn the heavy panels over the windows. Like the pocket doors, she'd left them open. Or was being off her medication making her forgetful?

Madison crossed to the window, then thrust the curtains aside. Two words had been emblazoned on the glass in red.

Get out!

* * * *

Detective Sherre Lorquet waited until the forensic techs left before turning back to the women seated on the couch. Jillian gnawed her lip, while Madison appeared angry, equally deflated. Her skin was sallow, but her eyes burned with an edge like cut glass.

Sherre had known both women for several years. The first to arrive on the scene when Boyd Hewitt was killed, she'd long since passed professional detachment. Madison and Jillian were among her closest friends.

Which made the call all the more irritating. She dropped into a chair with a faded paisley cover. Why Madison had chosen to buy the derelict property was beyond her. Furnished or not, cheap or not, the place was a relic. "One more time, Madison." Sherre consulted a small notepad. "Was the door locked when you got here?"

"I think so." Elbow propped on the arm of the sofa, Madison rubbed her forehead. "I didn't check. The door was shut. I know that much."

"And you used your key to get in?"

"Yes."

Sherre glanced to Jillian. The younger sister by two years, she appeared to be hanging on Madison's every word. With her empathic abilities, she was likely already mired in Madison's anger and frustration.

"You said you heard people arguing." Even with the pocket doors closed, Madison might have picked up on a conversation happening outside.

"Yes. A man and a woman."

"Could you tell what they were saying?"

"No."

Sherre's gaze flashed to the window where *Get Out!* had been scrawled in red. Likely spray paint, something forensics would be able to confirm. The culprit—or culprits—had taken the time to write the letters in reverse from the outside. When viewed from the room, the words were readable without mimicking a mirror effect. Whoever was responsible wanted the message understood clearly.

Her team found trampled grass, but nothing significant to identify footprints. Likewise, the slashed tires from the garage were apt to yield little. They'd been handled too many times. Jillian had been livid with her sister for not reporting the incident immediately, and Sherre had to agree. She was working with pieces when she might have had larger chunks of the puzzle if contacted at the outset.

"Let's go back to the pocket doors." Rehashing an event often jogged details in a victim's mind. "You said they were closed."

A nod.

"But you're positive they were open when you left the house?"

"They're never shut. They've been open from the time I moved in. I thought Jillian must have dropped by and closed them. The drapes were closed, too."

"And you were never here?" Sherre directed her question to Jillian.

"No." Jillian paced to the window, eying the ugly red letters emblazoned on the glass. "You're sure no one was in the house?"

"There's no evidence of forced entry. Nothing taken. Nothing disturbed." Sherre looked to Madison. "Who else has a key?"

"Just me and Jillian."

"And you changed the locks after settlement?"

"Yes. It's something we recommend all new homeowners do."

"Any idea why someone would want to scare you?"

Madison gave a chuff of laughter. "Aside from the obvious?"

"This isn't about Boyd. It's about you."

"My sister doesn't have enemies." Jillian moved behind the couch to rest her hands on Madison's shoulders. "I think she's right. The Porter brothers are dead, but Boyd ticked off a lot of people. Some of them might hold a grudge."

Sherre didn't need to be an empath to recognize the concern pulsating from Jillian. The younger woman had spent three agonizing years visiting Madison in Rest Haven. Sitting at her side, pleading with her to rejoin the world, living with the constant disappointment of a blank stare. Understandable that she'd hover.

"I don't buy it." Sherre slipped the notepad into the back pocket of her jeans. "Assuming there is someone with a score to settle over Boyd, what do they gain by scaring Madison?"

"Maybe they don't gain anything." Madison hesitated. "It could be about anger and paybacks."

"What makes you say that?"

"When I was leaving the store today, I ran into a guy in the parking lot. He told me Boyd had stiffed him for money."

Jillian's face paled. "Is that all?"

"No." Madison looked to Sherre. "He said there were a lot of people still ticked at Boyd, and I that should be careful. He wanted cash, but I told him if he didn't leave I'd scream."

"Why didn't you say something earlier?" Jillian sank next to her sister on the sofa, alarm evident in the way she gripped Madison's wrist.

"Because I was more focused on the problems here. The rest of it went out of my head."

"But the vandalism could be connected. How do you know the guy didn't follow you to the store? He could have been waiting for you."

"I don't think so. It seemed more random, like a chance encounter."

Sherre wasn't so sure. "Do you know who he was?"

Madison shook her head. "I just remember seeing him with Boyd. There were a lot of people who came and went from the house in those days. I didn't even realize Boyd was dealing. By the time I figured out what was going on, it was too late."

She'd been ready to leave him when Boyd was killed. Sherre still regretted Madison hadn't come to that decision earlier. "I can't do much if I don't know who the guy is. If he demanded cash or threatened you, that's attempted robbery."

"It wasn't exactly like that."

"Still—if you want to come down to the station, I'll have you look through some books. You might recognize the guy from a photo."

"I don't want to deal with it. Not now." Madison waved the suggestion aside. "I'm tired of the constant fallout from Boyd. If I think of the guy's name, I'll let you know. Otherwise, I just want to focus on what happened here."

"It's your call." Old properties were common targets of vandalism by kids, but slashed tires were personal. Cop instinct told Sherre the timing of running into someone from Boyd's past was more than coincidence. "At least give me a description of the guy." She'd go through the books herself. "I'll keep you posted on what I find."

* * * *

Madison used a handheld gardening spade to dig a small hole in the soil of Sylvia Stewart's grave. She added the daffodils, then stood back to survey her handiwork. After years of helping Jillian tend Gabriel Vane's resting place, it felt natural to look after Sylvia, her husband, and their son. She'd need to buy more flowers, remembrance offerings so Darrin and Nathaniel would know they weren't forgotten. Once she was more settled, she'd have to learn what she could about the family who'd occupied her home in the past.

A sensation of peace washed over her. Dusk was the time she loved best, especially with sweet florals and sun-warmed grass perfuming the night. The daffodils were so bright, they appeared luminescent in the twilight. Roth would be arriving soon, picking her up for dinner, but there was no reason to hurry inside.

On the veranda, she settled into a rattan rocker. After the turbulence of the day, it felt good to unwind. She'd made Jillian promise not to say anything to Roth about the tires, the warning on the window, or the guy in the parking lot. Whether or not the incidents were connected remained to be seen, but it seemed evident someone didn't want her here.

She needed to talk to Karen Randall and find out why the new agent had reacted so badly when she learned Madison had purchased the house. She could always call Corrine Charles, the executrix of Vera Halsey's estate, but didn't want to impose. Contact between sellers and buyers was conducted through respective agents and usually stopped after settlement. The fact that Madison *was* the agent—as well as the homebuyer—didn't change protocol.

"Hey. What are you doing back here?"

She glanced up to find Roth standing at the edge of the veranda.

He hooked a thumb over his shoulder. "I knocked but didn't get an answer. Thought I'd check around the side."

"Sorry." Madison hadn't heard him approach. She moved into his arms for a kiss. "It's such a nice night. I wanted some air."

His lips turned in a droll grin. "I would too if I lived in this dinosaur."

"I happen to like old homes."

"That's obvious. I've been replaced and neglected. At least I haven't been ousted by a dog."

"Jillian thinks I should get one." Something her sister had pressed only that afternoon after learning about the slashed tires and the threat on the window. "She offered to put me in touch with Blizzard's breeder."

Roth kept his arm hooked around her waist. "Probably not a bad idea, given how—"

If she heard "isolated" one more time, she was going to scream.

"*Rustic* the place is." Roth smiled down at her. After six months he'd learned to read her well.

"My schedule is too erratic for a dog. Maybe a cat."

"Great protection. If you're afraid of mice." He steered her from the veranda. "Are you ready for dinner?"

"Sure. I just want to switch on a few lights before we leave."

Independence aside, she feared returning to a dark house.

Chapter 4

March 24, 1878

Hollande withstood Sylvia Stewart's inspection, hands clasped in front of her, features arranged impassively. Nathaniel had warned her his mother would be difficult. After taking her on a tour of the home, he'd escorted her to his mother's bedchamber, made introductions, then left.

Sylvia sat enthroned in a chair before a brick fireplace, her blue-veined hands folded over an ebony cane. She was younger than Hollande expected, perhaps a few years shy of sixty. She wore her black hair in a severe top knot, wisps of gray visible at the temples. Thin-boned without appearing frail, she reminded Hollande of a sturdy tree defying the advancement of age.

"So, you're the girl my sons have employed to look after me." Sylvia's pale lips curled with distaste. She stood, then circled Hollande slowly as if evaluating her worth. Like one might a bauble or trinket for purchase.

Hollande held her tongue. She'd expected to feel a measure of kinship with Sylvia given they'd both become inconvenient to respective family members, but her empathy was one-sided. The older woman's resentment weighted the air with hostility.

"You don't look like much." Sylvia completed her circuit.

"I apologize if my appearance offends you."

"Hmph. Snippy thing." Sylvia resettled in her rocker. "Tristan, Nathaniel, and I have managed fine all these years. We have Annabelle to cook and clean. I see no reason to have another woman upset the balance."

"Perhaps, but your sons think differently." Nathaniel had introduced her to Annabelle Murray, the housekeeper/cook who spent a few hours each day preparing meals and tidying the rooms when needed. She looked no older than nineteen, dropped off by her young husband each day, picked up each evening after he completed his shift at the local sawmill.

"Why do you keep it closed up in here?" Unable to withstand the suffocating atmosphere any longer, Hollande crossed the room then tugged open the drapes. No wonder the woman was so miserable if this was how she lived. Through a cluster of rain-soaked trees fording the house, Yarrow Creek cut a blue-gray swath in the distance. Mist swirled above the waterline in filmy white patches. The view was steely and overcast, but at least the open curtains allowed light inside.

"Close those, young lady." Sylvia's voice carried the crack of the whip.

"Is it the rain you don't like?" Hollande faced her hostess, surprised by her tone.

Sylvia's lips compressed in a severe line. "It's the creek I have no wish to see. Ghastly thing." Her mouth puckered as if she'd encountered something sour. "Sit down." She used the tip of her cane to jab an adjacent chair. "As long as you're here, we need to understand one another."

Hollande closed the drapes then settled where directed. She thought of her room at home—the welcoming shades of cream and rose, the canopied bed with lacy coverlet, the tall windows overlooking cobblestone streets—and was suddenly homesick. How could Edgar have done this to her?

"I'm sure Nathaniel already instructed you about certain practices, but I intend to make them clear." Sylvia's stare was dark, a match for the dreary day. "You've been given the guest room on the first floor?"

Hollande nodded. The chamber was every bit as bleak as the rest of the house, with houndstooth wallcoverings and drapes so heavy they seemed better suited to a tomb. It was as though light and air hadn't been introduced to the place in...

She remembered when Darrin had died.

Thirteen years.

"Nathaniel and Tristan each have their own room, neither of which has any reason to be visited by you. Is that clear?"

Hollande flushed. "I assure you, Mrs. Stewart, I have no intention of becoming entangled with either of your sons." The mere thought made her bristle.

"Ah. So, you don't like to have your virtue challenged." Sylvia appeared to enjoy her outrage. "Stick to what you've pledged, and that is one obstacle out of the way." Stretching in her chair, she retrieved the fireplace poker. She prodded the logs in the hearth with surprising strength, sending the flames higher, much like Hollande's indignation.

"There is a room at the opposite end of the hall," Sylvia said.

"Your deceased husband's study." Hollande's back remained rigid, but she forced the edge from her voice. "Nathaniel said it is kept locked."

"At all times, in memory of Darrin." Sylvia returned the poker to its resting place. "You will have nothing to do with that room. Understood?"

"Perfectly."

"It is Nathaniel's practice to take dinner early then retire for the night. Once he does, you are not to disturb him."

Hollande nodded. Nathaniel had mentioned as much. Perhaps it was his way to unwind after tending to an acrimonious mother. "Is that all?"

"No." Sylvia stared down her nose. "As long as you are here, fetch me a cup of tea. Two sugars, no cream. Then you may go to your room and get settled. I do not expect to see you until dinner."

Hollande was only too glad to be dismissed. Feeling sick to her stomach, she served Sylvia her tea, then went downstairs to her room and closed the door. Nathaniel had placed her luggage on the bed. She dug in the smallest bag for a framed photo she was never without.

With Phillip's picture clutched to her chest, she collapsed on the bed and sobbed.

* * * *

Present Day

Dinner out with Roth was just what Madison needed. The evening allowed her to put the ugliness of the day behind her and relax with a glass of wine. They made plans to connect with Jillian and Dante plus a few mutual friends at Friday night's Fiend Festival, an event Hode's Hill held every June to honor an archaic urban legend. Madison had skipped the Memorial Day celebrations but looked forward to the Fiend Festival with its mashup of food tents, artisans, and bands. She needed a break from the house.

At home, she kissed Roth good night before locking the door securely. All went well until the rustling sound awakened her in the middle of the night. The moment she switched on the bedside lamp, the noise stopped.

"Damn it." Had she imagined it again? Maybe she'd been dreaming. She'd half convinced herself of the truth when she caught a flicker of movement beyond the balcony doors.

Madison's heart thudded. She turned off the lamp, slipped from bed, then tugged on a pair of jeans under her sleepshirt. Her cell phone was on the nightstand. She debated about calling nine-one-one, but she was two stories up. How could someone be on the balcony?

"This isn't happening."

Once again, she worried she might be experiencing side effects from stopping her medication. Dr. Kapoor would have surely told her if there was a risk. Maybe it had just been a bird or bat outside. She approached the doors, phone in hand should she need to summon help. It took only a few paces to see there was no one on the balcony.

Madison exhaled a ball of nerves. She wrenched open the door and stepped outside, embraced by the cool night. A yellow light moved along Yarrow Creek.

A light that looked like an old-fashioned lantern.

"That's it." She wasn't going to be scared from her home.

Back inside, she pulled on sneakers, shoved her cell in her pocket, then hurried downstairs. In the kitchen, she grabbed a flashlight before slipping out the rear door to the veranda. The light was still there, moving slowly, as if someone walked along the bank.

Looking for something.

The thought struck her from nowhere. Whoever carried that lantern was in no hurry, systematically moving back and forth, stooping occasionally for a better view. Could it be the person who'd slashed her tires? Who'd spray-painted the threat on the drawing room window? The man in the parking lot?

Madison opened her phone and scrolled through her contacts. She pressed Sherre Lorquet's number, watching the lantern as she waited for the ring.

Nothing.

She tried again.

The phone flashed *No Signal.*

Impossible. Her battery was fully charged, and she'd always had a strong signal before. Perfect.

Her gaze swept back to the light. She was too far away to detect a form in the darkness, but someone had to be holding that lantern aloft. The way it bobbed made her think of will-o'-the-wisps and other spooklights from folklore.

Keeping the flashlight off, she clung to the shadows and edged closer, dew-soaked grass muffling her footsteps. When she was near enough to detect a form, she squatted behind a tree and peered around the trunk.

There was no question her night visitor was a man. The breadth of his shoulders and the way he moved betrayed him. His clothing, like the lantern, was distinctly old-fashioned—boots, frock coat, and a shirt with a ruffling of white at the throat. Curiously, she felt no fear.

"Hello." She switched on the flashlight.

The man pivoted. Madison had only a second to catch a glimmer of dark gold hair and the shock of his expression before a shriek exploded above her. She recoiled, raising her arms defensively as her gaze was wrenched to the sky. A tornado of wind lifted her off her feet and hurtled her backward into a tree. When her body struck—head, shoulders, back— her legs folded beneath her.

She crumpled to the ground, a boneless heap, stripped of consciousness.

* * * *

Madison woke to the touch of sunlight on her face. With a groan, she scraped hair from her eyes and stared up at leaf patterns overhead. Memory slowly returned. The light by the creek, the strange man in old-fashioned clothing, the terrible shriek of sound followed by a cyclone of wind.

With effort, she pulled herself to a sitting position. A knot of pain bloomed in the back of her head. She prodded gingerly, discovering a lump that made her wince when she brushed her fingers over the top. Once on her feet, she took stock of several new aches. Lying on the ground had left her body stiff, but the pain in her right shoulder seemed related more to injury than a long night. Carefully, she rolled her arm to loosen the muscle, stooped for the flashlight, then picked her way down the bank.

Grass yielded where the ground sloped to the creek, ending in patches of dirt and boggy soil. Rocks, dried leaves, and reeds clustered at the edges. A myriad of trees bent over the water, including a few on the far side. Wherever she looked, the ground appeared undisturbed.

Like the drawing room.

Despite the closed pocket doors and drawn drapes.

Madison hugged her arms to her chest. It wasn't possible for someone to wade across the wide expanse of Yarrow Creek. Even if the man swam, which didn't seem likely given the way he was dressed, there should be footprints in the mud where he'd walked.

She massaged her temple, the ache in her head growing. She would have looked foolish dragging Sherre out of bed on a needless call last night. Foolish and hysterical.

No longer certain what she'd seen or heard, she headed back to the house. As she neared the veranda, the small cemetery to the rear made her draw up short. The daffodils she'd placed on Sylvia Stewart's grave—fresh and vibrant less than twenty-four hours ago—had withered into rotted brown husks, leeched of all life.

* * * *

Madison didn't catch up with Karen Randall until Friday morning. She found the other woman in the smaller of the realty firm's two conference rooms, a stack of printed letters, box of envelopes, and several packets of stamps spread over the table. As Madison stepped into the room, Karen scribbled her name at the bottom of a letter then stuffed it into an envelope.

"Hi."

"Oh! Hi." Karen gave a start of surprise.

"How are things going?"

"Fine." Karen sipped coffee from a blue mug. "There's a lot to do getting started."

"You'll be glad you took the time." Madison had come from the parking lot, loaded down with her laptop, purse, a stack of client folders, and her own cup of coffee. She shifted everything but the coffee onto the table and sank into a chair. "Has Glen hooked you up with a mentor yet?"

Karen grabbed a letter to sign. "Shelia Warburton."

"Shelia's great. Knowledgeable, too. She's helped me out more than once."

"How long have you been an agent?"

Madison hedged. Karen would have picked up on scuttlebutt around the office. Everyone knew Madison had spent three years in a care facility after seeing her husband murdered. "I've really only been active the last year or so." Wetting her lips, she shifted gears. "When we were talking the other day, you seemed a little frazzled when I mentioned I bought the house on Yarrow Creek Road."

"Frazzled?" Karen ducked her head to scrawl another signature. "I don't know what you mean." She busied herself with the letters, averting her gaze.

Madison sighed. "The house is really old, and I'm trying to find out whatever I can about the place. If you know something—"

"Like what?"

"I don't know." After several unusual experiences, she needed Karen to be forthcoming. "It's just...an odd place. You mentioned rumors. Said there were things that happened there."

"Yeah." Karen's hands stilled. She stared at the letters in front of her as if debating something. After a moment, she closed her eyes, drew a breath, then shifted her attention to Madison. "You remember I told you I had a cleaning business? Vera Halsey was one of my clients."

"The woman who owned the house?" Madison had never made direct contact with her during the sale. "I understand she passed away in a nursing home."

"That's what I heard, too. But she stopped my services months before she got sick. She was only in her early sixties, but something happened, and she started wasting away."

Madison had always assumed she was up in years, eighty or more. "That's horrible."

"Strange is how I see it." Karen smoothed an envelope between her fingers. "Everything about her was odd. The house, too."

"What do you mean?"

"I wish I could explain it better. I had two people working for me. Both said they'd quit before going back again. I was the one who ended up cleaning for Vera. After a while, I got used to"—she looked away—"things."

Madison's pulse ticked higher. "What do you mean?"

"I don't want to scare you."

Madison held her gaze.

"Okay." Karen leaned forward and lowered her voice as if sharing a secret. "It was just a sense of something always there...like being watched. The girls I had working for me said they heard people arguing when no one was around."

Madison's fingers tightened on her coffee cup. "Did you?"

"Once. Maybe twice. There were other things, too. Doors that shut on their own, cold spots, rancid odors. Sometimes I'd see someone from the corner of my eye and turn, but no one was there. Occasionally, some of my supplies would go missing only to show up in another room. The last week I was there, I swear someone tried to shove me down the steps."

"Did you ever talk to Vera about those things?"

"Not by choice, but she'd tell me whether I wanted to hear or not. She walked around the house whispering to herself. Sometimes she'd sit in the living room with a Ouija board and a black candle, staring off into space. She was the one who told me the place was haunted."

Madison felt the blood drain from her face. A strained laugh slipped from her lips. "Haunted?"

"Now you understand why I didn't want to tell you. Vera said there was something in the house. A presence that had been drawn by violence and stank of death. I know it sounds dramatic, but every now and then I'd catch a whiff of something foul. I thought the place had a sewage problem." The words spilled from Karen in a rush. "I hated going there. Almost like I could feel that *thing*, whatever it was she was talking about. She wasn't frightened of it, because it was contained and couldn't hurt her."

"Contained?"

Karen shrugged. "I know. Crazy, right? Vera said she was the first person who lived there who understood what it was. That was because her grandfather was a Stewart. She said he was descended from the original bloodline."

"The people buried behind the house." Madison's stomach contracted. She was sure her face was green, if not white. "Are you talking about ghosts?"

"Hey, you two. What's up?"

When Bruce Horton sauntered into the room, Madison nearly bolted from her chair. She'd been so intent on the conversation, she jerked, marginally avoiding spilling coffee into her lap. "Bruce." A nervous laugh escaped her. "Wow, you gave me a start."

"Sorry about that." He looked at her strangely. Probably remembering her history, which clung like a second skin despite her best efforts to banish it—*fragile. Ready to crack.*

"Thanks, Karen." She gathered her laptop, folders, and purse. "Sorry to run, you two, but I have a ten o'clock appointment."

She was out the door before either could challenge the lie.

Chapter 5

Dinner was strained, but Hollande expected no less. Sylvia's hostility was almost tangible, and while Nathaniel made a few attempts at small talk, he eventually gave up. Hollande wanted nothing more than to vanish into her room and retreat from the world in sleep, but she'd been hired as a companion to Sylvia. When Nathaniel announced he was retiring for the evening, Hollande retrieved her embroidery bag, then joined Sylvia in the drawing room.

"Can I get you anything?"

Sylvia's lips twitched in a frown. "I enjoy the quiet. And Tristan will be here soon."

Hollande took the snip as a warning to be silent. She settled in a chair by the fireplace, withdrew her embroidery hoop, and tried to concentrate on pleasanter times. Many evenings she'd stitch by the fire while Edgar read the newspaper and Carolyn penned a letter to family. In those days, all three had chatted about the latest news or events in town, and despite the dreadful loss of her parents, Hollande felt secure in her world. What could she possibly discuss with Sylvia—a woman who never ventured into Hode's Hill and had no friends to speak of? Her husband's death must have shattered her beyond comprehension to become such a recluse.

After five minutes, Sylvia spoke into the silence. "If my sons told you I'm ill, I'm not."

Surprised by her effort at conversation, more by the subject, Hollande glanced up with a start. The older woman regarded her steadily from a seat on the divan. Her skirt flowed around her in a black puddle, glimmers of firelight trapped within its inky folds. The dour fabric suited her, the only spot of color a gathering of pale-blue lace at her throat and wrists.

"I—" Overcome by awkwardness, Hollande struggled to find an appropriate reply. "I think they are more concerned with your well-being. And I'm afraid I learned of the situation secondhand. My brother is the one who spoke to Nathaniel. He informed me of the position only after giving my consent."

A severe black brow crept toward Sylvia's hair. "You mean to say he foisted this situation on you?"

Hollande lowered her eyes. "I can't truly fault him. He and his wife have a baby on the way, and Carolyn wishes to move closer to her family in Arbor Point. I lost my fiancé three years ago." Would that bring her closer to Sylvia? "Edgar had to sell our parents' home, so of course, he had to find a place for me."

Sylvia grunted in displeasure. "Men do not always know what is best for women." Something about her tone told Hollande she spoke from experience. "What happened to your fiancé?"

A blunt question from a blunt woman. Hollande dipped her needle into the hoop and forced herself to face the query head-on. "Phillip was a captain with Federal forces during the War Between the States. He was wounded at Gettysburg. Years later, the injury took a toll on his health." There was no need to mention the outcome. She wondered if she dared ask about Darrin. "You've been widowed for a long time."

"Some things you do know." Sylvia's gaze narrowed. She looked away, falling into stony silence. They remained like that until the sound of approaching footsteps drew their attention.

The stoop of Sylvia's shoulders vanished as her gaze swung toward the pocket doors. Hollande followed her glance, shocked by the sight of the man who strode into the room. At first, she was certain Nathaniel must have changed clothes to rejoin them.

"Mother, how good to see you." The newcomer crossed the room, then stooped to kiss Sylvia on the cheek. This had to be Tristan. Straightening, he shifted his attention to Hollande. "And this must be Miss Moore."

Hollande rose to her feet. "It is a pleasure to meet you, Mr. Stewart."

"Tristan, please, and the pleasure is mine. I'm sorry I wasn't here to greet you earlier." He had the same dark gold hair as his brother but wore it swept back from his forehead. Likewise, his eyes were the same amber, though somehow warmer. Perhaps it was nothing more than his ready smile and the openness of his features, so unlike Nathaniel's somberness.

"I'm sorry I missed dinner, but hopefully, Nathaniel and Mother kept you entertained."

Nothing could be further from the truth. "I think it's my responsibility to do the entertaining where your mother is concerned." She was conscious of Sylvia's glare, but the hostility evaporated the moment Tristan glanced in his mother's direction. The change that came over her face was startling.

"Come sit with me, Tristan. Tell me of your day." Sylvia patted the divan.

Bitter and resentful around Nathaniel, she fawned over Tristan. For his part, Nathaniel's brother indulged her, talking at length about his trip and various business associates in Curtisville.

Hollande found herself laughing over his many quips. He had a ready wit and a demeanor to put anyone at ease. *Charming,* her mother would have said. When Sylvia mentioned dinner warming in the kitchen, Tristan declined, saying he'd enjoyed a hearty repast before driving his carriage home.

"If anything, I feel my bed calling. It's been a long day."

Sylvia's face crumpled. "Not so soon." Her fingers coiled around Tristan's forearm in a grip that made the veins pop. "Sit with me a while longer. I've missed you."

For a second, Hollande imagined a flash of weariness in Tristan's eyes, but the trace was gone as quickly as it appeared. It was only when all three finally said good night, and Tristan escorted his mother up the stairs, that Hollande grew convinced his sparkling personality came with cost.

When he turned to face her, his features were crippled with exhaustion.

* * * *

Present Day

Madison had skipped last year's Fiend Festival, so the Friday night opening was her first in five years. Still reeling from what Karen told her earlier that day, she found it hard to focus on the activities. As usual, the city sectioned off an area of the riverfront, closing River Road to traffic. Festivalgoers wandered up and down the banks while others camped in lawn chairs, most clustered around a portable stage where the winner of the Fiend Contest would be announced.

Contestants vying for the title roamed the grounds in costume—caped figures dressed in black with leering devil masks or elaborate face paint. The Fiend of urban legend had terrorized Hode's Hill in the late 1800s, killing several women before being shot and plunging into the river. Though the creature's body was never found, the folklore surrounding its deeds grew stronger with each decade. In some ways it was odd celebrating a monster responsible for murder, yet like most archaic legends, the truth was taken with a grain of salt. The night came down to campy fun and a reason to celebrate.

Madison weaved between a hotdog stand and an ice cream cart, following Dante DeLuca and Jillian as they made their way further down the bank. Blizzard trotted at Jillian's side, a retractable leash hooked to the husky's bright blue collar. By mutual agreement, they'd chosen a pizza vendor as the spot to connect with a group of friends. A few minutes ago, Roth left to take a phone call, promising to catch up as soon as he was done.

Eventually, they located Tessa Camden with David Gregg, and Maya Hode with her husband, Collin. David, a senior detective with Hode's Hill PD, had been dating Tessa for over a year. Maya and Collin had married last September at the Hode estate, a sprawling manor on the opposite side of the river. Dateless at the time, Madison had attended with Jillian and Dante. Collin was so down to earth, it was sometimes hard to remember his family founded the town.

"I thought you'd be down on the stage with the mayor." Dante gripped Collin's hand.

"Headed there now." Hode Development sponsored the Fiend Festival each year, an association that put Collin's family in the limelight and required a short speech. "Shouldn't take long. Then I'm up for enjoying the festival like the rest of you." He gave Maya a kiss before sprinting off in the direction of the stage.

"Madison, where's Roth?" Tessa asked.

"He'll be here soon. He needed a quiet place to take a phone call."

"Good luck with that." David nodded to a group of boys racing between the food tents, his nephew, Finn, and Tessa's son, Elliott, among them. "Now that school's out, I swear the kids are on hyperdrive. This place is a zoo."

The others fell into easy chatter, prompting Madison to tug on Dante's arm. "Hey, can I talk to you a minute?"

"Sure." He seemed a little surprised but eased to the side, placing them a few steps from the main group. Engaged with Maya and Tessa, Jillian didn't notice. "Is something wrong?"

"Not exactly. I just—" How did she explain what she needed? It shouldn't be that difficult. Dante's given profession was artist, but he'd conducted enough séances to qualify as a medium. She'd never seen him in action but knew he was able to read folk memories when the impressions were strong enough. "I hope the art exhibit went well."

"Not bad." He shrugged. "Big cities are great, but it's nice to be back in Hode's Hill. Jillian said you got settled in the new house."

"That's what I want to talk to you about." She lobbed a glance to the side, making sure Jillian was still distracted. "The place is really old. It has a family plot with graves."

"I heard about those. Jillian seemed bothered by the idea, but you both know the seriousness of grave-tending." Dante shifted, allowing a young couple with a corgi to pass. The dog stopped every few feet to sniff the ground. When it reached Blizzard, the two circled each other, tails wagging. Jillian and the couple started chatting.

Madison shifted her attention to Dante. "The graves don't bother me, but I've had a few odd experiences. Then earlier today, I talked with a woman who used to clean the house. She had weird things happen while she worked there and is convinced the place is haunted."

Surprise crossed his face. "Does Jillian know?"

"No. And I don't want her to. But I want to understand what's going on. If you walked through the house, you might be able to pick up impressions. Folk memories."

"I don't know, Madison." He blew out a breath. "Your sister and I have a great thing going, and I don't like the idea of doing something behind her back."

"She'll worry."

"Of course, she's going to worry."

"More than she should. After Boyd and Rest Haven, she doesn't think I'm capable of managing on my own."

"That's not true." Dante held her gaze briefly before looking away. He seemed to debate the matter.

If there was another medium she could contact, she'd do it in a heartbeat, but there were too many frauds. Dante was the real thing, the first person to break through her walls after three years in a care facility. He looked the part of bohemian artist—long black hair secured in a ponytail, tears in his acid-washed jeans, a gold Saint Michael's medal looped around his neck—but he possessed a spiritual gift few people could match. More importantly, he cared about her and would never lie.

Which was why the predicament she'd placed him in made her feel deceitful.

"Hey, what's going on?"

Madison hadn't noticed when Jillian grew conscious of their conversation. The young couple with the corgi had wandered away.

"Your sister was telling me about her house." Dante left the comment open, giving her an opportunity to pick up the reins.

Damn him. She'd been stupid to think she could exclude her sister. "I asked if he could try to pick up some ghost impressions."

"Folk memories?"

"There have been some strange things I didn't tell you about, and I found out today the place is supposed to be haunted."

Jillian's eyes widened. "Were you *going* to tell me?"

Madison dropped her gaze. She was saved an answer when Maya interrupted to announce the group was heading toward the stage to hear the mayor's welcome address and Collin's speech.

"We'll be right there." Jillian shifted her attention back to Madison. Waiting. Behind them, someone yelled out an order for two slices of pepperoni. A mesh of spicy sauces and melting cheese wafted on the air.

Madison exhaled. "All right. I'll tell you everything that's going on, but not now. What if you both come over for dinner tomorrow night? I don't want Roth to know about any of this."

"No secrets?" Jillian's gaze held challenge.

"No secrets." Madison stooped to ruff Blizzard's fur when the dog butted against her. "How about six o'clock?"

"We'll be there," Dante answered for both. "Secrets aside, I'd like to see the place."

* * * *

Madison stood off from the group, shooting an occasional glance at her watch. Collin was on stage with the mayor, sharing sound bites about the founding of Hode's Hill and the legend of the Fiend. A large group had gathered, including over two dozen hopefuls for the Fiend contest. The mood was upbeat, the crowd pumped by the excitement of the annual summer festival. It wouldn't be long before the Fiend contestants took the stage, cheered on by whoops of encouragement.

Roth should have been back by now. She debated about texting him, going so far as to dig her phone from her purse. Before she could key in her security code, a man bumped her from behind.

"Oh, sorry." He reached out to steady her, and she glanced up into a narrow face with warm brown eyes. "I wasn't looking where I was going."

"That's okay." Madison offered a smile. He appeared to be a few years younger than her, with curly brown hair and an athlete's physique.

"I probably shouldn't be so focused on my phone. You know how it is these days."

"Yeah. Can't do anything without them." He extended his hand. "I'm Doug Crawford."

"Madison Hewitt."

"Nice to meet you, Madison. What do you think of the festival?"

"I haven't been here long enough to decide, but based on past experience, I'd say it's going to be a blast. I grew up in Hode's Hill."

"Me, too." He flashed an easy grin. "Hey, maybe we could check it out together. Have you eaten yet? I hear the pizza's awesome."

"Oh." She dipped her eyes, out of practice with the social scene and flirting. The fact Doug was even interested made her flush. "That's nice of you, but I'm here with someone."

"Namely me."

Madison jerked when Roth came up behind them. He stepped to her side, slipping an arm around her waist.

"My mistake." Doug held up both hands as if recognizing he'd crossed a territorial boundary. "We're good, bro." Then to Madison: "Nice chatting. Hope you both have a good time."

She glanced up at Roth as Doug sprinted away. "He was just being nice."

"Maybe." His mouth twisted in a frown. "It looked to me like he was hitting on you. I thought you were going to hang out with your sister and the rest of the group."

"I am." Madison pointed to Jillian, Dante, and the others, a few feet away, all focused on the stage. She'd lost track of Collin's speech. "I stepped back here to text you because you were gone so long. Was there a problem?"

"Yeah. A big one." He blew out a breath and pinched the bridge of his nose. "Alan's wife asked for a divorce."

Madison was sure she blanched. "That's awful." Roth's younger brother had taken a job transfer to Michigan last year, but they remained close, calling and texting several times a week. "Why would Bev do that? I thought they were good together."

"So did Alan. So did I." Muscles bunched in his jaw. "I guess the move put everything on edge. She said he's too controlling. He needed to vent."

"Is there any chance they can make things work?"

"It didn't sound that way. She left three days ago. He said she's coming back to Hode's Hill." He eyed her openly. "She's probably going to call you when she gets here. I think you should stay out of it."

Madison pulled away. "But she's my friend."

"And he's my brother."

The air sharpened with tension. Then, as if recognizing his belligerent mood, Roth puffed out his cheeks. He scrubbed a hand over the back of his neck. "Let's not argue. It's their problem, and they have to work it out. I want you to enjoy tonight."

Her demeanor softened. "I'd like you to enjoy it, too." She twined her fingers with his. "It's just so sad...Beverly and Alan."

"He said she was keeping secrets from him." Roth wrapped her in his arms, resting his chin on her head. "You'd never do that to me, would you?"

Madison thought of her slashed tires. The warning spray-painted on the drawing room window. Tomorrow night's dinner with Jillian and Dante from which she'd purposely excluded him. She leaned into his chest.

"Of course not."

* * * *

Doug Crawford took a long drag off his cigarette, then crushed the butt beneath his sneaker. Of all the shitty luck, he had to draw tails in the coin toss. He and Joey had chosen two women at random. Both looked unattached, attending the Fiend Festival with friends, date-free. Joey got the brunette, Doug the redhead. First to score a phone number—signaled by a ping to the other's cell—won fifty bucks and the right to crow.

Doug normally kicked butt when they played the game, but tonight, Joey walked away the winner. He'd not only scored the brunette's phone number but ended up going home with her clinging to his arm. So much for Doug's ride. Worse, thanks to Madison Hewitt's knuckle-dragger boyfriend, he'd struck out completely. Not wanting to cramp his friend's style, he told Joey he'd call an Uber.

Problem was, he didn't feel like bagging the night. Smarting from the loss and antsy with caged-up energy, he crossed River Road, cut over to Second, then ducked down an alley toward Fourth. The Fiend Festival had wrapped, crowds dispersed, but Pub Place—a stretch of eateries and bars—would be pumping out music and beers for hours. Plenty of time to pound down some microbrews. Maybe even land a legitimate phone number.

Halfway down the alley, Doug fished for another smoke. Brick buildings towered on either side, the south-facing facades of old homes that had been converted into office space. A law firm, ad agency, title company— all locked and shuttered for the night. Almond-shaped security lights sprouted over doorways and stoops, sleek glowing eyes that gouged yellow cones into the shadows. Somewhere far off in the distance, a train whistle pierced the night.

Doug stopped to light his cigarette, exhaling a long stream of smoke before tucking the lighter into his pocket. He threaded deeper into the alley, sidestepping a mangled Coke can and a grease-spotted container of French fries.

Hogs.

It pissed him off when people littered. Just not enough to clean up after them.

He took another drag on the cigarette, grimacing when he caught a whiff of something foul. A pocket of cold air hit him in the face. The stench mushroomed, slamming into him with the force of a sledgehammer.

"Shit!" His stomach seized. Gagging, he doubled over and spat phlegm. Worse than sewer gas or fermented garbage, the alley stank like something had gone belly up—festering in the sun until it was no more than a noxious smear of pus, gases, and ruptured organs. "What the fu—"

Every light in the alley died.

Doug spat bile. He looked behind him, confronted by a wall of darkness. River Road remained blocked to traffic. This deep in the alley, halfway to Fourth, closeted by buildings, not even ambient light made a difference. His breath plumed in the air, tinged with ice.

"Not freaking possible."

Not in June.

Doug tossed his cigarette, quickened his pace. There couldn't have been a power outage. Light glimmered at the extreme end of the alley where it yawned open to Fourth. What were the odds of all the building lights shutting down at once?

And what the hell was that freaking stench?

Something gurgled behind him, a noise like water slogging through pipes. Hair prickled on the back of his neck. He pivoted, aware of something hunkered in the alley—a blot of cold and death that made his blood freeze and catapulted his heart into a jackhammer.

Panicked, Doug launched into a run.

The creature was on him in an instant, slamming him face-first into the asphalt. His nose broke on impact, fountaining blood into his mouth. He tried to scream but choked on broken teeth and gravel. Couldn't see. Heard only that horrific, grunting gurgle.

Pain exploded in his skull, the back of his head sheared away. He wailed in red-veined terror, blubbering through a mask of blood, snot, and tears. Urine gushed down his legs, plastering his jeans to his crotch. It was all he could do to hold his bowels.

Crab-clawing, he inched forward, heaving out pleas, begging the God he hadn't prayed to in years to save him.

Pleasepleaseplease. Ohgodohgodohgod...

The thing on his back reared upward. He sucked a greedy gulp of air, struggling to get his hands under him. In a fogged, distant corner of his mind, he registered the bite of loose stones against his palms.

Doug scooted forward. Gained four inches before being flipped onto his back.

With the breath ripped from his lungs, he stared up into a face of nightmare. Of moldy, worm-ridden graves and death soil. The creature engulfed him.

He had only a second to prepare before his chest exploded.

* * * *

Frank Lange didn't make a habit of dragging himself into the office on a Saturday morning, but his boss wanted a new branding strategy for one of their top clients by Monday, and Frank was behind on putting something together. A bakery should have been a slam dunk. What kind of cretin didn't like cinnamon rolls or muffins?

But Ma's Buns had taken a publicity hit when Ma was caught in a compromising position with her much younger manager. Compounding matters was Ma's supposedly squeaky-clean image. The manager was a twenty-two-year-old girl who moonlighted at a strip club in Arbor Point. And of course, Frank inherited the whole mess.

Grumbling under his breath, he made his way through the reception area to his desk in the back. In some ways it was nice being the only one in the building. At least he didn't have to listen to Greta Walker, the new dynamo his boss hired, spout off about how many deals she'd closed this month. Let Walker try to salvage a business built by a fifty-eight-year-old grandmother who liked her lovers young, female, and slutty.

Frank dumped his briefcase on his desk, sucked a long draught from the lukewarm coffee he'd brought from home, then stretched, wedging a hand in the small of his back. He took his time booting up his computer, opening files, shuffling papers, fishing for a pen. All stalling tactics. He needed to get his act together and buckle down.

Except the plant on the corner of his desk looked like it needed light. His wife had delivered it one day last week to cheer him up. He didn't know how to care for the thing but felt obligated to try. Squat, bushy, and green, it had a dusting of yellow dots over pointy leaves.

Frank crossed to the window overlooking the alley and opened the blind.

His gaze landed on something sprawled on the asphalt. It took several seconds for his brain to catch up with the images. To register the glut of innards, blood, and body fluids. Ruptured torso. Butchered, strewn appendages. Half-eaten organs.

"He...ek." He made a sound like a mouse hyperventilating. Clamped both hands to his mouth and stumbled backward, colliding with his desk. *"Heekheekheek!"* Frank vomited, heaving coffee down the front of his shirt.

When he finally caught his breath, there was no one in the building to hear him scream.

Chapter 6

March 24–25, 1878

Hollande lay awake in bed, listening to the *click-click* of deathwatch beetles. The chattering was a familiar sound she associated with grief. After her parents died, she'd spent two nights sitting by their caskets silently reading the Gospel of Matthew. As was custom, the coffins had been placed in the parlor, allowing mourners to pay their respects. Edgar retired early each night, but she'd felt obligated to make certain her mother and father had crossed from one world to the next.

Despite advances to medical science, horror stories of loved ones buried alive still surfaced in the newspaper—that poor orphan child from Curtisville, dear Mrs. Buffington who'd lived down the street. She needed to be certain there was no life left in the bodies of the loving couple who raised her.

During those long nighttime hours, the only sound to infringe on the silence had been the active chatter of beetles hidden in the rafters and joists. It made her wonder if Sylvia had maintained a deathwatch beside her husband's coffin, listening to the same busy clicks.

Eventually, weariness overtook Hollande, and she fell into a restless sleep. Hours later, she woke to sunlight streaming through the windows, the day dawning free of clouds. The house seemed less imposing in the morning, and she made her way to the dining room for breakfast. Annabelle served her and Nathaniel, then left to carry a tray up to Sylvia. Hollande offered to take it, but Nathaniel shook his head.

"Let Annabelle. My mother is still adjusting to having you here."

Hollande picked at her eggs. She wasn't comfortable in her new position but feared what would happen should Nathaniel and Tristan decide to release her from employment. Would Edgar take her in, or would she be forced to secure accommodations in a boarding house?

Perhaps that wasn't such a terrible alternative. She would inherit a portion of money from the sale of her parents' home, a pittance compared to Edgar's, but enough to allow her to live modestly. Boarding homes were not desirable for those of genteel society, but she was beginning to realize how truly limited her options were.

Why did the dear Lord have to take Phillip from her?

"Miss Moore." Nathaniel's voice intruded on her thoughts. He'd been speaking while she wool-gathered.

"I'm sorry. What did you say?"

"I asked if you slept well."

"Oh. Yes." She could do nothing but lie. "The room is quite comfortable. Thank you for your concern." She added a sugar cube to her tea. "Will Tristan be joining us?"

"It's his habit to leave before dawn. Did you get a chance to meet him last night?"

She remembered the man with the ready smile, the easy demeanor. How could twins be so different? "I was in the drawing room with your mother when he returned home. We had a pleasant conversation."

Nathaniel grimaced. "That's Tristan. Always pleasant."

She wasn't certain how to respond. Perhaps bad blood existed between them. At the very least, Nathaniel appeared to harbor resentment for his brother. She wondered if that had always been the case, or if there'd been a time when they shared the closeness of siblings.

Lowering her gaze, she poked a potato wedge with her fork. The room felt overly large, much too big for the two of them. She tried to imagine it when Nathaniel and Tristan were small, Darrin and Sylvia happily married. Had the brothers chatted across the table, eager to finish dinner so they could race off to some shared adventure?

It was not her path to go down.

"The weather appears promising today. I thought I would ask your mother to take a stroll along the creek."

"That's not likely." Nathaniel slathered blackberry jam on a piece of toast. "She detests the creek."

Hollande recalled Sylvia's reference to the fast-flowing water as a *ghastly thing*. "Is there a reason for that?"

He chewed for a time, saying nothing while he sliced a slab of ham on his plate. Hollande grew uncomfortable with his silence. Obviously, she'd overstepped a boundary. She was about to make an inane comment when Nathaniel cleared his throat.

"My mother is a complex person. You'll come to recognize she has many idiosyncrasies, Yarrow Creek among them. As I told you yesterday, she is not entirely sound of mind."

Hollande bit her lip. There was no question Sylvia was a cantankerous woman, but she'd yet to witness a display of mental instability.

"It would help if I understood more about her." She set her fork down. "You've told me several times of her mental difficulties but have yet to elaborate."

He scowled, topping off his coffee with fresh brew from a silver pot. "What do you want to know?"

"Tell me about your father." Understanding the kind of man Darrin was might help her better relate to Sylvia and fathom why she was so bitter.

"He was a studious man but also a risk taker. My mother said he barely had two coins to rub together when they met. She married him anyway."

"She must have loved him a great deal."

"According to her, she didn't have eyes for anyone else." Nathaniel's face softened with the hint of a smile. "After they married, he invested what money he had. Fortunately, he chose wisely, purchasing a share of a quarry in Curtisville. Eventually, he earned enough to become a major stockholder, then owner. Tristan goes daily to supervise operations and meet with my father's business contacts. You might say he's the point person, while I oversee the detail work—books and correspondence—usually in the evenings."

That explained their differing schedules. From what she could see, the arrangement suited their opposing personalities. "I'm surprised your father chose Hode's Hill rather than Curtisville for his residence."

"He grew up here. Stewart Manor has always been my family's primary residence, but we maintain a townhouse in Curtisville. Tristan will sometimes remain overnight if the day waxes too old for the journey home."

Hollande sipped her tea. Given what Nathaniel said, his family was clearly well-off, yet the only staff she'd seen was Annabelle. No doorman or carriage driver. No groom for the horses. As far as she could tell, Tristan acted as his own driver to and from Curtisville, rising early to make the trip. A daily schedule of that degree had to be exhausting. No wonder he'd looked drained when he escorted his mother up the stairs last night.

"I'm surprised you haven't sold Stewart Manor and relocated to Curtisville. I would think living closer to the quarry would be easier for you and Tristan."

"Undoubtedly, but my mother will not hear of it. She insists on staying here."

"And yet she has no love for Yarrow Creek."

Nathaniel slid his plate aside. "I told you, she is set in her ways."

"Is that why she keeps your father's study locked?"

His gaze shifted to catch hers, a flicker of indecision in his eyes. It passed quickly. "You'll learn the truth sooner or later. Better that you do now. My father fell to his death from that room."

Hollande sucked in a tremulous breath. "I'm so sorry."

"He'd been drinking." Nathaniel's expression soured. "Tristan and I believe there must have been a problem at the quarry for him to imbibe to such an extent. My father rarely drank, but that night he consumed enough to wander onto the balcony in a perilous condition. He fell two stories to the veranda below. I was the one who found him the next morning. His skull had shattered in the fall. He must have died instantly."

"How dreadful." Hollande felt her features contort. "I did not mean to resurrect such unpleasant memories, Mr. Stewart."

"Nathaniel. If you are to live here—care for my mother—we should dispense with formalities."

"Agreed." She offered a tentative smile. In exposing his family's past, he seemed more approachable, less austere. "You must call me Hollande."

That hint of a smile again. It was amazing what the change did to his features, bringing light to his eyes, chasing off shadows. "Perhaps, since my mother has no desire to stroll near Yarrow Creek—and it is indeed a pleasant day, as you noted—you might accompany me on a walk."

Hollande drew back, surprised. "Why, yes." An odd fluttering rooted in her stomach. A quiver she hadn't experienced in several years. "I would like that, Nathaniel." Heat rose to her face, prompting her to lower her gaze.

She hadn't felt so self-conscious since meeting Phillip.

* * * *

Present Day

Detective David Gregg ducked under a barrier of yellow police tape, then made his way past several crime scene techs. Flagging Bob Anders, the nearest uniformed officer, he waved the man aside.

"Who was first on the scene?"

"I was."

Good. Anders was a solid cop. "What do we have?"

David had heard the radio call but wanted a firsthand report. From the looks of the activity, most of the department was on the case. Either in the alley, the building, or trying to manage the crowd out front. It hadn't taken long for the public to get wind something nasty had gone down. Several reporters and camera crews were tucked behind the police barrier, Christy Catterman of Channel 42 shouting questions to anyone who passed within range of her mic.

He rubbed his brow. The cop still hadn't said anything. It was going to be a shit-sorry day. "Bob?"

Anders's hands trembled as he flipped through several pages on a tablet.

David felt a stab of sympathy. "Bad one, huh?"

Anders gulped. Sweat stippled his cheeks, his skin colored the unhealthy gray of dishwater. "Eighteen years on the force, never saw anything like it. Whoever butchered that poor kid was one sick bastard."

"We got an ID on the vic?"

"His wallet was, um..." Bob swallowed again, consulted his notes. "Thrown clear of the pelvis and legs."

David glanced down the alley but couldn't see much for the millwork of techs and medical personnel crawling over the scene. "That bad?"

"I found pieces of the kid all over the place. Heaved twice before I could make a call." Anders rubbed his jaw. When he raised his head, his eyes were haunted. "According to his license, his name is—was"—he backhanded sweat from his chin—"Douglas L. Crawford of 163 Grove Circle."

"Anyone send a car?"

"Earlier. Apparently, it's the parents' place. The chief is talking to them at the station. He's been and gone."

"Witnesses?"

"None."

"Who found the body and made the call?"

Anders checked his notes again. "A woman named Greta Walker, but she wasn't first on scene. That was Frank Lange. Lorquet's inside with both of them." Anders jerked his head in the direction of the D. Bestman Ad Agency.

"Why didn't Lange call?"

"Couldn't. Walker said she came in early to get work done and found him cowering in a corner, clutching a plant. Couldn't get a word out of him."

"All right. I'll see what I can dig up. You got anything else?"

"Wish I didn't have what I do." Anders tucked his pad into his pocket. "No one deserves to die like that. That kid must have pissed off one mother of a nightmare. You know what's scary about the whole thing?"

"Other than the obvious?"

"Opening night of the Fiend Festival. Horrific murder." He jabbed his thumb toward the police barrier. "Catterman's going to spin the whole thing for sensationalism. By the time the noon broadcast hits, she'll be telling everyone the Fiend has come back to Hode's Hill—again."

* * * *

"You have to do something about those reporters. I don't want them out front."

Sherre Lorquet closed her eyes, striving for patience. If she'd heard the protest from Dwayne Bestman once, she'd heard it a dozen times. "It's a public street, Mr. Bestman. They're behind the barricade. That's the best we can do." She walked through the reception area, threading to the rear.

Bestman, a heavyset man with a bad buzz cut and black glasses, clung to her heels. "That's not good enough. Do you have any idea what this is going to do to my reputation? My company image? Why the hell did the kid have to get killed here?"

Asshat.

She balled her hands into fists, squashing the impulse to belt him. Insensitive bastard was like a gnat, constantly circling in her face. "Desmond." She summoned one of the uniforms. "Get Mr. Bestman a drink of water and keep him occupied in the lobby."

"I don't want any water."

"Sure, you do." Desmond clutched his arm and steered him toward the front.

Thank the Lord God Almighty.

Two other officers remained in the back where three desks, a copy machine, water cooler, and coffee station created a tidy workspace. Or, at least, it may have been tidy but for the medical paraphernalia strewn over the floor. Frank Lange remained huddled in a corner, clutching his plant. He'd been uncommunicative since she'd arrived. The paramedics had managed to secure a blood pressure cuff to his arm, but any attempt to coax him from his niche or remove the plant resulted in him shrieking like a banshee. Nearby, Greta Walker sipped coffee at her desk, hollow-eyed and shell-shocked. Sherre had spoken to her at length.

She motioned Officer Tom Brant closer. "Did you reach Lange's wife?"

"She's on her way. The chief had me send a car for her before he left." His gaze tracked to Lange, who had started rocking. "Poor guy. I can't imagine coming into work and finding something like that mess in the alley."

"At least he only saw the vic from the window." She glanced aside, spied David Gregg through the opening to the reception area. "Gregg's here. He's going to want to talk to Walker. Once he's done, take her downtown for a formal statement. And the moment we get anything intelligent out of Lange, I want to know."

Brant nodded, stepping clear as the senior detective approached.

"Hell of a morning." David's greeting told her he'd seen the body—or what remained of it.

"Did you talk to Clairmont?" The coroner should have been finishing up by now.

"Yeah. Not much shakes that guy, but this is one for the record books."

"He gave me a TOD as between ten and one."

"The Fiend Festival closed at eleven. Had to be after that, otherwise someone would have heard the kid screaming."

Sherre chewed the inside of her cheek. "He say anything about a murder weapon?"

"He didn't want to commit." David met her gaze.

She had the feeling he was thinking the same thing she was—that Clairmont probably was, too.

Nothing human could have committed that kind of slaughter.

* * * *

Saturday evening, Madison had just put a tray of stuffed mushroom caps in the oven when her sister arrived with Blizzard.

"I thought you'd be with Dante." She poured them each a glass of Riesling after they'd retreated to the kitchen. Blizzard made himself at home, sprawling in front of the door to the veranda while Jillian perched on a stool at the breakfast bar. "Is everything okay?"

"Fine." Jillian sipped her wine. "He got tied up at the gallery, so we decided to drive separately. He should be here soon."

Dante's gallery was located in the center of Hode's Hill. Catering to artisans, District Three featured his work plus that of other locals who wouldn't have a showcase otherwise. Painters, sculptors, even photographers found a home within the walls of his shop. Already independently wealthy thanks to a sizeable inheritance and trust fund, Dante maintained the gallery even when it occasionally dipped into the red.

Jillian rotated the base of her wineglass between her fingers. "Downtown has been so chaotic after what happened today."

"What do you mean?" Madison added a bowl of seasoned pretzels to the bar.

"You haven't heard? Didn't you turn on the news?"

"No. I worked in the yard, then I was busy in here." She didn't mention she'd used a utility knife to scrape *Get Out!* from the drawing room window. Yesterday, Sherre confirmed the lab results as spray paint, not that she'd expected any less. The effort she'd expended with soap, water, and elbow grease still irritated her. She hoped whoever was responsible had an allergic reaction to the paint.

"Then you don't know about the murder?"

Madison's stomach plummeted. She wedged her back into a corner of the bar. "Murder?"

"Last night. After the Fiend Festival." Jillian drew her wineglass closer, fingers growing white on the stem. "Someone was killed in the alley by the Bestman Ad Agency. The details are sketchy, but from sound bites the media is dropping, it must have been ghastly."

"That's horrible." They'd all had such a good time at the festival. "Do the police have any leads?"

"If they do, they're not saying. The victim was a young guy, about twenty-five, named Doug Crawford."

"My God." Madison collapsed onto a stool. Judging from her sister's expression, she must have looked like she'd seen a ghost.

Jillian gripped her hand. "Madison, what's wrong?"

"Doug. I know him. Sort of." She struggled to collect her thoughts. "Last night when you and the others were listening to Collin's speech, he bumped into me. We exchanged small talk. I think he wanted to hook up. He asked me to go for a slice of pizza, but Roth showed up."

Jillian blinked, wide-eyed. "You might have been one of the last people to talk to him. On the news they said he was killed after the Fiend Festival. You should tell Sherre. Or David."

"Jillian, this is awful. I mean..." Her stomach knotted. "What are the odds Doug would be the victim?"

"Calm down." As an empath, Jillian was likely bludgeoned with Madison's escalating anxiety. "Sometimes circumstance is nothing more than coincidence. What happened to Doug was a tragedy, but your connection to him was random. You more than anyone know the cost of having enemies."

Boyd.

For all she knew, Doug Crawford could have run the same risks as Boyd, made enemies every bit as ruthless.

"You're right." She gulped a mouthful of wine followed by a second when the first failed to calm her nerves. By now the mushroom caps would be sizzling. She hopped from the stool, forcing the ugly thoughts from her head. "I can't think about this now. I'll talk to David or Sherre tomorrow."

When she had time to place the events in perspective.

When the fear wasn't so throttling.

* * * *

Dante parked his 4Runner in front of the garage behind Jillian's Accord. The moment he stepped from the vehicle, his gut constricted in a hard knot. The energy coiled around Madison's home was palpable.

Not what he'd hoped to find.

The sun was only now beginning to slide between the trees, still hours from setting. He headed up the drive, then veered toward the side rather than continuing to the front porch. Given what Madison had told him about the home, she'd be hovering the moment he stepped through the door. Better to gather impressions on his own.

Yarrow Creek beckoned, prompting him to wander down the bank. At first glance the surroundings were peaceful, orchestrated by the drone of insects, rustle of cattails, and a gravelly chorus of bullfrogs. But as he gazed over the wide expanse of water, echoes of the past intruded. Words from another time, spoken in anger, snatched by the wind before he could decipher them. A bitter breath of winter blew across the creek, coaxing ice to the surface. The vision lasted no more than seconds, but it was long enough to convince him something vile had happened here.

Dante headed up the bank, deviating around the back of the house. He found the Stewart family cemetery neatly maintained and free of weeds. Like her sister, Madison took grave-tending duties seriously, raised on tales of the Third and Final Death. The plot probably hadn't been so neatly kept in decades. He extracted a slip of paper with names and dates he'd recorded earlier, then squatted to study the tombstones.

Darrin, Sylvia, Nathaniel.

Someone was missing.

Dante brushed his fingers over each stone in turn. The lack of sensation didn't surprise him. Folk memories resulted from life. Imprints of specific moments, anchored to time and place. Death's path was different. If there was darkness to be found in a graveyard, it was rooted in the nightmare creatures such places attracted.

According to Madison, the daffodils she'd planted on Sylvia's grave had rotted in less than twenty-four hours. But when he flattened his palm against the ground, he couldn't detect a trace of toxins. Finished with his inspection, he headed toward the front of the house. Cold spots bubbled around him as he neared the veranda. Unlike the heaviness by the creek, the pulses dissipated before he could focus.

No wonder Karen Randall told Madison the home was haunted. Without stepping inside, he'd discovered enough preternatural activity on the grounds to convince him Madison wasn't alone.

* * * *

David was still waiting on the coroner's findings when Bob Anders ushered a frightened-looking twenty-something to his desk. Amazing how he thought of anyone under the age of thirty these days. At forty-four, he was old enough to be the young man's father.

"Joseph Banco," Anders introduced the trim, dark-haired guest. Clean-cut and sharp-featured, the kid looked like he'd received the shock of his life.

Probably had. "Thanks for coming to the station." David motioned him to a wooden chair.

"Am I in trouble?" Banco eased to a seat as Anders left.

"I just want to ask you some questions."

"About Doug?"

"Yeah. I'm Detective David Gregg. Doug's parents said you drove him to the Fiend Festival last night."

Banco bobbed his head. Waited a beat, then licked his lips. "Should I have a lawyer for this?"

"You're not under suspicion. Not at this point anyway. Doug's parents already told us how close the two of you were."

"We grew up together." Banco swallowed hard. "Met back in fifth grade. I can't believe...when I heard..." Slumping in his chair, he made a choked sound and swiped at his eyes.

"Can I get you something? Coffee? Water?"

"No. I'm good." He sniffled, composing himself, then sat straighter. "Doug's dad called around seven this morning. He and Mrs. Crawford never realized Doug hadn't made it home until they saw his bed hadn't been slept in. That's when I found out, too."

Banco's information corroborated the testimony provided by Andrew and Paula Crawford.

"Then I heard the news. You know?" Banco's eyes were red-rimmed when he met David's gaze. "I was gonna come in...talk to someone. But that cop, Anders, showed up in a car. I want to help any way I can, but I still think maybe I need a lawyer."

"That's your prerogative. You're not being charged with anything." David consulted his notes. "Do you have an alibi for last night? Specifically, between ten and one?"

"Sure. I was with Maryjane Figg at the Knot. We were there until the place closed at two. Lots of people saw us. Talk to the bartender. We swapped stories about a dive bar in Curtisville. I think his name was Tony. Big guy with a snake tattoo on his arm."

David scribbled a note. Easy to confirm. "What about after two?"

"Maryjane and I went to my place. She was there all night."

If Banco's story checked out, he was in the clear. David didn't doubt the outcome. Murders were rare in Hode's Hill, but he'd seen enough killers to know the kid sitting by his desk wasn't one of them.

"Is Maryjane your girlfriend?"

"Not exactly. I met her last night. Doug and I...had a bet."

"Involving Maryjane?"

"Not just her." Banco sucked his bottom lip. He leaned forward, looking uncomfortable. "I know it's dumb. We picked two girls at the Fiend Festival we thought didn't have dates and flipped a coin. I got Maryjane and Doug got a redhead. I didn't know Maryjane's name then, but we hit it off."

"What was the bet?"

"First one to get a phone number won fifty bucks."

"Did Doug get a number from the redhead?"

"No. Turned out she was there with some guy. We screw up sometimes."

Stupid game, but David could see two testosterone-driven, twenty-somethings pumped by the idea. When it came to women, guys could be jerks. On the flip side, Maryjane Figg was capable of deciding whether she wanted to crawl into bed with someone she'd only just met.

"I'm going to need Maryjane's number."

"Sure." Banco dug out his cell phone, then pulled up his contacts. He rattled off the number, and David made a note to call her after he was done with the interview.

It had been a long day, far from over. He rubbed his brow. "Did Doug have any enemies you know of? Someone who might want to harm him?"

"No way!" The idea was clearly offensive. "He was a decent guy, you know?" Banco choked up again, folded back into the chair.

"Did he say anything about the redhead's boyfriend?"

"Not really. Just that he made it clear she was with him."

"Any idea who the girl was?"

"Yeah." Banco perked up. "Doug got her name before the Neanderthal warned him off—Madison something-or-other. Maybe Hawkins. No, that's not right." He frowned as if trying to drudge up the memory. A second later, his face lit up. "I remember. It was Hewitt. Madison Hewitt."

* * * *

Over dinner, Dante listened to Madison relay everything unusual that had happened in the house. Afterward, while Jillian helped her sister clear the table, he wandered off, preferring to explore on his own. Blizzard tagged along, following room to room, sometimes pausing in a doorway or hovering in the hall. By nature, animals were more receptive to supernatural activity, picking up vibrations humans couldn't feel.

Most humans.

Dante had no such problem. He'd experienced ripples of sensitivity since he was a kid, an ability that mushroomed at fifteen after his father died. Now, sixteen years later, he was still learning.

In Madison's bedroom, he walked straight through a cold spot, fully aware when someone touched his shoulder. The presence had been following him since he'd stepped onto the second floor. On the main level, he'd picked up snatches of a man and woman arguing, but the words had been too garbled to understand.

Head lowered, Blizzard padded to his side. The husky whined softly.

"You sense her too, huh?" There was something distinctly feminine about the presence.

Feminine and sad.

Whoever she was, she wasn't the only spirit in the house. Another presence lingered, hostile and bitter. That aura was strongest in the room at the opposite end of the hall, but he'd sensed its aggression the moment he'd stepped inside. It tainted the floorboards and walls, seeped into cracks and moldings. The spirit—whatever it was—had a chokehold on the place.

"Cold here, huh?" Dante scratched Blizzard behind the ears. Madison's bedroom was a hub of activity. His breath plumed in the air as he crossed to the balcony doors. The hostile presence loomed behind him, but the woman was there too, stronger somehow in her sadness.

The bedroom door slammed shut. An invisible force crashed into his back, sending him careening against the closet. Blizzard snarled, hair standing on edge.

"It's okay." Dante recovered quickly. He straightened his shirt. "I'm fine."

The husky backstepped, bumping into his legs.

"Yeah, I know you want to go. Our PO'd ghost wants me to leave, too." Dante laid a hand on the dog's head to calm him. He fingered the St. Michael's medallion looped around his neck—a medal that had belonged to his father and protected him from violent spirits more than once. The cold was beginning to fade.

"You're going to have to do better than that," he told the specter. "After some of the encounters I've had, you're chump change."

The door yawned open.

"Huh. Graceful now, are we?" He could no longer sense enmity in the room. Blizzard trotted into the hallway, and Dante followed.

"Oh, hey." He spied Madison at the opposite end, near the stairway. "I was just coming down to—" His voice cut off as the wrongness of the moment overtook him. While the woman's features were much the same, any resemblance to his girlfriend's sister stopped there. This woman wore a full-length gown with a pleated overskirt. Her hair was gathered into clips and pins in the front but hung loose over her back in a cascade of red curls. Melancholy clung to her like a cloak, magnified by the sorrow in her eyes. Before he could manage a single step, she vanished.

Blizzard padded forward, snuffling his nose against the carpet.

Throughout the entire otherworldly experience, the husky displayed zero aggression.

* * * *

Madison glanced up from her cell phone when Blizzard trotted into the drawing room, trailed by Dante. She'd missed a call, but the number was one she didn't recognize. Most likely a robocall or junk solicitation. Edgy since Dante left to investigate, she dropped the phone onto an end table.

"Well? Anything?" She leaned forward in her chair, a monstrous claw-footed thing left by the previous owner.

"Not much on this level." Dante settled on the sofa beside Jillian. "I picked up an audible manifestation earlier in this room. A man and woman arguing."

So she *had* heard something. "Could you tell what they were saying?"

"No, the incident was too quick, but the tone was unmistakable."

"What about the basement?" She thought of the old cistern.

"There's some kind of residual taint, but it doesn't feel spiritual. You've also got two outside areas with activity."

"Folk memories?" Jillian asked.

"These are different."

Madison looked between them. "I'm not sure I understand what creates a folk memory."

"Think of it as a moment frozen in time." Dante shifted, allowing Blizzard to settle on the floor near Jillian. "Something happens—usually horrific—and the incident replays over and over."

"You mean ghosts recreate it?"

"No. It's the memory of the event itself, imprinted in the place where the tragedy occurred. Like a TV episode on constant rerun."

"No one is really there," Jillian added.

Dante spread his hands. "Anyone receptive to the spirit world can usually sense folk memories."

Her stomach tightened. She regretted the slice of key lime pie she'd had for dessert. "Do you mean..." It was hard to force the words. To dial her mind back to the most heinous night of her life. "Boyd's death could have left a folk memory in our house at Mill Street?"

"Yeah." Dante blew out a breath. "It probably did. But it takes time for the residue to become visible. Decades, sometimes centuries. There's no rhyme or reason why some atrocities leave imprints and others don't."

She felt the blood drain from her face.

Jillian stretched forward to clasp her hand. "Put Boyd's death out of your head, Maddy. That's not why Dante is here."

"I know." She closed her eyes, tears burning the lids. "But the thought of his murder playing over and over..."

"No one will see it, Madison." Dante's assertion left no room for argument. "*You* need to stop seeing it."

She nodded. Snatched a tissue from a box on the end table. It was time to refocus. "You said you felt impressions outside." She dabbed her eyes.

"The graveyard?" Jillian guessed.

Dante shook his head. "Near the veranda below Madison's bedroom, and along the creek bank. The veranda is covered in cold spots."

Madison crumpled the tissue in her hand. "What about the creek?"

"That was different. I'm convinced something bad happened there. Not enough to create a folk memory, but enough to leave a hostile mark. My guess is it has something to do with your lantern-carrying visitor."

"He must have lived in the house. Do you think it could be Darrin or Nathaniel?"

"Maybe." Dante scraped a thumb across his chin. "But they're not the only male Stewarts who lived here."

"I know there were other generations."

"I'm talking about their generation. Last night after the Fiend Festival, I checked my grandmother's genealogy charts. Tracing family trees used to be a passion of hers. She tracked the lineage of most of the original families in Hode's Hill back to the founding of the town."

"I've seen her record book," Jillian inserted. "Sonia's details are incredible. We referred to the charts after Gabriel's remains were stolen."

Madison hadn't been to visit her ancestor's grave since settling on the house, leaving the tending of his plot to Jillian. She'd have to rectify that soon. It was their shared responsibly to see Gabriel Vane never experienced Final Death.

She concentrated on Dante. "Am I right that Nathaniel was Darrin and Sylvia's son?"

"Yeah. I wrote down birth and death dates for all three, and they match up with the dates on the tombstones."

"But?" Madison sensed something unsaid.

"Not all the members of the Stewart family are buried in that cemetery."

"What do you mean?"

"According to my grandmother's chart, Nathaniel Stewart had a twin brother named Tristan. She recorded his date of birth as 1844, but there's no reference to his death. She left the date empty."

A moment of silence hung over the group.

"Maybe he's buried somewhere else," Jillian suggested. "He could have moved away. Curtisville had more opportunity. Or he might have died during the Civil War."

"Could be." Dante leaned into the couch. "All of that aside, I need to tell you about the second floor."

Madison was so focused on Tristan, she'd foolishly forgotten the level where most of the supernatural occurrences had taken place. "Did you pick up anything weird in my bedroom?"

"It's one of two major hotspots. The other is directly opposite, at the end of the hall."

"You mean the room at the top of the stairs?" The previous owner had furnished it sparsely. Single bed, nightstand, bureau. Eventually, Madison hoped to convert the room to a home office.

"Yeah." Dante's gaze was steady. "Based on what I've experienced, there are two distinctive spirits in the house. Possibly more."

Madison gulped. "So, the place really is haunted?"

"There's no doubt. You've got a belligerent phantom—it threw me up against the closet in your room—and another, mellower ghost. That one seems sad about something. She's female, though I can't tell the gender of the first."

"Great." Just her luck. When she finally found the wherewithal to step out on her own, the property she bought could qualify for *America's Most Haunted Places*. Karen Randall only knew the tip of the iceberg.

"That's not all." The tone of Dante's voice made the hair prickle on the back of her neck. "The female ghost I mentioned? The first time I saw her, I thought she was you."

"*What?*" Her heart thudded.

"She was dressed like someone out of the 1800s. Her hair was longer, but aside from those two differences, you could be twins."

"Could she be Sylvia?" The thought disturbed her.

"No. This woman was young."

"What about before she had children?"

"I don't think so."

"Maybe Nathaniel had a wife?" Jillian ventured.

Dante shook his head. "According to my grandmother's charts, he wasn't married."

"Sonia could have gotten it wrong. She doesn't have a date of death for Tristan. One of them must have had a son, otherwise the Stewart line couldn't continue."

"My guess is Darrin had a brother. Someone who's not in the book. You know how sketchy old records can be."

Madison's head was spinning. "If the woman you saw wasn't Nathaniel's wife, or Sylvia, who could she be?" Her cell dinged with a text.

"Hired help wasn't uncommon in the 1800s. She could have been a servant." He fell silent, giving the matter more thought. "Maybe a relative or guest. Someone who stayed here."

"Someone who died here." Jillian sounded unnerved.

Madison retrieved her phone to check the message. The text was from Beverly.

Hi. Tried 2 call u from hotel. Did Roth tell u Alan & I split? I'm in Hode's Hill. Plez call when u can. A sad-faced emoji completed the message.

"Madison?"

"Sorry." She switched off the phone. Beverly had to be devastated, but she forced herself to focus on her own problems. "Don't bother suggesting I leave, because I'm not going anywhere. The previous owner lived here for over forty years. If the place was haunted and the ghosts were vindictive, how could she have stayed all that time?"

"You said Vera Halsey knew how to control whatever was in the house." Jillian's lips thinned into a white line, her voice marked by a brittle edge. Anger? Fear? Maybe both. "She *thrived* on the spirits of this house. Karen Randall told you she contacted them through a Ouija board."

"She also told you Vera was only in her early sixties when she died. That she grew sick and *wasted away.*" Dante's stare was direct, his hazel eyes near-black in the thickening shadows. Soon, she'd have to switch on lamps to hold the creeping twilight at bay.

Madison grew still. "What are you suggesting? That she died because of something in the house?"

"I don't know." Dante blew out a breath. "But I do know the veil between worlds should only be broached from dire need, and then only with the greatest respect and care. It sounds like Vera crossed the boundary for her own gratification. Repeatedly. That kind of experimentation is going to take a toll. I'd say she paid with her life."

"Dear God." Madison closed her eyes. Karen had told her Vera walked around the house whispering to herself. What if she'd been communicating with spirits that whole time? And what of the presence that had been *drawn by violence?* Could that be the malevolent phantom that attacked Dante in her bedroom?

She pressed her hands to her cheeks, her fingers like ice. "I'm not sure what to do. Every penny I have is tied up in this house. I can't walk away from it."

"You don't have to." Dante's assurance sent Jillian's gaze swiveling in his direction. Madison's sister clearly didn't like what she was hearing.

"I think Madison should leave. She can move in with me again until she sells the house."

"No." Madison's voice was sharp. "We've been through this. I'm not going anywhere."

"Let me do some research." Dante gripped Jillian's hand when anger flashed in her eyes. "I want to talk to my grandmother and see what she can remember about the Stewarts. Her grandmother Kaye passed down several tales that go back to that era."

"And what is that going to solve?" Jillian's expression remained flinty.

"The ghost who looks like Madison—I didn't sense danger from her. Even Blizzard was fine. He went on the defensive, snarling, when the other one attacked me, but he acted normal around her. Maybe I can find out who she is, or what happened that caused something malevolent to linger."

"But Madison could be in danger," Jillian protested.

"I don't think so. At least not from a paranormal aspect. Ghosts don't slash tires or spray-paint windows."

Madison drew a breath. "I'm hoping those were someone's sick idea of pranks."

"You should ask Roth to stay for a few nights." Jillian pivoted to face her, eyes wide. Unsettled, Blizzard stood and paced to the drawing room door.

"Jillian—"

"I'm serious. I don't like the idea of you being alone out here. Especially now that we know the place *is* haunted."

She was saved from answering by the ding of the doorbell. With a soft woof, Blizzard trotted into the foyer.

"Excuse me." Thankful for the diversion, she hurried after him. She wasn't expecting company, but Roth sometimes showed up on the fly. A peek through the window made her suck down surprise. "It's David." By the time she opened the door, Dante and Jillian had wandered into the foyer.

"Hi." He flashed a smile. "Mind if I come in?"

"Of course not. It's good to see you." She stepped aside so he could enter, then closed the door. "At least I hope it's good to see you." It was odd for David to visit, unless— "I hope you're not here in an official capacity."

"Not really. This is off the record." He exchanged greetings with the others and gave Blizzard a pat before refocusing on Madison. "Did you hear the news about the murder in town? Doug Crawford."

She nodded, her throat too constricted to speak.

"I talked to his friend, a guy named Joseph Banco. Last night at the Fiend Festival, he saw Doug talking with you."

Madison felt hot and cold all over. "He wanted to go for pizza." David was a friend. Dating Dante's cousin, Tessa, for God's sake. Just because she'd exchanged a few words with Doug didn't mean he thought she was involved.

"Can you tell me what he said?"

"Um..." She tried to remember. "He bumped into me, and I think I made a joke about paying too much attention to my phone. I was going to text Roth because he hadn't come back yet."

"Where was I?"

"You and Tessa—and everyone else—were by the stage listening to Collin. It was just a few minutes." She pushed hair from her eyes. "He asked me how I was enjoying the Fiend Festival, then asked if I wanted to grab a slice of pizza. He seemed like a nice guy."

"Was he agitated? Jittery about anything?"

"No."

"Could he have been distracted?"

She frowned. "What do you mean?"

"Did he seem worried someone might have been following him? Did he look around a lot?"

"No. None of those things. He asked about the pizza, I said I was with someone, and then Roth showed up. Doug backed off right away, apologized, and left."

"Did you see where he went?"

Madison shook her head. "I wish I could help you, David, but I only spoke to him for a few minutes."

"Okay. It was worth a shot."

"You don't have any leads?" For the first time that night, Dante looked uneasy. Tessa and Jillian didn't live that far from where Doug had been killed. Of course he'd be worried about them, just as Madison was.

"Nothing yet. I wish I could say if it was random or premeditated, but we're still trying to fit the pieces. I told Tessa to make sure her doors and windows are locked. Even during the day. Madison, Jillian, you need to do the same." He took a quick glance around the foyer. "Sorry to be the bearer of bad tidings. I know you only recently moved in, Madison. Your place looks nice."

"Thanks." Nice, if you didn't count the ghosts. "Do you want to come in for a while? See the rest of the house or have a drink with us?"

"Maybe another time. I've been working since early morning. I'm going home to crash." He opened the door, then paused on the threshold. "Oh, before I forget—I propped your mailbox by the garage."

Madison stared blankly. "What?"

"I didn't think you'd want it lying in the drive. It looks like someone backed into it."

Her stomach sank.

"Shit." Dante bolted past him on a trajectory for the garage.

A breath of cold scuttled up her spine. It couldn't have been that long ago the culprit had been skulking around. The mailbox was standing when Jillian and Dante arrived, which meant whoever battered the post from the ground had done it while the three of them ate dinner.

Another warning from her unknown tormentor to leave.

* * * *

"She's so damn stubborn." Jillian tried to keep the sourness from her voice, but an irritated tang slipped through. Seated in an Adirondack chair, she watched the frenzied dance of flames leap from the gas fire pit on Dante's patio. After leaving Madison—who practically shoved them out the door, insisting she would be fine on her own—they'd driven to Dante's sprawling home, tucked at the end of a cul-de-sac on the east end of town.

The custom two-story occupied a four-acre lot with an abundance of ground to the rear. Jillian usually enjoyed relaxing on the oversized patio, watching Blizzard roll in the grass. A peg in the ground kept him leashed with freedom to explore. Huskies off-rope were prone to run, even well-trained dogs like Blizzard. Right now, he was occupied watching a toad amble across a stone walkway.

"Madison is so determined to do everything on her own." Jillian couldn't help being irked by her sister's tenacity.

"Sounds like someone else I know." Dante flashed a grin from the adjacent chair. He passed her a glass of soda. "I remember when you were completely closed off to allowing anyone in your life."

"You would bring that up." She sipped her drink. "At least David was there and made a report of what happened."

The mailbox had been battered as if struck by a baseball bat or a car. A potential warning the same could happen to Madison?

"I'm still worried about the guy who confronted Madison in the parking lot." Her sister had finally managed to dredge a name from memory—Hocker—but couldn't remember details. She didn't know if *Hocker* was the man's first name, last name, or a nickname. David had promised to share the information with Sherre, stating they'd both look into any leads. "I guess I worry about everything after Boyd."

"Which is why your sister is insistent on staying alone. You need to cut her some slack."

"After everything you sensed tonight?"

"The ghosts?" Dante used a remote to toggle down the flames in the fire pit. "It's her choice. Her life."

Jillian blew out a breath. "I hate that you're right." The soft hum of tires approaching on the road made her realize how late it was. "That must be your neighbor."

She'd chatted with Dr. Grace Miner several times while staying with Dante, usually in the morning before Grace left to begin a ten- to twelve-hour shift in the ER. If she was arriving home, it had to be after eleven. Jillian debated about activating her cell to verify the time but couldn't summon the motivation. She dropped her head against the back of the chair, lulled by the soft chirping of crickets.

"I should get going."

The toad had made it into the grass and was in danger of being nosed by Blizzard.

"It's late." Dante dropped his hand over hers, lacing their fingers together. "Stay here."

Exactly what she needed to hear. "How did you know I didn't want to be alone?"

"Because you did loosen up and let someone into your life." He drew her to her feet. "Let's go inside. Madison will be fine."

A click of the remote extinguished the fire, plunging them into darkness. Dante crossed the patio, then bent to unleash Blizzard.

Jillian hugged her arms to her chest. Odd, how the absence of light made the dark seem sinister.

Or maybe that was just her fear of what was yet to come.

Chapter 7

April 12, 1878

Hollande carried Sylvia's lunch tray into the scullery, then set it on the table. The older woman had eaten little, preferring to be miserable company, complaining through the bulk of their time together.

No, she didn't want to take lunch in the dining room, nor did she care to go outside, listen to Hollande read, or play a game of fox and geese. Most vehement of all—she had zero desire to talk about her early years with Darrin. Did Hollande have no decency? She was a shrew for even making such an odious suggestion.

"I see the missus didn't eat much." Annabelle spoke over her shoulder as she kneaded dough on a floured board. A young girl with a thick braid of brown hair, she'd outgrown her initial shyness with Hollande, seeming to enjoy the presence of another woman in the house. They often conversed as Annabelle prepared food for the day. Given the cubed butter, milk pitcher, and sugar cannister on the counter, fresh biscuits would accompany dinner.

"She's exceptionally contrary today." After three weeks as Sylvia's companion, Hollande never knew if the woman was going to be amicable or cross. There were times she insisted on seclusion, others when she took pleasure in dominating a conversation. For the most part, she was agreeable in the evening when Tristan arrived home. On the occasions he chose to overnight in Curtisville, she turned prickly. A mood that lasted until he returned the following day.

Which explained her current behavior.

"Tristan didn't come home last night." Hollande carried dishes to the sink.

"I understand he's been staying in Curtisville more often." Annabelle wiped her hands on her apron before adding more flour to the board. She frowned in Hollande's direction. "You leave those be, miss. It's my job to tend the kitchen, including the scullery."

Hollande had stopped insisting Annabelle call her by her given name. Despite the girl's friendliness, the housekeeper kept an invisible boundary between them. It didn't matter they both held paid positions, Annabelle viewed Hollande's genteel upbringing as a station above.

"What would you have me do with myself?" Hollande spread her hands. "I feel useless when Sylvia is like this."

"There's no fix for it. Mr. Nathaniel and Mr. Tristan pay me to work, and I'll not have you aiding in my tasks. I made a fresh pot of tea, anticipating the mood of the missus." Annabelle nodded to a kettle on the stove. "I expected you wouldn't last with her today. Have a cup and keep me company."

"You take such good care of us, Annabelle. All of us." Knowing she wouldn't win the argument, Hollande did as instructed. Rather than sit, she cradled the cup in her hand and braced herself against the table. "Has Nathaniel returned from town yet?"

"Not that I'm aware of, miss."

He'd left before breakfast, appearing to be in the same foul mood as his mother. He'd been so pleasant lately, spending a good deal of time with her when she wasn't with Sylvia. They often took walks together or enjoyed the early hours of the evening by the fireplace before he retired to concentrate on business. Last night, he'd lingered longer than usual. Tristan never showed, choosing to stay in Curtisville, and Sylvia remained shuttered in her room.

Hollande was surprised by how comfortable she'd grown with Nathaniel—also how attractive she found him. Gone was the somber man of their first meeting. He'd become open, sharing tales of his younger years. How he and Tristan enjoyed swimming in Yarrow Creek as boys or racing horseback from town. Hollande had responded with memories of her own, talking about her parents and brother. When they eventually said good night, he'd escorted her to her room, his hand twined with hers. Later, she'd clutched Phillip's photograph to her chest as she lay in bed, her heart fluttering with butterfly wings. Confused by her feelings, she'd fallen asleep, only to wake in the morning to the sound of arguing. By the time she dressed and headed for the drawing room, Nathaniel was halfway to the foyer, Sylvia glaring daggers at his back. Hollande caught a glimpse of his face, his expression thunderous.

"Nathaniel?"

He drew up short as if seeing her for the first time. "Forgive me for not remaining for breakfast." His features softened only marginally. "I have matters to attend in town."

He left without another word, his stride purposeful as he headed for the carriage house. With a glance that could have curdled milk, Sylvia climbed the stairs to her room.

"Annabelle, are you aware of any disagreement this morning?"

"Disagreement?" Head lowered, Annabelle worked at shaping biscuits.

"Between Nathaniel and Sylvia. I thought I heard them arguing in the drawing room before Nathaniel left."

"I wouldn't know, miss." Annabelle's back stiffened slightly. "Surely if I did, I wouldn't linger. You know how the missus can be."

Sadly, Hollande did. Sylvia would have accused the girl of eavesdropping. "I just don't know what to do." She sipped her tea but had no true taste for it. "I've been useless at helping Sylvia. I fear she may dismiss me."

"Mr. Nathaniel would never allow that."

Heat rose to Hollande's face. Had Annabelle sensed the growing closeness between them? "What about Tristan?"

"I couldn't say. I've never met Mr. Tristan."

Hollande stared. "Never?"

"He doesn't come until evening, does he, being away at the quarry all day? I leave well before that."

"But there must have been times when he delayed in the morning? Stayed for breakfast."

"He's gone before I arrive. Usually grabs a meat pie or such to take with him." Annabelle fell silent and still as if internally debating a matter. Finally, she faced Hollande. "If you ask me, miss, there's something wrong between the brothers. I don't wish to speak out of turn, but I sense no great love between them."

Hollande's fingers tightened on her teacup, a sliver of cold knifing through her. Apparently, she wasn't the only one who'd noted Nathaniel's disregard for his brother. Yet only last night he'd spoken so fondly of their younger years. What could have happened to drive them apart?

"I think they intentionally avoid each other," Annabelle continued. "Make certain their paths don't cross. I only have sisters, but that's no way for siblings to behave."

It certainly wasn't.

Hollande's stomach knotted. Could their brotherly animosity have anything to do with the way Sylvia doted on Tristan? She'd only been a resident of Stewart Manor for a short time, but even to her it was obvious

Sylvia preferred one twin over the other. No wonder Nathaniel had been so sullen when she arrived. His brother spent his days in Curtisville, leaving Nathaniel the bulk of responsibility for their mother, yet she often snubbed him.

What a wretched circumstance.

Hollande enjoyed Tristan's company, but on the whole, spent far less time with him than Nathaniel. A few hours in the evening while he entertained his mother. In the morning, he was usually gone before she awoke. Only once, she'd caught him coming down the steps and managed a few snippets of small talk before he dashed off for another day at the quarry.

There's something wrong between the brothers.

Hollande met Annabelle's gaze, the cook's words ringing in her head. "How long have you been here?"

"Oh, not long." Annabelle turned back to the counter and began tidying up her mess. "Just a few months, but I'm determined."

"What do you mean?"

"There were several girls before me, but she drives them all away."

"Sylvia?"

Annabelle nodded. "If you ask me, she doesn't want another woman in the house."

* * * *

Present Day

Madison met Beverly early Sunday morning at one of their favorite coffee shops. Before Roth's brother and his wife moved to Michigan, she and Bev often grabbed a latte or flavored tea at the Chinkwe Beanery. The last time they'd shared one of the high tables by the window, Bev had been excited about starting a new life in Farmington Hills, but it was easy to see the move hadn't gone well. She looked haggard, as if she spent much of her time crying. Her latte stood on the table mostly untouched.

"Bev, I'm so sorry." Madison squeezed her friend's hand. "It's hard starting over in a new place where you don't know anyone."

"That's not it at all." Beverly dug a tissue from her purse. "I've started over before. I moved to Hode's Hill from Boston."

Before following Alan to Farmington Hills, Bev had a lucrative career as a physician's assistant. Employment she'd walked away from so Alan could accept a high-paying position with a tech firm. Madison could still recall how proud Roth had been of his brother when Alan received the offer.

"Everything was fine at first." Beverly blew her nose gently, then stuffed the tissue into her bag. "Or as good as it could have been."

Her tone puzzled Madison. "I don't understand. I thought you and Alan were great together."

"Sometimes." A weak smile turned her lips. "I was head over heels about him when we first met. He's a charmer, like Roth."

Madison could account for that. Roth always knew the right things to say. It hadn't been easy turning him down when he asked her to move in. Even though she wasn't ready to commit to that extent, it was hard to imagine a future without him. Just as it was hard to imagine Beverly and Alan headed for divorce.

"I should have known." Beverly turned her attention out the window where light danced off the Chinkwe River. A flat boat hugged the shoreline, a lone fisherman in the bow, silhouetted against the rising sun. "Farmington Hills was supposed to be a chance for us to start over. We'd been having problems for a while."

"I had no idea."

"Sometimes marriage just doesn't work." Beverly sipped her latte.

"Was there..." Madison found it hard to voice the thought.

"Another woman?" Beverly's laugh was hollow. "Nothing so obvious. It was the little things that started adding up. Getting upset if I went out with friends. Wanting to know where I was if I came home late from work." She shook her head. "The idiot. I was at *work!* Where else would I be? We argued a lot, even talked about separating; then the job in Farmington Hills came up. Alan said it was going to be a new beginning for us. He insisted the only reason he'd been disagreeable was because he was miserable with his job in Hode's Hill. I wanted to believe him. I wanted our marriage to work, so of course I jumped at the chance."

"Did Roth know all this?" She was surprised he'd never given any indication Alan and Bev were having problems. Then again, Beverly had never confided in her, either.

"I'm sure Alan told him. I should have told you, but I was afraid it could impact your relationship with Roth. You'd been through so much crap with Boyd, I didn't want to unload on you. And I really thought we could make it work in Michigan."

"So, what went wrong?"

At the entrance, a young guy with a laptop bag held the door for a mother pushing a baby in a stroller. The man headed for the counter, but the woman stopped near their table to eye a display of breakfast bars.

Bev picked at the cardboard band around her latte. "Everything started over again. Alan was critical about the jobs I applied for and made snide remarks about the way I dressed. If I went out alone on a weekend, he wanted an accounting of where I'd been." Her eyes welled. "He started to censor everything I did."

Madison passed her a tissue. "That's emotional abuse."

"Exactly. It's like the man I married turned into someone else. Jekyll and Hyde."

"You can't live like that. I never imagined Alan could be so controlling." Behind Madison, the barista called out a coffee order for *Joey*.

"Charm hides a lot. Now that I'm filing for divorce, I've decided to move home to Boston. I only came to Hode's Hill to tie up a few loose ends."

"I know it must be hard, but you're doing the right thing. Is there anything I can do?"

Beverly shook her head. "I already have a flight scheduled for mid-week. I'm going to move in with my parents until I find employment and can get back on my feet."

"Well, you're not staying in a hotel until you leave. I settled on my house the end of May. You can move in with me for a few days."

Beverly blinked, fresh tears in her eyes. "I don't want to impose."

"You're not. What kind of friend would I be if I let you burn money in a hotel where the food is overpriced, not to mention the room rates?"

"What about Roth?"

"Roth has no say. But, um..." Madison wet her lips. "There's one minor problem. The place is haunted."

Beverly choked on laughter. "What?"

"Excuse me." The intrusion of a man's voice made Madison raise her head. She glanced up to find the guy with the laptop bag standing off to the side.

"Are you Madison Hewitt?"

"Yes." She didn't recognize him, but sometimes a former client referred someone who was looking for a home. "I'm sorry. Do I know you?"

"Joey Banco." He extended his hand.

"Hi, Joey." She clasped her fingers around his, then indicated Beverly. "This is my friend Beverly McGrath."

"Hello." Joey nodded to Bev before refocusing on Madison. Nearby, the woman with the stroller was still trying to decide on a breakfast bar.

"This might sound crazy, but I saw you Friday night at the Fiend Festival. You were talking to my friend."

"Your friend?"

"Doug Crawford. The guy that was murdered in the alley."

Madison blanched. She was suddenly conscious the mother with the stroller had stopped reading ingredient labels and was staring at her wide-eyed. Several people in line at the counter turned in her direction.

"I..." The words stuck in her throat. "I'm so sorry about Doug. We only exchanged a few words."

"Yeah." Joey's voice was soft. "That's what he said, too. I wanted you to know..." He shifted, looking toward the ceiling as if to collect himself. His Adam's apple bobbed when he swallowed. "He was a good guy. I just..." Mouth set in a firm line, he met her gaze. "I didn't want you to have a bad impression of him. I sent him over to hit on you."

"What?"

"It was a stupid bet, but he was cool, okay? You should know that."

"Joey, I thought he was nice. If I hadn't already been with someone, I would have probably taken him up on his offer for pizza." She couldn't say for certain, but it was obvious Joey struggled from the loss of his friend. If a white lie could ease his pain, she'd toss on a few more.

"You knew that guy? The one who was killed?" The young mother edged closer, power bars clenched in her hand. In the stroller, her baby played with a plush green-and-yellow turtle dangling from the cross rod. A pink bow gathered the little girl's silky hair at the top of her head.

Just the thought of discussing murder in the presence of a child left Madison queasy. As if the mere mention of butchery could defile innocence. The mother seemed to have no such qualms.

"My boyfriend works with Christy Catterman. You know— Channel 42 News?"

Madison wanted to tell her to stop, but Joey looked enthralled.

"He's her cameraman and was there when the cops roped off the alley."

"I heard that Crawford dude was ripped up bad." A tall guy wearing a Stones T-shirt slipped from the line to plod closer.

Joey looked green. "The cops aren't committing to a cause of death. Not yet, anyway."

"I heard it was the Fiend."

"That's crazy." Madison bristled, irritated by the sensationalism. "People are going to spread rumors like that because of the timing after the festival."

"It's not a rumor." The mother dumped her power bars on the rack without looking. "Andy said cops were puking all over the place. They tried to cover it up, but there were pieces of the guy everywhere." As if worried the Fiend might burst through the doors at any moment, she snatched her baby from the stroller.

"Shit, man. What a way to go." The Stones guy screwed up his face.

Joey looked at Madison, a plea in his eyes to make the conversation stop. She felt helpless. "I wouldn't believe anything that isn't concrete fact."

"Yeah?" The Stones guy's voice held challenge. "Well, if it wasn't the Fiend, there's one sick mother of a killer rampant in Hode's Hill."

Madison caught Beverly's worried gaze and was suddenly thankful her friend would be leaving town.

* * * *

Roth was ticked. Hands stuffed in the pockets of his jeans, he paced the veranda as Madison sat in an old wicker rocker, trying to hold her emotions in check. She hadn't wanted to deceive him about Beverly, so she'd phoned after she and her friend parted ways at the Chinkwe Beanery. Bev returned to her hotel to pack, and Madison headed home to make sure the room at the top of the stairs was decent for company. Beverly laughed at the idea of ghosts when Madison finally managed to tell her of Dante's findings. At least having a guest for a few days would pacify Jillian. The idea did nothing, however, to placate her boyfriend.

"Why is she here?" Roth stopped mid-veranda, glance as terse as his voice.

"I told you. Because she's my friend, and I don't want her staying in a hotel." Madison was irritated having to justify herself. "Besides, I thought you'd be happy I have company given what I told you about the house."

She'd finally confessed everything that had taken place, both otherworldly and prank-related. At least, she'd told Roth the incidents were prank-related, choosing not to mention her encounter with Hocker. Not that it mattered. Roth had gone ballistic anyway, rattling off a string of reasons why she should have never bought the property. He wanted to rip the place apart in a search for clues that would lead to the culprit. Better yet, rip her tormentor apart. The idea of the place being haunted only seemed to fuel his reasoning. When she'd finally gotten him past the hurdle she'd concealed information, he'd zeroed in on Beverly.

"I don't want her talking trash about my brother."

Her spine stiffened. "Does Alan talk trash about Beverly?"

"That's not the point. Damn it, Maddy." He scraped a hand through his hair. "A divorce is personal. You shouldn't be involved."

"And neither should you." Hands clamped on the arms of the rocker, she tipped the chair forward. "All I'm doing is providing a place for a friend, so she doesn't have to dump a load of cash into a hotel until she leaves town." Bev had arrived before eleven in a rented Camry. She'd dropped her bags in her bedroom, cried on Madison's shoulder, then headed for Hode's Hill. "She's moving back to Boston. In a few days she'll be gone, and who knows when I'll see her again? She's here to visit friends and say goodbye, not to bash Alan."

Although from what Madison had heard, Alan could use a good bashing. Beverly planned to tell others the marriage simply wasn't working, avoiding specific details. Those problems had been for Madison's ears only because of her relationship with Roth.

"I hope he's nothing like his brother," Beverly had said as they'd left the café. "You deserve only the best. Especially after Boyd."

She looked at Roth, his posture rope-taut, cheeks mottled with the heat of anger, and wondered if he *was* the best. Maya had married Collin. Jillian and Dante were headed for engagement, and even Tessa and David seemed destined for a life together. Roth was *her* chance at happiness. She loved him. And yet...

"You can be so damn rigid at times!" Her voice came out harsher than intended. "This is my home, and I'll invite whoever I want." She had enough to deal with—a stalker, ghosts, a friend's marriage falling apart, the suffocating fright of a killer running loose in Hode's Hill. "Why are we arguing about Bev and Alan? I was so excited when I bought this house. I thought it was a step toward our future together. Something I needed to do before I could let go of the past, but I've had nothing but grief. Now, all I want to do is help a friend, and you go Rambo on me."

"Shit." Roth hung his head. A pulsebeat passed as he squeezed his temples between a thumb and forefinger. "You're right." The heat went out of his voice. "I'm sorry."

He squatted in front of the rocker, gazing up into her face. "Alan's my kid brother. I get overprotective. He got the brains between us, but he's not the best when it comes to relationships. He was burned a few times before I met you. I thought Beverly would be different."

Madison's anger faded. "He has to find his own way, Roth." She touched his face. Smoothed the hair behind his ear. "Let's not argue, okay?"

"Sure." He pressed his lips against hers, then drew back to hold her gaze. "I'll stay clear of Beverly while she's here, but if anything happens at the house—supernatural or otherwise—I expect you to call me. You should have told me what was going on from the start. No more secrets."

"No more secrets." At least she hoped.

* * * *

Beverly headed to bed early after a day of tying up loose ends and parting with friends—yet again. Drained, she fell into an exhausted sleep but woke abruptly in the middle of the night. Confused by her strange surroundings, it took a moment for the ugly reality of the last few weeks to crash over her.

Better she learned the truth about Alan now rather than later. She was still young enough to forge a life without him. Her former employer had offered to rehire her, but a clean break was needed. Hode's Hill was a place she would always associate with Alan. They'd started dating shortly after she'd arrived in town. In some ways, it felt like failure to return to Boston, but in others, moving home offered the fresh start Farmington Hills hadn't delivered.

Floorboards creaked softly beneath her feet as she wandered down the hall to the bathroom. There was zero chance of falling asleep again. The day had been brutal, leaving her mind stuck on fast-forward, one thought tumbling into the next like a constantly revolving hamster wheel. She hunted up a few Excedrin from the medicine cabinet, hoping to quell what promised to be a blistering headache.

Later, after dressing, she headed downstairs to the kitchen.

Coffee might help. Decaf, because the last thing she wanted was a stimulant that would keep her mind from catching up to the exhaustion of her body.

Maybe wine. She poked around in the refrigerator until she located a bottle of Riesling. Her first thought was to pour a small amount, just enough to take the edge off her clamoring thoughts. In the end, she grabbed a glass along with the nearly full bottle, carrying both outside to the veranda.

The setting was hard to beat. A starry night sky, moon-silvered trees, and a clear view to Yarrow Creek. Crickets and bullfrogs serenaded her as she settled into a wicker rocker. The whisper of the chair's runners against weathered flagstone blunted the edge from her nerves.

Madison had the right idea being on her own. She'd survived much worse than a divorce and managed fine. Beverly convinced herself she would do the same. The wine helped, cool silk against her throat when she swallowed. By the time she finished her third glass, she had a good buzz going, her muscles unspooling into loose thread. Screw Alan. Screw Farmington Hills. Life looked better through the haze of alcohol.

She melted into the rocker, tipping her head back to gaze up at the sky. Above, on the balcony, a woman leaned over the railing, staring down on her.

"Madison?"

Alarm rippled through Beverly. No, not Madison. She spun from the chair, splashing wine down the front of her shirt. That face—cold, bone-white, suffused by anger—did not belong to her friend.

Her heart thumped. Standing upright, she couldn't spy anyone on the balcony. Had she imagined those terrible features? Maybe a trick of moonlight or her overly taxed and wine-soaked mind? A far better thought than believing a withered crone had glared at her with such hatred.

Suddenly cold, she set her glass aside and hugged her arms close. The night crowded near, abruptly ominous, as if the shadows concealed unseen danger. Her head was pounding again, and her stomach roiled. She'd been stupid to drink so much wine so fast. She needed to pull herself together, stumble inside and into bed. But it was hard to move, the air abruptly freezing as if someone had thrown a switch, dropping the temperature twenty degrees.

She staggered toward the kitchen door, managing three feet before hitting a wall of stench so foul, she doubled up and gagged. Her stomach rolled over, protesting with a violence that dropped her to her hands and knees. Sobbing, she vomited onto the flagstones.

Something moved in the darkness. Something she couldn't see.

"Please, no." She could feel it. Malevolence. Hatred. A thing hideous and foul, so god-awful frightening, her muscles seized in terror. The reek of sulfur and carrion clogged her nose and bubbled into her throat. She curled into a ball, trying to make herself smaller. Whimpered and squeezed her eyes shut.

"Go away, go away." Should she try to run? Scream? A few feet and the thing would be on her. If she stayed, it might kill her anyway.

A rectangle of yellow spiked over her with an abruptness that made the dark recoil. The stench evaporated beneath a puff of creek-scented air. A symphony of crickets filled her head.

"Beverly? What happened? Are you all right?"

The alarm in Madison's voice wrenched Beverly from her cocoon of horror. A pitiful sound spilled from her throat as her friend crouched beside her. Behind Madison, the kitchen door yawned open, passage to a safe haven wrapped in light.

Beverly blubbered with relief and tried to climb to her feet.

Madison steadied her. "Your skin's like ice."

Her teeth chattered despite the return of warmth. "There was something here. In the darkness. Something evil." Her tongue felt thick, a tumbleweed that rolled sluggishly. The reek of vomit made her head spin.

"Were you drinking, Bev?" No judgment, just concern.

The evidence was everywhere. The empty wine bottle, the sour stench of sickness, her disorientation.

"You don't believe me. About...about..." What could she call it? "That *thing*." She sobbed harder.

"You've had a rough day. Come inside. We'll get you cleaned up." Madison guided her toward the door. Helped her upstairs, then out of her clothes.

Beverly collapsed on the bed with a lethargy she didn't think possible. "There was something outside. In the night." She closed her eyes, buried her face in the pillow. If only she could forget the taint of the creature. An unholy stain that oozed malice.

And death.

Chapter 8

April 14, 1878

"I do not want your flowers."

Hollande ignored Sylvia's biting observation and continued to arrange the daffodils she'd picked in a tall crystal vase. Standing before the window in Sylvia's bedroom, she allowed her gaze to wander toward Yarrow Creek. She'd found the flowers growing wild along the bank.

"If you don't care to walk outside, at the very least, I can bring its beauty inside for you. These will brighten your room." She cast a glance over her shoulder.

Sylvia sat enthroned in her usual chair before the fireplace, her face twisted in a disagreeable mask. The room felt stuffy to Hollande. She'd opened the drapes when she'd entered, whisking them to the side with a sweep of her arm. That had started Sylvia grumbling. The addition of the flowers only soured her further.

"Don't you like daffodils?" Hollande asked.

"Once."

"What changed?"

"You put your wretched hands on them. I pray the vile things will die quickly."

"Sylvia!" Hollande spun to face her. Each day it became harder to maintain a charade of civility. She twined her hands, sinking onto the edge of a straight-back chair. "Why do you detest me so?"

"You have no place in this house."

"You haven't given me a chance." She'd never met anyone as coldhearted and remote as Sylvia. The woman's animosity went beyond casual dislike, bordering on venom. "And you forget I did not choose this position, but had it thrust upon me by my brother."

"Then go burden him. I do not need you, and my sons surely do not. I have instructed Nathaniel to terminate your employment."

Hollande wilted inside. Nathaniel had said nothing to her. Just yesterday as they'd strolled along the creek, he'd drawn her close and kissed her. A proper kiss that made her heart quicken and senses reel. He'd told her he was falling in love with her. Shyly, she'd admitted to feeling the same. How love could bloom in such a hostile environment, she wasn't sure, but she and Nathaniel had found the promise of joy despite his mother's overbearing and shrewish nature.

Sylvia seemed to read her thoughts. "You will not get your claws in Nathaniel, lowly girl. No woman is good enough for my son. Either of them."

Hollande's back stiffened. "Is that why you argue?" She'd caught snatches of raised voices again only yesterday. She hadn't lingered, but Nathaniel's mood was dark when she came upon him an hour later. As they strolled along the creek, his despondency vanished. They hadn't talked of Sylvia or Tristan but spoke of pleasant memories—the first time Darrin took his boys to the quarry in Curtisville. Christmas in the house, when Nathaniel and Tristan helped their father haul a huge tree from the woods. Sylvia had made a large pot of mulled cider, and the family drank it together while stringing decorations.

Something clearly had gone wrong to change Stewart Manor from a place of idyllic bliss to the joyless crypt it was now. Darrin's death?

When Hollande gently prodded, Nathaniel shook his head and told her there were deeper, more destructive wounds in his family's past. He left it at that, refusing to say more, and she'd wisely let the matter rest. Perhaps Tristan would be more revealing of the problem if she pressed.

But he hadn't come home again last night, which accounted for Sylvia's foul mood today.

"It is no business of yours why my son and I argue," Sylvia snapped. "You would be wise to keep your nose out of our business—and away from my son. I am not blind to your attraction for Nathaniel."

Hollande felt heat rise to her face. Had Sylvia lingered by her bedroom window, watching as they'd strolled along the creek? Had she witnessed their kiss?

She stood, refusing to be intimidated, and stared down on the woman. "The attraction Nathaniel and I feel for each other is mutual."

"Is that so?" Sylvia's lips curled in an ugly grin. "Perhaps he may fancy you—a pretty face to turn his head. But I wonder if you would remain equally smitten if you knew his true nature. The sins he has committed."

Hollande's heartbeat pounded in her ears. Was Sylvia trying to frighten her, turn her from Nathaniel? "He is an honorable man."

With a snort of derision, Sylvia looked away, staring out the window.

Hollande could bear it no longer. "You are an impossible woman! I see how you treat Nathaniel. You are cold and distant with him, yet fawn over Tristan. It is shameful for a mother to blatantly favor one son over the other."

"You vile witch!" Sylvia shoved from her chair, her face the color of wine-soaked beets. "You know nothing of my relationship with Nathaniel. How much I need him, depend on him. My world would crumble without him." She thrust forward, inches from Hollande, her eyes blazing with heat. "That is why I will not allow you to get your hooks into him. Why I will fight to have you removed from this house. Now get out of my sight. I do not wish to see you again!"

Hollande slipped from the room and closed the door. In the hallway, she stood with her back pressed to the wood, one hand looped over the knob. Her legs trembled, but she didn't know if it was from fury or fear. One thing was certain.

She could not live like this.

* * * *

Present Day

Beverly was still sleeping when Madison left for appointments Monday morning. Not wishing to disturb her friend after such a rough night, Madison scribbled a note detailing her whereabouts, then left it in the kitchen by the coffeepot. She spent the morning working with a young couple she'd connected with through an open house, showing them several homes. Around noon, she sent Beverly a text but didn't hear back until nearly forty minutes later.

Roth just left.

Madison frowned at her phone when the message appeared on the screen. She'd spent the last hour at her office, reviewing comparable properties on her laptop for a listing appointment. There was no one else in her cubicle group, but she could hear two agents chatting by the copier. It sounded like Karen Randall had a showing lined up, and Shelia Warburton, her mentor, was explaining how to operate a lockbox.

Swiveling her chair to the side, Madison picked up her phone. She tapped out a quick reply.

What was he doing there?

It took only a moment for Beverly's answer to ping back. *I called him. Why?* She would have preferred Bev steered clear.

I didn't want to leave without seeing him. Tell u about it later.

Or Roth would. Madison was surprised he'd given his soon-to-be ex-sister-in-law the time of day, considering how irritated he'd been the other night. Maybe he'd had a change of heart.

She hesitated before sending a final thought. *Are you okay?*

Bev had been so disoriented last night, it scared her. Her friend enjoyed an occasional glass or two of wine, but Madison had never known her to drown her woes in a bottle. Then again, a divorce was the death of a marriage, trauma that might spur anyone into overindulging.

The reply was longer in coming back. *I'm ok. Sorry about last night. (a crestfallen-faced emoji).*

A smile tugged at Madison's lips. *Don't worry about it. Almost done here, then have listing appt. Depending on how it goes, could be few hours b4 I'm home. Need anything?*

Better judgment.

(laughing emoji) I've done worse. You'll get thru this. If u decide to go out, there's a spare key in drawer of foyer table.

(thumbs-up)

Madison signed off with a heart.

"Hi. How's it going?"

She glanced up to find Karen standing at the corner of her cubicle, a laptop bag hooked over her shoulder. The other woman was smartly dressed in black capris, wedge sandals, and a green-and-yellow striped blouse. She looked professional, yet casual.

"Good." Madison smiled. "How about you?"

Karen rubbed her hands together. "Nervous. I have my first showing this afternoon."

"Shelia's going with you, right?"

"Yeah, but she's letting me take the reins."

"You'll do fine."

"I hope so. The clients are supposed to be meeting us here in another fifteen minutes. How are things with you and the house?"

A loaded question. For a crazy moment, Madison considered telling her the place was home to several ghosts, including a woman who could have passed for her twin. "I'm still settling in." Something Karen said during their earlier discussion remained stuck in her head. "I know you told me about several of your experiences there. You said Vera Halsey talked about a presence that had been drawn by evil."

Could that be the malevolent ghost that attacked Dante?

Karen's eyes grew wide. "Have you felt it?"

"No." If there were ghosts in the house, they'd only manifested to her in cold spots, the occasional phantom argument, and the lantern-carrier by the creek. Too many people already knew Madison's past, including the years she'd spent with a damaged mind in a care facility. The last thing she needed was to start spreading tales about seeing spirits.

But Beverly had been terrified when Madison found her last night, insisting something *evil* lingered in the darkness. "I think maybe Vera played off folktales and rumors. Creaking floors and closing doors aren't unusual in an old house. Even drafts that create cold spots."

Karen appeared taken aback. "Are you saying the place *isn't* haunted?"

"I'm saying I think Vera liked to pretend it was." The best thing she could do was put an end to speculation and rumors. "I just wondered what she meant about the presence being contained."

"You said there's nothing there."

"There isn't, but I find the history interesting. Old houses have so much character. Vera sounds like she was colorful."

"No question about that." Karen hooked the strap of her laptop bag higher. "I'm glad the place is working out. I felt bad after I told you those things about the house, like maybe I scared you. I think I got freaked out working there because my workers were so afraid of the place. And Vera was bizarre. I have no idea what she meant about the presence being contained. She never explained what it was, but she said a lot of things that didn't make sense. Sometimes I think she was in a trance. Or high on drugs." Karen flashed a glance at her watch. "I better go. I want to set up in the conference room before my clients get here. Wish me luck."

Madison smiled. "Luck."

After the other woman breezed away, she sat back in her chair. She'd picked up nothing new from Karen. Maybe Dante would fare better when he talked to his grandmother about the Stewarts and their family history.

* * * *

Dante waved at yet another resident as he strolled down a central hallway for the Cottages at Chinkwe. The new senior living facility was being finished in phases with phase one complete, phase two under construction. His grandmother had been one of the first residents to move into Hode Development's newest community, thanks in part to Dante's strident media protests against the demolition of the old senior center, Pin Oaks. He and Collin Hode at been at odds then, butting heads at every turn. Two years later, they were close friends. More, the residents of Pin Oaks—many who had already transitioned to the Cottages—still loved Dante for the fight he'd undertaken on their behalf.

"There's my favorite grandson." Sonia DeLuca smiled as he stepped inside her practical but pristine apartment. The flow led him from a small entry to the living area a few steps away. A compact kitchen was situated to the right, a bedroom and bath to the left. Cozy, efficient, comfortable.

Sonia was seated on the sofa, her cream blouse a match for the overstuffed cushions.

"Your only grandson." Dante bent to drop a kiss on her cheek. "You're looking well, Grandma."

She always looked well, despite relying more on the use of a cane these days. Sometimes, she favored a walker in the apartment to get around, but none of that stopped her from dressing impeccably or making certain her pure white hair was neatly coiffed.

"I'll take the compliment. When are you going to get rid of that ponytail?"

Dante gave a short laugh at the abrupt change of topic. "It never bothered you before."

"You're getting older. Don't you think it's time to chop it off?"

"Jillian likes it."

"Lovely girl. When are you going to marry her?"

"What is this?" He sank beside her on the couch. "I'm here less than a minute and you're cutting my hair and planning my future?"

"I'm getting older." She shook her head as if finding the idea preposterous, or at the least disagreeable. "I want to know you're happy when I'm gone."

"Don't talk crazy. You're healthier than ninety-five percent of the people here."

"Maybe." She rested her hand over his, her skin carrying the touch of warm parchment. The scent of lavender and vanilla filled his head, reawakening memories of childhood. She'd filled the void left by his mother's passing, then later became his legal guardian when his father died.

She squeezed his fingers. "I'd feel more settled if I knew *you* were settled."

"I can't promise Jillian's answer, but there's a ring in the near future, if that's what you want to know."

Her smile bloomed. "Oh, I think I can guarantee her answer. Women know these things." She patted his hand. "Where is she?"

"Working. I thought you and I could talk. Do some reminiscing."

"About you?"

"About Hode's Hill. You know so much about the past."

She chuckled. "With reason. When you get to be my age, most everything is behind you. If we're going to chat, I should get you something to drink. What would you like? Coffee? Soda?" She reached for her cane.

"I'll get it." Dante stood. "What about you? Want anything?"

"Whatever you're having."

He was halfway to the kitchen when she called after him. "What do you think of the place?"

"It's nice." He'd been there before, but the building was still so new it carried the earmarks of recent construction—not a mark on the walls, cupboards that gleamed, carpet that carried a freshly-installed scent. She'd paid for upgrades to the unit, opting for higher-end amenities like a tiny fireplace in the living room and a walk-in shower with a tiled seat. Sonia DeLuca could afford to live anywhere, but she preferred to remain with the friends she'd made at Pin Oaks, many of whom weren't nearly as well-off.

"I think I'm going to have an accent wall painted in the living room. Rose, to match the carpet." That was an upgrade too. "Of course, I have a grandson who's an artist. Maybe he could paint a mural instead."

"He could." Dante returned to the living room with two glasses of Coke. Passing one to his grandmother, he resumed his seat on the sofa. "What would you like painted?"

"Let me think about it, and I'll let you know." Sonia sipped the soda, then set it aside. "Let's get back to why you're here. What's so pressing about Hode's Hill?"

"I was looking through your genealogy book the other day. Remember that?"

"How could I forget? I spent years working on that project before it became too time-consuming. By then, most of the work was done anyway."

"Do you remember a family named Stewart?"

Sonia's brows drew together. "There were several Stewarts, as I recall."

"Darrin and Sylvia. They owned a property off Yarrow Creek Road."

"Stewart Manor. It's still standing, isn't it?"

Dante nodded. "Jillian's sister bought it."

"Madison? Now that is a surprise. I should think that old house is a fossil by now. I remember Grandma Kaye once taking soup to a sick friend who lived there. I tagged along, and while she was inside, I played in the yard. I remember the place because of gravestones in the back."

"They're still there."

"Doesn't surprise me. As a child, I found the notion creepy. Now, I know such burial sites weren't unusual in the nineteenth century. Especially when a family had land."

"Your grandmother knew some of the Stewarts personally?"

"Apparently, but I couldn't tell you who. It was so long ago. I must have been six or seven at the time. All I remember were the graves." She looked aside, as if concentrating on something. "And the man. I'd forgotten about him."

"What man?"

"The one by the creek. It was starting to get dark. Near twilight, and he had a lantern. That's what made me notice. The light. I walked down to see what he was doing. When I asked, he said he was looking for someone. I remember he was dressed oddly, like a character out of a Dickens novel. He told me I shouldn't get near the water in the dark. That it was dangerous."

"Then what happened?"

She shook her head. "That's the oddest part. I can't remember. I think Grandma Kaye called for me, and when I looked back around, the man was gone. Later, when I told her about him, she said I must have imagined the whole thing. I guess that's why I forgot about it."

So, Madison wasn't the only one who'd seen a man in old-fashioned clothing by the creek. "Do you know anything about the history of the house?"

"Sorry." Sonia retrieved her soda for another sip. She turned the squat tumbler in her hands, her fingers as fine and delicate as the diamond-patterned glass. "All I really remember about the place is those gravestones. There were three."

"There should have been four."

"What do you mean?"

Dante dug a folded sheet of paper from the pocket of his jeans. "I made a copy of the page you drew up on the Stewart family tree." He spread it on the coffee table, then flattened it with a swipe of his hand. "See?" He directed her attention to the list of names she'd scrawled decades ago. "You indicated Darrin and Sylvia Stewart had twin sons—Nathaniel and Tristan. Nathaniel is buried on the property with his parents, but Tristan's grave is missing. You never listed a date of death for him either."

"That's odd." Sonia inched forward on the sofa, leaning nearer to study the sheet. "The line had to continue somehow." She pressed her lips together, saying nothing as she scrutinized the paper. Slowly, she ran a slender index finger across the names. "Now, I remember. Darrin had a brother. I think his name was Gerald, but I was never able to find any history on him. He lived elsewhere, but I believe one of his descendants eventually took over the house."

That would explain how Vera Halsey ended up in possession. "What about Tristan?"

"What about him?"

"Do you know what happened to him?"

"As I recall, I couldn't find any legitimate information. The consensus seemed to be that he died in an accident at a quarry. In Curtisville. Yes, that was it." She was confident now. "His family owned a quarry. That's why he isn't buried with the others. It's only my opinion, but he must have died after Sylvia and Nathaniel, otherwise they would have brought his body home. It's probably also why he never reclaimed Stewart Manor. His mother and twin brother perished at the house on the same day. I'm sure he wanted nothing to do with the place."

"Do you know what happened? To them, I mean."

"I'm afraid not. I suppose it could have been illness or some type of catastrophe. I often suspected a fire."

"That makes sense." He was thoughtful a moment, musing over the possibilities. There was no question tragedy was attached to the house, the only question was the manner in which it struck. Sitting in his grandmother's modern, brightly lit living room made the house seem like a tomb. He wondered if Jillian felt the pall hanging over the place, or if his perception was due to his unusual sensitivity.

His grandmother resettled into the corner of the couch, her gaze direct. "There's something you're not telling me."

She'd always been able to read him. "It's haunted."

Someone else might have laughed, but she was familiar with his gift, even if she labeled it superstition. "Did you have one of your feelings when you visited?" The way she said *feelings* left no doubt she considered his awareness questionable. She'd witnessed the same odd aptitude in her son, Salvador, Dante's father.

"A *feeling* that threw me up against a closet door."

Sonia let out a slow breath. "Perhaps you shouldn't go back there again."

"If there's danger for Madison, I need to get to the bottom of it."

Her mouth tightened. "I'm not a fan of what you do, but I know you've held séances in the past."

"True, but there are multiple ghosts in the house, including one that's hostile. Opening the veil to that kind of spirit would be disastrous. There's no telling the damage it could do."

"It sounds like Madison should move."

"That's what Jillian wants her to do, but it's not that easy. She has a lot of money tied up in the place, and it won't be a quick sale if she puts it back on the market." He was silent a moment, tugging a thumb and forefinger over his bottom lip. "Did *you* ever hear anything about the place being haunted?"

"Just the usual stuff. An old house at the end of a lane. A couple people would say bad things happened there, but that's all I remember."

"What about any house staff for the Stewarts? Did you come across anything about a woman who might have stayed there during Darrin and Sylvia's time?"

"I'm sorry, Dante. All I really know is what's on that paper." She indicated the sheet on the coffee table. "Grandma Kaye often talked about old times in Hode's Hill and stories her grandmother Sadie told her, but I don't recall anything specific about the Stewarts."

"If you do think of anything...remember anything, will you let me know?"

"Of course."

She smiled, and he was reminded again of how fortunate he was to have her in his life. Later, driving home, he ran their discussion through his head. He wasn't focused on the Stewarts so much as her. There was no question his grandmother was aging, but she was far from sickly or frail. Odd, how she could make him focus on matters without pointing them out directly.

Like the big house he'd inherited from his father. The place was a monstrosity, as she was fond of saying, part of the reason she'd chosen to live in Pin Oaks over staying at the sprawling contemporary. There were too many memories in the house. It would never do if he and Jillian moved forward with their relationship.

When are you going to marry her?

His grandmother knew how to be pushy.

She also knew how to prod him into action.

He was halfway home when he detoured onto the interstate and headed for Lilith Square, outside of town. The mall had four jewelers.

It was time to go ring shopping.

* * * *

Madison didn't leave her office until half past four. The listing appointment had gone well, with the seller choosing to sign all of the appropriate paperwork. She'd taken her time, explaining marketing strategy, listing details, then measuring the house. She snapped several photos for reference but would hire a professional photographer to do the job right. Afterward, she returned to her office to put the file together, schedule with the photographer, and finish several odds and ends.

When she finally got home, the smell of spicy marinara and oregano permeated the foyer.

"Beverly?" Madison followed the tantalizing odors to the kitchen, where she found Bev washing dishes at the sink. "What are you doing?"

"Oh. Hi." Bev glanced over her shoulder, her hands buried in soapy water. "Since you were working late, I thought I'd make dinner. I found some pasta in the cupboard. Mozzarella and sauce in the refrigerator."

"It smells great." Madison set her laptop bag and several folders she'd carried from work on the kitchen bar. She didn't see any pots on the stove. "What are you making?"

"Baked spaghetti." Bev nodded toward the oven. "It'll be done in about twenty minutes."

"Thank you. That's so much better than the tossed salad I had planned."

"We can have that on the side."

"You sure you don't want to become a permanent houseguest?"

Beverly laughed.

Madison removed a clean towel from a drawer by the sink. "How was your day?" The drawer stuck halfway when she tried to close it. Wedging her hip against the edge, she shoved until it lurched shut with a screech. "The kitchen can be a challenge."

"It has character." Beverly added more dish liquid to the sink. "I did have some problems. I couldn't get the pantry door shut."

"I'll take care of it. It gets stuck now and then." Madison grabbed a bowl from the drainboard. "Tell me how things went with Roth."

"Hey, I'll dry the dishes."

"You've done enough already. You're supposed to be a guest." She finished with the bowl, then snatched another. "And you're avoiding the conversation."

"Okay." With a resigned smile, Bev placed a pot upside down on the drainboard. "I guess it was stupid to call him. I always liked Roth, but he's convinced I'm at fault for the marriage failing. In Michigan, when I'd go out on my own, Alan suspected I was seeing someone on the side—something that couldn't be further from the truth. Roth appears to have bought into that. No matter what I said, he wouldn't listen."

Madison leaned against the counter, a glass in her hand. "Why do you think he came over?"

"I don't know. Maybe so he could tell Alan what I said. Anyway, it doesn't matter." Beverly let the water out of the sink, then used the sprayer to chase suds down the drain. "I didn't want to part on bad terms, especially since you're allowing me to stay here a few days. I made an effort. How Roth handles that is up to him. I just don't want to be the cause of problems between you two."

"You're not. And you won't be." Madison finished drying the pot, then added it to the cupboard. "I'm going to go change, then throw the salad together. Any chance you're up for a glass of wine?"

Beverly smiled. "No, thanks. I'll stick with ice water."

Ten minutes later, after changing into a pair of shorts and a pullover top, Madison returned to the kitchen. She poured herself a glass of Cabernet to the sound of a television game show drifting from the drawing room. Knowing Beverly was occupied, she dug a package of mixed greens from the refrigerator, then gathered cucumber, grape tomatoes, and shredded carrots.

The pantry door was stuck as Beverly said, but she managed to wrench it open. With the growing summer heat and humidity, the wood had swollen.

She switched on the overhead light and stepped inside. Having a walk-in pantry was a welcome perk of an old home, one that made stuck doors and screeching drawers tolerable. Eventually, she'd stock up on items, but for now the shelves were mostly bare. She'd pitched everything the previous owner had left, then given the shelves a good scrubbing. A few were warped, bowed in the center, but they did the job. The small enclosure smelled of aged wood and Pine-Sol.

Madison grabbed a box of croutons, tucking them into the crook of her arm before reaching for a bottle of olive oil. Something jostled against her, jarring her abruptly off balance. She stumbled into the rear wall, dropping the box.

"What the—?" She could have sworn she'd felt a physical presence, but maybe she'd bumped against the shelf before losing her balance. As she stooped for the croutons, she spied a small lever jutting from the floor behind the package.

Curious, she knelt to examine it more closely. Unlike the walls on either side, the rear was bare of shelving. The lever—a curved piece of metal—protruded from the base. Tarnished with the patina of age, the small device blended into the worn boards of the floor and walls. No wonder she'd never noticed it before. She pushed it with her thumb, but the mechanism remained locked in place.

Maybe the other way? This time, she tried pulling, but netted the same results. Using both hands did nothing either.

Stubborn thing.

Determined, she stood and pressed her foot on top, forcing the switch to the left. A scraping sound filled the pantry, followed by a hollow pop. Madison's gaze was drawn to the appearance of a crack in the wall, a dark splinter spanning ceiling to floor. Croutons and oil forgotten, she leaned against the wood. The panel swung open on a passageway cocooned in shadow. She caught a glimpse of a narrow stairway as a draft of musty air struck her face. Hesitating only a second, she slid her foot inside.

"Don't go in there."

Madison jerked at the sound of Beverly's voice. She glanced over her shoulder to find her friend crowded into the pantry, her face leeched of color.

"Bev?"

Shaking her head, Beverly took an unsteady step backward.

"Please, Madison. There's evil in this house. I don't think I can stay here anymore." She spun and fled, the sound of her sobs echoing in Madison's ears.

Chapter 9

April 18, 1878

Hollande read by the hearth in the drawing room while Tristan shared a late-night meal with his mother at the dining table. As was his habit, Nathaniel retired to work upstairs a half hour before his brother came home. Hollande had waited for the sound of Tristan's carriage out front but couldn't recall hearing the clop of hooves on cobblestones. Sylvia, however, had been certain he'd arrive.

"He'll be here."

Fifteen minutes later, he'd strolled through the front door to the utter delight of his mother.

"I've saved dinner for you, my son. Come sit with me and eat."

Tristan had barely managed a greeting for Hollande before Sylvia whisked him off to the dining room. Hollande didn't make an issue. Sylvia had been tolerable the last few days, even allowing her to read aloud from *Lorna Doone* while they took tea together. Harmony had reasserted itself between Nathaniel and his mother. They hadn't bickered in days, and although Nathaniel sometimes seemed gloomy, his demeanor with Hollande was attentive and gracious.

After he'd finished dinner, Tristan took brandy in the drawing room while Sylvia sipped tea. Hollande declined any refreshment, keeping mostly to herself as mother and son chatted. There was no question Sylvia needed time with Tristan to cast off her rough edges. She was almost pleasant when he was around. Certainly, she was devoted to him.

He brought more news of the quarry and shared a few tales of life in Curtisville. An evening party he'd attended at the request of a friend, a trolley ride to Arbor Point to meet with an engineer about equipment, the newest shops on Main Street.

Sylvia had no interest in quarry business. "Tell me about the party." Her eyes sparkled with delight.

Perhaps there'd been a time she enjoyed parties. When she'd visited with friends or entertained at Stewart Manor.

Tristan stretched his arm over the back of the divan. "Harry Kraner insisted I go. You remember him?"

"Oh, of course." Sylvia clapped her hands together. "He and your father were such good friends. I remember how he and Louise would visit in the summer, and we'd take chairs down by the creek. We'd sit and talk for hours with glasses of lemonade."

Hollande had only been half listening, but the mention of Yarrow Creek made her look up sharply. Since she'd been at Stewart Manor, Sylvia wanted nothing to do with the wide body of water behind the house. Even Nathaniel said she detested it. Apparently, there'd been a time when she felt differently.

"Tell me about the party," Sylvia urged.

"It was a small affair. Harry and Louise, along with a few other couples. We had roast duck with trimmings, then played parlor games. Lookabout was the favorite."

"Oh, yes, how I used to love playing that." Sylvia's eyes took on a distant glaze. For a moment, it was as if she stepped back in time. "You and your brother always insisted we play. I'd show you a trinket then hide it here in the drawing room. The first of you to find it was the winner. Do you remember?" She gazed at him eagerly. "When you were younger."

"I remember." Tristan's voice was soft. He looked away. "It's getting late, Mother. Perhaps I should escort you to your room."

Her face fell. "But I want to hear more. When you're here, I see so little of you. A few hours, then you're gone the next morning. Perhaps Nathaniel should go to Curtisville."

Tristan blanched. "What?"

"Yes. I think I will mention it to him."

"No." Tristan shot to his feet. "The arrangement we have is fine. I take care of the quarry, he sees to the books. And correspondence."

Sylvia stood. "We shall see about changing that." Her gaze slid to the side, taking in Hollande by the fireplace. "I think Nathaniel could do with time away from Stewart Manor." Once more, her face was closed and cold. Without waiting for her son, she strode from the room.

"Damn." Tristan dropped onto the divan. He propped his elbows on his knees, using both hands to scrub his forehead.

Hollande's stomach knotted. She understood part of Sylvia's reasoning. With Nathaniel in Curtisville, they would be separated. Sylvia no doubt hoped distance would put an end to their romance.

"I'm sorry, Tristan. This is my fault."

"No, it's not. It's always been her way to control those around her. Including her family. Sooner or later, it has to stop."

Hollande set her book aside. When Tristan wasn't doting on his mother or plying them with easy quips, he sounded much like his brother. Perhaps because, on this, they agreed. Nathaniel would no more want to go to Curtisville than Tristan wished to remain in Hode's Hill.

"I don't understand. The quarry belongs to you and your brother."

"It belongs to her. She is the matron with an iron first. We merely run it for her." He stood, sliding his hands into the pockets of his trousers. Firelight reflected off the taut lines of his face as he paced to the hearth. "You have no idea what Nathaniel and I do to placate her."

Hollande leaned forward, the rocker creaking with her movement. "Why?"

"The circumstances are difficult."

"Because of your father? Nathaniel told me what happened. How he died."

"My father's death is only part of it." His scowl dug deeper. "I am sorry I ever brought you here."

"*You* brought me? I thought Nathaniel—"

"It was my idea." He seemed to sense he'd spoken too freely. "I thought having a regular companion would convince her to abandon the past."

Hollande wet her lips, her mind fogged by confusion. Nathaniel had hinted of a dark family secret. Even Sylvia implied her son was guilty of something horrible.

"Tristan, nothing you say makes sense. Nathaniel is the same. You both hint of something terrible in the past, but neither of you are willing to address it. You won't even speak to each other. If you can't communicate with your own brother—your twin—how do you expect to make your mother listen to reason?"

"Nathaniel and I are not so distant as you think. I'm well aware of his feelings for you."

The admission caught her by surprise. "I...I'm sorry. I just assumed—"

"We talk in the evenings, late at night, after Mother has gone to sleep. It's best that way. I share news of the quarry, and he relays any changes regarding the business end. We often discuss other matters as well."

Heat rose to her face. "He told you of our feelings?"

"He loves you." His gaze softened. "I wish there were an easy path ahead, but my mother will make any union difficult."

As she feared. "I'm willing to take that chance." She squared her shoulders, sitting straighter. "For Nathaniel."

* * * *

Unable to sleep, Hollande rose early the next day. Up as the sun was struggling above the horizon, she fully expected to encounter Tristan, but he was nowhere about. Not even Annabelle had arrived yet. She donned a shawl and walked to the carriage house, guessing he was readying to leave.

He'd been fairly open with her last night. Nathaniel wouldn't talk to her of the past, but she'd made up her mind to learn the truth from Tristan. Unfortunately, by the time she arrived, he was already gone. Only a single carriage remained in the building, the one Nathaniel used for trips into town. Disappointed, she retraced her steps to the house. It must have rained overnight for the ground was soft and spongy, her shoes sinking into the soil, leaving indentations wherever she walked.

Strange that she hadn't noticed a single track at the carriage house. If Tristan had already departed, there should have been ruts from the wheels, hoof imprints where the horses passed. How was that possible?

Inside, she mulled the prospect over while heating water for tea.

The morning promised to be bright, the sky clear outside. Whatever ill weather came their way vanished with the night. If only she could chase off the issues between Sylvia and her sons so easily. The brothers had to stop indulging their mother's whims and enforce their own plan of action. It wouldn't do any good if Nathaniel went to Curtisville. Somehow, she had to make them see that.

There was no sugar in the pot Annabelle kept in the scullery, so Hollande headed to the pantry to rummage through supplies. She spied what she needed on an upper shelf in the rear corner. Just her luck. Someone had placed a large sack of flour against the wall, preventing her from reaching the jar. With effort, she wrangled the bag aside, budging it enough to glimpse a raised metal lever. As the bottom of the sack slid over the device, a hidden panel swung open in the rear of the pantry.

Dumbstruck, Hollande gazed into the darkened interior. Blood thrummed in her ears, but her wariness vanished quickly. She hurried to the kitchen, where she located an oil lantern.

The glow was more than enough to illuminate the passageway—a narrow flight of steps angling in both directions. The hem of her skirt stirred dust from the treads, but it was obvious she wasn't the only one to have passed this way. Someone had trampled a path in the middle of the stairs as if climbing up and down repeatedly.

Hollande moved carefully, her fingertips pressed to the wall for stability and guidance. The enclosure was cramped, claustrophobic, the angle precarious. A halo of light from her lantern picked up nests of cobwebs, wafting gray threads that faded into darkness as she descended. The air grew cooler and mustier the deeper she went, the steps ending abruptly before a solid wall. Uncertain what to do, Hollande pushed against the barrier, but it refused to budge.

She lowered the lantern to the base, searching for a lever, and found the device recessed into the floor. When she depressed the switch, a hidden door deposited her in the cellar. A few feet away, a sliver of light angled through the storm doors leading to the rear of the property. A convenient way for someone to enter the house unnoticed. But why, and where would they go?

Hollande returned to the passageway, shutting the door firmly behind her. She followed the stairs past the pantry to the second floor. Once again, she was greeted by a solid barrier and once again she discovered a lever recessed into the floor. Fearful of what she might find, she pressed her ear to the wood. Someone moved about on the other side, going through the morning routine of getting dressed. Water splashed in a bowl. Metal clinked on ceramic.

A razor?

When a man cleared his throat, Hollande had no doubt she'd discovered Nathaniel's bedroom.

* * * *

Present Day

Madison drove Beverly to the airport on Wednesday. Her friend had spent Monday and Tuesday night at a hotel. Though Beverly had been unable to explain why, Madison's discovery of the hidden stairway reawakened the trauma of the night she'd been drinking. Madison didn't challenge her reasoning. If she was more comfortable in a hotel, that was up to her. Bev had enough on her plate, and when it came right down to it, Madison couldn't deny the place was haunted.

She didn't explore the stairwell until after Beverly left town. Work kept her busy, and she continued to get together with Bev in the evenings, usually meeting for dinner in Hode's Hill. She talked to Roth a few times by phone, but he made no mention of Bev, a sore point between them. When Madison did finally explore the stairwell, she found it ended in the basement and one of the larger rooms upstairs. It wasn't uncommon for an old home to have a hidden passageway, though she couldn't conceive what this one had been used for. She'd have to ask Karen if Vera Halsey ever mentioned it.

Wednesday evening, Sherre called to say she'd had no luck in tracking down Hocker. Madison wasn't overly concerned, given there'd been no recent incidents of vandalism. Later, she occupied herself by cleaning the flowerbeds bordering the front porch. She'd yet to get a text from Beverly, but her friend was probably waiting until she got settled before letting Hollande know she'd arrived safely. Her flight should have been in by now.

Madison tackled the largest bed spanning the length of the porch first. She'd been putting off the chore for weeks, but the evening was pleasant, and the weeds were an eyesore.

She slid a cushioned pad under her knees, something she'd picked up at a home store, then tugged on a pair of flowered gardening gloves. A five-gallon bucket she'd discovered in the basement was perfect for holding clumps of crabgrass and spiky thistles pried from the soil. The routine of digging helped clear her mind of work, the house, even the rift between Bev and Alan. In many ways the task was therapeutic. She was twenty minutes into the job when overcome by the sensation of being watched.

The hair prickled on the back of her neck with a suddenness that made her still. Dropping a wad of crabgrass into the bucket, she swiveled to look behind her.

Small birds flitted in and out of a hedgerow bordering the street. A squirrel, clutching a nut in its mouth, scampered behind the garage at the bottom of the driveway. From somewhere farther down the road a crow cawed, answered by another. A light breeze skimmed through the grass and ruffled the decorative yard flag she'd added at the corner of the house.

Nothing out of the ordinary. If anything, the setting was idyllic, one of the factors she loved about the home. The property might be isolated, but the location was picturesque and serene.

Madison swiped the back of her wrist across her brow, mopping up sweat. The humidity was steadily building, leaving her hair sticky, clinging to her neck. Time to take a break.

She tugged off her gardening gloves, the pastel print already soiled with dirt, then dropped them beside the bucket. She'd grab a bottle of water, something to tie her hair back, then move on to the bed facing Yarrow Creek. The ones to the rear would have to wait. Given the overgrowth of weeds, Vera hadn't bothered with seasonal plantings, and no one appeared to have tended the landscaping after she moved into the nursing home.

Inside the foyer, Madison paused by a small table with a single drawer. She used it to store odds and ends—pen, paper, her spare house key, a flashlight, even a pink scrunchie to pull back her hair. As she fished the soft band from the drawer, she realized her key was missing. Beverly must have forgotten to return it. She could always get another made. Or maybe Bev had stashed it someplace else in the house.

In the kitchen, Madison grabbed a bottle of water from the refrigerator. The cool liquid felt good against her throat, reenergizing her to tackle more weeding. She needed to edge around the Stewart burial plot, too, but would likely put off the task until she focused on the beds in the rear. She was still contemplating her strategy when her cell pinged with a text.

Madison thumbed out her passcode one-handed.

Hi! The text was from Beverly. *Landed safely. Home with parents. Unwinding.*

Madison tucked the water bottle under her arm, freeing both thumbs to reply. *Good! Thanks for letting me know. Give yourself a few days to get settled. Call when you can.*

Will do.

Relieved her friend was safely in Boston, Madison was about to sign off when she remembered the key. *Um...question: Do you remember where you put my house key?*

A short delay before Bev's response. *The spare you told me about?*

Yes.

Never used it. Should still be in the foyer table.

That was strange. Maybe she'd overlooked it.

Ok. Must have missed it. Thanks. Take care and stay in touch. xoxo

Bev signed off with a heart emoji.

In the foyer, Madison combed through the table drawer, removing paperclips, stamps, even a few coupons she'd clipped for local restaurants. No key.

Had she used it and forgotten? Moved it somewhere else and the whole thing slipped her mind? Or maybe Jillian borrowed the key and didn't tell her, though her sister already had one of her own. With everything that had been going on, it would be easy to overlook. She decided to worry about it later.

Outside, she dropped her water bottle by the bucket, then stooped to retrieve her gloves—only to discover one missing.

The breeze was slight, not strong enough to blow something away, at least nothing as bulky as a gardening glove. She spun in a circle, glancing behind her. Crows still called to one another down the road. Chatting. Mocking.

She moved the kneepad, then the bucket. Fished inside the container, checked the flowerbed.

"This is ridiculous." Something must have dragged it off.

Her gaze tracked to the garage, where she'd last seen the foraging squirrel. Why would an animal carry off a glove? Spying nothing, she looked back toward the porch. The glove was fastened to the metal crossbar of her yard flag.

Madison's stomach knotted.

All four fingers had been sliced off.

* * * *

The missing key was the first of several items to disappear.

The next day brought steady rain, prompting Madison to hunt for an umbrella in the front closet. A fruitless search before scurrying out the door with a magazine clutched over her head left her frustrated and questioning whether she'd stored it there. On Friday, a book she'd set on the coffee table turned up in the bedroom Bev had used. Madison would have thought her friend borrowed it, except she was sure she'd left the book on the table *after* Bev flew to Boston. She was almost positive.

The missing key. The umbrella. Now the book.

She'd been off her meds for weeks. Was it possible she was starting to experience forgetfulness, or could something more sinister be at play? Karen Randall had said items would go missing only to appear elsewhere when she was working for Vera. Could ghosts physically move objects about? If she tore the house apart, would she find the key and umbrella in places she never expected? And if spirits were responsible for moving items, could they also be destructive—slicing the fingers from her gardening glove, slashing her tires? She hesitated to believe the incidents were the work of someone from Boyd's past—Hocker, perhaps—but what was the alternative? The only other unsettling thing that happened to her recently involved Doug Crawford. It was inconceivable to think his death might be related.

The ringing of her cell phone jarred her from her thoughts. She glanced at the display as she sank onto a stool at the kitchen bar. She'd been debating about what to throw together for dinner but had been too distracted by thoughts of ghostly predators and human stalkers.

She pressed to accept the call. "Hi, Roth."

"Hi." He sounded subdued, the timbre of his voice warm. "I'm sitting here on a Friday night, looking at a takeout pizza menu and thinking it's a lousy wrap for the week. I hate eating alone."

"Me, too."

"Good to know. How about something more eclectic and bar friendly?"

She smiled. "What did you have in mind?"

"The Knot." A small, artsy hole in the wall that served an upscale menu and craft beer. "I could pick you up."

She loved their veggie flatbread. "Or I could meet you there."

"That, too." They'd talked several times since the situation with Alan and Bev. Despite Roth's grudging acceptance of Madison's continued friendship with Beverly, something remained unsettled between them. One of the reasons she hadn't told him about the incident with the glove. He'd hit the roof anyway, insist she go to the police—*for a glove? Seriously?*—then vent about how isolated the property was.

Again.

"Meet me out front in an hour?" His voice drew her back to the present. She'd missed him the last week. "It's a date."

* * * *

The Friday night crowd pushed the Knot, a small restaurant with limited seating, over capacity. At least as far as booths and tables were concerned. Roth elbowed them a place at the bar when the hostess told them it would be a twenty-minute wait for a table. Madison ordered a Chardonnay, and Roth got a tall craft beer. The din of conversation and laughter competed with a pulsing blend of current hits and older music pumped through the sound system. Every now and then, a server hustled past with a tray of drinks or steaming food, the hearty aromas making Madison's mouth water.

"I'm glad we decided to do this." She swiveled on her stool, leaning close to Roth before taking a sip of her wine. "I missed you this week."

"How's it feel to have your house back?" Fishing about Beverly.

"Bev ended up going to a hotel Monday night. But I thought we weren't going to talk about her."

"She didn't stay with you the entire time?" He seemed surprised. "How come?"

Madison looked across the bar where two blondes and a brunette, all about her age, were laughing over something on the brunette's cell phone. She didn't want to talk about Bev's breakdown—*was it a breakdown?*—anymore than she wanted to talk about the dissolution of Bev and Alan's marriage.

"I think she felt more comfortable at the hotel." She sipped her wine.

Frowning, Roth leaned into the bar, wedging a forearm against the edge. "Because of my visit? I don't know what she told you, but *she* called *me*. I promised I'd steer clear of her, and I tried."

"I know, Roth. I appreciate it." She lowered her voice. There was little chance of anyone overhearing their conversation, but she was uncomfortable discussing Beverly. "She told me she called." Across the bar, one of the blondes talked animatedly with her hands, grinning as she relayed a tale that had her friends giggling into their wine. When was the last time she'd felt that happy?

Madison forced a smile at Roth. "Let's forget about Bev. I want to enjoy the night with you."

His smile was slower, but he nodded and clinked his glass to hers. Behind him, a young guy in a Yankees cap let out a whoop and blundered into his shoulder. Most of Roth's beer ended up on the bar.

"Hey!" Lurching to his feet, he flung drops from his hand.

"Oh, man. Sorry, dude." The kid, who couldn't have been more than twenty-one, if legal at all, grinned stupidly. "I didn't see you there."

"Look where you're going next time."

The kid was obviously inebriated. He waved to a table a short distance away where three other guys had degenerated into guffaws. Yankee-cap guy wasn't the only one who needed to be flagged. "My friends dragged me down here to celebrate my twenty-first. I'm legal, you know." At least one of them appeared sober. Probably the DD. "I was on my way to the head."

"I don't want to hear it." Roth grabbed a stack of napkins to sop up the $5.95 lager dripping from his arm.

"Uh...let me buy you a drink."

"Forget it. Just get out of my face."

"Hey, dude. I said I was sorry."

"Great. Now get out of here."

The kid finally got the message and shambled off to the bathroom. Swearing under his breath, Roth signaled the bartender for another beer.

Madison tried to remain neutral. "The guy said he was sorry."

"Yeah. I know." Roth shook his head then plunked down on the stool. He rubbed his forehead. "Sorry. I didn't mean to ruin the evening. I'm just wound tight over the whole thing with Alan. I've been thinking about visiting him in a few weeks. You know—guys and beers."

It sounded like a good idea. As a school teacher, Roth's summer was free. Seeing his younger brother could help him put everything in perspective. There was no question the two were close. She'd been so focused on helping Beverly, she'd overlooked how Roth must be feeling.

"I think that's a great idea." She laid her hand over his where it rested on the bar. "It would do you both good."

Her as well. With Roth occupied in Farmington Hills, she could focus on the house again.

And the ghosts.

It took another ten minutes for them to get a table. When they finally did, they were seated to the left of the door. A steady stream of people tracked past, coming or going through the entrance. The traffic seemed to bother Roth, who fidgeted and frowned as he studied the menu. When he asked their server for a different table, the frazzled-looking girl told him it would be a fifteen-minute wait if he wanted to switch. Madison was more than content to stay where they were but sensed tension building in Roth. She might have lost her empathic abilities when Boyd was killed, but knew enough to read body language.

"Roth, it's fine here."

"If you say so." They stuck it out, but the atmosphere grew strained all over again.

The situation went from bad to worse when Roth's bacon burger arrived with onion rings instead of fries. The server, a young girl with short-cropped black hair, apologized then scrambled off to get the fries. Somewhere along the line she got sidetracked. By the time she returned, Roth had almost finished his burger and was sitting with an empty beer glass. His irritation finally got the better of him. He demanded to know why he'd been unable to get a second drink when his first had been spilled by a kid who'd had too many and should have been cut off long before.

"I'm sorry, sir. I'm not sure who you're referring to." The girl's expression was equal parts apology and frustration. It was clear she was having a hectic evening. "We had someone call off sick, and I'm covering double my normal tables."

"That's not my problem." Roth's voice was stony.

She tried to smile. "I can offer you a coupon for a free appetizer the next time you come back."

"I'm not sure I will. This meal should be free of charge. My date's, too."

Madison was taken aback. "Roth, my meal was fine."

"That's beside the point. I'm not going to throw away good money for lousy service." He leaned forward to study the plastic nametag pinned to the girl's shirt. "Juni. See if you can find the manager."

Madison wanted to crawl under the table.

The girl's face drained of color, but the clench of her jaw indicated her pallor came from indignation rather than shame. "Give me a minute." Her voice was tightly controlled. Icy. When she strode off, Madison gathered her purse.

"I'm going to wait outside."

He appeared thunderstruck. "What?"

"This is your fight, Roth." She was mortified by his animosity. Yes, there'd been a couple of slipups, and the service could have been better, but the place was packed to the rafters and the waitstaff was obviously doing their best to keep up. It wasn't worth making an issue. If Roth felt that strongly, he could call and speak with the manager the next day.

"I thought you'd support me." He apparently considered himself the injured party. "It's been a disaster since we walked through the door."

"You made it a disaster." Couldn't he see that? "You've been on edge since we sat down at the bar. I was looking forward to a nice evening and—"

"So, you're saying I ruined everything?" The belligerent edge of his voice told her there'd be no reasoning. He was determined to argue. It was a side of him she hadn't seen before. Was this payback for how she'd supported Bev?

"I'm not going to get into a public squabble."

He'd been talking loudly enough to make several diners stare in their direction. Without giving him a chance to respond, she edged her way through the crowd, then out the door.

In front of the Knot, people milled on the sidewalk, a few with drinks in their hands. Most were talking or laughing as they waited for a table. She envied their easiness and casual chatter. She was so tired of feeling down. The situation with Bev, the ghosts plaguing her house, a stalker who liked to mutilate gloves and slash tires—now the spat with Roth—it was becoming too much. Maybe her sister was up for company. She dug out her phone, thumb poised to dial, when she remembered Jillian telling her she and Dante had plans for the evening.

The thought of Dante started a domino effect that had her thinking of ghosts again—which spurred a memory of Bev's meltdown and her friend's hysteria about the house. Madison shoved her phone in her purse and glanced across the street.

She'd left her Civic in the parking garage on the corner of Fourth and Third. It was a beautiful evening, a half hour from sunset. She should collect her car, go home, and put everything out of her mind. Yarrow Creek would look idyllic this time of night, stained with the copper glow of a fat, dying sun, the water deep violet where trees blocked the light. Dr. Kapoor used to encourage her to picture such places when she was feeling anxious or low. Tranquility to deter whatever problem reared its head.

"Hey." Madison was jolted back to the present by Roth's appearance at her side. He rolled his shoulders, looking slightly contrite. "Sorry I made a scene."

She glanced behind him toward the Knot. "Did you see the manager?"

"No. I told the waitress to forget it."

"You don't sound happy." Roth didn't like being wrong.

"Can we just drop it?" He wrapped his fingers around hers, holding her hand. "It's Friday, and there's plenty of night left."

"I think I'm going to go home."

The downward curve of his lips indicated it wasn't the answer he'd hoped for. "Can I at least walk you to your car?"

"Sure."

They didn't say much as they crossed the street, even as they entered the garage. Roth seemed to be thinking, head lowered, brows drawn together. "I guess I was a jerk, huh?"

"You've been better." Her Civic was wedged between a Subaru Outback and a Grand Cherokee.

His smile reached his eyes. "Maybe we can do dinner the right way another time."

"I'd like that." She leaned into his embrace, accepting his kiss. When she drove away, she glanced into the rearview mirror.

He was still standing where they'd parted, head bowed as he punched something out on his cell phone.

* * * *

Juni Gold had a splitting headache. Her feet were killing her, and her back ached. She normally would have been out of the Knot by eleven twenty, but with Emily calling off sick, it had taken longer to cash out. She didn't know if her friend was truly sick, or if Em simply decided to blow off her shift. She was probably off somewhere with her new guy, a hunky blond named Norman.

Juni unwrapped a piece of spearmint gum, pushed the soft rectangle into her mouth, then crossed the street to the parking garage.

She would have never thought a *Norman* could look like a poster boy for ripped abs and pumped biceps, but this one did. Lucky Em. Hopefully, one of them enjoyed a good night, considering she'd worked her tail off. Even the tips had sucked. There were a few gems in the group, especially early on, but most had been meager. Probably because she was stretched too thin, couldn't cover tables like she should, and the kitchen kept screwing up her orders.

She'd almost lost it over the jerk with the onion rings who'd wanted French fries. Anyone else would have taken the free appetizer coupon she'd offered and been done with it, but not mister-stick-up-his-butt-get-the-manager-asshat.

Remembering didn't help her headache. She quickened her pace, hustling through the garage to the stairwell. Her Kia Soul was halfway back on the second level. She could have used the elevator but didn't like the idea of riding alone. The last thing she wanted to do was get stuck in an elevator at half past midnight. She and Em always walked from the Knot together. When she wasn't with her friend, there was usually someone leaving the same time she did.

Not tonight. Not only had it taken longer to cash out, but Tony had asked her to stay behind to talk. She was more than ready to leave the place by the time she finally caught up with him. She normally got on well with the Knot's manager. He was friendly and easy-going and liked to mingle with the customers. He'd even roll up his sleeves and tend bar when needed. Not much got to him, but tonight he'd been frazzled. Told her he'd gotten a call from a customer who'd complained about her attitude.

He said you refused to get me when he asked.

That's not true!

She'd been on her way to track down Tony, when a few minutes after making his demand, the French fry bastard spotted her across the room and flagged her over. He'd told her to forget about it. Thrown a couple bills on the table—enough to cover the check, no tip—then left. She thought that would be the end of it, but he'd apparently changed his mind, calling to complain not long afterward.

When Juni explained her side of the story, Tony eased up. He told her not to worry, that there was no pleasing some people. He hated to suck up when his staff had done nothing wrong, but part of customer relations was being able to eat a few dollars. He planned to send the guy a voucher for a free entrée, end of discussion.

Juni appreciated the way he stood by her, but the conversation made her even later leaving the restaurant. A few cars remained scattered in parking stalls when she stepped onto the second level. The Knot closed at eleven, but several of the pubs along Fourth would stay open until two. And on Friday night, there was still a smattering of traffic in the distance. She spied headlights here and there, visible through the wide, fresh-air openings.

Just her freaking luck one of the overhead lights near the stairwell was out. The darkness made her jittery and tense, her mind racing to the guy who'd been killed in the alley. Doug something-or-other. The cops said not to worry, the killing probably wasn't random. Doug must have known his murderer and all that bullshit, but some people were whispering about the Fiend.

She quickened her pace, shoes echoing against the concrete. Garages were creepy any time of day, but night was a hundred times worse. She hustled toward her car, rummaging in her bag for her keys. Why hadn't she gotten them out before leaving the stairwell?

Stupid!

At least the steps had been brightly lit. Her fingers closed on the fat key head just as the entire garage plunged into darkness.

Juni froze, terror spiking up her spine, a curse ripped from her lips.

She bolted for her car, trying to navigate by the faint glimmer of ambient light. She didn't care what had caused the blackout—power failure, mechanical problem—just wanted the hell out. Was someone watching? Hiding? Lurking?

It was impossible to gauge where to slip her key in the lock when she reached her vehicle. Why hadn't she paid for the damn upgrade and gotten a keyless entry? She jabbed—once, twice—trying not to think about the damage her blind stabs did to the metallic green paint. Her hands shook. When had the garage gotten so god-awful cold, like someone dumped a shitload of winter over it?

Cell phone.

She could use the flashlight app!

Brilliant girl.

Something moved behind her.

No, no. Just her crazy-hyper imagination. Nothing there. *Silly, silly Juni.*

She groped in her purse.

Sensed the thing again. Rising up. Bulky. Black.

"Who's there?"

Hyperventilating. Terrified. Hand fumbling blindly in her purse.

Oh, God! Oh, God! Oh, God!

A wall of stench closed around her, so rank she choked on bile. She was crying now, unable to stop.

"Please, please..." The bag tumbled from her hands, fingers so frozen she couldn't bend them. Something watched from the darkness—crouching, waiting to spring.

Evil. Evil thing!

Juni blubbered. Tried to run but stumbled to her hands and knees. "Help me! Someone, please help me!" She crawled forward.

Sobbing. Screaming. Gagging. Fully conscious when claws sliced into her legs and wrenched her backward.

She shrieked. Rolled onto her side. Flailed wildly with her arms.

Strike. Hit. Survive.

A small halo of yellow light blinded her.

"Hey, lady, you okay? What's going on?"

The claws released her. A man's concerned face bobbed behind the orb of a flashlight.

The stench shifted away from her.

She tried to yell. Tried to tell the man to run, but it was too late. The flashlight flew from his hand as the thing bowled him over. His wail of terror nearly stopped her heart. She clamped her hands over her ears, huddled against her car, and wedged into a ball.

When Tony found her eight minutes later, all she could do was scream.

Chapter 10

April 20, 1878

Hollande followed a footpath to Yarrow Creek, with the midmorning sun climbing overhead. She'd yet to see Nathaniel, but Sylvia was once again in a foul mood, sequestered in her room. Hollande had attempted to deliver a breakfast tray but ended up leaving it in the hallway when the older woman refused to answer the door. When she could finally escape, she was glad to be outside where the freshness of spring replaced the stuffiness of the house.

In another month, the trees would be bursting with leaves and color. Already, bridal wreath and dogwoods had begun to bud. Bluebells and primrose grew wild along the creek, dotted among clumps of daffodils. Hollande loved the perky yellow blooms, but any time she tried to bring a bouquet into the house, Sylvia threw the flowers away. She cursed the daffodils as *frivolous and worthless*, saying they reminded her of Hollande. The older woman's tongue sharpened each day until Hollande was frequently on the verge of tears.

She hates me, she'd complained to Nathaniel last night.

She's trying to drive you away, my love. Do not let her win. Give me but a while longer, and I promise to rectify the situation.

Hollande didn't understand how he planned to change his mother's attitude, but when he took her in his arms and kissed her, she thought of little but her love for him. He did not go to Curtisville as Sylvia proposed, nor did Tristan return home. One or both must have spoken to Sylvia in private and refused her suggestion, a unified stance for which Hollande was grateful. The thought of being separated from Nathaniel made her ill. By the same token, it was clear Tristan's absence robbed Sylvia of what little pleasure life brought. Did he fear returning because she might once again insist he stay?

Hollande sat on the trunk of a fallen tree near the creek's edge. The water ran high and muddy, typical for early spring when rains were frequent. It had stormed again last night, the gloomy weather adding to the dismal air of Stewart Manor. She was thankful the rain had passed, the ground heated by the sun, no longer boggy. If only the atmosphere in Stewart Manor could be the same.

"I thought I might find you here."

Hollande hadn't heard Nathaniel approach. She gave a small jolt when he sat down beside her. "I...I wanted some fresh air."

"Needed is more likely." He took her hand, gently rubbing his thumb over her knuckles. "Annabelle just left. She told me what a wretch my mother was this morning."

Hollande looked away. "No different than usual." She couldn't stop the thread of bitterness in her voice. After a month subjected to Sylvia's viperous nature, her outlook was bleak. She loved Nathaniel but wasn't sure she could continue to bite her tongue given his mother's constant berating. Oh, to voice what was in her heart!

You evil shrew of a woman! You are a miserable crone who takes delight in making everyone around you miserable.

She tightened her hands, her gaze focused across the creek where a blackbird pecked among toadstools. Better to look there than let Nathaniel see the disappointment in her eyes. He promised to remedy matters, but she saw no means of escape from Sylvia's thumb. Not as long as Nathaniel's mother controlled the quarry.

"I know it is unfair to you." Nathaniel's voice was grim. "The situation with my mother is difficult. Do you remember what I told you about her the first day we met?"

His question caught her off guard. "That she was ill."

"More than that."

Hollande studied his face, the intensity of his eyes. As if he willed her to see more than the obvious. "That she had good days and bad." She thought back to that first meeting in the drawing room, Nathaniel distant and cold. A man who seemed to have no joy in life. "That her sickness was of the mind."

"Yes."

Hollande waited for more, but he didn't speak. Her focus narrowed, scattered birdsong and the warble of the creek fading into background noise. The way he looked at her...the way the light struck his face, curved along his cheek. What was she missing?

"You don't see it?" he prodded.

"Nathaniel..."

He exhaled and looked away. Planted his feet apart and laced his hands between his knees. "Do you see how fast the water is running?"

It took her a moment to catch up with the change of topic. Her gaze flashed to the creek, then back to him. "Yes. There was a storm last night."

"Tristan and I used to go swimming when we were boys. Fishing, too."

"Not when the water was like this."

His mouth tightened. "No. Our father taught us to be careful. Not only in the spring, but winter could be dangerous as well, especially when the headwaters to the north overflowed. There were thaws when the creek climbed close to the house." He shook his head with a soft snort. "Tristan loved the water, far more than I ever did."

"Does he miss it?"

Nathaniel stared blankly. "What?"

"Now that he's in Curtisville? Even today, my brother enjoys a spot of fishing—though he'll be the first to tell you he is a city-dweller." She recalled Sylvia talking about the creek with Tristan. "Your mother said she and your father would often sit by the water with friends and talk for hours while sipping lemonade." As before, the revelation struck her as strange. "I guess there was a time when she enjoyed coming down here."

Nathaniel nodded, his expression bittersweet. "That was a long time ago. So much has changed since then." Turning to face her, he gathered her hands. "There is a part of me that wants to tell you to leave. To run far away and forget you ever stepped foot within Stewart Manor. But the selfish part clings to the hope that you are my future. My nights are haunted by the fear that one day you will awake and decide you are unable to love someone as flawed as I."

Hollande's heart broke. "Nathaniel, why do you torture yourself?" She gripped his arm, clung tight. "I have professed my love and look forward to the day when I will be your wife. You *know* the obstacle in our path, the person who stands between us. I am not asking you to choose. I will gladly care for your mother all of her remaining days if she will allow me the privilege. Does she fear I will take you from her?"

He bowed his head. "Dear God. It is so much more than that."

"Then let us face it together." Hollande stood. "I cannot help if you will not be truthful with me. There is something you and your brother refuse to acknowledge. It's in your actions and the words you don't say. Nathaniel—please." She knelt before him, her fingers coiled around his wrist. "If it relates to your father's death, however painful the outcome, your mother must face it."

She thought of the locked room at the end of the hall. The hidden staircase that led to Nathaniel's bedchamber. Was he slipping out at night, meeting with Tristan for reasons the brothers were unwilling to divulge? Tristan said he and Nathaniel routinely talked after their mother fell asleep. Were they plotting to take control of the quarry? If they believed Sylvia was mentally unstable, it made sense they would take action to secure Darrin's legacy. Could that be why Nathaniel asked her to be patient? It was only a matter of time before he and Tristan had matters in hand and relegated their mother to an institution where she could receive proper care?

Perhaps hiring Hollande was the first step. A test to see if Sylvia would respond to someone else. Given her disposition had not improved, but had worsened, they might be investigating medical alternatives.

Hollande's stomach curdled. She'd heard horror stories of asylums, but surely Nathaniel and Tristan would house their mother in a reputable facility. If only she better understood the nature of Sylvia's illness.

"Your mother is resentful and demanding but appears to be of sound mind."

Nathaniel laughed bitterly. "She lives in the past."

Back to the room at the end of the hall.

"Perhaps it is unhealthy for her to keep your father's room sealed the way she does."

"That is not her choice."

"I don't understand." Sylvia made it clear from the start that Darrin's study was off limits.

Nathaniel drew her to her feet. "The locked door is my doing. And until you and I are able to secure our future, it must remain that way."

* * * *

Present Day

I'm alive. I didn't die.

The trauma Juni endured in the parking garage refused to fade. She hunkered beneath the blankets of the hospital bed, hugging Percival, a blue-eyed stuffed zebra, to her cheek. Emily had swung by her apartment, grabbing the fluffy toy from Juni's bed before descending on her in a torrent of tears and hugs. She'd stayed through breakfast, fussing like a mother with a two-year-old, pouring orange juice, adding cream to Juni's coffee.

For hospital food, the meal wasn't bad, but Juni ended up pushing scrambled eggs around her plate while trying to choke out details of the attack. Em told her to stop thinking about it, stop talking about it. Thank God the pain meds muted the worst of the horror.

Did Emily even believe her? What about the cops who responded to Tony's desperate phone call last night? There was no denying her legs were slashed and bandaged. She couldn't remember the number of stitches the wounds required, but the damage was substantial.

Some pervert psycho, Emily said.

No.

Juni squeezed her eyes shut.

Something inhuman. No one would convince her otherwise. The thing had lurked in the darkness, attacked her, then turned on the poor man who'd tried to help. She could still hear him screaming. Smell his blood mingling with hers on the concrete floor of the garage. If only Em had stayed longer, she might have been able to doze. Sleeping was hard when she was alone, the remembered terror leaving her afraid to close her eyes.

What if the creature was still out there?

"Juni Gold?"

She jerked, glancing up to find a man and a woman standing at the foot of her bed. There was something vaguely familiar about the man. Tall and lean with rugged features, he carried himself in a way that said *veteran cop,* despite his casual attire. Silver threads glinted in his black hair, and a light stubble of beard contoured his jaw. Had he been in the garage? Talked to her?

"I'm Juni." She kept her arms locked around Percival, her safety net.

"I'm Detective Gregg. This is Detective Lorquet."

Juni's gaze tracked from the man to the woman. She was a good deal younger but looked every bit as competent. Blue eyes, dusky skin, long black hair. Juni didn't recall seeing her before, but last night was a fog. She was glad the bed by the window was vacant, allowing her to wallow in confusion without the judgment of a roommate.

"Did you...did you find the thing that attacked me?"

"Thing?" Gregg motioned to two chairs. "Mind if we sit down?"

She shook her head. Gregg took the chair beside her, while Lorquet chose to sit on the foot of the mattress, facing her.

"Why did you call it a thing?" Lorquet asked.

"Because that's what it was."

"Did you see it?"

"Yes—maybe." She clutched the zebra tighter. "Some."

Part of her wanted to take Emily's advice and shut the memory from her mind, but the other part didn't want anyone to suffer what she'd gone through. "What about the man? The one who tried to help me? Is he okay?" The memory of him coming to her aid lived like a cancer in her gut. If not for him, she'd probably be dead.

Lorquet and Gregg exchanged a glance.

"I'm sorry, Juni," Gregg spoke quietly. "He didn't make it."

"What? No!" Her stomach catapulted into her throat. "Oh, no, no, no!" She buried her face against Percival. After a moment, Gregg slid a hand onto her shoulder.

"We believe it happened quickly. He likely didn't suffer."

"But it has to be the same thing that attacked that guy in the alley and ripped him apart." She wiped a hand under her eyes, mopping up tears. "How could he *not* suffer?"

Lorquet grabbed a box of tissues from the bedside table. Returning to her seat on the mattress, she passed them to Juni. "The man who tried to help you—Stanley Reed—died from lacerations to the neck and chest. His attacker was swift and didn't linger. There was no dismemberment."

Juni crushed a tissue against her eyes.

Stanley Reed.

A name she would never forget. He'd saved her life.

"Juni." Gregg withdrew a pen and a small tablet from his shirt pocket. "We need you to walk us through what happened last night. Everything."

She blew her nose. "So much is a blur."

"It's important you remember. If we're going to catch this killer, we need you to concentrate."

She sniffled. Nodded. Between the medicinal smell of the place and the emotional trauma from last night, she was beginning to grow queasy. "What do you want to know?"

"Start at the beginning," Gregg coached. "When did you get to the garage?"

"I think it was almost midnight."

"Is that normal for you?" Lorquet asked.

"No. But it took me longer to cash out because I was covering for my friend, Emily. She'd called in sick, so I took her tables for the night." Juni wiped away fresh tears, snatched another tissue from the box. "Then

Tony—he's the manager—asked me to stay because a customer called to complain about me. He wanted my side of the story."

"Tony VinCarey?" Gregg flipped back several pages in his tablet. "He's the one that found you in the garage and called nine-one-one."

She nodded.

"What was the complaint about?"

"Stupid crap." Her stomach roiled when she told them about French Fry Man. The damn bastard had effed up everything. If she'd left the Knot on time, she might have missed the killer, and Stanley Reed would still be alive.

"Do you know this guy?" Gregg wrote something in his tablet.

"I've seen him around. The woman he was with, too. They come in now and again, and I've seen the woman at the Knot with a few of her friends."

"Do you know their names?" Lorquet asked.

Juni shook her head. "Oh—wait. I heard the woman call the guy Roth. I remember because I thought it was an unusual name. Too bad he was such an A-hat."

The detectives exchanged a glance, something silent passing between them.

Gregg cleared his throat. "Describe the woman he was with."

"Um...red hair...slim. Maybe late twenties or early thirties. She could do a lot better than the French fry creep."

"Did you ever have any problems with this guy, Roth, before?"

"No. I told you—he was just a jerk in a foul mood. If it weren't for him, I would have gotten out of the Knot earlier. Maybe poor Mr. Reed wouldn't be dead." She choked back a sob, fighting tears.

Lorquet pulled the rollaway table close. She filled a cup with water from a plastic pitcher, then passed it to Juni. "Tell us what happened when you got to the garage."

"Everything was okay until the lights went out." Juni sipped, surprised at how good the water tasted. She hadn't realized her throat was so dry. "I was on the second level, almost to my car when everything went black."

"That's interesting." Gregg scribbled in his tablet again. "The lights were active when the first responders arrived on the scene."

The only light Juni remembered was the small orb of Stanley Reed's flashlight bobbing in the blackness. Her pulse triple-timed as cold reality washed over her.

"Then someone had to be there...shut down the lights. Someone was stalking me." She choked on a cry. "What if he thinks I saw him? What if he tries to come in here?" Panic was setting in, turning her fingers to trembling sticks.

"You're safe in the hospital." The firmness of Detective Gregg's voice was calming. "More than likely you were a random target. In the wrong place at the wrong time. We'll start by looking into workers who might have access to the electrical system and the knowledge to shut it down. Also, past employees of the garage. Is there anyone who might hold a grudge against you?"

Her stomach dropped. "Then you're saying it wasn't a random attack?"

"It's a standard question, Miss Gold."

"No." She shook her head, lowered her eyes. "No one."

"Did your doctors tell you about the damage to your legs?"

"Several deep cuts on each." She thought she might be sick. Recovery was going to take time, an equation that didn't work well with the burden of monthly rent. Tony had already been to visit and told her they'd work something out. She had vacation and sick leave accumulated, and when she was ready, there might be bookwork she could do from home.

"It's time you tell us about the actual attack." Detective Lorquet spoke into the silence, the only noise to intrude on the stillness the distant shuffle of people in the hallway.

Nurses, visitors, orderlies. Juni learned to tune them out not long after she'd awakened.

"Can you describe the person who attacked you?" This time it was Gregg talking.

Juni molded her lips, sucking like a fish. Someone had sliced up her legs, but her mind kept telling her it was some*thing.* "I want to believe it was a person. But that's not what I saw."

"What did you see?"

"Blackness." She didn't want to remember. Hugged Percival closer. "It was a presence more than a thing. Dark...evil." There were no other words that fit. A single tear trickled down her cheek. "It didn't make a sound, but I could feel it. Smell it. The stench was so bad I thought I might throw up. I got as far as my car but couldn't get the lock open." She wiped the tear away, looked from one detective to the next. "My legs weren't cut with a knife. You both know that. *I* know that. You're not going to find this thing by looking at employees of the garage. It's not *human.*"

She started sobbing in earnest, all the horror of the previous night washing over her.

"I'm sorry, Juni." Detective Gregg slipped his tablet into his pocket and stood. "I know this has been difficult. You've been very helpful. We'll give you a break now. I'll send a nurse in to check on you. Detective Lorquet is leaving our contact information on the nightstand."

Through her tears, Juni was vaguely aware of Lorquet placing two business cards on the table.

"Try to get some rest." Gregg walked around the bed, toward the door. "If you think of anything that might be helpful, please give one of us a call."

"Wait—*wait!*" It was all she could do to force the plea through her tears. She raised her head, catching a blurry glimpse of the two detectives by the door. "There's something else you need to know."

Last night in the darkness, one single, impossible element had burned into her mind.

"It had wings."

* * * *

Sherre said nothing for a time as David wended his black Mustang through downtown traffic. The Saturday morning rush was never as busy as workday congestion, but still heavy enough to clog several intersections. As David idled the Mustang at a traffic light on River Road, she let her gaze skim to a paved path paralleling the Chinkwe.

Several people occupied benches, chatting or bird watching. Others strolled with dogs, some talking on cell phones. The usual assortment of joggers, walkers, and bicyclists added to the lazy weekend atmosphere. A pleasant setting. Serene.

Could one of those people unknowingly be their killer's next victim? She needed a kick in the butt for even considering the crazy idea that lodged in her head at the hospital. She was a cop. And cops examined physical, logical evidence.

But...

"Trauma can do strange things to a person," she said at last. The light turned green, the string of cars rolling forward, then fanning out.

"You're talking about Juni and her vision of wings?" David switched to the left lane, passing a silver Volvo on the outside.

Gregg would have been the last person Sherre thought would take the girl's tale at face value. "You believe her?"

He shrugged. "People are capable of disconnecting when someone threatens their life. Who knows what someone in Juni's situation might imagine? Could also be our killer was in costume."

She hadn't thought of that. *God, let it be true.* Then she could put her idiotic idea to rest.

Except it wasn't that simple. There were still the cuts on Juni's legs, the lacerations on Stanley Reed's chest, and an autopsy report on Doug Crawford that contained paragraph after paragraph of anomalies. The county coroner believed Crawford's death was the result of an animal attack.

Yeah, right.

She'd been skeptical from the start. A wild animal in an urban town like Hode's Hill?

But what was the alternative?

Because Clairmont hadn't been able to identify the type or breed of animal, his report had been forwarded to three different wildlife experts, including one at a state university. So far two had responded, unable to offer anything to fit the profile. The remaining contact—the director of a prominent East Coast zoo—had yet to respond but indicated he'd received Crawford's report and was looking into it.

Sherre held little hope he'd produce a match. A part of her was convinced a wild animal wasn't responsible, just as a part believed no human could have committed the crimes. That's what she got for becoming embroiled with Dante DeLuca and Jillian Cley. There'd been a time both were convinced monsters from Hickory Chapel Cemetery had descended on the town, causing accidents and killing innocent people. Initially skeptical, Sherre couldn't discount a number of bizarre tragedies *had* taken place.

God help her for contemplating a monster now.

"You don't think our killer was in costume?" David turned the car onto Third.

"I'm not sure what to think." Sherre frowned as they passed a dry cleaner. She'd been so wrapped in her thoughts, she'd lost track of their route. "Where are you headed?"

"The Knot. I thought we'd talk to Tony about French Fry Guy."

"You mean Roth?"

"If it really was Roth." He stopped for another traffic light. "Don't you think it's odd Roth talks to Doug Crawford and he winds up dead? Then he complains about Juni, and she's attacked. He's connected to both victims."

"If that's the case, so is Madison." Sherre hated venturing the idea, but her friend had also crossed paths with both.

"Yeah." David sounded subdued. He slid the Mustang into a parking space two doors down from the Knot.

"It's coincidence." Sherre wasn't ready to let the idea go. "Roth and Madison are our friends. We know them. Know what kind of people they are. Neither would have anything to do with murder or assault. Plus, you're forgetting something."

He killed the ignition. "What?"

"Neither Roth or Madison are connected to Stanley Reed."

"That we know of. It's also possible Reed was just in the wrong place at the wrong time and was never an intended target."

Sherre mulled it over as she watched three teenage girls cross the street with the WALK signal. "You think Juni was. If that's the case, why didn't the killer finish the job?"

"Someone scared him off after he finished with Reed?" David draped a forearm over the steering wheel.

Sherre didn't buy the logic. "There were no other witnesses. If the killer was frightened off, it had to be something else that sent him running."

"Tony was the one who found Juni." David jerked a thumb toward the Knot. "I talked to him last night, but he might remember something new now that he's had the perspective of distance."

"How do you know he's even here?"

"I called from the hospital when you were using the restroom." The sliver of a grin curled his lips. "How about it, Lorquet? My money's on a guy in costume. If you want to prove me wrong, you're going to have to come up with something substantial."

Like a monster.

She knew exactly who to see to find one.

* * * *

Dante was surprised when Sherre asked to meet with him and Jillian, hinting her visit was tied to the monsters of Hickory Chapel Cemetery. She'd contacted Jillian, not needing to look further for Dante, who'd been lying in bed beside his new fiancée when her cell rang.

He'd taken Jillian to dinner last night, then later proposed over a bottle of wine while they stargazed from her rear deck. He might have planned the event with more fanfare, but Jillian didn't seem to mind, dissolving into tears when she accepted his proposal. They'd already visited Madison, sharing their news, but made time for Sherre before heading off to see Dante's grandmother. Jillian had been eager to show the detective her engagement ring, and after a round of well-wishes and congratulations, the three sat at Jillian's table to discuss the reason for Sherre's visit.

Dante listened silently as she told them about Stanley Reed, killed in a parking garage while trying to help a girl named Juni Gold. "You need what?"

"I need to know if a monster is loose in Hode's Hill."

He could only guess what the statement cost her. Sherre was one of the last people to believe in his gift. She'd attended a séance of his over a year ago, the single skeptic in the group. It was only after he'd summoned the ghost of Gabriel Vane that she'd grudgingly admitted he *might* be able to breach the supernatural realm.

"Are you talking about the Fiend?" Jillian fiddled with her new ring, twisting the diamond nervously. "Oh, that poor man, Mr. Reed."

The jittery restlessness was a sign she struggled to squash her empathy, no doubt already imagining what Reed's loved ones were feeling. If she didn't break the connection, her pupils would bloat into engorged black pools. The change made her seem otherworldly, or—in the view of those who didn't know her—a freak. In public, she used tinted glasses to shield her eyes, but she was among friends.

"Jillian." Dante folded his hand over hers. "Let go of Stanley Reed." He kept his voice low. Soothing. He understood all too well the price of a preternatural gift. "Sherre was asking about the Fiend."

Blizzard left his spot in front of the French doors, padded to Jillian's side, then settled next to her chair. It never failed to amaze Dante how the husky acted as a buffer for her emotions.

"Not the Fiend." Sherre's voice brought Jillian back to the moment.

She blinked and focused on the cop. "Then who?"

"I don't know." Sherre rubbed her brow, frustration in her voice. "I don't buy any of the garbage that witch Catterman swills on TV. She's only in it for the ratings. Yeah, we've got a sick, sadistic killer. The coroner thinks an animal butchered Crawford. He'll probably come back with the same for Reed, even though he wasn't dismembered. All of that aside, forget the Fiend."

"We're back to monsters." Dante sensed where she was headed.

"Exactly. I need to know if everything is still..." Sherre fumbled for words. "On the level with Hickory Chapel."

Jillian looked puzzled. "I don't understand."

"Now that Vane's bones are back in his grave."

"Oh." The realization dawned on her face. "You think that something escaped Hickory Chapel Cemetery?"

Something, as in *monster.*

"Not possible." Dante dismissed the idea. Gabriel Vane had suffered a terrible fate when his life ended, but as the first buried in the cemetery, he'd become its guardian. He was also protector over the Hode's Hill residents with ancestors interred there. "Vane's presence wouldn't allow anything to escape."

Dante was well acquainted with the lurid creatures that inhabited the cemetery, having seen them firsthand. Monstrosities with deformed bodies and protruding eyes. Things that oozed pus, crawled on all fours, or slithered on greasy bellies. Creatures with tattered wings, forked tongues, and barbed tails. He'd lived with the images since he was fifteen and his father died. Since he'd heard a ghost bell toll in Hickory Chapel, sending a high school friend to his death. Less than two years ago, he'd watched a swarm of nightmare beasts suck the life from a killer. Jillian had witnessed that same gruesome death, something neither of them would ever forget.

"I would know if something escaped from Hickory Chapel."

Jillian might be connected to Vane, but he was connected to the cemetery.

"I thought you might say that." Sherre leaned forward, both hands cupped on the edge of the table. "I can't believe I'm freaking buying into this, but Juni Gold said the thing that attacked her had wings."

Jillian balked. She knotted her fingers in Blizzard's fur. "Wings?"

Dante wasn't ready to concede. "Someone in costume?"

Sherre shrugged. "That's what David thinks."

A man Dante respected. Gregg had been a cop for a long time, first on the scene when Dante's high school friend, Spencer, was killed. He spread his hands. "David's a smart guy."

"David doesn't know you can see monsters." The corner of Sherre's mouth curled.

Back to that again. Damn, but she'd become a believer. He glanced at Jillian. "You once told me that cemeteries attract creatures of darkness. Maybe you need to explain that to Sherre."

Jillian drew a breath, shifting her attention to the cop. "Because it's a place of death, things of darkness are naturally drawn to cemeteries. They feed on the end of life and the sadness of burial. Graveyards are hallowed ground, but many people of the Old World believed each needed a protector. The first person buried on the site became its guardian."

Sherre's gaze was steady. "Like Gabriel Vane?"

Jillian nodded. "But sometimes that wasn't the case. If the belief wasn't in place at the founding, there wasn't a spirit to keep the darkness confined."

"So, what you're saying is that any other cemetery in Hode's Hill might not have the same protection as Hickory Chapel? Which means, if I'm to believe this insanity—and God help me for entertaining the idea—some freakish monster escaped and is on a killing rampage?"

Jillian nodded.

"Why now?" Sherre didn't mince words. "Why not a year ago? Five years ago? Ten years ago?"

Dante frowned. She had a point. "What's different?"

"That's what I need you to find out." She cast him a challenging glance. "Will you talk to Juni Gold? Maybe it really was a guy in costume who attacked her."

"And if not?"

"You're an artist. If she described what she saw, do you think you could draw it?"

"You mean like a police sketch?"

Sherre grimaced. "This isn't going any further than between the three of us—but, yes."

Drawing monsters. It wouldn't be the first time he'd undertaken the task.

"Sure." What the hell? He was the only resident monster expert Hode's Hill had.

Chapter 11

April 25, 1878

"I will not tolerate your stubbornness!"

The angry shriek of Sylvia's voice was the first thing Hollande heard when she entered Stewart Manor. As was becoming her habit, she'd risen early and taken a walk by Yarrow Creek. Despite Sylvia's dislike of daffodils, Hollande had picked a small bouquet, intending to put the flowers in her room. She hesitated in the foyer, hearing the low rumble of Nathaniel's reply behind the closed doors of the drawing room. His words were indistinguishable, but the sharpness of his tone was clear.

A second later, Sylvia's banshee screech cut into the foyer. "I will never forgive you for this! Never!"

More words from Nathaniel. Hollande thought she caught her name and drew nearer.

"That wretched girl is responsible. This is her fault!" Sylvia hurled the accusation like a knife. "You cannot take him from me."

Hollande was almost to the door, drawn despite her reluctance to eavesdrop, when she heard Nathaniel speak plainly.

"Tristan is not returning."

Sylvia screamed something unintelligible, her fury followed almost immediately by a loud crash. Before Hollande could catch her breath, the doors flung open and Sylvia stormed from the room. The moment she spied Hollande, her eyes blackened with rage. A gnarled, bent finger jabbed in Hollande's direction.

"You! I will not forget what you have done."

"I—" The sheer hatred in Sylvia's voice left Hollande at a loss for words. She clutched the daffodils tighter.

Sylvia's lips curled. "You have no more backbone than those simpering things you insist upon bringing into my house." Eyes blazing, she leaned forward, her face inches from Hollande's. "*My* house. Remember that when your world falls apart, you odious, lowly girl."

Nathaniel stepped into the doorway. "*Mother!*"

The crack of his voice boomed through the foyer but had no effect on Sylvia. Back rigid, head held high, she climbed the steps to the second floor without a backward glance.

Hollande realized she was shaking. Tears burning in her eyes, she looked to Nathaniel. "What have I done?"

"Nothing." He clasped her arm and led her into the drawing room.

The first thing Hollande noticed was the tea service. A china pot and cups lay shattered on the floor in front of the divan. As if someone had swept everything from the sofa table in a fit a rage. She had no doubt who that someone was.

"I have never known your mother to be violent in her anger." Hollande set the daffodils on the table, then crouched to pick up the broken pieces. Hot tea puddled about the shell of the ruined pot, the cups like broken eggs. She used cloth napkins to blot the liquid.

"Leave it. I'll take care of it." Nathaniel was still incensed, his voice edged with frost. "She is beyond reasoning. Beyond sanity." He squatted beside her, picked up several pieces of broken china, then banged the shards onto the table. "I cannot tolerate her presence much longer." Blood squirted between his fingers. "Damn!"

"Nathaniel! You've cut yourself." Hollande turned his hand over to reveal a gash angled across his palm. She pressed a clean napkin to the laceration before folding his fingers to hold the makeshift compress in place. "Go into the kitchen to tend this. I'll finish here."

His face was flushed from anger. "It is not your place to clean up my mother's mess."

"Nathaniel, please. Do as I ask and see to your wound."

He hedged. Grunted an affirmative, then headed from the room.

Hollande wilted onto the floor. If Nathaniel and his mother could no longer speak civilly, what was to become of her? What of her love for Nathaniel?

That wretched girl is responsible. This is her fault!

Sylvia's shrill accusation pinged inside her head.

Perhaps it was time she packed her bags and took lodging in a boarding house. Edgar had sold their parents' home, setting money aside in an account for her. She also had what she'd saved from her month as Sylvia's companion. Perhaps with time and distance, Sylvia would become less volatile and Hollande and Nathaniel could plan their future. As it stood, her presence was akin to the fuse on a powder keg.

Yes. She would leave.

Hollande stood, smoothing the wrinkles from her dress with unsteady hands. She would tell Nathaniel her decision and pray there was a way for them to build a future from there. Let Sylvia realize she didn't have designs on the house or quarry. All she wanted was a life with the man she'd fallen in love with.

Hollande drew a breath, steeling herself to confront Nathaniel with her plan. He would not be happy. Would likely even try to talk her out of it, but she'd reached the point where living with Sylvia was intolerable, the woman's explosive moods a destructive cancer.

It was one matter to live with someone who was difficult, another to reside in the same house with a woman who detested you. As Hollande debated the matter, it occurred to her that maybe Nathaniel wasn't the one to tell. He would try to dissuade her, and they would fall back into the same repetitive pattern. What she needed was an ally, someone with Nathaniel's best interest at heart. Someone who understood Sylvia's volatile nature and was an expert at defusing her moods.

There was only one person who fit that description.

Tristan could help.

* * * *

Present Day

Madison woke to the sound of weeping.

At first, she thought she was dreaming, then realized the muffled crying came from the hallway. Ambient light bled into her bedroom from a window she'd left open to the night. The musky scent of creek water permeated the air, layered with the honeysuckle that grew wild along the bank. The balcony doors were shut, locked securely, drapes wide, inviting moonlight and long tree shadows to prong across the rug.

When the weeping continued, she swung her feet to the floor. Maybe Jillian had a fight with Dante and dropped by seeking solace. God forbid anything bad happened between them, but who else could be crying?

"Jillian, is that you?" Madison strode toward the door.

The sobbing stopped abruptly.

She moved from the room into the hallway, the short step bringing her up against a wall of cold that made her breath plume with frost.

A woman with long red hair stood at the end of the corridor facing her. Dressed in old-fashioned clothing, she might otherwise have been Madison's twin. An aura of profound sadness clung to her, grief magnified by the tears streaked over her cheeks. Her skin gleamed the pale white of cameos, her eyes dark cerulean.

In the frigid air, Madison longed for a robe. She clutched her hands, fear prickling goosebumps up and down her arms. "Who are you?"

The woman said nothing.

"Is...is there something you want from me?" Her knees trembled, pulse palpitating in her throat. There was no doubt this woman was pure spirit, the ghost Dante had seen.

The phantom glided to a closed door in the middle of the hallway, her body transparent, blurred slightly as if viewed through rain-streaked glass. Without a sound, she pointed, then vanished into the room.

"Wait!" Madison lurched forward. Shivering in her skimpy sleep shirt, she thrust through the doorway. The ghost was still there, standing in the far corner where a secret panel opened to the hidden staircase Madison had discovered. Before she could collect her breath, the woman disappeared behind the door.

"No." She knew where the steps led—down to the pantry, then farther to the basement. A dark, narrow passageway without light. It took less than a minute to race back to her room, shove her feet into flip-flops, and snatch her cell phone. When she finally ventured into the passageway, Madison used the flashlight app on her mobile to guide her.

A few bare bulbs hung scattered above the staircase, but all had burned out ages ago. They'd been too high to replace. Eventually, she'd hire someone with an extension ladder, but for now, the app provided enough light to see by.

"Please...are you here?"

She sensed when she passed the pantry, kept going farther down the narrow steps into the basement. There, she was able to flick on a light, but the power didn't work. Either that or the ghost's presence kept it from functioning. Another time, the lack of illumination might have sent her scrambling up the staircase, but she'd moved past fear and operated solely on adrenaline.

The ghost hovered by the cistern, her cerulean eyes locked on Madison.

"Is there something you're trying to tell me?" Madison wet her lips. Took a cautious step forward. "I don't know what you want from me."

A slender finger directed her attention to the cistern. Roth had wrangled the heavy lid back in place but hadn't bolted it to the floor. Surely, the spirit did not expect her to move the lid and look into the hole. She wasn't certain she had the strength to heave the stone cover aside, even if she wanted to—which she most assuredly did not.

With a guarded glance for the spirit, Madison inched closer. The woman's features were sharper now, hazy at the edges like a hologram slightly out of focus.

Madison's breath caught. "We look so much alike."

The ghost dipped her head, a slow nod.

"Did you live here?"

Another nod.

Madison's throat was dry, her heart hammering so fiercely it was hard to articulate her thoughts. "Are you one of the Stewarts?"

The ghost shook her head.

Cold spots swelled in the air, ice on Madison's skin. She fought to keep her teeth from chattering. "Do you have a name?"

Silence.

Perhaps the phantom couldn't speak. If Dante were there he'd know how to communicate, but Madison was at a loss. She was about to venture another question when an arctic gale blew through the room, hurling Madison off her feet. She was thrown against the wall, the light on her cell snuffed into darkness. A scream ripped from her throat as the face of a crone-like woman swelled in front of her—black hair, hooked nose, twisted features. The eyes blazed with hatred.

"Get out!" The visage ballooned three times in size, the mouth spitting words like daggers. *"Get out of my house, or I will kill you!"*

Madison's eyes rolled into her head. Mercifully, she fainted.

* * * *

Dante waited until Sunday to see Juni Gold. Originally, Jillian planned on going with him, but when he stopped by her brownstone, she told him Madison had phoned, horribly upset. Something supernatural had happened at the house, but she wouldn't say more.

First Sherre's report of wild animals, then Madison's metaphysical experience. Dante was starting to believe a creature—monster, phantom, *whatever*—was running amok in Hode's Hill. God help the town if the place was under paranormal attack. They'd had Vane as a defense the last time, but Dante had no idea how to eliminate the threat now. He planned to swing by Madison's house after his visit with Juni. While he was at the hospital, Jillian would stay with her sister, taking Blizzard for company.

It didn't take him long to find Juni in a room just off the nurses' desk on the fourth floor. A petite girl with short dark hair and large blue eyes, she was sitting up in bed, leafing through a celebrity magazine when Dante stepped into the room.

"Hi. Juni Gold?" He carried a sketchpad under his arm, a pencil tucked behind his ear.

"I'm Juni." She was probably attractive when she wasn't looking wary, bored, or frightened. Right now, her expression was a combination of all three. "Who are you?"

"Dante DeLuca." He offered a smile.

"You're the guy Detective Lorquet wanted me to see." An edge of suspicion crept into her voice as she eyed him up and down. Faded jeans, deck shoes, slip-on shirt, ponytail. Probably not what she was expecting given a cop referred him. "I've seen you before. You made all that noise a few years ago about Pin Oaks. You didn't want them to tear it down."

"Guilty."

She ditched the magazine, then pulled a stuffed zebra onto her lap. "My friend's grandma lived there. She was glad to have someone looking out for her."

"Where's your friend's grandma now?" Dante eased into a chair, setting the sketchpad on his lap.

"The Cottages at Chinkwe."

"My grandmother lives there, too. It's a good place."

"Emily thinks so." Her expression grew quizzical. "How come you want to talk to me?"

"Didn't Detective Lorquet explain?"

"Not really."

"How are you feeling?"

"Okay, I guess."

"Are they going to let you out of here soon?"

"Later today. Em's picking me up after she finishes her shift at the Knot. She's going to stay with me tonight." Juni worked a loose thread on the blanket between her fingers. "I wasn't looking forward to being alone."

"Because of what happened?"

She nodded, silent a moment, then cast him a sideways glance. "Are you a cop?"

"No."

"Consultant?"

"No."

A look of horror crossed Juni's face. "You're not a reporter, are you? Those idiots won't leave me alone, especially that Catterman diva with Channel 42."

Dante gave a short laugh. "No, I'm not a reporter. I'm an artist. I own the District Three Gallery on Chesterfield. Other than that, I might be able to shed some light on what happened to you." He hesitated, rethinking what he'd said. "Depending on what you tell me."

"What do you mean?" The wariness returned to Juni's gaze.

"Detective Lorquet said you think something attacked you. Not someone. Some*thing.*"

"She didn't believe me. Neither did her partner. The older guy—Gregg."

Dante scratched his cheek. He wondered how David would feel being labeled *the older guy.* "From what I understand, you told a pretty incredible story."

"If you're here to mock me, you can take a hike." No mistaking her hostility. The girl had suffered a horrific attack, only to be told it couldn't have happened as she remembered.

Dante couldn't fault her belligerence. "What if I said I believed you? That I've seen...monsters."

She stared as if uncertain how to respond. Dante didn't give her the chance to consider a reply.

"I'm sensitive to the spirit world. Detective Lorquet knows that. It's why she asked me to talk to you."

"Are you saying you're psychic or something?"

"Not exactly." Dante made a waffling motion with his hand. "I can't predict the future, but I can communicate with the dead and see into the spiritual realm." No sense mentioning folk memories. "I don't normally volunteer that kind of information, but since you claim to have seen something incredible—"

"Not *claim.* I *did.*" Juni leaned forward, her eyes fired with intensity. "It had wings."

"Tell me about it."

She blinked. "What do you mean?"

"Can you describe it?"

She recoiled, retreating against the pillows piled at her back. A nurse bustled past the doorway, pushing a blood pressure cart. Juni's gaze flicked to the hall before returning to Dante. She hugged the zebra to her chest, lashes dipping against her cheeks.

"I don't like thinking about it." Her voice was thin, barely audible.

"I wouldn't want to, either." Dante drew the chair closer, lowering his voice in what he hoped reflected trust and understanding. "Look, Juni, I know it isn't easy talking about these things. I've been there myself, treading a line between belief and denial. But Detective Lorquet took you seriously enough to ask that I see you. A man died trying to help you."

Juni nodded, tears filling her eyes. Her bottom lip trembled.

"That thing is still out there." Dante flipped open the drawing pad. "You know what a police sketch artist does?"

Another nod.

He withdrew the pencil from behind his ear. "Then how about you talk, and I draw?"

* * * *

"Ghastly, huh?" Dante handed Sherre the sketch he'd put together from Juni's descriptions. The creature was enough to turn even a cold-blooded killer into a whimpering pile of blood and bones.

She stared at the paper. "What is it?"

"A ghoul."

"You say that like you're certain."

"I am."

Rather than meet at the police station under the scrutiny of prying eyes, Sherre had suggested a walk-up soup counter on River Road. A half dozen wrought iron tables ringed by chairs occupied the sidewalk, tucked under a striped green awning. Only one other table was occupied, most people choosing to carry their food to the benches strung along the Chinkwe. Of the two locations, Sips and Soups was less congested, better for contemplating killers and monsters.

Dante dug into a bowl of corn chowder as Sherre studied his sketch.

"You're a damn good artist." She'd ordered iced chai but had barely touched the drink. "This is too realistic for my taste. There's absolutely no way this is someone in costume."

He'd thought the same. It hadn't been easy getting Juni to remember. He'd needed to mentally guide her back to that night, forcing her to recall a situation she wanted to forget. He'd spoken much like he did when summoning a spirit, opening the door to broaden her mind and reach beyond surface memories. At first, all she could recall was the presence of something dark and malevolent, an odor like rotting meat strung with bat guano. Once she focused on the creature's wings, Dante was able to steer her beyond her fear and the blackness.

Juni had been stunned to have the beast's shape develop in her mind. To realize, despite the horror of the attack, she absorbed more than she'd imagined. An exercise in mental recall, Dante's prompting had dredged a fully formed beast from her memory. A thing with thick-veined wings, scaled flesh, and scythe-like claws. The creature's face was elongated, mottled with pustules and open boils. Bags of rotting flesh sagged over a narrow snout ridged by knots of bone. Exposed fangs curved from upper and lower jaws, ending in deadly points.

"Your wildlife experts aren't going to find that in a textbook or case study." Dante nodded toward the drawing.

Sherre's fingers tightened on the paper. "Where will we find it?"

"A graveyard. Ghouls are attracted by death." He leaned back in his chair, momentarily distracted by the blare of a horn. Across the street, a cab driver waved a city bus from his lane. If only their problem was as simple as shuffling an obstacle aside. "In folklore, ghouls robbed graves and feasted on the bodies of the dead."

"If that's the case, then why is this thing attacking living people?" Sherre laid the sketch on the table. "More importantly, how do we get rid of it?"

"It likes dark places. Light will send it fleeing."

"Interesting. All the victims—Crawford, Gold, Reed—were attacked at night. Gold said the lights in the garage went out right before the thing struck."

"I buy that." He leaned back in his chair. "Not all, but some supernatural entities can manipulate electricity. Stanley Reed showed up with a flashlight. It's probably what saved Juni's life. The thing turned on him then fled to escape the brightness."

Sherre looked doubtful. "We're talking about a flashlight beam."

"That might not seem like a lot to you or me, but to a creature that needs darkness to exist, any light is lethal."

"Is that how we kill it? With light?"

Dante chewed the inside of his cheek. He wished he had a concrete answer, but ghouls crossed spiritual domains. Phantoms and ghosts he understood, even monsters, but a ghoul adhered to the laws of neither. It might materialize in physical form or choose to remain unseen. The only trait he knew for certain related to the creature's ability to kill. It had to be visible to slaughter its victim.

"I'm not sure how we kill it. Light's a possibility. Maybe fire."

"Great." Sherre's tone implied his answer was anything *but* exceptional. "If you don't know for sure, who does? You're my monster expert."

"The first step is to figure out where it came from." He shoved the empty bowl of corn chowder aside. "It had to be confined somewhere or there would have been attacks before this."

Sherre tilted her tea, looking into the plastic cup as if the answer lay there. She pursed her lips. "You're sure it has nothing to do with Hickory Chapel?"

"Positive."

"Should you ask Jillian?"

"I don't have to. I know more about what's contained in that graveyard than she does, and—"

Contained.

He stopped suddenly, the single word striking with the power of a thunderstorm.

"Huh?"

"I've got an idea." Damn, what if he was grasping at straws?

"Are you going to share it?"

"Not yet." He stood, gathering his trash, anxious to be away. "Keep the sketch. I stopped at the office supply store on Hudson and made a copy."

"What the hell am I going to do with a sketch?" Anger crept into her voice. "I can't put out an APB on this thing. DeLuca, I've got people dying."

"I know that." He dumped the trash in a can, already backing away from her. "Give me a day or two. I'll call you."

She lurched to her feet. "Where are you going?"

"To see Madison—and hopefully, get an answer."

Chapter 12

May 3, 1878

"You're so quiet, miss."

Annabelle's observation drew Hollande from her thoughts. She forced a smile, smoothing the strings of her Dorothy bag between gloved fingers. There was a nip in the air this morning, the day dawning unusually crisp for early May. Based on the chill, it may not have been the best time to undertake a trip to town, but it was the one Annabelle set aside for her monthly supply run. She would select the necessary items needed for Stewart Manor from the Hode's Hill general store—everything from dry goods to perishables, and select sundries requested by Sylvia—then Mr. Yetzer, the proprietor, would arrange to have them delivered the next day.

The trip was Hollande's first venture into town since moving to Stewart Manor. She'd communicated with Edgar by mail, and he'd visited only last week to tell her of the funds he'd secured in her name at the local bank, providing her with the appropriate paperwork.

Caro and I will be leaving town for good next week. She needs to be close to her family. The baby and all...

Hollande had maintained a stony silence while he squirmed through a series of excuses for deserting her. She was surprised how easy it was to play on his guilt. When he'd first told her of his plans—selling their parents' home, securing her employment without her consent—she'd accepted his judgment, behaving as a dutiful sister. But she was no longer the same person. Stewart Manor had changed her. Her love for Nathaniel gave her the courage to manipulate Edgar as he'd repeatedly done to her. When he left, she'd provided him with instructions on what she required him to do.

"Miss?"

"I'm sorry, Annabelle. I was wool-gathering." Hollande cast aside her thoughts. "How inconsiderate, when you've permitted me to tag along. I never did learn to handle a carriage."

"'Tis nothing really. Especially a wee surrey, like this." Annabelle gave the reins a jostle as the horse trotted up the lane away from Yarrow Creek. The buggy was the smallest of the carriages owned by the Stewarts, ideal for short jaunts. Nathaniel held no qualms about allowing Annabelle to take it to town, something the girl told Hollande she'd done regularly since assuming the position of housekeeper and cook.

Despite the chill, the day was pleasant, with trees dressed in greenery sprouting fresh buds. Birds maintained a busy chatter. The steady clop of the horse's hooves against the hard-packed soil combined with an occasional squeak of the buggy seat for a soothing rhythm.

"I haven't been to town in over a month." Hollande tried to quiet her nerves.

"I think Mr. Nathaniel was pleased you'd have a day out of the house." Annabelle slanted a troubled glance in her direction. "I know things haven't been good with the missus."

Hollande suppressed bitter laughter. "The situation couldn't be worse." She worried her bottom lip between her teeth. "I hope her incessant dislike of me hasn't colored her impression of you."

"She remains as sharp-tongued as ever. That one has never been fond of me."

"And yet you stay?"

"With reason." Annabelle shifted her attention to the easy bob of the horse's head as the gelding ambled down the road. She flicked the reins to pick up the pace. "Me and my mister want to start a family. That takes money, so we've been trying to save what we can."

"I'm sure you could find a better situation than Stewart Manor." The words no sooner left Hollande's mouth than she regretted the comment. Nathaniel needed someone to see to the house given his mother did little but brood and make demands. Who was she to encourage Annabelle to leave his employment?

"Maybe. But when the missus stays clear, my position is pleasant enough." Annabelle gave a slight shrug. "Plus, I worry about Mr. Nathaniel and Mr. Tristan. If I let the missus drive me off like she's done with the previous help, where does that leave the brothers? I'll tell you where." She leaned closer to hammer the point. "Scurrying to find another replacement. Yet again."

Hollande glanced aside, fixating on the expanse of rolling hills. Her stomach plummeted. "Annabelle, I don't know how to tell you this..."

"Tell me what?"

She drew a breath, forcing her gaze back to the girl who'd become a friend. Her nerves faltered, as did the courage she'd marshaled only that morning.

"When we reach town, I won't be returning to Stewart Manor."

* * * *

Present Day

When Dante arrived Sunday afternoon, Madison relayed the same story she'd told Jillian earlier—seeing the ghost of the woman who looked like her, following the spirit to the basement. The appearance of the haggish, floating face shrieking threats, each word thrown like darts.

Get out of my house, or I will kill you!

"Do you believe me?"

"Of course." Dante was puzzled she'd ask. "Why wouldn't I?"

"I don't know." Madison massaged her temples.

Seated on a stool at the kitchen bar beside Jillian, she looked worn out, emotionally and mentally exhausted. Like her sister, she cupped a glass of lemonade. Dante had the feeling if he gripped her fingers, he'd find them icy, even shaky. Blizzard lay a few feet away, ears forward and alert as if listening to the conversation. Madison had invited them to stay for an early dinner. Based on the aroma wafting from the oven, whatever she was cooking promised to put the corn chowder he'd eaten to shame.

"I'm starting to wonder if I'm imagining things." Madison cast him a questioning glance. "Maybe I need to see Dr. Kapoor again."

"Your psychologist isn't an exorcist," Jillian spoke up immediately, her voice honed with a sharp edge. She wouldn't want her sister falling back into old patterns. "The only demon you needed to banish was Boyd, and you've done that."

"But maybe there are no ghosts in this house." Madison wasn't ready to abandon the idea. "Vera could have used a hallucinogen to see spirits. Something airborne..."

Jillian frowned. "You're grasping at straws."

"And a hallucinogen-induced vision doesn't shove you into a closet door." Dante pushed away from the counter. "I think I'm experienced enough to recognize the presence of a ghost when I encounter one."

Madison deflated, her shoulders drooping. "True. I just don't know what to do. I wasn't scared before, but last night was terrifying. It must be how Beverly felt when she claimed something was after her."

"Beverly?" Dante cast Jillian a glance. "Did you know about this?"

His fiancée shook her head. She studied her sister. "What happened with Beverly?"

"I guess I didn't tell you."

"No."

Madison swiped a thumb down the outside of her glass, collecting a film of condensation. "I didn't see any reason for her to pay for a hotel, so I invited her to stay with me while she was in town."

Jillian's brows rose into the fringe of her hair. "I bet that went over well with Roth."

"He wasn't happy by a long shot. He blames her for the divorce, since she's the one initiating it." Madison pressed her lips together, adding a terse shake of her head. "I love Roth, but sometimes he can be shortsighted. We ended up arguing about Bev. Thankfully, we were on the veranda, so she never heard us. Or maybe she did, and that was part of the reason she got drunk that night."

"I didn't think Bev was a drinker."

"She's not. But she must have been upset enough to overindulge. I'd gone to bed but got up in the middle of the night for a bottle of water. I was in the kitchen when I heard her sobbing outside. Not the kind of crying you do when you're upset. More like she was scared out of her wits."

Dante frowned. "What was she doing out there?"

"I don't know. When I found her, she was curled up in a ball, hugging herself. She'd gotten sick—I guess from the alcohol—and was talking crazy."

"What do you mean?"

"She kept insisting there was something in the darkness. She said it was evil. I've never seen anyone so terrified."

Jillian shifted on her stool, her eyes wide and dark. "What was it?"

"She couldn't say. She called it a *thing*." Madison shrugged. "Honestly, there was nothing there, but Bev insisted. She was really worked up about it."

Dante's gaze flashed to Jillian. He knew his fiancée was thinking the same thing he was. Sherre had come to see them because Juni Gold believed she'd been attacked by a monster—a *thing*. He'd given that creature an identity. A ghoul attracted to cemeteries and death.

And there just happened to be three gravestones lined up behind Stewart Manor.

* * * *

Madison sensed something unsaid passing between her sister and Dante. The sudden silence that fell over the room chased cold up her back. An unsettling feeling that whispered Bev's histrionics weren't the meltdown she'd originally assumed.

"Out with it. What aren't you telling me?"

Jillian bit her lip. "Sherre came to see me and Dante yesterday."

"About?"

"Do you remember Doug Crawford?"

"How could I forget?" The brutality of his death would haunt her for a long time to come.

"There was another murder Friday night." Jillian's gaze dipped momentarily before returning to her face. "A man was killed in the parking garage on Fourth when he tried to help a waitress from the Knot. Something attacked her when she was walking to her car."

The floor gave beneath Madison. "Oh, my God. I parked in that garage. Roth and I were at the Knot Friday night. When did this happen?"

"After midnight. I'm surprised you haven't heard it on the news."

She shook her head, trying to process the information. "I haven't had the TV on. Does Sherre think it's the same killer?"

"Looks that way." Dante pulled a square of folded paper from the pocket of his jeans. "The waitress survived but insists whatever attacked her wasn't human. She described it the same way Beverly did—evil, malevolent—but said it had wings. Sherre sent me down there to see if I could sketch what she saw."

Madison watched as he unfolded the paper, heart thudding against her ribs. When he stepped closer to the bar, sliding the drawing onto the counter, her mouth went dry. "What is that thing?"

"A ghoul."

"Attracted to cemeteries and death." Jillian's face was white, her words a whisper.

"Or graves." Dante looked between them. "Like the three out back."

Madison swallowed hard. "You think it's connected to the house?"

"Look at it this way—Vera Halsey said there was an evil presence here. One drawn by violence and death. According to Karen, Vera wasn't afraid of it because it was *contained.* What if that presence escaped?"

"How?" Madison's stomach was in knots. She found it hard to tear her gaze from the drawing of the ghoul, a creature rendered so lifelike by Dante's skill. She shuddered under an imagined chill.

Jillian touched the edge of the paper. "Could it be related to the experience Madison had last night?"

"The ghost." Of course! She was an idiot for not seeing it earlier. "The woman who looks like me. She led me into the basement. To the cistern." Pieces fell into place, jigsawing together in her mind. "I remember when Roth unbolted it, the smell was atrocious."

Dante's gaze narrowed. "Are you saying it was sealed?"

"Yes." Why hadn't they left the damn thing alone? "Roth helped me clean the basement shortly after I moved in. Because the lid was bolted so securely, he was sure there had to be something inside." She shrugged, feeling foolish. "Like hidden treasure. It was kind of a game."

Dante slumped against the counter. "A deadly one."

"You don't think—" She looked from him to Jillian, and back again. "No. I don't believe it. I was in the basement when Roth removed the lid. There was nothing inside. Just—" Words failed as the memory of that moment struck with sudden insight. She tightened her fingers around her glass, knuckles bleaching white beneath the pressure. "Every light in the room went out—like something snuffed them all at once. It was horribly cold, and there was an odor. I can't begin to describe how revolting it was."

"Juni mentioned an odor."

"Juni? Is that the waitress from the Knot?" Too many coincidences. Madison thought she might be sick. "The server Roth and I had Friday night was named Juni. I saw her name tag. I remember feeling sorry for her because she got Roth's order wrong. He was upset and gave her a hard time."

"Like he was upset with Beverly?"

And Doug.

Madison pressed both hands to her stomach, fighting nausea. "What are you saying?"

"I don't know. But one ghost led you to the basement to find something. Another tried to drive you out." Dante folded the paper, then shoved the drawing back into his pocket. "I think it's time I take another look and see what's down there."

* * * *

Blizzard padded down the basement steps ahead of them. Once on the lower level, Dante took his time examining the hidden staircase Madison found, then turned his attention to the cistern. When he'd been in the basement before, he'd only given it a cursory once-over, too focused on the paranormal activity on the upper floors. Had that been by his design or the unconscious prompting of something else? The presence that infested the house was stronger than he remembered on this level. That could be the result of the supernatural encounter Madison experienced last night or because something didn't want him scrutinizing the cistern.

As he moved closer, Blizzard passed him, snuffling toward the base. Halfway through the investigation, the husky backpedaled with a growl.

"Not too pleasant, huh?" Dante squatted by the lid, placing a hand on the dog's collar. The trace of an unpleasant odor made him grimace. He cast a glance over his shoulder at Madison. "Do you have a septic problem?"

"No." She inched nearer. "But now and then, I notice a smell like raw sewage. Just a hint, then it's gone. Karen said she noticed the same thing when she worked here."

Jillian stood by her sister. "I'm sure a ghoul doesn't smell pleasant."

Madison hugged her arms to her chest. "I'm not sure this is a good idea."

"It's the only one I have." Dante grunted with exertion as he worked at moving the lid. It was heavier than he'd thought, forcing him to stand, using his legs and back for extra leverage.

"If there was something in there, Roth and I would have seen it."

"You said the lights went out." The stone made a grating sound as he forced the cover inch by strenuous inch from the opening. The veins popped in his forearms. "Ghouls are fluid and can move through air, materializing and disappearing at will." The stench hit him in the face, an abominable odor that made him gag and stagger backward. "Shit!" He dropped the lid, pulling his foot clear seconds before the heavy stone hit the floor.

"Oh, that's awful." Jillian covered her nose and mouth with both hands.

A second or two was all it took for the reek to vanish, but the residue remained clotted in Dante's nose and mouth. He spat into the open hole, dragged a hand across his lips, then looked to Madison. "Do you have a flashlight?"

Her face was pale. "Anything for my soon-to-be brother-in-law." She managed a shaky smile, defusing the edgy tension hanging over the room. After rooting on a nearby shelf, she passed him a slender light with a black barrel.

Dante activated the beam and dumped light into the hole. Jillian and Madison inched closer to peer inside while Blizzard nosed around the rim.

"There's nothing down there." Jillian sounded almost disappointed. "There has to be something to explain what's going on."

"Whatever was there escaped when Roth opened the cistern." Dante had no doubt whatever had been contained—as Vera Halsey phrased it—used the opportunity to slip free. If it was a ghoul as he suspected, it might have attached itself to Roth. Could a creature, initially drawn by violence, feed off someone's anger? "It looks to be about ten feet deep, cut like a well. It's hard to tell from up here."

"I don't understand why the ghost led me here last night." Madison shook her head. "Why would she want me to look in the cistern if there's nothing inside?"

"Good question." Dante switched off the flashlight. "I guess there's only one way I'm going to find out."

Madison appeared puzzled. "How?"

"By going down there."

Chapter 13

May 3, 1878

Hollande waited outside, choosing a rocker on the covered front porch of the boarding house. It would only be a matter of time until Nathaniel showed up. She chose to pass the hours with a book, though her thoughts frequently strayed from the pages.

Edgar had secured the lodgings per her instructions. After his last visit to Stewart Manor, he left with a single bag of her belongings, the luggage already in place in her room when she arrived. The items would be enough to see her through the next week until she decided on a course of action. By then she hoped to have secured Tristan's help. Nathaniel had borne the brunt of his mother's care for years. If she spoke to Tristan, explaining their desire to marry, she hoped he might intercede on their behalf. Perhaps move his mother to Curtisville where she could reside with him. Hollande had no designs on Stewart Manor—she found the home depressing—but if Nathaniel wished to remain there, they had to find a workable solution for Sylvia, and that meant including Tristan.

She glanced up from the book, her attention drawn by the jangling approach of a carriage. The boarding house occupied a corner, wedged between a seamstress's shop and a narrow alley. The late day sun dipped behind the roof of an adjacent haberdashery, splaying shadows over the lawn. Despite the hour, a number of people still meandered on the sidewalks and street. All the better when Nathaniel confronted her. He was less likely to make a scene with gawkers lingering nearby.

The carriage rolled to a lurching halt in front of a wooden gate. The entrance sign—a square board proclaiming "Rooms and Meals" in white paint—suffered from weathering, leaving "Roo s and eals" as the establishment's primary recommendation for lodging.

Nathaniel jumped to the ground, tossing the reins aside before the gelding came to a thorough stop. Expression fierce, he stormed through the gate, up the walkway, and onto the front porch.

"Hollande." Spying her in the rocker, he clomped across the plank boards, halting when he towered above her. "Annabelle said you're not returning to Stewart Manor."

"No." She steeled herself, voice firm. If she wanted a future with this man, she needed to survive the storm of the next few minutes. "I've decided it's best to remain in town until—"

"Until what?" He latched onto the word, bending down to grip both arms of the rocker.

"Nathaniel, do not make a scene."

The calmness of her voice had the desired effect.

He stalked to the porch railing. "You have already done that. Leaving without confiding in me. Taking up lodging in this..." He grimaced, motioning to the building at her back. "*Place.* The idea is reprehensible, far from suitable accommodations for a woman of genteel standing."

She closed her book with a snap. "They are suitable for me until we resolve our problem."

"That being my mother."

"I do not wish you to choose between us. I merely need time away from Stewart Manor for my own sanity. The atmosphere is poisonous."

"I am to blame."

"How can you say such a thing?" Hollande stood, tuning out the activity on the street. It pained her to see the grief on his face. "You are not the one who belittles me. Who makes no effort to show kindness or even a measure of common courtesy." She stepped beside him, laying a hand on the sleeve of his greatcoat. "It is no healthier for you than me to reside there."

"I've been aware of that for some time. I had hoped your presence would change matters."

"As you've said, but my presence has only served to inflame the situation." The truth stung.

Nathaniel was silent a moment. Finally, he shifted his attention to the entry of the boarding house. "How did you secure lodging here?"

"Through my brother." Hollande presented her back to the street, standing shoulder to shoulder with him. "I sent a travel bag with Edgar when he visited last week and instructed him to make the arrangements."

Nathaniel balked. "And he agreed to this?"

"He didn't have a choice. He and Carolyn plan to leave town for good this week. I played on his guilt for deserting me."

"He crumbled far too easily, but I should not be surprised. It is a weak and selfish man who plans his sister's employment."

"True." She offered a slight smile. "But we would never have met otherwise."

"That's beside the point. I do not like you residing here. At least allow me to put you up in proper lodgings."

"And become a kept woman? I think not."

Before Nathaniel could reply, a man wearing a gray overcoat and fingerless gloves exited through the front door, onto the porch. He inhaled deeply, savoring the fragrance of late day air. Short and rotund, he had an ample belly that stretched the seams of a garishly yellow waistcoat.

"Oh. Right then. Didn't see you there." He flashed a grin when he took notice of them. "Stuffy as all get-out inside with the gas lanterns. You've got the right idea taking some fresh air." He tipped his top hat then ambled from the porch, through the gate, and down the street.

"Probably headed somewhere for whiskey." Nathaniel scowled while watching his progress. "I don't like the looks of that man."

"I understand he's a traveling salesman. Tonics, I believe."

Nathaniel wheeled on her. "Snake oil?"

She fought the urge to laugh. "Don't be ridiculous. And if he is, he's only passing through. Mrs. Shaver, the landlady, does not allow anything untoward beneath her roof. He will not be permitted to peddle his wares here."

"It's not his wares I'm concerned about."

The outrage in his voice was flattering, but nothing she would allow to sway her. "My lodging is temporary, Nathaniel. I merely needed a quick means of escaping your mother's hostility. Together, you and I will find a solution. If that takes more time than less, I promise to seek more suitable accommodations."

He grumbled something under his breath but appeared slightly mollified. "Very well." He gave a clipped jerk of his head. "I have belabored the problem too long. If my mother does not wish you to reside in Stewart Manor, she can reside there herself. Alone."

"You would desert her?" Shock made Hollande gape.

"She has Annabelle."

"She tolerates Annabelle barely more than she does me. Your mother will come to ruin in that rambling house. Please." She squeezed his arm, unwilling to let him do something he might later regret. "Give me time to put my thoughts in order. If you proceed rashly now, I will blame myself for prompting your actions. We both need a few days apart. Distance to think clearly."

Distance that would lead her to Tristan.

Nathaniel gazed down on her. "For you, I would wait a lifetime."

* * * *

Present Day

Monday afternoon, Dante returned to Madison's home with the necessary equipment to explore the cistern. June evenings meant extended daylight, but given the danger of a malicious ghost, he preferred to work when the sun was close to zenith. Both Jillian and Madison helped him set up, ensuring everything was in place and ready to go not long after one o'clock.

The basement was well illuminated with fresh bulbs. In addition, he arranged several battery-operated flood lamps near the cistern. If needed, the excess brightness would banish anything supernatural when activated. As an added precaution, he sprinkled the pit with holy water.

"I feel like we should have a priest." Madison gnawed on a thumbnail.

"That still might be a possibility." Dante double-checked the climbing rope he'd secured to an overhead beam, ensuring the knot was tight. The other end was clipped to a harness looped around his waist and legs. The cistern would be a tight fit, but he anticipated enough room to maneuver. Applying tension to the rope, eliminating slack, would force the harness into a seat, allowing him to inch down the wall.

Or so he hoped.

He fingered the St. Michael's medallion looped around his neck. He was rarely without its protection, especially when the chance existed of confronting something supernatural.

"Now I regret never going rock-climbing with you." Jillian appeared as worried as her sister.

"Everything will be fine." He would have preferred to have David, Roth, or Collin there in case he needed someone to haul him out, but circumstance hadn't played out that way. David was convinced Juni's attacker was a nutcase in costume, and Roth was responsible for opening the cistern in the first place. Other than unearthing a shitty odor, he would say the whole thing was a waste of time. Collin, who was well acquainted with ghosts and Dante's talents after encountering the spirits of Lucinda Glass and the psychotically twisted Josette, was tied up on a job out of town. Hopefully, Jillian and Madison, acting together, would be able to pull him up if he ran into trouble.

"You both have your gloves, right?" He looked between the sisters, who hovered nearby with Blizzard. Each nodded, indicating the heavy gloves he'd provided in case they needed to grip the rope.

"Okay, then here goes nothing." Dante tucked his ponytail up under a yellow hardhat. A square headlamp was strapped to the brim, a smaller flashlight secured to the harness.

"Wait." Jillian rushed forward before he could step into the pit. Pushing on tiptoes, she wrapped her arms around his neck and gave him a quick kiss. "Be careful."

"You know what to do if anything supernatural happens?"

"Activate the floodlights."

"And?"

She rolled her eyes. "Worry about my safety and Madison's before trying to help you. Dante, if you really think I'm going to leave you stuck in a hole—"

"Just take care of yourself and your sister." Before she could protest, he eased into the cistern. He'd only inched a few feet down the wall, the harness snapping into place, his head just below the opening when a fetid stench wafted up on currents of air. "Gad!" He should have brought a mask. It would be his own stupidity if he ended up hurling.

"What's wrong?" Jillian's worried face appeared above the opening.

"Nothing. Just..." He swallowed hard, breathing through his mouth. "Stinks." Darkness clustered around him the deeper he went, the light overhead retreating. His headlamp picked up chipped edges of rough stone, clots of dirt and grime. Now and then a spider scuttled into a crack or crevice. Pockets of eggs clung to the walls in various places, cottony white balls waiting to hatch long-legged arachnids.

He used the flashlight from his harness to angle below. It had been hard to gauge the distance from above, and he realized he'd probably misjudged by several feet. The air grew damper as he inched his way down the filthy hole, chill and clammy with moisture. He'd have to trash his clothes. Good thing he'd picked his rattiest jeans and shirt to explore the disgusting pit.

Near the bottom, the beam of his flashlight settled on a grubby dirt floor just as the flash of a folk memory struck.

Can't breathe...need help...

What's become of her? Angry...maddened...

She wouldn't...not when I defended her...

How could I have been so wrong...

The stench became unbearable, clogging his nostrils, sucking air from the pit like a vacuum. He panted for breath, barely conscious when his feet touched the ground. His chest contracted. Expanded. Shot pain across his ribs.

He stumbled to his knees, hands sinking into muck. Rancid cesspools festooned with shards of glass, tattered cloth, unspeakable silt he didn't want to contemplate. He heaved up his guts.

"Dante!" Jillian's shrill cry ricocheted into the pit.

The rope snapped, plummeting down on top of him. Overhead, the circle of light at the mouth of the cistern vanished, snuffed in the wink of an eye. The grate of stone echoed in his head as the heavy lid thudded into place, sealing him inside.

"Jillian!" He dragged his hand across his mouth, slumping against the filthy wall behind him. The glow of his headlamp defined sharp edges of gray and white scattered on the muddy ground.

He winced.

Dante switched off the headlamp to conserve the battery. The only light that remained was the smaller flashlight, a beam that barely penetrated the darkness when he angled it above his head.

"Jillian!" The echo of his voice bounced against the walls, tumbling back like dropped stones. No wonder Madison's violent specter hadn't materialized earlier. Why chase him off when it could entomb him? The spirit was smart enough to peg him as an enemy. Someone who could summon it, potentially even banish the wretched thing if he pulled out all the stops. Stupidly, he'd allowed himself to become trapped.

He had to believe Jillian and Madison hadn't been hurt. Scared, frightened, but physically unharmed. Until they could get help, he needed to conserve air and keep his wits about him. Imagine himself in a cave instead of an ungodly pit.

With—he grimaced, playing the flashlight over the dingy gray remains—human bones.

* * * *

Madison paced in the ER waiting room. She couldn't recall how long Dante was in the airless cistern. She and Jillian had tried, but had been unable to wrangle the lid free, almost as if something kept it locked in place. The entity finally released its hold when the ambulance crew arrived. By the time they hauled Dante from the cistern, he was filthy and unconscious. Neither she nor Jillian could explain how the ponderous lid had been locked in place, but the EMTs wisely left it up to the police to sort out if they should be booked for attempted murder. Fortunately, Sherre's arrival put an end to any such foolishness, and the incident was written up as an accident.

The paramedics hooked Dante to portable oxygen, and he roused long enough to utter a single word—*bones*—before falling back into a stupor. The last Madison had seen of Sherre, she was busy ordering two uniformed officers to dump light into the cistern.

Madison drove Jillian to the hospital but hadn't been allowed to accompany Dante to a treatment room. While her sister trailed a doctor and nurse down the hall, Madison was relegated to waiting in the ER. She placed a phone call to Roth, then flipped through two magazines without registering more than an occasional photo. People came and went—pushed in wheelchairs, trailed by anxious family members, cradling broken limbs, ushered by orderlies. All the while a white-faced wall clock marked passing seconds and minutes as if they were hours.

Finally, Roth appeared. Madison spied him striding down the hallway and rushed to meet him.

"Let's talk somewhere more private." Without giving him a chance to reply, she led him to an alcove further down the corridor.

Once away from others, he gripped her elbow. "What happened?"

Only two words, but it was all the prompting Madison needed. Tired of keeping everything pent inside, wondering if she was crazy, she babbled the entire story. The ghost that looked like her, the black-haired crone, the ghoul, Beverly's meltdown, the hidden staircase, the cistern. *Everything* came pouring out, including tears.

"That's it." Roth's tone mangled fury and concern into a heated knot. "You're done with that house. You're moving in with me."

Madison wiped her eyes. "I am done with it. I stayed with Jillian last night."

"Jillian? I told you before, you could move in with me."

"I know that. Just—please." She couldn't contemplate a permanent commitment. Not now. "You haven't asked about Dante."

"How is he?"

"He was unconscious when they took him from the hole. They kept oxygen on him in the ambulance, but I haven't heard anything since we got to the hospital. Jillian's with him now."

"Why didn't you tell me you planned this stupid stunt? I could have hauled him out."

"I know." She bit her lip, hating herself for the shortsightedness. "I should have insisted. Dante didn't think you'd understand or even condone—"

"What? That he's some kind of carnival fortune-teller?"

"See." Her back stiffened. "That's *exactly* why I couldn't tell you."

"Damn it, Maddy, there was nothing in that hole. You were there when I opened it." Roth cast a glance around as if realizing his voice had grown sharper. When he spoke again, his words were measured. Lower and reasonable. "You can't seriously believe that some invisible ghoul was imprisoned in a cistern. That's crazy."

Of course it was crazy, but she was intimately acquainted with the bizarre. She'd faced terrors no sane person should ever have to confront. Through it all, Jillian had stood by her. Dante and Sherre, even Maya and Collin. If push came to shove, Tessa and David would be there too, but Roth had always been the cynic in their group. Was it any wonder she'd excluded him today?

"Did you ever believe me about anything?"

"What do you mean?"

"About Boyd."

"That he was murdered?"

"No." He still didn't understand. Her eyes were dry now, no more tears. "That I was an empath. That I *felt* him die. That I lived every painful, agonizing second of his death."

"Madison, don't do this."

"If you love me, you have to accept that I'm not crazy."

"I never said you were."

"Not in words." That was the rub. She looked down the hall. Watched a young couple leave the ER hand in hand. The man lifted his arm, looping it around the woman's shoulders. Hip to hip, they continued toward the exit.

"Why drag up Boyd now?" The edge was back in Roth's voice.

A hollow emptiness rooted in her stomach. "Because if you believed me about him, you'd believe me about what happened today." She was tired, frustrated. With a shake of her head, she stepped past him, intending to return to the ER. "I can't argue about this now."

"I'm not arguing." He caught her arm, holding her in place. "Why did you call me?"

Because she'd needed someone. Because—even as she gazed into his eyes, clear and nonjudgmental—she'd wanted his support. "I'm frightened. I wanted you with me."

He hooked his arm around her shoulders. Pulled her close just as she'd seen the man offer comfort to his girlfriend or wife. When she leaned into his chest, he kissed the top of her head.

"I'm here," he whispered. "I'm not going anywhere."

Chapter 14

May 6–7, 1878

Hollande waited three days before hiring a carriage and driver to take her to Curtisville. She wanted to ensure Nathaniel believed she was settled in the boarding house before vanishing for an extended time. As it stood, she didn't know how long she'd be away but paid her room in advance for another week. With any luck, she'd be able to convince Tristan to return with her almost immediately. Naturally, there would be affairs he would need to place in order, warranting the quarry ran smoothly while he was in Hode's Hill. In light of his frequent trips, he likely already had short-term measures in place.

She found the carriage comfortable but the journey longer than anticipated. It amazed her Tristan undertook the trek as often as he did. Perhaps a regular routine made the excursion less grueling.

Several miles from town the lead harness broke, and she was forced to whittle away the hours while the driver made repairs. By the time he deposited her in front of the Curtisville Hotel, the sun was already setting. With no idea where Tristan lived and certain the quarry office would be closed, Hollande booked lodgings then joined a few other patrons in the dining room for the evening meal.

The dinner was filling, a hearty portion of roast beef and potatoes served on bone china, with apple cobbler for dessert. She sat with an older couple who were passing through town on the way to Philadelphia for their grandson's wedding. Gray-haired and cheerful, they held hands often and laughed frequently, clearly in love after many years together. Their closeness made her hope she and Nathaniel would someday be so blessed.

Once in her room, Hollande changed into a sleeping gown then collapsed into bed, exhausted from travel. That night she dreamed of the carriage house at Stewart Manor, and the absence of tracks the morning she'd gone looking for Tristan. She slept later than planned, but still made time for breakfast and tea before going in search of Nathaniel's brother.

In the hotel lobby, she stopped at the front desk, where a thin man with short black hair and a prominent mustache read from a newspaper spread on the counter.

"Excuse me, sir."

"Yes, miss?" He was attentive immediately, the same man who'd provided her room key last night. "How may I be of service?"

"Could you please direct me to the Stewart Quarry? I'm afraid I don't know my way around Curtisville."

"Stewart Quarry?" Brows knitting, he puzzled over the name. "Oh! You must mean the S & K Quarry. You can find the office on Eighth Street. That's just down several blocks, then one back." He pointed the direction through the main window.

"S & K." She nodded, realizing she'd never asked Nathaniel the name of his family business. "Thank you."

Outside, she found any number of carriages on the street, open and enclosed, several for hire. She'd brought extra funds, not knowing how long she'd be in town, but the day was pleasant, the sidewalks bustling with activity, so she decided to walk.

Curtisville was larger than Hode's Hill, and she immediately found herself enthralled by the broad avenues, towering buildings, and myriad of shops, clubs, and eateries. She hoped she didn't appear backward, a mouse in a country dress, but judging by the women she passed, her attire was acceptable. Perhaps a little out of date, but clean and well-tailored. She regretted she'd neglected to bring a parasol, but minus that oversight, she fit in fairly well. Every gentleman she passed tipped his hat, and several ladies offered smiles. Eventually she arrived at the S & K Quarry office, a squat building with a stone façade and ornate gas lanterns flanking a maple-hewn door. Inside, she found a man with wire-rimmed spectacles sitting behind a broad desk on which several ledgers lay open.

"Hello." His smile was earnest, a little too eager as he came to his feet. "How may I help you?"

"I'd like to see Mr. Stewart."

"Stewart." The smile dimmed slightly.

"Yes, I realize I don't have an appointment, but Tristan knows me."

"You wish to see Tristan Stewart?" The smile vanished completely, replaced by an air of confusion. "Miss—?"

The question dangled between them.

"Moore. Hollande Moore."

The man rolled one hand over the other, tugging his fingers. "I think perhaps there must be a mistake. You're not from around here, are you?"

"Hode's Hill." A sliver of something—annoyance? bewilderment? impatience?—pinged in the back of her mind. She glanced around the office, noting two wing chairs by a table littered with periodicals. Several framed photographs of a rock quarry adorned the walls, and a wooden shelving unit held maps, rolled and stored in cubby holes. No one else appeared to be about, though a hallway branched off to the right.

"Is Tristan in today?"

The man opened his mouth. Clamped it shut without speaking.

"Herbert, did you get those statistics from Benningham?" The question preceded a bald man down the hallway. He drew up short when he spied her, a look of surprise crossing his face. On the portly side, he was nonetheless compact with an average frame and a broad chest. His brows were thick and heavy, the color of printer's ink, his eyes the faded brown of bark.

He dropped several papers on Herbert's desk. "Why didn't you tell me we had a visitor?"

"I...uh, Mr. Kraner..." Herbert couldn't seem to find his voice.

Hollande latched onto the name immediately. "Are you Harry Kraner?" Tristan had mentioned him during one of his visits with Sylvia.

"I am." Mr. Kraner stepped forward, gathering her fingers into his palm. He placed his other hand over hers in greeting. "And who do I have the pleasure of addressing?"

"Hollande Moore."

Herbert cleared his throat. "Miss Moore is here to see Mr. Stewart."

Mr. Kraner cast a frowning glance at his clerk.

"Mr. *Tristan* Stewart," Herbert clarified.

"I've come from Hode's Hill." Hollande didn't understand the delay. "If Tristan is not in at present, perhaps you could direct me to his townhouse. I assure you we are acquainted. He and his brother employed me to care for their mother, Sylvia."

"Sylvia." Some of the color leeched from Mr. Kraner's face. He licked his lips. "Perhaps you should come to my office, Miss Moore." He extended his arm, indicating the way.

Hollande was not immune to the pointed look he cast at the clerk.

"No interruptions, Herbert."

"Yes, sir."

Mr. Kraner escorted her down the hallway, then into a large but cluttered office. "Please, have a seat."

He indicated a straight-backed chair before a mahogany desk. Nearby, a credenza and hutch ate up wall space. Across the room, twin bookcases held rows of narrow ledgers, the skinny volumes offset now and again by fat binders sprouting pages at the top. A shuttered window with a view of the street overlooked a table where a map was pinned in place.

"Thank you." Hollande settled in the chair as Mr. Kraner took the seat opposite, behind his desk. She clutched her Dorothy bag on her lap. "Thank you for seeing me. It was never my intention to disrupt your day."

"Of course not." The smile he'd graced her with earlier returned as he shuffled papers aside. "You mentioned Sylvia Stewart."

"Yes. Tristan and Nathaniel hired me to look after her. I understand you and your wife were friendly with Sylvia and her deceased husband."

"For many years. Darrin and I were business partners."

"Oh." She hoped her shock didn't show. Nathaniel had never mentioned Darrin having a partner, and Tristan had spoken of Harry Kraner as if he were someone his mother may have known long ago.

Tell me about the party, Sylvia had pleaded.

Harry Kraner insisted I go. You remember him?

It was one matter to recall a friend you hadn't seen in years, but a business partner was not likely to be forgotten.

"I'm sorry." Heat flooded her face. "I thought Darrin owned the quarry?"

"He did. But he allowed me to purchase shares as he'd once done. In those days, he and I, Sylvia and Louise, were like family. We had such good times together, until..." A shrug. "Sylvia grew ill. Mentally, as I'm sure you're aware. She began imagining things."

"Such as?" She'd come to see Tristan, but Hollande couldn't allow the opportunity to pass. There was so much about Nathaniel's family she didn't understand.

"That I was trying to cheat Darrin. That Louise and Darrin were having an affair." Mr. Kraner shook his head, as if even voicing the words reeked of incredulity. "Nothing could have been further from the truth. In time, my wife and I had to stop visiting Stewart Manor. Darrin knew Sylvia's grip on reality was deteriorating but resisted placing her in an asylum. Instead, he backed off from the business, making me a full partner. That was when Stewart Quarry became S & K Quarry."

All the more reason for Tristan to assume additional responsibility for his mother's care. "If that's the case, I don't understand why Tristan devotes so much energy here. Surely, he can spend more time in Hode's Hill and leave the quarry in your hands."

Mr. Kraner canted his head, studying her as one might scrutinize an unusual problem. "You did say Tristan and Nathaniel hired you?"

"Yes."

"And you've spoken with Tristan face-to-face?"

"Yes." She was growing tired of his questions.

"My dear, I'm afraid that's not possible."

"Why not?"

"Because Tristan Stewart died thirteen years ago."

* * * *

Present Day

"Do you have any idea how scared I was?"

Jillian paced while Dante finished dressing. The hospital had kept him overnight for observation. She'd stopped by his house to gather clean clothes for him, then waited in his room while he showered. Discharge papers were in the works. In the meantime, he pulled on the jeans she'd brought, then slipped a blue T-shirt over his head. His hair was wet and loose, hanging in a riot of curls down his back.

"Things didn't go exactly like I planned." He sat on the bed to tug on his shoes. "Yesterday is a blur. Tell me what happened after I went into the cistern."

Rehashing those moments was not something she wanted to do, but they were in too deep. Her, Madison, Dante, even Sherre and Roth. Toss in Dante's discovery of bones in the pit, and David was also involved.

"Everything was fine, then the lights cut out. I tried to get to the floodlights, but it was as if something held me back." She shivered, remembering the bite of cold on her skin—skeletal hands, icy fingers. She hadn't seen a thing, but the abhorrent touch ripped a shriek from her lungs. Later, Madison had told her she'd experienced the same thing.

"When I did get to the lights, they wouldn't turn on. I kept flipping the switch, but nothing happened. Then I heard the lid of the cistern fall in place and knew you'd been sealed inside." She pressed her hands to her stomach, feeling nauseous. "Dante, you could have died. Maybe this phantom should be left alone. At least, maybe you should defer to someone else."

"Like a priest?" He finished tying his shoes, then stood and pulled her close. Silent a moment, he stood with his chin resting on the top of her head. "I've thought of that, but I'm not ready to give up."

Exactly what she expected him to say. "What if I am?"

"You're not thinking straight."

"I think I'm the only one who *is*." She drew back, frowning up into his eyes. "You said yourself that spirits are dangerous. This one is lethal."

"But we discovered its secret."

"What do you mean?"

"The bones in the cistern. You did tell Sherre, right?"

Jillian nodded. "She and David had a team there last night. I heard the remains were removed and are being examined."

"There's no telling how long they laid there." Dante paced to the window.

His room occupied a corner of the third floor with a view of the walk-path along the Chinkwe. A jogger ran past with a leashed labradoodle, making her think of Blizzard. She was rarely without the husky but had chosen to leave him at home despite his certification as a therapy dog. He'd sensed the spirit last night earlier than her or Madison, releasing a snarl seconds before the lights went out. After that, her screams had drowned out his angry growls. She had to wonder if a ghost could harm an animal.

"I suppose it could have been an accident." She thought of the skeletal remains.

"No." Dante twisted to face her. "Whoever those bones belong to, the cistern was sealed to keep them inside. The person was probably alive when they were pushed into the pit."

Her stomach flopped. "Pushed?"

"I don't think whoever it was went willingly." He ran a hand through his hair, raking the long, wet strands from his face. "The spirit who resembles Madison wanted someone to discover the body. She wouldn't be concerned with a crime that happened after she died. That means the murder must have occurred during her lifetime. The victim was probably her or someone she knew."

Murder. She hated the sound of that word. "You're speculating."

"Makes sense, doesn't it?"

She had to agree. Worse, he seemed focused on getting to the bottom of what happened. In spite of her fear, she understood his motivation. He knew what it was like to be sealed in that wretched hole. He'd been shuttered among the stink and the muck with his air depleting. Whoever perished in that pit had suffered a horrible death.

She thought she might be sick.

"I had a folk memory."

Jillian was grateful when Dante's voice startled her from her thoughts. "When you were in the cistern?"

He nodded. "It wasn't much, just pieces. I couldn't latch onto a steady impression, but it involved a woman. I got the sense she betrayed the person whose memory I stumbled over."

"You think she's the phantom?" Odd how they had whittled things down to the *ghoul* and the *phantom*.

"Yeah, I do." Anything else he might have said was cut off by the ringing of his cell phone.

Dante slipped the mobile from his pocket. Frowned when he glanced at the screen. "My grandmother. She doesn't need to know I'm in the hospital or what happened."

"I agree." She'd learned long ago some circumstances were best kept secret.

Dante pressed the connect button. "Hi, Grandma." A pause. "No, that's okay. I'm with Jillian." More silence, this time longer. He slipped his free hand into the pocket of his jeans and paced between the TV and the opposite wall. "How do you know her? Uh-huh. Yeah. That would be great."

Jillian couldn't make sense of the one-sided conversation. When he finally said goodbye and disconnected, she looked at him expectantly. "What was that about?"

"We need to call your sister."

"Why?"

"My grandmother has a new neighbor at the Cottages."

"That's nice." It seemed odd Sonia would call simply to relay that information. "What does that have to do with Madison?"

"The woman's name is Margaret Irving. It turns out she enjoys genealogy."

"I'm glad Margaret and your grandmother have something in common, but I still don't see how that relates to Madison."

"Because Margaret's great-grandmother was Annabelle Murray." He tucked his phone in his pocket. "Annabelle was the housekeeper at a place called Stewart Manor."

Chapter 15

May 7, 1878

Hollande lurched to her feet.

"Why are you playing these dreadful games with me?"

Mr. Kraner remained seated, but sadness touched his eyes, mingled with an emotion that made her queasy. Pity? Did he think she was deranged, mentally damaged like Sylvia?

"I assure you, Tristan did in fact die thirteen years ago, Miss Moore." His voice was sad but firm. "His death followed shortly after Darrin's. A week. Two at most."

"That's not possible." The room closed in on her, shrinking as she spoke. A stab of wooziness made her clutch the edge of the desk to keep from swaying.

"Please sit down." White-faced with alarm, Mr. Kraner hustled to her side. He guided her to the chair. "Perhaps I should have Herbert fetch smelling salts."

"No." One by one, all the nuances she'd chosen to overlook bombarded her. In the entire time she'd resided at Stewart Manor, she'd never seen Nathaniel and Tristan together. Not once. There were never two brothers, only one. A man she thought she'd loved. A man who'd tricked her into believing his twisted charade.

"I've been so foolish." Tears stung her eyes.

There hadn't been tracks around the carriage house because Tristan never needed transportation that day. Whatever game Nathaniel played, he'd left an open loophole the morning she'd gone exploring.

Hadn't she followed the hidden staircase to his room? It must have been easy for him to retire each evening, change his clothing, then use the secret passage to descend to the basement. All he had to do was slip from the house through the storm cellar doors. He probably kept a second carriage stowed up the road. The property was large and rambling, with more than enough acreage to hide a vehicle. A short jaunt by foot, then he returned as Tristan in the coach.

Such a carefully plotted, elaborate hoax.

Why, why, *why?*

Sylvia treated him as Tristan. Called him by the name of her dead son. And Nathaniel acted so very, very different, playing the part of his twin to perfection.

He'd made a fool of her.

Hollande wiped her eyes. Before she could rummage in her Dorothy bag, Mr. Kraner produced a clean handkerchief.

She gave him a watery smile. "You must think me deranged."

"Not at all." He wheeled his chair from behind the desk to sit closer. "I think you are confused."

Her laugh was bitter. "*Duped* is the word I will use. Would you be so kind to tell me the truth, as Nathaniel and his mother have both led me to believe Tristan is alive."

"I do not know the whole of it, only that Tristan perished in Yarrow Creek. It was during the winter. The water ran high from snowmelt, which is probably why he was swept away so quickly."

And that's why Sylvia hates the creek.

"Nathaniel was there but was unable to save him." Mr. Kraner shook his head. "I've heard Nathaniel wandered the banks of the creek with a lantern for months afterward, searching for his remains. He was determined to give his brother a proper burial, but Tristan's body was never found."

She wanted to feel sorry for the man she loved, but anger overrode any residual compassion she might otherwise entertain. Trying to compose herself, she raised a hand to her mouth. "This is all so overwhelming. Looking back, I realize Nathaniel only ever referred to Tristan. And Tristan—or the man I thought was Tristan—to Nathaniel. I never saw them together. Nathaniel is quite the actor."

"Do not judge him too harshly." The sincerity of Mr. Kraner's tone surprised her.

"You do not understand." She dabbed her eyes with the handkerchief. "We spoke of marriage. The lies I have discovered cannot be forgiven."

"A harsh judgment. Did you believe Nathaniel to be an honorable man prior to today?"

"Naturally. I loved him." She stifled a sob. "I love him still, but this..." She spread her hands. "How can there be an explanation for such deceit?"

Mr. Kraner inhaled deeply. He slumped in his chair, eyeing her as a kindly father might a daughter. "Perhaps you should ask him."

* * * *

Present Day

Madison didn't arrive at the Cottages at Chinkwe until after Dante and Jillian were already there. She'd been delayed writing up an agreement of sale for a buyer who'd popped out of the blue. Not that she minded unexpected deals. This one came from a client she'd shown a handful of investment properties to over a year ago. The man phoned to say a duplex in his neighborhood had gone on the market, and he wanted to place an offer. She'd written it up and presented the contract all within several hours—a cash deal with a quick settlement. The seller had been eager to accept.

By the time she reached the Cottages, it was after two on Wednesday afternoon. She cut a path through the lobby then threaded down the hallway, already familiar with the layout from a previous visit. The first level of the three-story building featured a dining hall, recreation area, library, and media room. She found Dante and Jillian seated at a square table in the recreation area with a petite woman who appeared to be in her mid-eighties.

"Hi."

"Hey." Dante stood. He looked better than the last time she'd seen him. Good color, with only a smudge of shadow under his eyes, his hair scraped back in a tight ponytail. He indicated the woman who worked at piecing together a jigsaw puzzle. "This is my grandmother's friend, Margaret Irving."

"It's nice to meet you."

"You, too, dear."

Madison glanced around the room, noting other residents engaged in card games or talking in groups. A few, like Margaret, worked at puzzles. Others chatted as they colored between the lines of detailed illustrations with brightly hued pencils. More than one of the agents Madison worked with had taken up the popular hobby of adult coloring books as a way to unwind.

"I don't see Sonia." She'd thought for certain Dante's grandmother would be there.

"She said the air conditioning was too cold and went upstairs to grab a sweater." Dante made room for her to sit, then resumed his seat. "I offered to get it for her, but she wanted the exercise."

"She gets around just fine, that one." Margaret studied a puzzle piece with opposing knobs before fitting it into a partially constructed section.

"You seem to do well, too," Jillian commented.

"So they tell me." Her eyes crinkled at the corners when she smiled. "My granddaughter's a physical therapist and keeps me current with exercises. Of course, at my age, it's about keeping the mind as sharp as the body." She tapped a wrinkled index finger against her temple. "That's why I do puzzles, read, and keep a journal."

"You're ambitious."

"Prudent." She sorted through a pile of random puzzle pieces. "I enjoy mental stimulation, and maintaining a journal preserves the past. That's how Sonia and I got on the subject of genealogy. She saw me writing one day, and I told her I developed the habit from my mother. She learned it from her mother and so on. Kids today have no desire. It's all about gadgets and pushing buttons." Her gaze flecked to Madison. "I understand you bought Stewart Manor."

"The old house on Yarrow Creek Road?" Madison nodded. Even knowing the name of the family who'd lived there, she'd never heard the property referred to by such a regal title. It carried an antiquated yet grand ring. "It's a beautiful home. Several of the rooms need repairs, but it has a lot of character."

Sometimes she forgot the vintage embellishments that made the home so appealing. Original woodwork, interior transoms, pocket doors, keeping cupboards, and the serene location along the banks of Yarrow Creek. Despite everything that had taken place, she hated the thought of selling it. "I understand one of your ancestors worked there."

"My great-grandmother, Annabelle Murray. She was a housekeeper for the original owners."

"Darrin and Sylvia Stewart?" Dante prompted.

"Not Darrin. He'd passed on by the time Annabelle was hired."

"Do you know what happened to him?"

"I've only heard stories. Grandma Ida said there was an accident and he fell from a balcony. He must have broken his neck." She added two pieces to the sky, blue tiles streaked with white.

Madison bit her lip. Would Darrin be angry enough to haunt the house?

"But that wasn't the real tragedy." Margaret slid another tile into the ragged frame of the puzzle. A picnic basket nestled on a blanket gradually took shape. "My understanding is that something horrible happened in the spring of 1878. I was only five when my great-grandmother died, but sometimes Mama and Grandma Ida would discuss the past. Whatever happened that spring, Great-Grandma Annabelle never returned to Stewart Manor."

"That was when Sylvia Stewart and her son Nathaniel died." Jillian latched onto the time frame. "Both on the same day."

Madison had been thinking the same thing. Definitely the makings of a tragedy. She gazed at Margaret. "You said your great-grandmother kept a journal?"

"It was lost long ago."

She deflated. There had to be something Margaret could tell them. "I'm trying to research the history of the house. Is there anything you can share about the people who lived there? Anything that might help?"

Margaret was silent a moment as if cataloging her memories. She smoothed a wispy strand of hair behind her ear. "I understand Grandma Annabelle was poor when she went to work for the Stewarts. From what I recall of family history, she was paid handsomely. Mostly because the atmosphere in the home wasn't conducive for a young lady at that time, hired help or not. Several other women left employment after only a few days."

"Why would they do that?"

"Because of Sylvia Stewart." A soft chuckle. "I remember Grandma Ida saying Annabelle often described Mrs. Stewart as *viperous.* Can you imagine such a thing?"

"I wonder why she stayed," Jillian murmured.

"Other than the funds?" Margaret plucked a puzzle piece from the pile. "Probably because of Hollande Moore."

The name was new to Madison. "Who is that?"

"A woman who resided there for a brief time. I'm not positive, but I believe she may have been hired to look after Sylvia. She and my great-grandmother became friends."

"Was Sylvia ill?"

"Not physically. I never heard it said outright, but I got the impression she suffered from a type of mental illness." Margaret resumed building the picnic basket, trying a second, then third piece, when the one she'd selected didn't fit. She sighed. "I don't appear to be getting anywhere with this puzzle."

"I think you're doing great." Dante wedged a loose piece between his thumb and forefinger. "I couldn't make heads or tails of this." He dropped it into the pile of fragments. "Is there anything you can tell us about Tristan Stewart?"

"The twin brother? Only that he was often away in Curtisville, overseeing the family quarry. I have no idea what became of him, or even the nature of the tragedy that took place. It's the one thing Great-Grandma Annabelle refused to talk about." She glanced at her watch. "I'm afraid I have to leave now. My granddaughter is coming, and I promised to meet her in the lobby. She's taking me to pick out some new summer blouses. I hope I've been helpful."

"Amazingly." Dante spoke for all of them. "There's just one other thing I have to ask—you wouldn't happen to know what Hollande Moore looked like?"

Margaret clapped her hands. "That's something I can answer. Great-Grandma Annabelle often talked about how pretty she was. She said Hollande had long red hair and blue-green eyes. She called her the perfect definition of a lady."

* * * *

"Now we know who our mystery ghost is." Dante passed Madison a glass of white wine.

She accepted it with a thank-you, then curled her legs beneath her onto the plump cushion of a patio chair. The smell of barbeque chicken wafted from a gas grill tucked in the corner of Jillian's deck. Since Madison was presently staying with her sister, they'd chosen to throw an easy dinner together that could be eaten alfresco. To the left of the French doors, Blizzard lay with his head on his paws enjoying the late afternoon air. Every now and then, his ears twitched or swiveled as he picked up the sound of cars on the street below.

Dante nestled the wine bottle in an ice bucket, then sat beside Jillian on a settee.

"Hollande Moore." Madison sipped her Chardonnay. "How does that give us leverage?"

"She has to be the woman who resembles you. The one who led you to the cistern."

"And the body."

"Our murder victim."

"You say that like you're sure."

"I was trapped in that airless pit, remember?" He stretched an arm over the back of the settee. "I guarantee you no one went down there voluntarily, and if they'd fallen in by accident, the lid wouldn't have been bolted shut."

"I suppose." She sighed. "Have either of you heard anything from Sherre about the bones?"

"No." Jillian set her glass on a low table, then settled into the crook of Dante's arm. "I'm sure it will take time to identify the remains, especially if it turns out to be someone who died over a century ago."

"So why would Hollande Moore lead me there?"

"Good question." Dante chewed his lower lip. "I wonder if the bones had anything to do with the tragedy Annabelle wouldn't talk about. One thing's certain—if Hollande is our mystery ghost, then Sylvia must be the hostile presence in the house."

Jillian twisted to gaze up at him. "Why not Darrin or Nathaniel?"

"Because your sister said the face she saw—the one that warned her out of the house—was female. And given what we know of Sylvia—that she was probably mentally unstable with a nasty disposition—it all fits."

"Perfect." Madison drew a breath. "A psychotic ghost. Even after all this, I don't want to sell the property. How do I get rid of her? I want my home back."

He was silent for a while, then crossed the deck to check on the grill. "She's there for a reason. We need to find out how she died."

Blizzard watched attentively as Dante used a pair of metal tongs to rotate pieces of chicken. The sweet, smoky smell of barbeque wafted across the deck to Madison, reminding her of childhood summers with her parents and Jillian, more recent ones with Boyd. Her deceased husband had been fond of outdoor cooking, going so far as to haul their small grill into the yard off-season. Strangely, the thought of Boyd didn't spark the trauma it normally did. Instead, she focused on the residue his death may have left behind. She prayed no one ever discovered the imprint of his murder, but if folk memories were real, they constituted windows to the past. Which led her to what Dante told them earlier.

"You said you picked up bits of a folk memory when you were in the cistern. I don't want you going back into that pit, but do you think there's a way you could sense what happened from the outside?"

"Maybe."

Jillian shifted uneasily. "I'm not sure about this." She glanced at Dante. "The last two times you or Madison went into the basement, something bad happened. Maybe we should wait to see if Sherre can turn up anything on the bones."

"That's going to take too long." Dante shut the lid of the grill, then hung the tongs from a hook on the side. "It could be months."

"Wait a minute." Madison uncurled her legs. "By now, she should at least know if the remains belonged to a male or female victim. If Sylvia died in the cistern—if someone killed her—that could explain why she's haunting the house. Maybe the grave out back doesn't hold a body. It could be a remembrance marker."

"You're forgetting the one for Nathaniel with the same date of death." Dante retrieved his wineglass from the table. "I don't think the remains belong to Sylvia, but I do agree we should check with Sherre to learn what we can. I want to try to dredge up the folk memory again, too."

"Dante." Jillian shot him a troubled glance.

"Don't worry, I'll be better prepared next time." He plucked the bottle from the ice bucket. "Who wants more wine with their chicken?"

* * * *

Sherre was seated at her desk, elbows propped on the edge, head in hands when David Gregg walked up behind her.

"What are you reading?"

She gave an involuntary jerk, pulling her attention from the papers spread in front of her. "The report from our zoological friend on Doug Crawford's autopsy." David dropped into a chair on the other side of her desk. She shoved the file across to him. "Same as our other two experts. No idea what did the killing."

"No reference to *who* anymore?"

"I'm past that. You should be, too."

He scowled at the report. "So, if it's not an animal, and we have no match for a weapon, what's that leave?"

She knew exactly what it left—a dredged-from-the-Netherworld ghoul. Too bad Gregg was a veteran detective who'd built his career on connecting dots. He might act on gut instinct, even cater to it, but he'd stopped believing in hobgoblins as a kid.

Intent on tuning out the clatter of the squad room, she settled back in her chair. The click-clack of keyboards, orbiting ring of a phone, and conversations volleyed between detectives and uniformed officers faded into the background. The place was busy for a Thursday afternoon, the upside being there were no new killings to investigate.

"What do you think of Dante DeLuca?"

"He's a friend, almost family." David pulled the zoo expert's report into his lap, sifting through the pages. "You know damn well I've been seeing his cousin for over a year."

"Did he or Tessa ever mention his unusual skillset?"

"Art?"

"The other one."

He frowned. "Yeah, I know he has some kind of freak affinity for the supernatural."

"What if I told you I once attended a séance he held and am completely convinced he summoned a spirit from the dead?"

"Oh, yeah?" David smirked. "Who?"

"Gabriel Vane." She tossed the name, aware of the implosion it would make. *Boom!* An open grave, missing bones, a dangerous killer who'd threatened Tessa's son *and* David's nephew. That was the kicker.

Sherre leaned forward. "I'm not easily swayed, but I know what happened that night. What I heard and saw. There's no way Dante could have pulled off a scam, and no reason for him to. If you don't believe me, ask Tessa. She was there."

With an exasperated puff of his cheeks, David flipped the folder onto her desk. "Get to the point. What do you want me to believe?"

Sherre slid open her pencil drawer. God forbid anyone but David see the drawing tucked inside. She could already hear the other detectives ragging her.

How are you gonna do a lineup on that one?

Damn. Looks like my ex-wife.

New hot date, Lorquet?

"According to Juni Gold, this is what attacked her." She passed David the sketch.

He looked from the drawing to her face. "How'd you get this?"

"I sent Dante to the hospital to do a sketch based on Juni's description."

"Shit." With a look of disgust, David swiveled his chair to the side. He webbed a hand over his face, waited a beat, then met her gaze. "All right, I'll bite. What the hell is it?"

"Dante says it's a ghoul. Some kind of monster that feeds on violence and death."

"You put out a BOLO on this you might as well kiss your career goodbye."

"No kidding. I'm not freaking stupid." She'd debated the wisdom of sharing the drawing with him, but the alternative was worse. Something was killing, and unless they found the thing and stopped it, someone else would die. "Stanley Reed's wounds matched Crawford's—what was left of him." They'd both seen the autopsy report. "Clairmont couldn't identify what killed either victim, and our three wildlife experts came up blank. That is not some creep in a costume." She jutted her chin to indicate the sketch.

"I thought Juni couldn't remember much about her attacker?"

"Dante has a way of guiding people to retrieve memories."

"How do you know he didn't *guide* Juni into seeing what he wanted her to see?"

"You know him better than I do. You're dating his cousin. Would he do that?"

David swore under his breath. It was the reaction she'd hoped for. They both knew Dante had nothing to gain.

"So now what?" David tossed the sketch on her desk.

She snatched it before the drawing attracted unwanted attention. "We need Dante for that." Her cell phone rang. Sherre glanced to her mobile, noting the number on the screen. "Looks like we're in luck. That's him now."

Chapter 16

May 11, 1878

Hollande spent four days in Curtisville before finding the gumption to return to Hode's Hill. Nathaniel would have surely called at the boarding house by now and discovered her missing. When leaving, she hadn't provided notice of her destination, but with minimal detective work he would have been able to string the pieces together. She'd paid a week of room rent in advance, indicating she planned to return within a few days. And if he checked with the carriages for hire, he'd learn she'd secured transportation to Curtisville. By now, he must have realized she'd discovered his secret.

Would he avoid her or spin more lies?

Twilight had fallen by the time the carriage she employed deposited her at Mrs. Shaver's boarding house. Hollande found the landlady sipping brandy in the parlor. A rotund woman with a large bosom that routinely and alarmingly threatened the seams of her dresses, she ran the establishment with the help of her son, Felix. Her husband had passed over a decade ago. Or so Mrs. Shaver was quick to tell Hollande when she first arrived.

Whether that personal disclosure came from chattiness or a desire to garner sympathy, Hollande was never certain. The older woman ran her rooms-for-rent business with a firm hand, but not without a fondness for gossip. By contrast, Felix was backward and slow. While his mother favored evenings with a night cap, Felix often sat quietly with a checkerboard, playing both sides of the game. Tonight, he was nowhere in sight. Neither were any of the other residents.

"Hello, Miss Moore." The steady creak of Mrs. Shaver's rocker echoed in the stillness as she wobbled the chair's runners back to front and back again. A crystal decanter filled with amber liquid stood on a doily-covered table beside her. The room was stuffy, gas lights sucking up the air, but she didn't seem to mind. Based on the ruddy glow of her cheeks, she'd been imbibing for some time.

"Good evening." Hollande bobbed her head. The return trip had been wearisome, and after her discovery in Curtisville, all she wanted to do was retire. She hoped the woman wouldn't want to chat.

"Would you like to join me for a brandy?" Mrs. Shaver smiled, exposing a gap where her upper right incisor once rested. The fault of a shoddy dentist, she'd told Hollande one morning while dishing up breakfast.

"Thank you, no. I'm rather fatigued and think I'll retire." She clutched her travel bag in both hands, holding it in front of her skirt. Hopefully, the landlady would recognize her need for rest after a long trip.

"There are leftovers from dinner in the kitchen. Would you like me to put a plate together for you to take to your room?"

Hollande hadn't eaten since leaving Curtisville but, surprisingly, wasn't hungry. "No, I'm fine."

"As you please, though if you ask me, a skinny thing like you could do with a bit of extra meals. You probably haven't eaten at all."

"I ate in Curtisville."

"Ah, yes. Curtisville." Mrs. Shaver sipped from her crystal glass. "Your young man was quite distressed when he learned you'd headed there. Apparently, he made an inquiry of a carriage driver for hire."

"Nathaniel was here?" She'd suspected as much but still couldn't mask the distress in her voice.

"Three days in a row. I told him you would surely be back, as you'd only paid for a week."

"I plan to pay for more."

"You are welcome to stay." Mrs. Shaver set her glass on the table. "It's my pleasure to host you, but your young man may have other ideas. He left you a missive."

"A letter?" Hollande's stomach tightened.

"I had Felix place it in your room no more than an hour ago. Had you arrived prior to dinner, you would have encountered Mr. Stewart."

Hollande hoped she didn't blanch. The last thing she wanted to do was see Nathaniel. Not now. At the same time, she couldn't help wondering about the contents of his letter.

"Thank you, Mrs. Shaver." She shifted her travel bag to the side.

"He used to come to town, you know. Sometimes with his father."

That stopped her. Hollande canted her head. "You know Nathaniel?"

"In a manner of speaking. I know him like most people in Hode's Hill, from seeing him about. The stray encounter here and there. Would you like to know more about his family?" She indicated the divan across from her. The cushions, once a vibrant rose, had faded over the years. Pink afghans hid most of the wear.

Hollande hesitated. As tired as she was, she was tempted to remain. The older woman had a fondness for gossip. Some of what she said might lack for accuracy, but there was usually a measure of truth even in hearsay. Odd that Nathaniel never mentioned he knew her. Was that because he didn't want Hollande asking her questions about his family? About Tristan?

She crossed the room, then sat down. "Nathaniel hired me to care for his mother, Sylvia."

"Sad, what happened to her, isn't it?" Mrs. Shaver topped off her brandy. "Are you sure you wouldn't like a drink, Miss Moore?"

"No, thank you." Hollande tried not to fidget. If she allowed Mrs. Shaver to control the conversation, there was no telling how long it might drag. "I'm not sure I know what you mean. About Sylvia."

"The way she changed, of course. Back when her boys were small, she used to visit our store. Me and my mister ran the place together. After he died, it was too much for me, even with Felix. When the boarding house became available, it seemed the wiser investment. This property wasn't pristine, mind you." She raised her gaze to the ceiling as if encompassing the whole building. "It took fixing, but I was able to pitch in with Felix. Now, of course, I'm older. There are days I swear my knees don't want to function. Did I tell you how bad they get when the weather turns damp?"

"Yes, you did. I'm sorry for that." Shortly after she'd checked in, Hollande had been treated to the full scope of Mrs. Shaver's ailments. Including the story about the dentist who'd let her suffer with an abscessed tooth for two days before deciding to pull it. If Hollande didn't steer her back on track, the older woman was likely to venture into details of bunions and home remedies for insomnia. "Did Sylvia bring Nathaniel and Tristan to the store?"

"The twins? Oh, yes!" The question seemed to work. "What delightful boys, too. Pleasant, well-mannered, but a bit impish...enough so there was never a doubt they got up to mischief. Tristan seemed to have his mother's eye more than Nathaniel, but she doted on both. I couldn't say how old they were when the lot of them started to curdle."

"What do you mean?"

"We saw less of Sylvia in town. The boys still came now and again. Handsome men they grew into, both of them. They were always good with Felix, even though everyone knew he was slow, poor soul." She stroked a bit of loose hair hanging from her bun, a faraway smile on her face. "No matter who came—Nathaniel or Tristan—Felix would tag along like a puppy. They'd buy him a bit of candy, then sit and chat with him out front of the store. Folks would always stop to say hello, sure to include Felix. That's the only time they paid mind to my boy, when one of the brothers was with him." Her expression soured, mouth twisting into a bitter grimace. "Nathaniel barely acknowledged him when he was here."

"I'm sorry." A stab to the stomach made Hollande tense. "He must have had a reason."

"Time. That's the reason. It makes monsters of us all." Mrs. Shaver's eyes were suddenly watery. She wiped away a tear. "I know his mother never recovered from the loss of her husband, but even in the years preceding Darrin's death, Sylvia was different. She made fewer trips to Hode's Hill, and when she did come, she never had a kind word or smile. She was suspicious of everyone. Folks started to whisper behind her back. Said she wasn't right in the head. I missed the woman who liked to chat while her boys roamed around the store."

Hollande thought of Harry Kraner's words.

Sylvia grew ill. Mentally, as I'm sure you're aware. She began imagining things.

Mrs. Shaver shifted in her rocker, smoothing her skirt with a backward swipe of her hand. "Sad, really. I know it must be hard for the brothers. Their father passed on, their mother unstable. Once Darrin died, we rarely saw either of them in town."

"Pardon?"

"I understand Tristan prefers Curtisville to Hode's Hill—or so several of the housekeepers who tried to work at Stewart Manor have said. Miss Moore?" The landlady's voice sharpened with concern. "Are you well? You look suddenly pale."

"I..." Hollande fought a swell of nausea, certain her face had bleached bone-white. "I'm sorry. I suppose it's the travel catching up with me." She pinched her cheeks in an effort to restore color. "Please forgive me. I really should retire now."

"Of course. You've had a long day."

Hollande mumbled a parting good-night, retrieved her travel bag, then swept from the room. She'd been so devastated by what Harry Kraner told her about Tristan, she never stopped to consider the damaging scope of

Nathaniel's deceit. He hadn't created his lie for her. The elaborate hoax was one he'd maintained for thirteen years.

Allowing everyone in Hode's Hill to believe Tristan was alive.

* * * *

Present Day

"A male victim, likely between the age of eighteen and thirty." Madison read from the notes Dante had scrawled on a tablet while talking to Sherre. She glanced up from her seat on the sofa, squinting against the glare of light spilling into her sister's brownstone. "That's it?"

"For now." Dante adjusted the curtains at the bow window, then dropped into a sand-colored recliner. "According to her, the remains have been shipped to a forensic anthropologist. The county coroner thinks the bones are old. Could be over a century, but more study has to be done to determine the date."

"So, it's definitely not Sylvia in my cistern."

"Or Hollande." Jillian tossed a squeaky toy in the direction of the kitchen, watching as Blizzard bounded after the lime-green crocodile. Seated on the floor, her back to the sofa, she twisted to gaze up at Madison. "For all we know, it might not even be someone who lived there."

"I'd bet money Sylvia is tied to the death."

Dante's observation surprised Madison. "Because of the folk memory you had?"

"*Pieces* of a folk memory." He snagged the crocodile as Blizzard passed, drawing the husky toward him, then wrangling the toy free. With a flick of his wrist, he sent it soaring to the foyer, grinning as the dog bolted in pursuit. "If I can clear the distractions and the negative energy from the basement, I should get a better impression."

"We could do it together." Jillian pressed her shoulder against Madison's knee, her focus on Dante. "We did that once before. With Gabriel."

"Yeah." Blizzard dropped the toy at his feet. Waited patiently and attentively for him to pick it up. He gave it another toss, back toward the kitchen. "Gabriel wasn't dangerous. My gut tells me that's not the case this time."

"It doesn't matter. I want to help my sister."

Madison looked between them. "What are you talking about?"

Jillian scooted up onto the sofa. "When you were in Rest Haven, Dante and I worked together to find out what happened to Gabriel. I opened my empathy to him, and that sharpened his ability to read a folk memory he wouldn't have been able to sense otherwise."

"With Jillian's help, it was like looking through a magnifying glass." Dante stood, then paced across the room. Near the doorway to the kitchen, Blizzard plopped on the floor, sandwiching the crocodile between his front paws. The husky gnawed contentedly.

Madison turned to her sister. "I don't want you doing anything that's risky."

"Memories aren't ghosts. They can't hurt you. They're just impressions of something that happened in the past."

"Then why is Dante reluctant?"

"Tell her." His words were directed at Jillian.

She heaved a sigh. "Because I'll see what happened. And because I'm an empath, I'll feel what happens, too."

"No." Madison shot to her feet. "Absolutely not!"

"Maddy—"

"Don't even try to convince me. We think someone was killed in that cistern. *Murdered.* Are you forgetting I know exactly what that feels like? Experiencing Boyd's death almost shattered my mind. I'm not about to let that happen to you."

"This is different. I don't know the person."

"Murder is murder. I don't care if you know them or not." Madison wheeled on her. "My God, Jillian, you fall to pieces just *thinking* about the victim of a crime. You're *overly* sensitive. What do you think experiencing death is like?"

She'd probably pushed the line with that one but didn't care.

Wide-eyed and silent, Jillian stared up at her. She swallowed hard. "It's the only way."

"No." Madison folded her arms over her chest. "We'll find another."

"There is one." Dante paced closer. "I'm not saying it would be easy, but—"

"Tell us."

He blew out a breath. "You were an empath once, Madison."

She tensed involuntarily. "I was."

"That ability is still there."

"No. It died with Boyd."

"You think it did because you're too frightened to try. Afraid that if you do—if you connect with someone—you might not be able to disassociate in time. You're terrified of ending up in another Rest Haven."

"Dante, stop." Jillian stood beside her sister. "I hope you're not headed where I think you are."

Madison's mouth was dry. She wanted to tell him everything he said was off base, but he was glaringly on target. As if he could see inside her head, prodding awake the secret fear she worked daily to bury. "I...I haven't opened myself like that in a long time."

"But you could. If you really want to know what happened in Stewart Manor, you could be my conduit."

"Absolutely not." Jillian was adamant. "It's a bad idea."

Madison wasn't so sure. She closed her eyes, building resolve.

"Okay." The word slipped from her lips in a whisper. "Tell me what I have to do."

* * * *

"How long do you plan on staying with Jillian?"

Roth's words drew Madison from her reverie. She'd been staring at the sixty-inch TV in Roth's living room for the last ten minutes without registering a single scene of the movie she selected. She couldn't remember the title, just that when he'd scrolled through the offerings from his cable company, she'd chosen a romcom in hopes it would stop her thinking about tomorrow. Nibbling her fingernail wasn't going to change the fact she'd agreed to use her empathy. Not the basic sensitivity most people possessed if they allowed themselves, but the acute connection of an empath.

"I'm sorry. What did you say?"

He clicked the remote, lowering the volume on the movie. They sat side by side on his sofa, his arm looped over her shoulders. A sleek black coffee table held a bottle of red wine along with a tray of crackers, assorted cheeses, and dips. She'd barely touched any of it.

Roth drew his arm free, leaning forward to slide the remote on the table. "I don't think you're watching this." The film wasn't one he would have chosen anyway. He was probably glad for her distraction. "I asked how long you planned on staying with Jillian."

"Oh. I'm not sure, but I am antsy to return to the house."

"You really want to go back there?"

"It's my home. Ghosts and all." She gave a short laugh, surprised she could find humor in the thought.

"If there are ghosts—and I'm not saying I believe that—what happens when you get rid of them? There's still a human stalker who's made it clear you're not wanted there."

Hocker, if it was him. "Whoever that is hasn't bothered me for a while." How many other "Hockers" were hidden in Boyd's past? Bad pennies waiting to surface, reminding her exactly how dangerous her husband's contacts had been.

Madison retrieved her wine from the table. The glass was embellished with a gold tint, matching the tall, skinny lamps flanking the couch. Her home, antiquated and in need of repairs, was a stark contrast to Roth's contemporary one-floor condo.

He scowled. "A stalker is a stalker. What are you going to do if the creep comes back? I worry about you being alone out there."

"If there's a problem, I'll call Sherre." Madison wedged her shoulders in the corner of the sofa to face him. "I'm more afraid of the ghosts than any human predator. Dante thinks if he can pick up a folk memory tomorrow night, we should be able to figure out who died in the cistern. That could be the key to unlocking the whole puzzle."

"You put a lot of faith in him."

"Of course. He's trying to help me."

"What about me?" His brows rose with the challenge. "I want to help, too."

"I know." Madison swirled a finger over the top of her glass.

"But you already told me you don't want me there." His voice soured, indication of nursing a grudge.

She couldn't fault him. Before they decided to unwind with a movie, she'd explained Dante's plan. Given what happened the last time she embraced her empathic abilities, she'd wanted Roth aware of what she intended to do. Of what might go wrong.

He'd been irked, accusing Dante of placing her in potential danger. When he insisted on being there, Madison had been forced to say no, convinced his emotions would be volatile. The distraction would be too much for her, and the negative energy would hinder Dante.

Roth had conceded only when she wouldn't budge, but demanded she call the moment the experiment was over, promising to be there within minutes.

"There *is* something you can do for me." By excluding him, she'd bruised his ego and wanted to make amends. In addition, his mention of a stalker was a blunt reminder Stewart Manor lacked the security of a newer home. "Maybe we could meet at the house tomorrow afternoon."

"Why?"

"Remember the storm doors in the basement? The latch is flimsy. I'd like to have them locked from the inside with a cross brace or chain. I want to make sure the only way they can be opened is from the cellar."

"You mean you haven't already? That should have been one of the first things you did as soon as you started having problems. I could have taken care of it for you ages ago."

"I know. I guess it slipped my mind."

"No wonder. Dante has you chasing ghosts and ghouls." He crossed the room to hover in front of the balcony doors, wineglass clutched in his hand. Tension left a visible line across his shoulders, cording the muscles in his neck. "I'm tired of having you in danger."

"I understand, but the house is important to me." She stepped to his side, surprised by the surge of emotion his words provoked. Despite the ongoing problems, she felt connected to Stewart Manor. To the people who'd once lived there, and the lonely graves out back. "I don't want to argue."

"Neither do I, but how do you think I feel?" Roth glared down on her, a tic in his jaw. "You're going through all this crap, and I can't help. Worse, Dante's grasping at straws. He's playing on your weaknesses to make himself look important."

Madison gaped. "How can you say that? He's your friend."

"Not as long as he continues to put you at risk. I don't like you seeing him."

"That's not your choice." Heat rose up the back of her neck. A stray thought left her reeling. "Roth...are you jealous of Dante?"

"Don't be crazy. I'm just ticked he's using you."

"He's helping me."

"Call it what you want. He's still the one who comes out looking like a hero."

She'd heard enough. Without a word, she strode across the room, snatched her purse from an end table, then headed for the door.

"What are you doing?" Roth didn't move.

"Leaving."

"I thought we were going to watch a movie together. That you were going to spend the night."

"That was before."

"Before what?"

"Before you turned into a jerk."

Madison stormed from the condo.

* * * *

Dante stepped inside the foyer and switched on the light. He usually stayed overnight with Jillian, but now that Madison was living there again, he felt it better to come home. He'd gotten so used to Jillian's brownstone, the sprawling mansion he inherited from his father seemed emptier than usual. Plenty of space, all hollow save for memories and furniture.

He walked down the main hallway, through a vaulted great room, then into a large, open kitchen decked out in granite and stainless steel. After rooting through the refrigerator for a bottle of sparkling water, he slumped into a chair at the breakfast table, backed by floor-to-ceiling windows on three sides.

Dante dug out his phone, randomly thumbing through email. Most of the messages related to his gallery, but there were a few from friends, one from Sherre. Her note was short, likely kept that way in case it leaked into the wrong hands.

David has bought in. How do we track this thing?

After their phone discussion the other day, he'd asked for more time to get back to her. She'd provided him with the few available details about the bones in the cistern, but he hadn't been able to offer much in return. At least she seemed to believe him about Roth unintentionally releasing the ghoul from the pit.

Not that she had much choice. What had Holmes said?

When you eliminate the impossible, whatever remains, no matter how improbable, must be the truth.

She and David Gregg were out of alternatives. He typed out a quick reply.

Give me until tomorrow night. Trying something with J and M. Should have more details when we're done.

He hit SEND, was about to flip to a message from an artist interested in displaying her work, when the overwhelming sensation of being watched struck him.

Dante stilled. He slid his gaze toward the windows, but it was pitch black outside, eleven sixteen at night. Anyone—or any*thing*—lurking beyond the glass would see him, backlit by kitchen light. The idea made him feel like a plastic duck in a carnival game, waiting to be picked off.

Stupid.

He crossed the room, flipped off the light, then stood for a moment, breathing heavily in the shadows. Every nerve ending in his body sprang awake, his sensitivity to the spirit world prodded into hyper mode.

The thing was out there.

The ghoul.

He had no idea what he'd done to attract it. Maybe stumbling over the bones in the cistern. If gut instinct served, the damn monster had been entombed with the victim for over a century. Whatever its reason, the creature was now on the hunt, and he'd become its target.

Dante shoved his phone in his pocket, then rummaged through a utility drawer until he found a flashlight. He debated about taking a knife, finally pulling a chef's blade from a holder on the counter. What he needed was a flood lamp, but the ones he used as a defense during séances were ringed around the cistern at Stewart Manor.

He cursed, weighing his options. If the ghoul was there for him, it might not bother anyone else. By the same token, Grace Miner, the ER doctor who lived next door, usually rolled in after eleven. Her normal habit was to leave her car in the garage while she walked down the driveway to check the mail. If the thing decided to scrabble in her direction, she wouldn't stand a chance.

Decision made, Dante pulled out his phone and placed a quick call to Sherre.

"Lorquet."

"It's here." His voice was low, his gaze pinned to the windows. He caught the whiff of something foul.

"DeLuca? Where are you?"

"My place."

"What—"

"Hurry. Out back. Bring flood lamps."

He clicked off before she could say another word. Then steeling himself, knife in hand, he crept toward the door.

Chapter 17

May 12–15, 1878

Nathaniel arrived at the boarding house the day after Hollande returned to Hode's Hill. Mrs. Shaver trudged up the steps to her room to inform her of his visit.

"He's downstairs waiting for you, dear."

Seated in a chair by the window, Hollande dipped a needle into an embroidery hoop. "Please tell Mr. Stewart I do not wish to see him."

Mrs. Shaver's face crumpled. "But he keeps returning every day."

"That is his prerogative."

"Surely, you can spare some time."

"No, I cannot." Mouth pinching into a white line, Hollande lowered the hoop to her lap. When she spoke again, her voice was rigid. "Thank you, Mrs. Shaver."

The older woman finally took the hint and left. Alone, Hollande plucked a piece of parchment from the end table beside her chair. Her gaze dropped to Nathaniel's strong handwriting, slanted over the paper. She'd read the message several times since opening the envelope last night, the words ingrained in her head.

Please allow me the chance to explain. If afterward, you wish never to see me again, I will understand. It will break my heart should you choose life without me, but if that is your desire, I will honor your wish.

Hollande bowed her head. She pressed the letter to her lips, fighting tears.

* * * *

Nathaniel returned the next day. Again, on the following, then again, the day after that.

Realizing he would continue to persist, Hollande finally agreed to see him. Because she didn't want prying eyes or ears during their conversation, she asked they speak someplace private.

Nathaniel appeared relieved. Whether that came from having a chance to explain, or because seclusion would allow him to maintain his charade, she wasn't sure. It wouldn't do for anyone to overhear him talking about his dead brother who lived in Curtisville.

He suggested a carriage ride, and Hollande consented. He might have deceived her, but his treachery would not extend beyond the hoax. She had no fear riding from town with him but sat stiffly in the open coach as he guided the horses down the main thoroughfare, then onto a narrow lane bordered by fields and trees.

The day was gorgeous, sun-golden, touched by a whisper of breeze. Fluffy white clouds moved slowly across a sapphire sky, the grass a vibrant blend of greens. Spring had finally arrived, chasing off the gray dismal weather of March and the rainy weeks of April. But for the knot of emotions in her stomach, she would have enjoyed the pleasant afternoon.

"You've barely said a word to me." Nathaniel sent her a sideways glance.

He'd arrived in the larger coach, not the small surrey Annabelle used. The vehicle was comfortable with a high back and dual lanterns secured to the sides for use at dusk. Nathaniel set a leisurely pace, no doubt buying time for discussion.

"My understanding was you were going to do the talking. *Explaining.*" Hollande winced, annoyed she came off sounding like a shrew.

"Very well." His Adam's apple bobbed when he swallowed. "Would you like me to start with something specific or—"

"Tristan." She whirled to face him, the name ice on her tongue.

Nathaniel drew the carriage to a halt. "You already know. He died thirteen years ago."

"Then why—"

"Did I pretend to be him?" He didn't let her finish the thought. "It's complicated."

"I'm listening." She wanted to hear something. *Anything* to explain why he would deceive her and an entire town.

Nathaniel squinted into the sun, gazing off across an expanse of rolling hills. "I became trapped in a nightmare of my own devising. You don't know how many times I wanted to tell you. Even started to tell you. The whole reason I hired you was an attempt to end the hoax. I thought if my mother had a companion, someone she could relate to, she'd let Tristan go."

"Nothing you say makes sense. You're talking in circles."

"I killed my brother."

"Nathaniel—" She'd heard wrong. Yes, that was it. Of all the things she imagined he might say, murder never entered her mind.

"I told you my father fell to his death when he was drunk." He twisted to face her, the brim of his top hat slanting shadow across his eyes. "That's not true. At least, I don't believe it."

"But you said he was upset about the quarry. That something must have happened to make him overindulge that night."

"If he was upset, it was because he'd run out of options for my mother. You see her as she is now, but there was a time when she was happy. When she and my father were in love and the house was filled with laughter. I was sixteen when I first suspected something was wrong. The deterioration of her mind was a gradual process, not something that happened overnight. It isn't easy watching someone you love transform into someone you barely recognize."

"I'm sorry."

Nathaniel threaded the reins through his hands. "She began to anger with little or no provocation, becoming enraged over trivial matters, accusing friends and family of plotting against her. After a while, she started imagining things. My father stepped down from the quarry to spend more time with her. She should have been placed in a sanitarium, but he didn't have the heart. He loved her too much. In the end, she dismissed his devotion, convinced he had a mistress."

"Harry Kraner's wife."

"I see he told you." Nathaniel grimaced. "I think my mother went to see my father the night he died. She must have confronted him about Louise. I'm not sure what happened afterward, or how he fell from the balcony, but I have an uneasy feeling she was involved."

"What do you mean?"

"Something about that night has never set well with me. When I found my father the next morning, his clothes reeked of bourbon. Almost as if someone had doused him with it, in an attempt to make it look like he'd been drinking."

Hollande felt sick. "Your mother?"

"I pray not, but something doesn't add up. When I told Tristan, he denied the possibility. Even when our father spoke to us of her mental instability, my brother refused to believe the worst.

"One evening, I found him by Yarrow Creek and shared my suspicions about our father's death. He grew angry. Hostile. I tried to reason with him, assuring I wished no harm to come to our mother. That having her incarcerated wouldn't restore our father's life, but for her own well-being she should be placed in a facility where she could receive proper care."

"An asylum?"

"It is an ugly word. Tristan took exception, and our argument turned to blows. By that time, I was as furious as he was. I must have shoved him. I never intended for him to fall into the creek. I tried everything I could to reach him, but he went under and didn't resurface."

"I'm so dreadfully sorry." The story was not at all what Hollande expected.

"I waded in after him. Let the current take me where I'd seen it sweep him, but I couldn't find him. I searched for hours. Diving under the water, combing the banks. He was gone."

"Mr. Kraner said his body was never found."

"No." Nathaniel heaved out a breath. "My mother refused to accept his death. Her mind was already fractured, but losing Tristan sent her plummeting into an abyss she had no desire to escape. After a while, she started calling me by his name. I'd correct her, but it never did any good. She'd insist I was my brother. Hour after hour, day after day, week after week. Eventually, there came a point where I grew tired of arguing and conceded. I was responsible for taking my brother from her. How could I refuse her need, when I was guilty of killing him?"

"But you didn't. Tristan's death was accidental."

"An accident that never would have happened were it not for my anger."

"Tristan was angry, too. You just told me that. He was equally at fault for your confrontation."

Nathaniel looked away.

"You have blinded yourself to Tristan's responsibility."

"Perhaps."

Not the answer she hoped for. When he maintained a stony silence, she sighed. "Does your mother truly believe you are your brother?"

"When I am in character, yes. At first, I spent all of my hours playing his role, then little by little I allowed moments of myself to slip through. My mother embraced those as well, assuring me she was pleased to have both sons again. After that, I divided my time as Nathaniel and Tristan. My mother would brook no mention of Tristan's death, therefore I was forced to let others think he was truly alive. As the years passed, the hoax became more elaborate." His mouth tightened in a bitter smile. "There is a hidden passage in the house that allows me to slip outside undetected."

Hollande decided against mentioning she knew of the staircase. The revelation served no purpose.

"I retire for the evening, change clothes, then make my way outside."

"And Tristan's carriage?"

"Hidden in a grove of pine trees several miles down the road. I make sure my mother hears it coming when I return as Tristan. I've been lax maintaining those pretenses since you've arrived." He glanced toward the horse, watching as the gelding idly cropped grass. "Even so, I am trapped. I've performed the role of my brother for so long, I see no way out."

"But you can refuse."

"As I've tried. Everything has changed since you came to Stewart Manor. I had hoped you would free my mother from her delusions, but instead I'm the one who has to break free. Since your arrival, I've told her more than once I will no longer play her game. Why do you think she made all that noise about Tristan staying at the house and me assuming his place in Curtisville? It was a threat to force me into behaving. She's aware of my feelings for you. In the role of Tristan, I wouldn't be able to act on them. Instead, I called her bluff. I told her I would share everything with you."

"That's why she's so hostile toward me."

"She sees you as coming between her and Tristan. For *you,* I want this wretched charade to end."

"But I thought your mother controlled the quarry?"

"Something else I've allowed her to believe. She doesn't realize my father sold the bulk of his shares to Harry. These days, checks are mailed directly to my bank. She lives in the past. Not only with Tristan, but the quarry as well."

"And the room at the end of the hall? Why do you keep your father's study locked?"

"Because I'm not sure what the sight of that room would do to her. It's where they argued, and where he met his end. As unstable as she is, I don't want to resurrect those memories. She's convinced he fell from the balcony as a result of his own failings. Once she told me she suspected his death was an act of suicide. I do not believe my father killed himself, but I may never know the truth of what happened that night."

"Nathaniel, this is all so twisted."

"Yes, but one thing is not." He claimed her hands, clasping them tight as he gazed down at her. "And that is my love for you. If you will only give me one more chance, I promise to set everything right. Come back with me to Stewart Manor. Resume your place in my home. This time as my wife."

Hollande gasped.

"I will tell my mother of our plan to wed. Because my father could not place her in a sanitarium, I will honor his wish and purchase a smaller house in town for her residence. She will have staff and the necessary care to live out her remaining years as she pleases."

"But Stewart Manor is her home."

"No longer. I have catered to her delusions for too long. It is time to purge my life of her manipulation and poison. Stewart Manor can be filled with light and laughter again. Please, Hollande. Say you will marry me."

She hesitated only momentarily, conscious their union would not be without obstacles. Even if Sylvia no longer resided at Stewart Manor, she would remain an intricate part of Nathaniel's life, and by extension Hollande's. In time, the people of Hode's Hill would learn the truth about Tristan, and Nathaniel would be forced to endure the fallout.

Was she strong enough to rise above the web of deceit crafted by his mother?

"Yes, Nathaniel. I would be honored to become your wife."

* * * *

Present Day

Dante activated the flood lamps in the rear of the house, bands of stark white illuminating the paver patio. His gaze skimmed across sectional sofas, a dining set, the stone fire pit, and a granite bar. For the first time since inheriting the house, he regretted not having motion-triggered lights installed. If he stayed where he was—surrounded by brightness—and waited for Sherre, he might come out of this alive. If there was ever a time Grace Miner needed to be late, it was tonight.

The whiff of odor he'd caught earlier swelled stronger. With it came the sense of creeping darkness. He flicked on the flashlight, angling the beam over the lawn where the floodlights didn't reach. Clusters of bushes, trees, and ornamental shrubs leapt back at him. No sign of the ghoul, but the beast would remain invisible until it struck. Dante's heartbeat quickened. His hand grew sweaty on the knife.

Maybe he should go back inside, wait until he saw the flash of oncoming headlights. With luck, Grace might even be late. Sometimes the ER backed up. Sometimes she stopped for milk or bread on the way home.

He'd almost talked himself into the idea when he heard a car approaching. Far too soon for Sherre.

A wall of stench struck him. "*Gad!*"

The reek in the cistern had been abominable, but this rated supreme on a Richter scale of foul. Fighting the urge to retch, he folded in half. Cold pelted him like hurled chunks of ice. Before he could straighten, every light in the yard died. In the abrupt, suffocating blackness, night became a tomb. He could no longer hear the chatter of crickets, whisper of wind, or the approach of Grace's car.

Dante toggled the switch on the flashlight, but the bulb refused to ignite.

"Shit." He'd known damn well the ghoul would strip every active source of illumination before it attacked, but he'd let fear override reason. If he'd only kept the flashlight off, he might have been able to crank the beam when it counted. Now he was screwed.

His breath plumed in the air, frosted and white, his heart a rabid jackhammer. He inched away from the house, around the first sectional on the patio. In the eerie quiet, he half imagined the hum of Grace's car in her driveway.

From nowhere, a fetid gust of wind buffeted him. The gale lifted him off his feet and flung him backward into a chair. He spilled onto the paver stones, the cumbersome seat toppling with him, pinning his leg under the edge.

Dante gave one solid kick, propelling chair and cushion over the patio in a juddering slide. Before he could climb to his knees, something sharp lanced across his cheek.

Black. Oily. Reeking of death.

Talon or pinion.

Blood dribbled onto the stone. His blood. He lashed with the knife, meeting nothing but air. A quick roll to the side sent him scrambling to his feet. Somewhere in the back of his mind, he registered the absence of a car engine, prayed Grace had retrieved her mail and was tucked safely in her house.

"Come on, Sherre. Where the hell are you?"

Another battering wall of stench. The reek of the Netherworld. An odor that clung to tormented ghosts, creatures that fed on flesh, faceless things that slithered underground. Dante spat on the stone, gagging when bile bubbled into his throat. The ghoul was near. So close, he thought his limbs would seize in terror.

There was a damn good chance he was going to die tonight, butchered and mauled by a creature that feasted on death. He was close to hyperventilating, his heartbeat ratcheting into the stratosphere.

The darkness shifted. Oozed like liquid.

Dante caught a glimpse of claws, tasted dung when the ghoul's breath wafted across his face. He screamed a curse, slashed wildly with the knife. The back of his calves banged against the firepit, the impact and resistance dumping him onto his butt. He was still sucking air when the ghoul materialized. Black on black, leaking pus and slimy secretions.

He heaved to the side, collided with a table, and sent its contents spilling onto the ground. A deck of cards, an empty beer bottle he'd neglected to trash, and the remote for the fire pit. He flung the bottle at the beast's head. Watched it soar harmlessly past and thud on the grass. Fat lot of good it did.

In the distance, the screech of tires and a pulsing strobe of red and white signaled Sherre's arrival. The slam of a car door rebounded through the night, followed almost simultaneously by another.

The ghoul bellowed. Vaulted onto the fire pit and swept a talon at Dante's head. He dove clear, groping for the remote.

Come on. Come on.

"DeLuca!" Sherre raced across the lawn, fumbling with a lamp.

"No! Don't use the floodlight!" The ghoul would flee, chased by the burst of illumination. Right now, he wanted the monster tethered exactly where it was, talons locked over the rim of the pit, wings stretched to the sky. The damn thing looked like a grotesque phoenix straddling a pyre.

"Let's see if you can burn, bastard." He jabbed the remote. Fire blazed to life, clawing up the ghoul's legs, rupturing flesh, cracking scales like eggs. The creature flung back its head, shrieking unholy agony to the sky.

"*Now!*" Dante ordered Sherre.

She activated the light. Another burst to life half a foot behind her.

Dante shoved backward, crab walking until he could scramble upright. From the corner of his eye he saw David sprint to the opposite side of the patio. Together, the detective and his partner trapped the ghoul in the crossbeam of their lamps.

The creature screamed. Hissed and wailed, spitting fury and terror. The fire held it prisoner, flames gutting its legs and belly, drenching the night with the stink of burning meat. Within seconds, the floodlights mounted on the back of the house surged to life. Even the solar lamps lining the walkways sputtered awake with a weak glow.

The ghoul folded, slumping over the rim of the pit. Chunks of scorched and bloody flesh sloughed from the beast's body onto the ground. Fire flickered over its scales, climbing higher to engulf its head. Warily, Sherre and David approached from opposite sides, lamps targeted on the motionless creature.

"I wouldn't freaking believe this, except I'm seeing it." David's voice held a mixture of disgust and wonder, layered with unease. "Think it's dead?"

"Yeah." Dante wiped blood from his cheek. "I also think we're going to have a crowd, between the police cruiser out front and the way that thing was screaming. Half the neighborhood probably heard it. Hopefully, they can't smell it."

"I'll take care of it." Sherre jogged away, speaking into her mic.

David switched off his flood lamp. He gave Dante a quick once-over. "Are you hurt?"

"Hurt? No. Shaken up and in need of a drink? Yeah."

"Figure out what we can do with the carcass, and I'll buy you one. If Christy Catterman gets wind of this, Hode's Hill will become the local freak show."

Dante glanced off to the side where Sherre was already heading to the front of the house. "We could dump it somewhere and hope it's never found."

"Looks like it's going to be a bitch to move. And it's not exactly aromatic." David grimaced. "Did it stink like this when it was alive?"

"Worse." The adrenaline crash struck without warning. One minute, Dante was standing, the next he slumped into a chair. He dropped the knife and greedily sucked air.

"Hey, I think I should call a doctor." David's tone registered concern. Dante waved him off. "I just need a minute."

It was several before Sherre returned. "I sent the gawkers on their way. Told them a dog caught a fox. Most of them bought it, the rest will have to wonder. If the precinct logs any calls, they're aware we have the situation in hand." Her gaze strayed from the ghoul to Dante. "I don't know how you lasted against that thing, DeLuca, but you'll never hear me bash any supernatural warnings you spiel again."

"Same here." David eyed the ghoul. Most of its lower body was blistered and charred. A long gray tongue curled from its mouth, dripping mucous and drool onto the stones. "I have a feeling it's going to be a long night."

Sherre lobbed him a questioning glance. "Why is that?"

"Because we're going to have to find a way to move this thing."

"And do what with it?"

"Haul it to the incinerator. Best way to get rid of garbage is to toss it in with the trash."

* * * *

Madison wasn't sure how to handle Roth the next day. He arrived at Stewart Manor in the afternoon as they'd planned before their date soured the previous night. She was surprised to find him standing on the porch, a bag from the hardware store parked at his feet when she opened the door.

"Hi." Hands stuffed in the pockets of his jeans, he gave a contrite shrug. "I was afraid you wouldn't answer."

"What are you doing here?"

"I bought a heavy-duty chain and a padlock to secure the cellar doors from the inside." He indicated the bag. "We talked about that last night, remember?"

She crossed her arms. "You mean before you turned into a jerk?"

Roth scraped a hand through his hair. "I'm sorry, Madison. I don't know what came over me. I've been worried about you, and hearing how Dante wants to use your empathic abilities set me off. I couldn't take that anger out on you, so I blasted him."

"And now?"

He didn't answer immediately. "I realize no matter how much I worry, the decision is yours. That aside, I hope you understand where I was coming from. Knowing what happened to you after Boyd—"

"This is different." She cut him off before he could reawaken her fears. She'd spent the night at Jillian's brownstone, twisting and turning in the spare bedroom, mentally preparing herself to embrace the empathy she'd abandoned after her late husband's death.

"If you say so." Roth offered an apologetic smile. "I trust you."

Exactly what she needed to hear. Stepping clear, she invited him inside. They chatted briefly before he headed to the basement to take care of the cellar doors. Later, Madison offered to make lunch. Roth declined, settling for an iced soda. He provided her with the key to the padlock he installed, then left shortly before three. She kissed him goodbye and promised to call later that night.

After he was gone, she headed outside. The rear flowerbeds required weeding. When she was through, she trimmed the high grass around the Stewart family graves, pausing over Sylvia's. All indications pointed to the Stewart family matriarch being the malicious ghost who haunted Stewart Manor, but Madison couldn't understand why Sylvia was set on driving her from the property.

Vera Halsey had lived there for decades. Could the problem be Madison's likeness to Hollande Moore? According to Margaret Irving, Hollande was hired to care for Sylvia. Maybe the older woman had resented her interference. Even worse, Hollande might have mistreated her. Whatever the answer, Madison hoped Dante would be able to unearth the reason later that night.

She couldn't continue to impose on her sister, especially now that Jillian and Dante were engaged. Life was starting to make her feel like a third wheel. Sooner or later, she was going to have to make a decision about the house and whether or not she intended to keep it. Stewart Manor didn't seem nearly as threatening during the day, but personal experience taught her that wasn't always the case.

Back inside, she spent a few hours catching up on paperwork, checking email, and exploring real estate listings for buyer clients. By the time dinner rolled around, she was too nervous to eat and merely picked at a handful of grapes and crackers.

Dante arrived with Jillian at half past eight. He looked haggard, like he'd barely slept, but offered a reassuring smile when she greeted them at the door. Jillian unfastened Blizzard's leash inside the foyer, then gave her a hug. She was pale and jittery, slanting more than one wayward glance in Dante's direction. The undercurrent between them was palpable, especially for an ex-empath.

Madison's stomach knotted. "Is something wrong?"

"We'll tell you later," Dante said.

"I think you should tell her now." Jillian's lips flattened in a tight line. "I wanted him to postpone this, but he's too stubborn."

"What's going on?" The knot in Madison's belly ballooned in size. "Did something happen?"

"That's putting it mildly."

"Let's not fight in front of your sister."

"We're not fighting!" Jillian balled her hands, glaring at her fiancé. "Excuse me for being freaked out you could have died."

"*What?*" Blood thundered in Madison's ears. "Dante, what is she talking about?"

He heaved a sigh. "I was going to wait to tell you. I didn't want to distract you from what we're doing, but maybe it's better you know up front. Then you won't be worrying about the ghoul."

"What about it?"

"It's dead."

"Dante killed it." An icy sliver of admiration wormed under the anger in Jillian's voice.

If Madison had a chair to sink into, her legs would have buckled. "How?"

"For some reason it zeroed in on me last night." Dante clearly didn't want to make a big deal out of it. "The thing caught me outside, and I ended up torching it on the fire pit."

Madison choked on shock.

"I made a call to Sherre before it attacked." Dante's voice reached her through a fog. "She and David showed up, and the three of us got rid of the carcass."

"This is my fault." Madison sank her fingers into Blizzard's fur when the dog pressed against her. The husky seemed to recognize she needed the support.

Jillian frowned. "What are you talking about?"

"Last night...I was with Roth and we argued. He was angry at Dante because of what we're planning to do. He was being ridiculous. For a minute, I even thought he was jealous. I left in a huff."

"So, the thing *was* tied to Roth." Dante didn't sound surprised. "It's the only logical explanation."

"Is Roth in danger?"

"No, and I don't think anyone else is, either. The ghoul's dead. It's not coming back."

Madison suddenly understood her sister's frustration. "We should put the folk memory off to another night." Her gaze settled on Dante. "Until you've had a chance to recuperate." Why hadn't she noticed the thin gash angled over his cheek before? Was the cut a result of his encounter with the ghoul?

"I'd rather do it now. The ghoul was attached to this house because of a history of violence and death. Now that it's gone, it might be easier for me to read any folk memory that exists. The longer I wait, the fainter that memory might get." He looped an arm around Jillian's shoulders, tugging her close. "I'm fine. Just tired." He kissed his fiancée's temple, then drew back with a grin. "At least Sherre was able to feed Christy Catterman enough garbage to keep her happy."

"What do you mean?" Like everyone else, Madison was familiar with the Channel 42 reporter.

"After we got rid of the thing, Sherre concocted a story about a rogue bear. Trapped, shot, and disposed of. The public no longer has to worry about psychotic killers. Catterman ate it up and ran the story earlier today."

She decided not to ask how Sherre managed to bury a bogus incident report. Between her and David, the two detectives had enough clout to pull it off.

"Dante visited Juni Gold earlier, too." Jillian lobbed him a conciliatory glance.

"She deserved the truth. She was terrified the thing would come back. Now she doesn't have to be afraid."

"Neither do we. And Roth never has to know." Madison was grateful the creature was gone. More so that Roth would never learn he was indirectly responsible for choosing the ghoul's targets. "I still don't understand why it attached itself to him."

"He freed it." Dante seemed to think the explanation was sufficient.

"But I was there, too."

"You didn't unbolt the cistern, Roth did. Other than that, we may never know why the thing chose him." He drew a deep breath. "Let's get started on the folk memory. I don't want to lose the twilight."

"Okay." Madison led the way to the rear of the home, then down the basement stairs. The mustiness of the cellar struck them the moment they descended the steps. Blizzard headed to the cistern, pausing to snuffle around the base. The worst of the odor was gone, as if banished with the death of the ghoul. Only a faint sulfuric taint remained, lingering like the hint of ozone after an electrical storm.

Madison switched on the remaining lights, leaving the flood lamps for Dante. Three squatted on the floor where he'd placed them before his disastrous accident in the cistern.

"I see you padlocked the storm doors." Jillian glanced from the heavy chain and lock to her sister. A furrow of worry creased her brow. "Was someone in the house? Did that creep who slashed your tires come back?"

"No, but I thought it best to make things as difficult as possible. Roth chained that up for me earlier today. He was upset I hadn't done it sooner."

"Smart man. I agree with him."

Madison's gaze strayed back to Dante. He stood over the cistern, staring down into the pit. Was he remembering his harrowing time trapped inside, air depleting? She shivered. "I still don't understand why we're doing this so late in the day." If Sylvia had been able to seal Dante in the cistern with the sun near zenith, how much more powerful was she likely to be with daylight hovering on the cusp of night?

"Dusk is the perfect time." Dante crossed to the flood lamps. "Or in the old vernacular—eventide." He activated one light after the other, toggling them on, then shutting them off. When he was through, he switched off the overhead bulbs she'd activated, leaving only the one by the stairway lit. A skinny swath of yellow pitched over the floor, casting the rest of the basement in shadow.

Madison's heart crawled into her throat. "I thought we wanted the lights?"

"Normally I'd agree, but for this I don't want barriers, and light is a barrier." He moved back into the darkness, closer to the cistern. "At eventide, the veil between worlds grows thin. Twilight is a transitional phase, best for reading folk memories."

"I thought you could read them any time of the day?"

"I can. But if you remember, this one was spotty. Fragmented. That's why I need your help, and why I chose dusk to experiment. We need to do this now."

Madison inhaled to calm her nerves. "What should I do?"

"I'm going to concentrate on the cistern. As an empath, you can sense what others are feeling. I want you to focus on me, open your thoughts, and embrace what I feel."

"Like I did with Boyd." Why did she have to think of that now?

"If anything goes wrong, promise you'll sever the connection." Jillian squeezed her fingers in an icy grip.

Too tense to speak, Madison nodded. Her sister's face glowed shell-white in the semi-dark. She was certain she looked every bit as ghostly, all color leeched from her skin. She wet her lips. "I'm ready."

"Good." Dante shifted his attention to his fiancée. "Jillian, if anything goes wrong, I need you to activate the flood lamps."

"I will." She hooked her fingers through Blizzard's collar, keeping the husky at her side.

Already Madison's empathic abilities swirled sluggishly awake. She sensed Jillian's nervousness and fear, Dante's determination. When he crouched by the cistern and pressed his fingertips to the edge, her awareness swelled. A door long closed suddenly opened. Instinctively, she recoiled, remembering the funnel connection responsible for dumping the agonizing moments of Boyd's death into her head. Every thought, sensation, and excruciating second of horror.

The frenetic up-and-down plunge of the butcher knife. An explosive blast of pain boiling blood into her lungs. Choking on fluid, unable to breathe. Darkness and blackness. Screaming and terror. Sucking life.

This is what it feels like to be murdered.

Her legs weakened. She sank to the floor, terrified of going back to that moment in time. To the horrific memory responsible for gutting her mind, reducing her to a near-catatonic husk. Jillian's voice came from far away followed by a feather brush on her shoulder. Her sister's touch was insubstantial. Distant.

Madison was already someplace else. Dante met her gaze across the basement, driving the memory of Boyd from her head. In the moment their eyes met, her husband's death was thrust from her thoughts, replaced by another.

Another murder. Another time.

Madison cast off the last of her fear and let the folk memory engulf her.

Chapter 18

Hollande packed her travel bag while Nathaniel waited in the lobby of the boarding house. Afterward, she said goodbye to Mrs. Shaver, who hugged her with a telltale gleam in her eyes.

"Should you need a room, you're always welcome here. That said, I wish you the best in your new life."

"Thank you." Hollande bobbed her head. She avoided mention of her impending nuptials, despite Mrs. Shaver's sly observation. Sylvia deserved to learn of the wedding first, an honor accorded to the mother of the groom.

Not that Sylvia would celebrate.

Hollande suppressed a sigh, vowing to stop measuring her future by Sylvia's whims. Nathaniel was anxious to begin their life together, determined they would wed as soon as he was able to arrange clergy. She'd never seen him so happy, his contentment drawn from their impending marriage and the relief of finally putting the ghost of his brother behind him.

I only regret I do not know the resting place of his bones.

Sadly, Hollande doubted he ever would. By the time they arrived at Stewart Manor, the silver of eventide cloaked the grounds. Nathaniel helped her from the carriage, and she stepped to the ground, pausing to appreciate the heady musk of late spring. The warm-water scent of Yarrow Creek.

Once inside, he deposited her travel bag in her room. The items she'd left behind before leaving for Curtisville were all still there. A surprising find, as she could easily envision Sylvia disposing of them. Even more startling, a bouquet of daffodils stood in a milk glass vase on the bureau. She paused to finger a silky petal before glancing to Nathaniel.

"For you. Something to welcome you back."

"Thank you." Heat flooded her cheeks.

Before she could recover her poise, he approached and gripped her hands. "I promise there will always be daffodils in the spring. Aster in the fall. Boughs of greens in the winter."

She couldn't imagine a better life than the one they would share together. "What of the summer when flowers are at their peak?"

"We have no need. You outshine the most dazzling blooms of the season." Nathaniel pressed his lips to hers. When he drew back, his gaze was filled with promise. "Wait for me in the drawing room. I'm not sure how long I'll be detained with my mother."

"It doesn't matter." Hollande repeated the vow he'd made before she departed for Curtisville. "For you, I would wait a lifetime."

* * * *

When the minutes stretched with agonizing slowness, Hollande grew worried. Unable to remain seated, she paced from the divan to the fireplace. A few seconds more, and she wandered to the window. Outside, darkness blanketed the grounds, night falling swiftly once the sun set.

How long had Nathaniel been gone? Shortly after he headed upstairs, she'd heard shouting—Sylvia's voice, though she'd been unable to tell what the woman was yelling. The words didn't matter, for her tone was defiant, bristling with anger. Hollande almost wished Annabelle was there to keep her company. She would miss her friend but hoped once Sylvia was settled in town, Annabelle would make the transition with her. She seemed to be one of the few people Sylvia tolerated to a degree. Hollande would visit, of course. Nathaniel, too, but—

Her thoughts scattered at the sound of footsteps in the foyer. For one off-kilter moment, she recalled how she used to listen for Tristan's arrival on nights he promised to visit. Before she could banish the memory, the doors to the drawing room banged open.

Sylvia appeared, framed on the threshold, a cast iron poker clutched in her hand. Flecks of blood glistened on her cheek.

"Sylvia?" Hollande backed against the window, her voice lurching up an octave. "Where is Nathaniel?"

"With Tristan."

"What do you mean?" Fear clawed awake in Hollande's stomach. This couldn't be happening—the spatters of blood on Sylvia's face, the end of the poker oily and dark. Nausea boiled into her throat. *"Nathaniel!"*

"He can't hear you. If you think he's going to rescue you, lowly girl, you're sadly mistaken."

"Why...why would he need to rescue me?"

"Why do you think?" Sylvia circled the divan. "You took Tristan from me. I took Nathaniel from you."

"You can't mean that." Her gaze darted to the blood-streaked poker. Dear God, had this depraved woman killed her own son? Hollande refused to believe Sylvia capable of such wickedness, but that left an equally grim alternative. Nathaniel must be grievously injured, possibly dying. It was imperative she reach him.

She retreated in the opposite direction. "Sylvia, *this is madness.*"

"Odd you should choose that word." A grim smile twisted Sylvia's mouth. "My husband insisted I was mad. Rather than own up to an affair with that trollop, Louise Kraner, he threatened to place me in an asylum. Can you imagine the audacity?"

Mute, Hollande shook her head. Perhaps if she kept the woman talking, focused on the past, she could slip free. Reach Nathaniel and render whatever aid he required. She inched toward the doors, Sylvia drawing closer.

"You wonder why his study is kept locked?" Her foot collided with an end table, but she never slowed her pace. "I'll tell you why. We argued on the balcony. He and I, the man who vowed to love me above all others. How could he betray me with her?"

"I—" Hollande had no words. Too late, she realized Sylvia was systematically herding her into a corner. Her back bumped against the fireplace where it met the wall.

"Do you know what I did?"

"No." She didn't want to hear any more, frightened of learning the truth.

"I pushed him. Sent him plummeting to his death. At least it should have been his end, but the lecher was still alive when I rushed outside. I found him with broken legs, bleeding from the head. He begged me to help him. Said none of what happened was my fault, that he loved me all the same." Her eyes glazed over with a faraway look. "Why do you think he would say that?"

"I don't know." Hollande wanted to sob.

"I can still see him lying on the cobblestones, beseeching my help."

"Please stop." She buried her face in her hands.

"I picked up a rock and bashed in his skull. Later, I dumped bourbon over him to make it appear he'd been drinking. Too sloshed to know what he was doing. I left him for Nathaniel to find the next morning."

"*You are a madwoman!*"

"Yes. Yes, I am." Malice gleamed in Sylvia eyes. "Who else but a madwoman would manipulate one son into posing as another?"

Hollande moaned. She thought she was going to be sick. "You knew all along it wasn't Tristan?"

"Of course. Didn't I tell you I needed Nathaniel more than you'd ever realize?" She leveled the poker between them, pinning Hollande at the waist. "Nathaniel made Tristan live again. Before you came, he played the part almost every night. We were happy, the three of us."

Bile burned the back of Hollande's throat. "You need help, Sylvia."

"Then you showed up and started putting ideas in Nathaniel's head." The older woman continued as if she hadn't heard. "Suddenly, he wanted a life of his own. A wife and a family. A life that didn't include his brother."

"His brother is *dead!*"

"Do you think I don't know that?"

"You played on Nathaniel's guilt for pushing Tristan into Yarrow Creek. He loved his brother. Tristan's death was an accident."

"It was murder." Sylvia leaned close, her eyes gleaming like flint. "I know, because I'm the one who killed him."

* * * *

Present Day

Madison tensed when the folk memory struck. One minute she was staring across the basement at Dante, the next her surroundings blurred. When she blinked away the distortion, she spied an older woman in a long gown standing by a wooden shelf.

A prickling of fear crept up Madison's back. This had to be Sylvia, her black hair knotted into a severe bun. She occupied herself inspecting jars of fruits and vegetables, dismissing each as if none suited her needs. Behind her, the cistern made a dark hole in the cellar floor, open and filled with water.

Madison gasped when the storm doors flung open. Then her consciousness spiraled away, claimed by another.

Tristan staggers down the steps. He has no clue how long it's been since he hauled himself from the punishing waters of Yarrow Creek. He thinks he may have spent a day or more stumbling up the rocky shoreline from where the current carried him. He knows he passed out more than once, waking to the hot clutch of fever. His clothes are torn and ragged, splotched with mud and blood. The jagged rocks of the creek bottom have ripped chunks of flesh from his arms and legs. His hair is plastered to his face, and his throat burns from spitting up water and bile. He shivers, greedily drinking in the limited warmth and half-light of the basement. The hour is early enough that shadows have yet to fester in the corners. Even so, the glow from a lantern brightens the gray surroundings.

"Mother." He stumbles to his knees at the bottom of the steps.

She swivels from a shelf where she is examining vegetables canned earlier that fall. Her mouth rounds into a perfect O when she spies him. A jar of greens slips from her fingers and shatters at her feet.

"Tristan!" She is at his side in a matter of seconds, bending to brush the matted hair from his brow. "Oh, thank God, you are alive." Her lips are warm and dry as she covers his cheek with kisses, unmindful of the dirt and blood.

There are bits of old leaves and grass snagged in his hair. He is sure he must stink, but she does not seem to mind. He rests against her, thankful for her warmth. His life has been one of eternal cold since stumbling from the creek, but for the hot, gummy moments when fever claims him.

"Nathaniel said you were dead. That he pushed you."

He is so tired, his limbs weighted with heavy fatigue.

"It wasn't his fault." His voice is raw, a painful grate that makes him wince. He is more to blame than his brother and has no wish for Nathaniel to harbor guilt. "We argued. It is my fault for striking him."

That altercation seems a lifetime ago. As children, they often tussled as boys will, but as men they have always settled differences with thought and words. Why had he been so angry?

"Was your argument about me?" There is something in her tone he does not recognize. A darkness that creeps like thickening fog.

Tristan has lost track of the days but knows it cannot be long since Nathaniel found their father's broken body on the cobblestones. Since he insinuated their mother may have been involved and the prudent action would be to consign her to a sanitarium.

Tristan loves her more than life, but he has endured days of despair, death shadowing every step. He has had time to ponder mortality, question his father's abrupt end and her ever-erratic behavior. For too long he has

*chosen to live in denial, casting the burden of doubt on Nathaniel. Perhaps
the need for truth stems from the pain throbbing through his battered limbs
or the spool of light from the lantern welcoming him home. Whatever the
source, he must be fully assured of his mother's innocence.*

Now. Once spoken, forever done.

"Yes." *It is difficult admitting the truth. He wishes he could wind back the
clock to a time when he was certain of her virtue.* "We argued about you."

*His mother grows still, fingers settling where she'd been stroking his
hair. She does not draw away.* "What about?" *Her tone is casual.*

*He wonders why she is not more concerned for him—calling for help,
summoning his brother—but he is the one who first ventured down this
vexing path.* "How did Father die?"

He senses a tensing of her muscles.

"How do you think he died?"

*Dread blooms in his gut. There must be a reason she chooses to parry
his question with another.* "I want to believe he fell."

She draws away, climbing to her feet. "Would it bother you
if I pushed him?"

Unable to process her words, he stares, certain fever has addled his brain.

"Oh, Tristan." *Her smile is indulgent.* "Don't you see? He deserved to
die. He spurned me for Louise Kraner."

"No." *He is uncertain if he groans the protest or spits the refusal in
denial. Either way, her admission flays his heart.* "Mother, no—"

"You don't wish to hear the answer?" *She appears puzzled, as if unable
to comprehend why he would venture the subject, then recoil.* "The fall
didn't kill Darrin. I would have preferred that, but I had to finish the
deed with a rock."

He gags. Hocks up water. Bile.

"You poor dear." *She bends to stroke his hair.* "This will be our secret.
You have always been my favorite."

*The pain of his heart overrides the torture of his body. Moisture pools
in his eyes.* "Mother, you need help."

"Don't say that."

"Father knew it, Nathaniel does, too. I've been blinded by my love for
you. None of this is your fault."

"Your father said the same thing right before I crushed his skull."

*Tears stream down his face. He envisions dying by the hand of a loved
one. Imagines his father's grief, the last heartbreaking seconds of his life.*

"I promise, Nathaniel and I will take care of you. Secure the proper
help. Doctors who can treat you." *He tries to climb to his feet, but the*

last of his strength deserts him. He crumples against the lip of the cistern, overcome by memories of the woman who raised him.

Who fussed over his bruises when he was a child, played games of hide-and-seek, and delighted in his laughter. He is vaguely aware when she moves away, her footsteps pat-patting against the cellar floor. He doesn't understand what she is up to until he sees her retrieve a jagged chunk of glass from the broken jar. Even then the truth doesn't fully register.

It is only when she returns and crouches at his side... Only when she smiles, whispering how much she loves him... Only then that he understands the full scope of her madness. He is blindsided by her swiftness, unprepared when the glass punctures his throat. Within seconds, blood floods his lungs. He wheezes for air, fighting for life, desperate to stem the draining flow.

But she is already manhandling him, forcing him toward the well of water cut into the floor.

"Rest sweetly, my son."

He is still alive when she dumps him into the cistern.

Madison broke the connection. Overcome, legs weak and unable to support her weight, she sagged to the floor.

Jillian was beside her in a pulsebeat. "What happened?"

"I was able to dredge up the folk memory with Madison's help." Dante switched on the overheads, sending a welcome flood of light through the basement.

Jillian looked between them. "And?"

"Sylvia killed her son." Madison hugged her arms close, chilled to the core. "She slit Tristan's throat then dumped his body in the cistern."

"You saw that?"

"I wish I hadn't." She wiped away tears. When Blizzard nuzzled under her arm, she buried her face in his fur. "He was hurt, and she killed him. What kind of mother could do such a thing?"

"But I thought...I thought he lived in Curtisville?" Jillian appeared at a loss.

Madison didn't have the fortitude to answer. She let Dante explain what they'd seen, along with details about the brothers, Darrin's death, and the shock of Sylvia's betrayal. By the time he was through, she'd recovered enough to climb to her feet. Jillian kept an arm around her waist as if fearful she might fall.

"Then Nathaniel is the ghost who haunts the creek at night, searching for his brother. He must have gone to the grave thinking he was responsible for Tristan's death."

"No wonder Sylvia tried to drive me from the house." Madison's spine stiffened with bitter resolve. "She didn't want me learning the truth."

"It looks that way." Dante seemed wearier than when he'd arrived. "Why don't we get away from here? Go upstairs."

Madison was only too thankful to leave the cistern behind. She feared seeing Tristan's face every time she stepped into the dismal cellar. Strangely, something had changed. A brightening of sorts despite the dusk still huddled outside. Almost as if a veil had lifted, displacing a layer of gloom.

Upstairs, Jillian shooed Madison and Dante into the drawing room, then rounded up bottles of water from the kitchen. Curled in a fat easy chair, Madison accepted hers with a smile but didn't bother twisting off the cap. Her sister passed her a sweater, and she gratefully huddled into the warmth.

"I hope this is the end of folk memories and ghosts." Jillian plopped down beside Dante on the divan.

"Me too." Madison glanced at Dante, wanting reassurance.

"Maybe." He swigged a mouthful of water, then set the bottle on the coffee table when he was through. The room was quiet, restful in a way it hadn't been before. "Sylvia's dirty secrets have been exposed. A woman who kills her husband is evil enough, but one who kills her husband *and* her son?" He grimaced. "The ghoul must have been attracted by Tristan's death, then burrowed in the cistern. It might have stayed there for decades. My guess is that after Sylvia died, the pit was sealed over, and the creature became trapped inside."

"We still don't know what happened to her or Nathaniel." Madison picked at the label on her bottle, a nervous gesture to keep her fingers from trembling. She'd been connected to Tristan in the final moments of his life. Not nearly as intensely as her one-time link to Boyd, but enough to leave her queasy and shaken.

"It's possible we may never know." Dante tugged the tie from his hair. He dropped his head against the sofa, his gaze fixed on the ceiling. With his legs sprawled before him, there was no mistaking the height of his exhaustion. "I won't swear to it—mainly because I'm not functioning anywhere near capacity—but the house feels different."

"What do you mean?" Madison sat up straighter.

"The presence I felt before...the one that permeated the walls and floors." He rolled his head on the backrest to look at her. "It's gone."

A sliver of hope wormed into Madison's mind. "Do you think learning the truth about Tristan might have loosened Sylvia's hold on the house?"

"Let's hope." Dante stretched, expelling a yawn. "As much as I'd like to speculate more, I'm burnt out. I think I've reached my limit."

She'd been selfish to keep pushing. "You and Jillian should go home."

Her sister glanced at her in alarm. "What about you?"

"I promised Roth I'd call and let him know how everything went."

"And then?"

Madison read between the lines. *You're not going to stay here, are you?*

"I'll head back to the brownstone. Tomorrow, I'll decide what to do about the house." She didn't add she'd likely spend the night. After everything that happened, it was the only way to discover if Sylvia's ghost was truly gone.

She saw Dante and Jillian to the door, then returned to the drawing room to call Roth. He answered on the second ring, and she assured him everything turned out fine. She didn't go into details, uncertain he'd believe her anyway. He wanted to drive over to see her, but her energy was running nearly as low as Dante's. She told him she planned to spend the night at Jillian's but hoped to see him tomorrow. When she hung up, she soaked in the quiet, thinking about all she'd discovered that night. About the three graves behind the house and the absence of a resting place for a son betrayed by his mother.

She punched out a familiar number on her cell.

"Lorquet."

"You can stop your search."

"Madison?" A frown crept into Sherre's voice. "What are you talking about?"

"I know who died in the cistern."

"How?"

"It doesn't matter. You need to focus on Tristan Stewart. He deserves closure."

Chapter 19

May 15, 1878

Hollande shook her head, unable to believe her ears. Sylvia relayed Tristan's death as if reciting a memory of little consequence.

"You killed him." Her back was wedged into the corner, stone fireplace on one side, wall on the other. Sylvia stood in front of her, the cast-iron poker a barrier between them. "You killed him, then let Nathaniel go on believing he was responsible for his brother's death. You murdered one son and destroyed the other."

"How else could I keep both?"

Hatred shot through Hollande, crushing her fear. "You evil, despicable woman." She acted without thought, lashing out and thrusting the poker aside. The defiance earned her a second, perhaps two. She scrabbled from the corner, snatched a vase from the nearest table, and hurled it at Sylvia's head.

The older woman ducked, striking out with the poker at the same time. Heavy iron cracked against Hollande's wrist, shattering the bones in one fell stroke. She screamed, stumbling into the divan, nearly overcome by a sickening wave of agony. Somehow, she managed to shove free. Her fingers closed over the spine of a book buried in the cushions. She flung it behind her, then lurched for the door, never waiting to see if the missile struck its target. She bolted from the room and raced for the stairs, intent on reaching Nathaniel as quickly as possible. She was halfway up the steps when Sylvia appeared in the foyer.

"Where are you going, girlie? I thought you wanted to take care of me?"

Hollande sobbed. She cradled her broken wrist to her chest, tripped on her skirt, then frantically clawed upright. Everything would be fine when she reached Nathaniel. She had to keep going. Close her mind to the pain, the fear.

At the top of the steps, she found the door to Sylvia's room standing open. Something about the way it yawed listlessly made her gut balloon with fear.

"Nathaniel." She blundered inside, wrenching to an immediate halt. He lay sprawled on his back, one arm flung above his head, blood pooled on the floor beneath him.

"*No!*" Hollande dropped to her knees. She tried to manhandle him onto his side, but with her broken wrist, his bulk was too great. "Nathaniel, please! Please!" There was nothing she could do but bow over him, cradling him close. Somewhere in the back of her mind, she registered the slow progress of Sylvia's footsteps advancing up the stairs. "Nathaniel, you can't leave me. I can't go on without you."

But she had to. It was that or die at the hands of a madwoman. In a few more seconds, Sylvia would reach the top of the stairs.

Hollande raced for Nathaniel's bedroom, intent on the hidden passage that would lead to freedom. The room had been locked from the inside. Seconds later, Sylvia appeared behind her, slowly plodding down the corridor. Hollande dashed to the next room but found that locked as well.

This isn't possible.

She staggered down the hall, every step sending fresh pain through her butchered wrist. At the end of the corridor, the door to Darrin's study swayed on its hinges. If Sylvia had set a trap, she had no choice but to embrace it. Desperate for a place to hide, she slipped into the room then slammed the door. When she gripped the knob, it came apart in her hand.

"No! Please, no!" Someone had battered it repeatedly, making the lock useless.

Hollande spun, her gaze raking the room. There had to be something she could use as a weapon.

In mockery, the fireplace stood cold and black, both the poker and ash shovel missing. Cobwebs sprouted from lampshades and glommed into corners. Open to the night, the balcony doors sang like a siren, but death lay that way. Darrin was proof of that.

She crossed to a cherry desk coated in dust, then rummaged through the drawers until she located a letter opener. The blade was blunt, but with enough force, it might do the same damage as a knife. In the hallway, the steady tramp of Sylvia's footsteps drew nearer.

Hollande backed toward the balcony, the makeshift weapon clutched in her good hand. Even if she managed to clamber over the railing, the drop to the veranda was too great, the unyielding surface sure to break bone. Her best chance was to stand and fight.

Sweat trickled down her neck. Her heart beat faster and mushroomed into her throat.

Sylvia flung the door wide. She paused on the threshold, hair sweat-matted to her temples, eyes stygian in the sallow mask of her face. Her fingers twitched on the iron poker.

Hollande forced herself to block the image of Nathaniel—his skull crushed, blood pooling on the floor beneath him. "Please, Sylvia. It doesn't have to end this way. I can help you."

"I don't need help." Her voice was dispassionate, tainted by the cancer of madness. "You never should have come here." She hefted the poker. "I can't change the past, but I can make certain this house becomes your tomb." Without warning, she lurched forward, swinging the rod like a club. A violent displacement of air fanned over Hollande's face.

She hurled herself onto the balcony, a step from death on the unforgiving stones below.

"Mother!" Nathaniel's voice cracked across the room. Only it wasn't Nathaniel who stood framed in the doorway. He'd cast off his coat and swept the hair straight back from his forehead. Blood coated his temple where Sylvia struck him, but it was Tristan's gaze that held her transfixed. Tristan's face.

She dropped the poker. What little sanity she'd clung to vanished in the blink of an eye. "Tristan, you've come back to me. Truly come back this time, my beloved son." She raised her hand imploringly.

Unmindful, Nathaniel brushed past her. He crossed to the balcony, where he gathered Hollande into his arms.

Tears flooded her eyes. "I thought I'd lost you."

"Never." He buried his face in her hair.

Sylvia's maddened cry ripped them apart. Hollande had only a second to recognize the rage on her face—eyes white and wide, spittle flying from her lips—before Nathaniel flung her aside. He never had a chance to brace himself. Sylvia plowed into him, and as one they plummeted in a freefall over the balcony's edge. The sickening thud of flesh on stone sent Hollande scrambling to the railing.

"*Nathaniel!*" She bent over the side, the image below turning her bones to liquid. Her knees buckled, and she slid to the ground, cheek pressed tight to the wrought iron slats. She no longer felt the pain in her wrist. Didn't care that Sylvia's skull had shattered on impact.

She couldn't bear the sight of Nathaniel's dead, vacant eyes staring up at her.

* * * *

Present Day

The clock beside Madison's bed slogged through the minutes. Finally, unable to sleep, she scribbled Jillian a note saying she was headed to Stewart Manor. If Sylvia's ghost was truly gone, the sooner she embraced the property, the better.

By the time she pulled into the driveway, the digital readout on her dashboard stood at twenty-two minutes after midnight. Roth's car was parked off to the side, away from the road where it wouldn't be seen. He didn't have a house key, making her unable to fathom a reason why he would be there at such an odd hour. As she climbed the steps to the front porch, it crossed her mind he might have decided to recheck the storm cellar doors to ensure they were secure. Nothing else made sense. She should be grateful he worried about her, but there was something disturbing about him poking around the house when she wasn't there.

She discovered the front door unlocked, a dim square of light spilling from the drawing room. Had he entered through the basement, then climbed the steps? The rest of the house was dark, shadows nested in corners near the staircase and the narrow, gaping mouth of the hall. Stillness weighted the air, broken abruptly by the sound of something tearing. A nerve of disquiet prickled Madison's spine.

"Roth?" She set her purse on the entrance table, then crossed to the source of shallow light. "My God!"

A scene of madness greeted her. Chairs overturned, pillows slashed and oozing stuffing, lamps broken on the floor. In the center of the chaos, Roth pivoted to face her. He clutched a long knife in the fingers of a black-gloved hand.

The air left her in a rush. "What the hell are you doing?"

"I..." His mouth pumped soundlessly. He licked his lips, frozen in place, then took one halting step forward. "Madison...I can explain."

"No." Heat engulfed her. Scorching, furnace-hot, chased by a rock-hard jab to her gut. "No, you can't. You just tore up my house." No wonder the ghoul had latched onto him. He was as much a monster as the creature he'd once unwittingly fed. "How did you get in here?"

And then it dawned on her. Roth had visited Beverly. Afterward, the key from the foyer table was missing. At first, she'd thought her friend had taken it, then that she'd misplaced it.

"You..." Her breath bottomed out in her lungs, throttling the flow of air. "You have my key." What an idiot she'd been! Stupid, gullible, too blind to see the obvious. "You've been sneaking into the house, moving things around, trying to scare me."

She folded onto the couch, unmindful of the ruined cushions, chunks of stuffing strewn around her. Her heart slammed against her breastbone with the force of a battering ram. "You were the one who slashed my tires, left the dead squirrel on the porch, and painted the threat on the window. You've been spying on me. Stalking me." It was never Hocker or anyone else connected to Boyd's past. All those vile nasty tricks—the mailbox, the gardening glove. She pressed her fingertips to her temples, fighting the urge to vomit. "Were you trying to drive me crazy?"

"Madison." His Adam's apple bobbed as he swallowed. "I did this for you."

"For me?" She wasn't certain if she wanted to laugh, scream, or cry. "No, Roth. This is sick. There's nothing you can say—"

"I wanted you to sell the house." He blurted the protest, cutting her short. "Move in with me. I wanted that from the beginning, before you even bought the damn place. How many times did I tell you? Plead with you? I thought if you were scared enough, you'd come to your senses. I did all of this because I love you."

Madison was living a nightmare. "You don't do this to someone you love." Disgust robbed her of tears. "You're like Alan. You want to control me, like he tried to control Bev." Why hadn't she seen it before? His bursts of irrational anger, his attitude toward Dante, his badgering to sell Stewart Manor.

"People need to be controlled when they don't know what's best for them."

"I can't listen to this." Madison raised both hands, enforcing a barrier between them. She stood. "We're through. I'm calling Sherre."

"I can't let you do that."

Her patience was shot. "What the hell does that mean?"

"You're not thinking straight." Roth stepped near enough to touch her, but she didn't flinch. "Once you realize everything I've done is for us—for our future together—you'll come to your senses."

"You're living in a fantasy world. The only thing I realize is how blind I've been." A vinegary laugh burst from her throat. "I should be grateful for what you've done. At least you showed your true colors before I got in too deep, like Bev did with Alan."

She turned away, intent on heading for the foyer to retrieve her purse and cell phone, but Roth's fury buffeted her before she managed a step. With her reawakened empathic abilities, there was no escaping the fallout.

Fingers clamped on her upper arm. He whipped her about.

It may have been that he only intended to continue their argument, but her gaze locked on the knife. She thought of Clive Porter, who'd restrained her while his brother butchered Boyd.

A different house—Mill Street.

A different intruder—a killer jacked up on drugs.

The walls and floor drenched with blood when the slaughter was over. *No, no, no!*

Madison screamed. She swung her fist, knuckles clumsily connecting with Roth's cheek. The blow surprised him more than stunned him, but those precious seconds bought her freedom. She scrambled clear of the sofa and bolted for the door.

Roth was quicker. He grappled her from behind, his fingers knotting in her hair. When he pulled, she thought her scalp would split open. Her head collided with the coffee table, launching black spots behind her eyes. He wrenched her to the floor, then tossed the knife.

"Madison!" Straddling her, he pinned her wrists above her head. "Stop fighting me!"

No, no, no!

She screamed louder, still stuck in the horror of being trapped by Boyd's killers.

"Don't you get it?" His face loomed over hers, mottled red, his eyes a cesspool of fury. "I love you! I've always loved you. You belong to me! No one else. Not that jerk at the Fiend Festival. Not Dante. Not even your sister."

She twisted a hand free. Flailed at his face.

"Let me go!" Her nails sank into flesh. Dug deeper, then ripped free. Blood dribbled down his face.

"I told you not to fight." He jammed her wrist to the floor.

For a second, she thought her bones would pop. A sudden blast of cold air plugged the scream in her throat. The icy explosion lifted Roth like a rag doll and hurled him across the room. His back struck the wall with a resounding thud. He crumpled to the floor, a useless heap of arms and legs.

Madison climbed unsteadily to her feet. It took her a moment to understand what had happened. A tall man, wearing a greatcoat and boots, towered over Roth. His form was insubstantial, but at the same time strikingly clear, his hair tinted the dark gold of lantern light. She recognized him immediately—the man she'd seen searching the creek bank, holding a lamp aloft as he searched for his dead brother's body.

Roth whimpered, curling in on himself. "Don't hurt me."

"Nathaniel." Madison spoke directly to the ghost.

At the sound of his name, he shifted to face her. His gaze held a troubling mix of sadness and gratitude.

"You gave my brother back to me by revealing the truth. You freed his spirit from an unjust grave. For that, you deserve the truth as well."

The voice was in her head, the specter motionless across the room. Roth continued to cower against the wall.

Cold spots bloomed around her, bursts of frost that chilled her blood. The weight of a hand settled on her shoulder as featherlight as the room was cold. She blinked aside a ripple of distortion to find Hollande Moore gazing into her eyes. Her heart jolted when the ghost flowed into her body, joining their thoughts and emotions as one. The history of Stewart Manor unfolded in Madison's mind like a dying rose, petal by decaying petal. The torment was real when she watched Sylvia take Nathaniel to his death, claiming both their lives in one final, insidious act.

"You have found your brother now, his spirit freed, your long search over," Hollande addressed Nathaniel using Madison's voice. "We once vowed we would wait a lifetime for each other. There is no longer anything to chain us to this place. Will you now walk with me in the next life?"

"Come with me." Nathaniel extended his hand. *"In my heart, you have always been my wife."*

Madison jerked as Hollande's ghost departed her body. Across the room, the two spirits embraced, becoming one. Within seconds, they faded from view, the cold in the room gradually dissipating.

Stewart Manor was officially free of the dead.

Madison looked to Roth still balled up by the wall. "Are you hurt?"

"No." His voice was a weak whisper. "Call Sherre. I won't try to stop you."

* * * *

Present Day
October 23

Madison layered a cable-knit sweater over a lightweight turtleneck and jeans, then carried her coffee outside. The fall air was temperate, crisp at the edges. She settled into a patio chair, grateful for the rays of a fat morning sun that stained the veranda gold. Around her, the yard exploded with color—cinnamon, mustard, and orange. Shrubs and trees shaded Yarrow Creek with jeweled and gem-bright leaves. Cattails sprouted among the reeds, offset by clusters of late-blooming goldenrod. Her first autumn in Stewart Manor promised to be beautiful. The thought made her thankful she'd held onto the house even during the worst times. There hadn't been a single ghostly appearance since Nathaniel and Hollande departed. No cold spots, odors, or creaking doors. All that remained was the tragic history of the Stewarts, as much a part of the structure as its limestone foundation.

It had taken some doing—with intercession from both Sherre and Collin Hode—but she'd managed to have Tristan's bones returned. She'd paid to have him interred in the Stewart burial plot with the rest of his family. When she'd placed flowers on all four graves in late August, the blooms remained fresh for days, withering at a natural pace.

In mid-September, she'd stood as maid of honor at her sister's wedding. Afterward, Jillian moved in with Dante. Neither were in a hurry to sell their homes, but she'd recently placed Jillian's on the market and was in the process of working to find them something new.

Roth left town a week after the incident at Stewart Manor. In the end, she'd decided against pressing charges, wanting to move forward with her life. He flew to Farmington Hills to visit his brother as once planned, and Alan talked him into staying. Yet another stalling point she'd overcome. Finally, after Boyd, after Rest Haven, and what would have spiraled into a toxic relationship with Roth, she felt like a new person.

As Madison sipped her coffee, she spied someone moving through the trees along the creek. A man in a long coat with dark gold hair. Doubt beaded goosebumps down her arms. The ghosts were gone, yet there was no mistaking Nathaniel's coat or hair. He even held something aloft. A lantern?

"Nathaniel?" The name left her lips in a whisper of shock. She set her cup aside, then bolted down the bank. "Nathaniel!" Forceful this time.

He whirled to face her, flashing a surprised smile. "Hey."

Up close, she realized she'd confused a stranger with Nathaniel. This man wore a duster, not a greatcoat, and his ash hair was woven with brown threads. He held a 35mm camera with a thick strap and a lens nearly as fat as it was long. Of course, Nathaniel didn't haunt the banks of Stewart Manor.

She felt suddenly foolish and struggled to recover her poise. "What are you doing here? Do you know you're on private property?"

"Sorry." His grin morphed into something slightly apologetic. "I parked a mile or two down the road to shoot the creek." He indicated the direction he'd come. "I didn't realize I strayed. I thought I heard you call 'Nathaniel.'"

"You remind me of someone I knew." For as much as she resembled Hollande, his features were a near-perfect match for Sylvia's son. That couldn't be coincidence.

"I'm Julian Pryce." He offered his hand.

"Madison Hewitt." The grip of his fingers was firm.

"Is that your house?" He indicated the rear of Stewart Manor, visible through the trees.

"Yes."

"It looks like a great place. Probably loaded with history."

A smile flitted over her lips. "You could say that." She nodded to the camera. "Are you a professional photographer?"

"Project manager. Photography's a hobby. By trade, I work for Hode Development."

"With Collin?"

"You know him?" Julian's eyebrows climbed into his hair.

"He's part of my circle of friends. His wife and my sister used to be neighbors."

"Small world I guess." Julian hooked the camera over his neck. "I don't know Collin that well, but I thought enough of him to take the job when he offered. I started last week."

"Congratulations. A project manager with Hode Development is a huge accomplishment."

"So I hear. I'm from Curtisville, but Hode's reputation is well-known."

At the mention of Curtisville, Madison fought to keep her expression under control. What were the odds? "Then you're new to town?"

"Yeah. Which explains why I didn't know I was on private property. Sorry about that."

"It's okay."

"Well...it was nice meeting you. I don't want to hold you up." He turned, ready to head back along the shoreline.

"Um, wait." She swallowed hard. Starting over sometimes meant embracing what felt right. "Would you like to have a cup of coffee? I just made a fresh pot."

He hesitated. "Are you sure?"

"Yeah. I'll show you the house." She smiled. "I might even tell you some of its history."

"That sounds great."

As they walked up the bank, she couldn't help wondering if he wasn't already familiar with it—back to front, and back again.

If she didn't know better, she'd think Hollande Moore had something to do with him getting lost.

A THOUSAND YESTERYEARS

In case you missed it,
keep reading for an excerpt from the first Point Pleasant novel,
available now from Lyrical Underground.

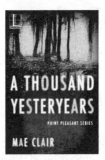

Behind a legend lies the truth . . .

As a child, Eve Parrish lost her father and her best friend, Maggie Flynn, in a tragic bridge collapse. Fifteen years later, she returns to Point Pleasant to settle her deceased aunt's estate. Though much has changed about the once thriving river community, the ghost of tragedy still weighs heavily on the town, as do rumors and sightings of the Mothman, a local legend. When Eve uncovers startling information about her aunt's death, that legend is in danger of becoming all too real . . .

Caden Flynn is one of the few lucky survivors of the bridge collapse but blames himself for coercing his younger sister out that night. He's carried that guilt for fifteen years, unaware of darker currents haunting the town. It isn't long before Eve's arrival unravels an old secret—one that places her and Caden in the crosshairs of a deadly killer . . .

Learn more about Mae at
http://www.kensingtonbooks.com/author.aspx/29541

Prologue

"Do you think Caden Flynn will go?" Eve Parrish kept pace with her friend, Sarah, as a brisk December wind pushed them down Main Street toward the Crowne Theatre. Eager for a glimpse of the movie poster that had everyone in the tiny river town of Point Pleasant, West Virginia talking, she barely felt the sting on her cheeks. Her mother would box her ears if she knew what Eve was up to, but all the boys at school said the poster hung in the window, plain as day for anyone to see. That had to mean she could sneak a peek. She was twelve now, practically a teenager.

Her parents had called *The Graduate* racy, and Mrs. Quiggly, who sold brown eggs and fresh milk from her farm outside town, said the poster was shameless. She wanted to bring a petition against the theater and make them take the "vile thing" down.

"Silly, busybody," Aunt Rosie had chided behind her back. Never one to get hung up on proper behavior, Aunt Rosie did artsy things like taking photographs and hosting moonlight picnics for friends. She even had a darkroom in her home and occasionally sold shots to the local paper who proudly displayed them with the byline *Photo courtesy of Rosalind Parrish.*

"I heard Caden tell Wyatt Fisher they should take their girlfriends to see it," Sarah said, interrupting her thoughts.

Eve gasped. It was bad enough the boys might see a movie as shocking as *The Graduate,* but more appalling that girls would go, too.

"Maybe they'll chicken out." She had a hopeless crush on Caden, an awkward situation given he was eighteen and the brother of her friend, Maggie. Although careful not to make a fool of herself whenever Caden was around, she usually ended up tongue-tied.

Sarah shrugged and tugged the collar of her coat higher against the wind. Several cars drove by in the pre-holiday rush, the glow of headlights holding the night at bay. Sunset was still a half hour away, plenty of time for Eve and Sarah to reach the theater and ogle the poster. The movie didn't open until next week, but the buzz it generated had already swept through their school.

"I wish Maggie was with us," Eve said with a touch of melancholy.

Sarah rubbed her reddening nose. "Me, too."

The walk to the Crowne was only a few blocks from the Parrish Hotel, owned by Eve's parents and Aunt Rosie. Despite the short distance, it was cold enough to make her wish she'd brought a scarf. At least she'd have something titillating to share with Maggie once she saw the poster. Maybe her gushing about how improper the advertisement looked would make her friend smile.

"Do you think she really saw the Mothman?" Sarah's voice was barely audible. Nervously, she glanced over her shoulder as if fearing the giant birdlike humanoid would sweep from the sky. "Was she near the TNT?"

Eve shook her head.

A remote area of dense woods and small ponds, the TNT had once been used to store ammunition during World War II. Eve's father had taken her there on a few occasions, allowing her to explore the abandoned weapons "igloos." But ever since the Mothman was first spied in the region, she hadn't been back. Her father said bad things happened there, and Mrs. Quiggly insisted the place was a haven for UFOs.

"She was visiting Nana and followed Mischief into the Witch Wood."

A fat orange tabby, Mischief belonged to Maggie's grandmother, an elderly woman who everyone called Nana. She lived in a sprawling house snuggled up to a thicket of woods at the farthest end of town. Eve and Maggie had dubbed the thicket the "Witch Wood" after discovering a sycamore tree that resembled an old woman with legs.

"But it's too cold to go into the Witch Wood now," Sarah protested.

Eve nodded. She, Maggie, and Sara occasionally played there, but usually in the spring and summer when the trees were green with leaves, making it easy to catch caterpillars and grasshoppers.

"Maggie was afraid Mischief would get lost."

Sarah made a *pffing* sound. "As if! He's always getting into trouble and always finds his way home. I wish she hadn't followed him."

"Me, too." Eve bit her bottom lip, worrying it between her teeth. She'd visited her friend for a brief time yesterday, finding Maggie huddled beneath the blankets in her bedroom. She hadn't been to school for three days. "She's afraid to go outside."

They had almost reached the theater. Farther down the street, traffic was lined up at the red light that led to the Silver Bridge. Her father would be home soon, returning from Gallipolis, a neighboring city nestled on the Ohio side of the river. He'd headed there earlier in the afternoon to meet a friend, and like everyone else, would need to cross the Silver Bridge.

"I heard the Mothman's eyes are red," Sarah said.

"Maggie thought so. She told me when she couldn't find Mischief, she got an odd feeling, like something bad had happened. Her skin broke out in goose bumps."

Sarah's eyes widened. She rubbed her nose again. "My mom says people get a weird sensation when they see the Mothman. I've heard her talking about it to my dad when she thinks I'm not around."

"My parents do the same thing." How strange to be focused on something scary when everything around them reflected the festive mood of the coming Christmas holiday. The streetlights on Main were decorated with cheerful ribbons, wreaths, and pinecones, and a lighted Christmas tree brightened the display window of G. C. Murphy, the local five-and-dime. At the store entrance, a man in a Santa Claus suit called out holiday greetings and beckoned shoppers inside. A sense of excitement and seasonal cheer hung in the air.

"Maggie was scared." Eve wet her lips, remembering what her friend had told her. "She thought she heard a noise. Like scraping, or someone digging."

"What did she do?"

"She crept closer, but stayed hidden behind the trees. At least, she thought she was."

There was no mistaking Sarah's nervousness as she squeezed her mittened hands together. "But she wasn't?"

Eve shook her head, only then realizing how frightened she was for her friend. A lot of people thought the Mothman was trying to warn the town about something terrible, like a looming disaster, and that's why it kept reappearing. But Maggie said the creature was awful. A hideous monster with hateful eyes that bored into her soul. Those who'd seen it said its eyes were so ghastly, they couldn't recall any other feature of its face. Rumored to be at least seven feet tall, it had large wings that allowed it to fly vertically like a helicopter. Most said it was gray in color, and the Mothman's terrifying eyes glowed scarlet even in the daylight.

"She got close and peered through the trees," Eve explained. They stopped in front of the theater, but the poster they'd come to see no longer felt important. Someone blew a horn as the light for the Silver Bridge turned green, but traffic remained at a standstill. "That's when she saw it, crouched on the ground."

"What was it doing?" Sarah's eyes filled with fear.

"Maggie didn't know. It was hunkered down with its wings draped around it like a cape. Then it turned and saw her, and she screamed."

Sarah looked like she wanted to do the same.

A chorus of horns blared from the stalled traffic, causing Eve to knit her brows. "Why do you think all the cars are backed up like that?"

Sarah appeared too focused on the story to pay attention to the vehicles bottled up at the entrance to the Silver Bridge. "Did she run? Did it chase her?"

"Of course she ran. Wouldn't you?"

"I would have screamed my head off."

"Me, too." Her heart kicked into a prickly rhythm. Was it because of her fear for Maggie, or the cold sensation that crept over her as she stared at the unmoving traffic two blocks away? Instinctively, she headed for the backup, Sarah keeping pace beside her. "Maggie heard it chasing her, but she managed to get away and run to Nana's home. She didn't tell anyone about it until two days later. She pretended to be sick so she wouldn't have to go to school."

"But Dr. Pullman couldn't find anything wrong with her." Sarah's observation was half question, half statement.

"Nope. And that's when she had to tell the truth."

"How awful." Sarah soaked in the story as they continued walking, seemingly unconcerned they hadn't stopped to gawk at the poster for *The Graduate* as planned. The sidewalk was busy with Christmas shoppers heading in and out of G. C. Murphy and the local bank.

Any other time, Eve would have delighted in the festive mood, but something didn't feel right. Was she the only one who sensed the ominous undercurrent in the air? And why were there so many birds flitting around overhead, as if they couldn't find a place to rest?

"What happened to Mischief?" Sarah asked.

"He came back later. I heard he was fine."

"He's such a bad cat." Sarah shook her head. "I feel just awful for Maggie. Do you think anyone believes she saw the Mothman?"

"Her parents didn't. They tried to convince her she saw a large bird or something."

"What about Ryan and Caden?"

Ryan was Maggie's other brother. Only a year older than the three of them, they often hung out with him and his friends. Fun and kind of goofy, he was unlike Caden, who Eve thought as dreamy and mysterious as an ancient knight.

"She said Ryan believes her, but Caden thinks she's overreacting."

"Well, he is eighteen." Sarah shrugged. "He's one of them. An adult."

How could she have a crush on an adult? "My mom was talking to Mrs. Flynn earlier, and she said Caden was going to try to get Maggie to go Christmas shopping tonight. You know how she's wanted to visit that new department store in Gallipolis? He thought that might get her out of the house."

"I hope it worked."

"Me, too." Eve's stomach did a queasy flip-flop. Did she really hope so? It would mean Caden and Maggie would be on the Silver Bridge. "It's getting near dinner time. If it worked, they're probably headed back right now." *Like my dad.* "Do you notice all the birds?"

Sarah eyed the sky. "Yeah. Weird, isn't it?"

More horns from the stalled traffic.

"Something's wrong." She started walking faster, bypassing the Santa who waved shoppers into the five-and-dime with a hearty "ho-ho-ho." As the doors opened and closed, the cheerful notes of "Jingle Bells" carried onto the street, spurring her into a jog.

"Eve, wait." Sarah hurried to catch up. "What's wrong with you?"

"The traffic." Goose bumps broke out on the back of her neck. "Look." She'd never seen it stacked up like this before. Friday nights were always busy, especially around rush hour, but even with the addition of Christmas shoppers, there were far too many cars.

The pungent tang of exhaust snarled with the rumble of idling motors as they neared the entrance for the bridge. From her vantage point on the sidewalk, she spied the tall rocker towers erected against the sky. The sun had yet to set, the fiery ball ebbing toward the horizon, painting the silver framework with splashes of tangerine and copper.

"The light's green," Sarah said at her side. "Why aren't they moving?"

Eve glanced at the traffic signal just as it cycled to yellow, then red. Not a single car had inched forward. "The light must be out on the Ohio side. Everything's backed up."

"So people are going to be stuck on the bridge."

Like her father. Like Maggie and Caden.

It shouldn't have bothered her, but an unsettled feeling gnawed at the pit of her stomach. The Silver Bridge defined Point Pleasant, much like the Parrish Hotel. Eve had been on the bridge once when the rocker towers swayed slightly, but her dad had told her they were designed to be flexible, and she shouldn't be afraid. The towers moved with suspension chains to help reduce strain on the bridge piers. She didn't understand the construction, but knew the people of Point Pleasant were inordinately proud of their beloved Silver Bridge.

Sarah shook her head, apparently deciding they'd seen all there was of interest. "Hey, we missed the poster for *The Graduate*. Let's go back."

Eve nodded, trying to mask her uneasiness. "Okay. If my dad's on the bridge, he's going to be stuck in traffic anyway."

She started to turn from the sight when a deafening boom split the air like thunder. A woman's shrill scream knifed deeply into her bones. Within seconds, the terrified shriek was echoed by a dozen more voices raised in horror. Those stalled in traffic poured from their vehicles. On the ramp for the Silver Bridge, reverse lights flashed as cars tried to back away from the traffic signal amid a mad chorus of blaring horns.

"Oh!" Sarah shrieked. "Oh, no. No, no, no!"

Her friend lurched forward, rushing toward the bridge, and Eve jerked in her wake as if pulled by an invisible string. A sob built in her chest. It wasn't happening, couldn't be happening! But even before her gaze fell on the rocker towers looming above the Silver Bridge, she understood the horrified screams, the frenzied bleat of car horns, the chaotic cries of starlings wheeling overhead.

As if trapped in a slow motion bubble, the solid framework twisted sickeningly above a bridge crippled with stalled traffic. Christmas shoppers, truckers, workers returning at the end of the day, even visitors crossing from state to state. How many lives were clustered in that frozen string of cars? Her father. Her friend. Caden.

"Daddy." The name was a pitiful squeak, pushed past the lump in her throat. She lurched another step, vaguely conscious of people swarming past her. They came from cars and stores, from traffic that had stopped haphazardly on Main Street. Screams and voices that made no sense. Birds shrieked above her. Somewhere in the background "Jingle Bells" still played through the open doors of the five-and-dime. Even the suited Santa raced past, waving and hollering for people to get off the entrance ramp.

A scream built in her lungs. Someone yelled for police, someone else for an ambulance. Three steps ahead of her, a woman huddled on the street, hugging a small child to her chest. From the look of the open car door behind her, she had been on the ramp but managed to scramble free, abandoning a brown station wagon. Both the woman and the child were sobbing.

No more than thirty seconds had passed, Eve was sure. Why couldn't she scream? Why couldn't she look away from the twisting rocker towers? In the span of a single heartbeat, they collapsed, the entire bridge folding like a mammoth deck of cards. A heap of metal, steel, and headlights plummeted into the Ohio River.

Eve stumbled to her knees, the scream in her chest ripped lose in a mournful wail.

In little more than sixty seconds, the Silver Bridge was gone, claiming the lives of those she loved.

Chapter 1

June, 1982
Point Pleasant, West Virginia

Eve Parrish stared through the windshield of her Toyota Corolla at the two-story house her aunt had bequeathed to her in her will. A house she remembered fondly from childhood, it had been in her family for four generations, just like the old hotel in downtown Point Pleasant.

Tightening her grip on the steering wheel of the parked car, she vowed to worry about the hotel later. *One problem at a time.*

At twenty-seven, it was staggering to find herself the sole owner of her family's homestead *and* the Parrish Hotel. She'd inherited the latter after her father died, and Eve's mother had signed her ownership of the property over to Aunt Rosie. Not long afterward, her mother had uprooted them, determined to put the tragedy of the Silver Bridge in the past. It had always been Aunt Rosie who came to visit Eve and her mom in Pennsylvania.

But Aunt Rosie was gone.

Why couldn't she have told them about the cancer? Eve would have done something, anything to help. Insisted she get treatment.

"She didn't want treatment," Adam Barnett, Rosie's lawyer had explained as he'd passed her the keys for the hotel and the house earlier that day. "She went quickly, which is how she wanted it."

Eve swiped a tear from her cheek. Aunt Rosie had planned to marry in the summer of '68, but the Silver Bridge altered those plans. Shaken by the tragedy, Eve's aunt had called off her engagement to Roger Layton and never married. Was that why she'd allowed herself to go so quickly once diagnosed with breast cancer? Did she think no one loved her?

A spasm of guilt twisted Eve's stomach. Her small apartment was only six hours away in Harrisburg, but her mom had drilled a steady dislike of Point Pleasant into her head from the time they moved away. It was the place where her father had met his end in the icy waters of the Ohio River only weeks before Christmas and a hotspot for bizarre Mothman and UFO sightings. Was it any wonder her mother had insisted on burying the town in their past?

Right or wrong, Eve hadn't returned in fifteen years. She barely recognized the sparse streets now, so changed from the thriving river community she remembered. She'd been glad to see the Crowne Theater still in operation, but saddened to know G. C. Murphy's had closed its doors. How she, Maggie, and Sarah had loved their soda fountain.

Taking a deep breath, she popped the door on the Corolla and stepped onto the street. Aunt Rosie's house—the same house in which her father and his sister had grown up—was located several miles from downtown Point Pleasant. Every bit as imposing as she remembered, the large two story was offset by a covered porch and a towering chestnut tree in the front yard. Her father had once hung a tire from the lowest branch at Aunt Rosie's behest so Eve and her friends would have a swing when they visited.

Reluctantly, Eve glanced to the house next door. Not quite as large, the cheerful colonial looked in far better condition than the imposing structure Eve had inherited. The paint appeared fresh, the shrubs neatly trimmed. Colorful blooms had already sprouted in the flowerbeds, and a pot of pansies welcomed guests to the front porch.

She'd spent countless afternoons playing in Maggie's home. Countless Friday night sleepovers when they'd stayed up late eating Mrs. Flynn's peanut butter cookies and giggling about boys. She'd never told her friend about the crush she'd had on Caden, but Maggie had known. Best friends always did. Unlike his sister, Caden had survived that fatal night on the Silver Bridge.

With an inhale of determination, Eve hooked her purse onto her shoulder. She would leave her overnight bag and suitcase in the car for the time being. She'd packed light, hoping to finalize plans for the house and hotel within two weeks. Hopefully, Adam Barnett could recommend a real estate company capable of handling residential and commercial sales.

He'd warned her about the break-in. "Nothing taken, it appears. Just vandalism. It happens sometimes when a house sits empty. Probably teenagers looking for a thrill. I had all of the damaged items removed and disposed of as you requested."

The key turned easily in the lock. According to Mr. Barnett, the vandals had gained entrance through the screened porch in the rear, and then busted the kitchen door. Both doors would require reinforcing. With any luck, the rest of the damage would be minimal.

As she stepped inside, a swarm of memories assaulted her. The house smelled stale, closed up for too long, but a trace of Aunt Rosie's signature scent lingered beneath the mustiness. A light bouquet that whispered of spring flowers and clover. On the heels of having visited her aunt's grave at the cemetery, the fragrance brought tears to Eve's eyes. Hugging her arms close to her chest, she blinked them away.

Mr. Barnett had made sure all of the utilities were working, but it was stuffy in the house. She'd have to set the ceiling fans to circulate the air. At least no one had covered Aunt Rosie's pretty furniture with those dreadful white sheets people used when closing an estate.

Her aunt had kept most of the furniture Eve remembered from childhood. The gold and crystal lamps on the end tables were new, but the heavy-footed couch and easy chairs upholstered in crimson brocade were as she remembered, if faded from time. Black walnut tables and thick butternut drapes covered with climbing grapevines accentuated the décor. Surprisingly, there was little damage to the room.

Tracing her fingers along a chair rail, she headed for the dining room. Whoever bought the old monstrosity would have to crave a home with character. It certainly had that. From its wide windowsills to arched openings and massive moldings, it echoed the detailing of a different time.

In the kitchen, she found the door leading to the screened porch reinforced with plywood to prevent further break-ins. The upstairs fared worse. The room her talented aunt had employed as a dark room had been completely ransacked. Mr. Barnett had been hesitant to volunteer the information but said there were chemical spills, and many of her aunt's beloved photos had been found torn and littered on the floor. Looking at the damage, Eve felt a slow burn of anger that someone would destroy her aunt's work. They had no right! As if in mockery of the act, the vandals had used black spray paint to leave a large squiggle on the wall like a brand. Stupid, stupid kids.

Two of the bedrooms had barely been touched, but the last—her aunt's room—had suffered nearly as badly as the dark room. The contents had been dumped from the dresser and closet. At least Mr. Barnett had seen to it that her aunt's lovely clothing had been piled on the bed for her to sort through and replace. Someone had obviously overturned the bureau—

the mirror was shattered— and the bedspread had been ripped off and thrown on the floor. This time when the tears welled, she couldn't stop them. It wasn't fair. Her aunt had been taken prematurely at forty-nine by an ugly disease, and this is how her memory was honored? Lifting a soft terry robe from the bed, she inhaled her aunt's scent and pressed the fabric to her cheek.

"I'm sorry, Aunt Rosie. I'm sorry I wasn't there for you when you needed me."

Eve jerked reflexively when a sharp pounding interrupted her thoughts. Given the vandalism she'd witnessed, her heart lurched frightfully, sending a flutter through her stomach. It took a few seconds before she placed the sound as someone banging on the front door. Mr. Barnett had indicated someone from the sheriff's office would likely stop by to talk to her about the damage. She hadn't expected them so soon, but was eager to learn the details of the report. Tucking a stray strand of hair behind her ears, she hurried down the steps, then yanked open the door.

"Why hello there." The petite woman standing on her front porch offered a friendly smile.

"I…" Eve mentally stumbled, her mind doing cartwheels. Something about the woman was familiar. The appearance was off—there was gray in the woman's hair that hadn't been there before, and her eyes looked watery, not bright like Eve remembered—but the inflection of her voice was the same. She swallowed hard. "Mrs. Flynn?"

"I saw your car. Maggie said you were coming."

"Excuse me?"

Her dead friend's mother smiled indulgently and patted her hand. "It's all right. I realize things are different now." Turning, she roamed to the edge of the covered porch and rested her hands lightly on the railing as she gazed over the front yard. "Maggie has waited a long time for you, Eve."

Flummoxed by her unexpected arrival and the strange comments, Eve trailed after her. "Mrs. Flynn? I…don't understand what you mean." Surely, her best friend's mother wasn't discussing Maggie as if she were still alive. Perhaps the woman was ill. Her odd behavior made the whole scenario seem like a dream.

A car passed in front of the house, sending a flutter of leaves into the yard on a puff of air. The breeze smelled of honeysuckle and exhaust, and a clingy kiss of sunlight warmed Eve's face. She couldn't be dreaming.

"Did you know they didn't find her body until June of '68?"

Eve bit her lip, uncertain how to respond. When her mother had uprooted them the spring after the bridge collapse, the bodies of three victims were still missing. She'd later learned that Maggie's remains had been located during the summer, but there was no talk of returning for the funeral. Her mother wouldn't hear of it.

"I'm so sorry." At least her father's body had been discovered in the debris pile on the Ohio side of the river, allowing him the dignity of a proper burial. Not Maggie. For nearly six months, her remains had been battered and misshapen by the cold currents of the river. If the knowledge ripped at Eve's heart, how much more the heart of her friend's mother?

"Would you...would you like to come inside?"

"No thank you, dear." Mrs. Flynn turned to face her. "I just wanted to welcome you back. Maggie asked me to."

Oh, God. The woman was certifiably crazy.

She might have contemplated the thought further but for the arrival of a police car in front of Aunt Rosie's house. Mrs. Flynn shook her head at the sight, then quietly left the porch without so much as a goodbye. She was halfway across the yard when the man in the car stepped onto the street.

"Mom," he called.

Mom?

Eve felt her eyebrows launch into her bangs as she watched the man dart around the rear of his car to greet Mrs. Flynn on the grass. They exchanged a few soft words before the woman continued her path back to her home and the man jogged toward the porch. As he hustled up the steps, Eve got the shock of her life.

"Ryan?"

"Hey, you remembered." Maggie's brother grinned and extended his hand.

When she slid her fingers into his, he yanked her close, hugging her tightly. In no time, she found herself laughing breathlessly.

"It's so good to see you, Ryan." She hugged him back, delighted by the warmth his unexpected presence brought. "Mr. Barnett never said you worked for the sheriff's department."

"Yep. A sergeant." He tapped the badge pinned to his neatly pressed uniform, then held her at arm's length, his smile igniting a sparkle in his blue eyes.

It was hard to believe the skinny thirteen-year-old she remembered had matured into such a tall, broad-shouldered man. His black hair, no longer curly but wavy, lay tousled over his brow, his grin as infectious as always.

"God, it's good to see you after all these years." Ryan seemed reluctant to release her. "I ran into Adam Barnett at the bank, and he told me he'd given you the keys. I can't believe you're really here."

"I can't either." She hugged him again, then laughed. "You got so tall."

"And you got so…" He paused and wiggled his eyebrows, molding his hands in the shape of an hourglass. "Curvy."

She swatted his arm. "You always were a trouble-maker. Do you want to come in for a while? The house is a wreck, but—"

"Actually, that's why I'm here. I wanted to go over the vandalism report with you." He sobered abruptly and stepped away. "And I'm sorry about my mother. I hope she didn't say anything to upset you."

"No, I…" How did she explain the odd conversation? She'd only been in Point Pleasant a short while. The last thing she wanted to do was offend a childhood friend by pointing out that his mother was off her rocker.

Ryan shook his head, clearly conscious of what may have been said. "Sometimes she gets confused and gets caught up in the past."

Eve let the remark slide without comment. "I was just going to get my bags out of my car." She steered the conversation elsewhere. "Maybe you could give me a hand?"

"Sure."

Together, they trudged to her Corolla. Ryan grabbed her suitcase and overnight bag while Eve snatched a jacket from the backseat along with a few boxed goods she'd brought for the trip. Later, she'd hit the grocery store and stock up on perishable items. At least the refrigerator was in working order.

In the house, Ryan carried her luggage upstairs while she detoured to the kitchen with her small parcel of crackers, instant rice, and peanut butter. She wished she had something to offer him, but the best she could manage was peanut butter and crackers. Mentally, she bumped the grocery store higher on her to-do list.

"I put everything in the spare bedroom for you," Ryan announced, entering the kitchen. "I guess you saw Rosie's room is a mess."

Eve added her box of instant rice to the nearest cupboard, nudging aside several cans of Campbell's soup left behind by Aunt Rosie. A vivid memory flashed through her mind as she recalled her aunt feeding her tomato soup and a grilled cheese for lunch on a brisk autumn day.

"Her dark room, too." Eve shut the cupboard and turned, bracing her back against the counter. "The vandals hit the upstairs hard. Do you have any idea who would have done such a thing?"

"Afraid not." Ryan motioned her toward the dining room. "Let's sit down."

At the dining room table, he withdrew a folded sheaf of papers from his breast pocket. "I thought you should have a copy of the vandalism report."

Eve eyed the papers he handed her. It was standard stuff—date, time, damage done. "Who reported it?"

"No one. I still live next door with my mom. It's um…complicated." He cleared his throat awkwardly. "After Rosie died, I kept an eye on the place. Several days after her death, I was walking around the house when I noticed the door on the screened porch had been busted. I guess the vandals chose it because it was hidden from the street. Easy entry."

"Did they take anything?"

"Not that I could tell, but Rosie isn't here to answer that question. I should have said it before, Eve, but you have my sympathies." He covered her hand with his where it rested on the table.

She managed a wan smile and nodded a thank you. It was good to see him again, a familiar face that made the shock of returning to her childhood home less traumatic. Even if he was grown, no longer the thirteen-year-old boy she remembered, he was still the brother of her one-time best friend.

"So you think it was just kids out for some fun?" She winced, unable to comprehend how anyone could view destroying the home of the recently deceased as entertaining.

He hesitated. "It looks that way."

"Is there something you're not telling me?"

"Nothing of importance." He patted her hand again and stood, then paced a short distance away. "What are you going to do with the place?"

The million-dollar question. "Sell it, of course." It hurt to say, as if she was turning her back on Aunt Rosie and all her aunt held dear. "Vandalism aside, the home needs work to make it desirable. I'm no expert, but it looks like it could use a new roof and several of the rooms should be repainted. If I want to put it on the market, I'm going to have to fix it up first." It was a sobering thought. "I don't suppose you could recommend someone?"

He surprised her with a quick answer. "Do you remember Caden?"

"Your brother?" Her heart lurched again. How could she forget her childhood crush?

"He has a contracting business. Home remodeling, repairs. That sort of thing."

"It sounds ideal." For some reason she hadn't considered encountering him when she'd returned to Point Pleasant. "Do you have a phone number for him? I'd like to talk to him about taking on the repairs."

"How about if I have him stop by tomorrow? Will that work?"

"Perfect." She was planning on addressing the hotel tomorrow, something that would probably take most of the day. "Do you think he can stop early? Around nine? I was planning on visiting the hotel later."

"It shouldn't be a problem." He shot her a sideways glance as if measuring her reaction. "The hotel is still the center of town."

"I thought as much." Eve glanced at her hands, thinking back to the years when her parents and Aunt Rosie had made the hotel the focus of their lives. It had been her family's defining legacy long before she was born. Her great grandfather Clarence had paid for its construction in 1922, then quickly turned the establishment into a thriving operation, bolstered in part by Point Pleasant's blossoming river trade. It hadn't taken her more than a few hours in town to realize those days were nothing more than a memory. "I noticed things are different."

A shadow crossed Ryan's face. "A lot's changed since you left."

Acknowledgment

Thank you to my fabulous critique partners for your insightful feedback and suggestions during the developmental stages of this novel. I count myself fortunate to be part of such a dedicated and helpful group.

To my wonderful editor, Paige Christian, your expert input is invaluable. It is a pleasure to work with you and all of the team at Kensington Publishing/ Lyrical Underground. I am so thankful to be part of the Kensington family!

To my readers who continue to support me by purchasing books and leaving reviews, you make the writing journey worthwhile. It is my goal to make each release every bit as entertaining as the last, if not more so. I hope you've enjoyed Eventide and the entire Hode's Hill Series.

Finally, to my family, friends, and especially my husband, thank you for your unwavering support throughout the years. The writing life is not for the faint of heart, but through your belief and encouragement, I've been able to make that dream a reality.

Meet the Author

Mae Clair opened a Pandora's Box of characters when she was a child and never looked back. A member of the Mystery Writers of America and Thriller Writer's International, she loves creating character-driven fiction in settings that blend contemporary and historical time periods.

Wherever her pen takes her, she flavors her stories with mystery, suspense, and a hint of the supernatural. Married to her high school sweetheart, she lives in Pennsylvania and is passionate about urban legends, old photographs, a good Maine lobster tail, and cats.

Discover more about Mae on her website and blog at MaeClair.net.

Printed in the United States
by Baker & Taylor Publisher Services